I0771502

THE EVERLOVE CHRONICLES
A PRINCESS AND THE PEA RETELLING

BITTER AND SWEET

CHRISSY Q MARTIN

Copyright © 2025 by Chrissy Q Martin

All rights reserved.

No part of this publication may be reproduced, distributed, or transmitted in any form or by any means, including photocopying, recording, or other electronic or mechanical methods, without the prior written permission of the publisher, except as permitted by U.S. copyright law. For permission requests, contact Swimmer Girl Books.

The story, all names, characters, and incidents portrayed in this production are fictitious. No identification with actual persons (living or deceased), places, buildings, and products is intended or should be inferred.

Book Cover by GetCovers

Map Illustrations by Chrissy Q Martin

For Christy

Thank you.

Here's to many more adventures with my bestie!

Krusteei
Thalassos
Fisk
Cularis
Ryutoa
Varglais Ocean
Mylania
Valeyn
Ilzchen
Somniara
Lanark
Terhen Sea
The Mystic Lands

The Greater World
N
W
E
S
Voneira
Rugosa
Bevisser
Azura
Great
Lake
Caerowan
Swendale
Navarez
Maurgel
Montagnia
Verdelle
Antella
Treis
Orannver
Nagisara
Dagon

CHAPTER ONE

FIA

"If you don't want to find yourself at the end of my sword, you will do as I say." My voice is harsh. My narrowed eyes stare out of my hooded cloak at the young man with his scrawny arm outstretched over the well. "Put the kitten down."

"No one's going to miss one kitten." The rough looking youth wiggles the ball of fur in his hand. I've seen this bully around the fishing village before and never had a good feeling about him. "And it's a runt. It's best I put it out of its misery."

He extends his hand out even further over the deep well as he holds the kitten by the scruff of its neck. The gray tabby kitten gives a helpless mew which only helps fuel my anger.

"If you drop that kitten," I say in a gruff voice, "I'll show you what it means to be dropped down a well."

"Ha!" A single solitary laugh emerges from the young man's mouth. "I'd like to see you try."

"Put the kitten down now or I will."

"Oh." The bully's jaw falls in a mocking way as he mimics dropping the kitten. I hold my breath and tense, ready, but he doesn't let go of the helpless animal. "I almost lost it."

"I will only tell you one more time." Anger pierces through every word as I tighten my fist and get ready to grab the sword beneath my cloak. It's at times like this I wish I had magic to smite every stupid human being. It's only bullies who pick on those smaller than themselves, and I wish I could turn this guy into a cat for wanting to throw a kitten down the well for the sheer fun of it. "Put. The. Kitten. Down."

"Who are you to be ordering me about?" the young man sneers.

Suddenly a sword appears and the sharp tip points at the bully's chest.

"You would be wise to obey Her Royal Highness," a stout soldier says. He wears a navy blue Ryutoan royal guard uniform. "Princess Fia is ordering you to put the kitten down."

Reimund, my bodyguard and personal time exterminator, bounces the tip of his sword up and down in front of the village hooligan while I roll my eyes. I thought I was stealthy enough to lose my royal guard, but Reimund bested me. Again.

The bully pulls the kitten to his chest while scrutinizing me. His dark eyes narrow and he stares hard, trying to peer at me as my face is hidden by the folds of a hood. I won't reveal my face and give everyone the satisfaction of knowing a princess resides under the cloth. I didn't want anyone to know I was here. I only wanted a few minutes to myself until I spotted this oaf about to drown a kitten.

Tentatively, with his eyes on Reimund, the bully places the kitten on the ground at his feet. It is not my orders he obeys, but Reimund's. Or it's his fear of the sword. I should have pulled mine out.

"Be gone!" Reimund shouts and the young man takes off in a run.

I stoop over and pick up the helpless little runt and cradle her to my chest. "I was doing quite fine on my own." I rigidly stand and avoid eye contact with Reimund. The kitten's body settles into the swell of my chest, and I cover her with my palm to keep her warm.

"I could see that, Your Highness." Reimund sheaths his sword. "But I'm tasked with protecting you."

"I don't need protecting," I complain. "I was trying to do the protecting."

"You have rescued yet another magnificent beast," Reimund says, and I can't tell if he's joking or being serious.

"She is magnificent." I give the tiny kitten a small pat on the head.

I prefer to be serious; with the occasional sarcastic comments or witty banter most people don't understand. I'll assume Reimund is serious, though I'm usually wrong about people. They can be far crueler than they appear.

"Perhaps there's something your new magnificent charge would be comforted by." Reimund walks to the side of the well opposite me and bends over out of my sight. When Reimund stands, he holds another kitten, nearly identical to the one I hold, except slightly larger.

"Come, Princess." Reimund hands the second kitten to me. "I believe you'll find some milk for these creatures back at the castle. They can join your other rescues."

If it weren't for the two tiny animals cradled in my hands, I would be running toward the sea and away from my guard for a moment's peace. But these kittens meow with hungry bellies, and I won't leave them to starve or be thrown into a well.

"Very well," I say with an added huff. I still don't have to be happy about having a guard follow me. "Lead the way."

Reimund extends an arm out in a gallant gesture. "You must lead the way, Your Highness. I shall follow wherever you go."

Under the folds of my hood, I roll my eyes and stomp past him. A rotation of guards has been assigned to me since my twin brother disappeared nearly six weeks ago. Reimund is the only guard I haven't outwitted. I carefully place the kittens in the pockets of my cloak and set off.

The village is alight with the beginnings of a new day. Small fishing boats which pushed off much earlier in the morning are now returning with their catches to sell at the market or trade. The smell of fresh bread lingers with the odor of fish and the salty sea. It's not the most pleasant of scents, but it's easy to get used to and comforts me. I may live in the castle, but the smell of the village is the scent of home.

Rather than heading straight back to the castle, I meander slowly through the market stalls. I turn my head back to Reimund, his eyes are firmly on me, and I know I won't be able to lose him here.

"Have you had your breakfast?" I ask.

"I missed it due to an early morning activity," Reimund replies, no trace of emotion on his face. I was the early morning activity when I abruptly left the castle and tried to lose Reimund in the expanse of grass between the castle and village.

I carefully check the kittens in my pockets before pulling a coin from the depths of one. I hold it out to Reimund. "Buy us some pastries from one of the stalls. I'll let you choose."

Reimund presses his lips together, and I'm not sure if I detect a faint smile. All my guards have a serious look, but Reimund is the only one without a touch of distaste to his face. I don't prefer having a guard, but Reimund is the one I tolerate best.

"I shall not fall for this trick, Princess. If you desire pastries, you must purchase them," Reimund says.

"No trick." I wave the coin. "I promise."

Reimund keeps his pink lips pressed together and eyes the coin. "I know your word to be true, but you'll have to indulge me this time and purchase the pastries you desire."

Reimund has the right to be wary, before I made a promise. If I hadn't made a promise I would likely dodge away as he bought pastries, but when I make a promise, I keep it. I made a promise to my brother, and I intend to keep it, but have not yet found a way to do so. This morning was a test run, and I failed.

I purchase two pastries topped with tart jam and sweet custard. Reimund gladly takes one and we eat in silence as we walk the main path to the castle. I may not apologize verbally for my actions, but I let my actions speak for themselves. Sweet pastries are an apology.

Back at the castle, Reimund stands nearby in the stall as I feed the kittens. They eagerly lap up the fresh milk but have more covering their faces than they get in their belly. It makes me smile in delight.

A member of my father's personal guard enters the stable and inclines his head to Reimund. I try to ignore them as they whisper, but it's hard not to be curious. I suspect what they're talking about, and it's not going to be anything in my favor.

"Princess Fia." Reimund addresses me as the king's guard takes a step back.

"Yes?" I run a finger over the smaller kitten's tiny head and down its back.

"Your presence is requested in the throne room," Reimund says.

I sigh. "Requested or required?"

There's a beat of silence. I keep my eyes on the kittens lapping up milk.

"Required," Reimund replies, and I hear the apprehension in his voice. "You are being summoned."

I certainly know what I'm going to encounter. My twin brother was summoned to the throne room, and Fynn was given an ultimatum. It's now my turn.

"Alright." I pick up the kittens and stomp over to Reimund. "Hold these for me, please."

Reimund takes the kittens, one in each hand, and trails after me as I follow the king's guard. It's never a good thing to be summoned to the throne room by the king.

I may not have the threat of a curse hanging over my head like my brother, but I have a threat I can't thwart with marriage or true love's kiss.

CHAPTER TWO

EMERIC

I no longer have the threat of death hanging over my head, but I do have the expectations of a kingdom to live up to and a castle to help run.

"I think it should be split pea soup," a young cooking apprentice declares.

"I think it should be a hearty beef stew," the head cook says with lifted eyebrows. "What do you think, Prince Emeric?"

I think I shouldn't have been called to settle such a petty dispute. When a person has faced a fierce water dragon because of a fairy decree issued on an eighteenth birthday, a kitchen conflict over what type of soup to serve seems trivial.

"Make both," I reply with little emotion. "Some guests may prefer a lighter vegetarian soup, while others prefer meat."

"Very wise, Your Highness," the head cook says with one curt nod. The apprentice only has a smug smile on his face.

I can't believe they would argue over soup when not long ago our castle was under siege, and we were rationing supplies to feed the villagers and castle workers within the stone walls.

"Is there anything else you require of me?" I ask without the lengthy exhale I want to do.

"No, thank you," the head cook replies. "The next banquet menu is settled, and breakfast is being served."

I trudge into the hallway. I've gone from training my younger brother to survive a deadly quest to settling verbal disputes in the kitchen, but it doesn't instill any confidence in my abilities. I once thought I could do anything, to only find I'm severely lacking.

It's one thing to face an old fairy decree which requires you to make a sacrifice to a dragon after your eighteenth birthday or become a slave to the High Fae, but it's another to fail when you're heir to the throne.

The Swendale dragon decree is an agreement made over two hundred years ago between the High Fae King Alberic and my family's ancestor King Aberthol Swen. As the blood of Swen's attracts dragons, a decree was signed to ensure fairy magic provides invisible protection of Swendale's borders from dragons. If a Swen crosses the borders of the kingdom and leaves Swendale, the protection is void and they risk their own life. Payment for the protection falls to the sovereign's male heirs. After their eighteenth birthday, a male heir has twenty days to seek out a dragon and offer an acceptable sacrifice or become a slave to the High Fae.

I failed to make a sacrifice, and the task was left to my younger brother, Leo, when he turned eighteen. I had two years after my failure in which to contemplate my death and enjoy what I could before it became Leo's turn to sacrifice. According to the decree, if Leo died, I would die. If he failed, we would both become slaves to the High Fae. I trained Leo with a sinking feeling he would die or fail. Not one male ancestor in Swendale's history ever returned from sacrificing to a dragon. They either perished or became a slave to the High Fae.

I'm alive today because Leo didn't fail. I've always outshone Leo, but the one time it counted for something, he was the shining star. He made the sacrifice I couldn't. I'm trying to take account of what I do have because I didn't expect to live this long.

During what I thought was the two years I had left to live between my eighteenth birthday and Leo's; I took advantage of all the guilty pleasures in life. I was bitter and desperate, and indulged where I shouldn't have. I used my power and looks. I'm aware I'm attractive to many young women, especially ones with a thing for ruggedly handsome men with dark hair and dark eyes. Even more women love an heir to the throne. But good looks and being a prince can't help when it comes to dragons and war. And now - when there's no longer a timeline on my life, things look a little different.

"Hello, Prince Emeric." A pretty kitchen girl bats her long, dark eyelashes at me as I pass through the hallway. She ducks into a curtained alcove, but not before throwing me an inviting look.

A few months ago, before Leo's eighteenth birthday, I would have followed the pretty young woman. Desperate to fill my short time with pleasures of any kind, I would let any woman kiss me if she offered. Now, the ticking time limit on my life has stopped, and the desperation is replaced with emptiness. I'm not sure what I'm supposed to feel, what I'm supposed to do, or what to fill the emptiness with.

I walk past the alcove where the kitchen girl waits for me. She'll be disappointed, but I have larger matters waiting for me. As heir to the throne, and having survived the dragon decree, the queen of Swendale has taken a larger interest in making sure I'm prepared to take the throne someday. Swendale hasn't had a king in centuries, and I'll be the first. My mother is set on making sure I'm up to the task. Most days I shadow her and do her bidding. Any romantic notions with other women are no longer a pressing issue, learning from my mother is the bulk of my time.

"Emeric." Queen Adelinde, my mother, smiles at me when I enter the large banquet hall in the center of the castle. It's where we eat our meals and most of the daily tasks of castle life are completed.

"Hey, Em." My younger sister, Adette, looks up from a plate of biscuits and gravy. She's a younger version of Mother with long, golden brown hair and blue eyes. I tend to take after Father with his dark complexion and dark hair, while Leo is a mix of both our parents.

Adette keeps her eyes fixed on me as I take a seat. She's always observing things and knows more than she lets on. At one time, I suspected Adette would be heir to the throne, as Swendale has a history of ruling queens because of the dragon decree doing away with any male heir. But with Leo and I both alive, Adette is relegated to third in line.

"Did you settle the quarrel in the kitchen?" Mother asks.

"I told them to mix the two flavors of soup," I reply. "We'll be having pea stew at the banquet."

Adette snickers and then straightens up when Mother narrows her eyes at the unprincess like behavior.

"We may need a pea with one of our guests," Adette says.

"Adette." Mother shakes her head at my sister, and I have no idea what transpires between the two of them.

"Who exactly are these guests?" I ask, suspecting something is being kept from me. We're expecting travelers from the neighboring kingdom of Montagnia, the same kingdom which put us under siege two months ago.

"I understand the Duke of Locksley has a proposal," Mother says. "He is sending his daughter, Lady Oria, as his ambassador. She has spent the past few years in Verdelle, under their protection while Morella ruled Montagnia as regent. Lady Oria is returning to her home now that King Gareth is back in power."

Morella was a ruthless regent of the kingdom south of our border. Peace has returned under the rule of the rightful leader, King Gareth. Even though we're on good terms with King Gareth, there are many obstacles to overcome to undo the damage Morella caused. Trade routes were closed for many years, and it takes proposals and meetings to reopen them.

"Does the proposal involve reopening the trade routes with southern Montagnia?" I ask.

Duke Riker Robin oversees the area of Locksley in southern Montagnia. His region has mines which once traded their valuable resources for Swendale's honey, beeswax, and wool. Swendale is the only kingdom with the special Abella bee, which produces honey and wax known for healing powers. While Swendale is a self-sufficient kingdom, trade with other countries is sometimes necessary.

"There will be some talk of trade and other things," Mother vaguely replies and picks up a paper in front of her. Her eyes look at the written words on the paper rather than at me.

I notice Adette place a hand over her mouth to hold in another snicker of laughter.

"What is this about?" I ask, blinking slowly. I'm missing something.

"What do you think of marriage?" Mother asks, her eyes peering over the paper at me.

"Marriage?" The word bursts out of my mouth.

Chapter Three

FIA

"Marriage?" I sputter and my body freezes. My ears ring and I must have heard wrong.

Marriage is the last word I expected to hear from my parents. They know I have no intentions of marrying and would prefer to spend my life alone. I can't think of a man I would enjoy being married to, nor a man who would enjoy being married to me. It would be a punishment for both of us. Plus, I never want to have children.

"You will marry," my father, King Kenneth of Ryu-toa, tells me with a flat gaze.

"Are you trying to punish someone by having them marry me?" I ask.

My parents are aware of my bad attitude towards marriage and love, and I can't see it changing anytime soon. Watching their loveless marriage has strengthened my opinion to remain single. An unknown man out in the Greater World may be my true love, but it doesn't mean I need to find him and marry. True love is rare, and it can stay lost and unfound. I plan to never let anyone know I have a true love.

"Marriage is not a punishment." Father's voice is stern, meaning I shouldn't question him. "It's a duty."

"It may have been for you." I clench my hands into fists, discreetly hidden in my pockets. I plan to question him. "It is only the men in our family who are required to get married before eighteen to avoid turning into a dragon. I do not have the same curse upon me. Why then do I need to get married?"

"Your brother..." Father's voice trails off. He rarely talks about Fynn since he left.

In a rare show of emotion, Father reaches over and places a large palm on Mother's small hand. They sit side by side in their ornate throne chairs on a raised dais. Father's chair, of course, is much larger and more exquisite than Mother's.

"What about Fynn?" I ask, speaking the name most castle workers, guards, and villagers won't dare speak around my parents or me.

The rumor is Fynn ran away to elope with his old flame, Camille. I know the truth. Fynn left with Camille, but to help her escape a forced marriage and let her marry the kitchen boy she fell in love with. Fynn also went in search of his true love to thwart the curse upon him.

There are whispers of another rumor. That Fynn didn't marry by his eighteenth birthday and transformed into a dragon.

I don't know the truth, but I plan on discovering it. Our shared birthday was a week ago. Fynn is either a dragon, married to some girl to prevent the curse, or he found his true love.

Fynn was desperate to discover his true love and stop the curse. I read if you put fresh rosemary under your pillow while you sleep, you'll dream of your true love. Fynn agreed to attempt it, if I would also. My true love appeared in a vivid dream, but I lied to Fynn and told him I didn't have one. Fynn's dream was hazy, and I took him to a seer named Sibylla for clarity. Sibylla told Fynn his true love was a princess in an enchanted sleep. Fynn left to find her. He returned home after a failed attempt with a sleeping princess in Montagnia.

We knew of another sleeping princess, one from a fairytale. A century old tale out of Somniara about an enchanted princess asleep in a palace covered with thorns. The princess had to be Fynn's true love. I helped Fynn arrange a trip to Somniara with Camille. As much as I want to not believe in true love for myself, I want to believe in it for Fynn.

He deserves true love.

I promised Fynn I would find him, human or dragon, one month after our birthday. I've been planning and plotting to leave since the day I turned eighteen.

"Fynn was heir, and he didn't live up to his duty," Father says. "The responsibility now falls to you."

I clench my jaw. If the Tanin curse was on me, I would choose to become a dragon over marrying. I would avoid ascending the throne and continuing the curse.

"Female royals in Ryutoa don't have a place in the line of succession," I repeat from my well-engrained lessons on the laws of Ryutoa. "I am not heir, nor can I ever be."

"That is true." Father's voice echoes in the vast room.

"It's a stupid law," I say with a shake of my head. "If succession followed the order of birth, regardless of gender, I would be heir to the throne."

Fynn may be my twin, but I'm a few minutes older than him.

"Ryutoa's succession doesn't work that way." Father's voice is still calm, but I'm sure I can get him to pick up the tone and volume. This conversation is bound to stoke his anger.

"You're king." I stare hard at Father as Mother quickly wipes a tear from her cheek. I hate to bring up Fynn in her presence as she always cries, and tears from other people make me uncomfortable. "You can change the law."

"I may be king, but I can't change this law." Father looks at me with his steely blue eyes. They darken like a stormy sea when he gets angry. I'm making it wavy, and a storm is brewing. "It is tradition."

"Traditions can be broken," I retort with a glance at Mother. She sinks into her chair, aware of what's coming and braces herself.

"The curse on the males in our family is a tradition, and yet, it can't be broken," Father answers.

"You've never tried!" My passion is aroused before Father's.

"I know Fynn was trying and where did that get him?" Father twirls a corner of his curly mustache. Is he gloating?

"At least Fynn tried!" Father doesn't know Fynn left for Somniara, because he was forbidden from going there. "And he could return."

"There was a report of a dragon in Ilzchen the day after Fynn's birthday," Father reminds me, and I flinch.

He says, 'the day after Fynn's birthday', as if I don't share a birthday with him. There was no celebration for my eighteenth birthday.

"The reports claim there were two dragons, not one," I say, with a slight bitter edge. I'm not mad at my brother, but rather my father. "I doubt Fynn turned into a dragon and found another dragon quickly. The timing may only be a coincidence."

"It hardly matters. Fynn may return as a man or as a dragon," Father says, "but we still need a plan in place for succession."

"What plan do you have if Fynn doesn't return?" I ask, knowing there are no male heirs after my brother.

"There could be an heir," Father says, his hard eyes still on me. Mother won't look my way.

Father always has a plan, and I know he regrets not taking action with his plan for Fynn earlier. Fynn's luck is now going to be my misfortune.

"Our family lineage is recorded and straightforward. There are no heirs," I say.

I poured over our family history when I was trying to find a way for Fynn to avoid the curse bestowed upon males in our family. Generations of Tanin men have married before their eighteenth birthday, disappeared, or transformed into a dragon. Other Tanin's have been killed by the fire of a Tanin male transformed into a dragon. Survival in this family is difficult, which is why Fynn needed to escape.

Now it seems my fate may be the same as my brother's. I need to marry or escape.

"There could be an heir," Father says in a voice which makes the hair on my arms stand up. He leans forward in his throne chair and places his elbows on his knees.

My toes tap against the two-hundred-year-old stone floor as I think, and then my foot stills when a thought comes to me. A horrid thought.

"Succession of the Ryutoa line is males only and the next in line after Fynn would be-"

Oh, no. They can't want this for me. I don't want this for me. This has to be a cruel and unusual joke. It's very nearly a curse.

"Your son," Father fills in.

"No!" I narrow my eyes and clench my fists together. Father stares as hard at me as I stare at him. "I don't want children. Nor do I want to get married."

"It is your duty," Father says, while Mother still avoids looking at me. Her normally perfect posture is slouched in her throne chair, and she looks tinier than normal.

"No!" I shout. "It is not my duty. It is yours. Mother is young enough. You could have another child or two."

My parents married at eighteen and had Fynn and me at twenty years of age. Mother is still of childbearing age. She gave her husband an heir to the throne once, she could do it again.

"I can-" Mother's small voice cracks. "I cannot."

She shrinks into herself, and while I'm not one for emotion and embraces, I have a tiny desire to rush to my mother and wrap my arms around her.

"Your mother cannot bear more children," Father says, after a quick look at his wife. "The burden is now yours."

"Thank you," I say sarcastically. "Thank you for saying what it truly is. A burden. I'll have to carry a child for you to have an heir."

"Yes," Father replies, not understanding my sarcasm.

"What if I have to carry many children before I have a boy?" Rage rolls around in me like a storm building at sea. I inherited some things from my father, but his throne will never be one of them.

I'm not fond of the archaic rules in our kingdom for succession, but I haven't fought them because I have no desire to rule here. Though, I think I would be a far better ruler than most men who have led Ryutoa.

"Then so be it," Father says. "You'll have as many children as you need."

"Children are not a commodity," I seethe through my teeth.

I hate feeling as if Fynn and I were born only to preserve the Tanin line in Ryutoa. Though I can't think of another reason my father would have had us. It wasn't because he wanted children for a family.

"Royal children have duties," Father says. "You have privileges and with those privileges comes a price."

"Then I give it up!" I yell again, flapping my hands around as if I can swat this away. "I no longer want to be a princess."

Fynn wanted to trade places with me and not have a curse upon him, and now I'd gladly trade with him. Let me become a dragon and see what I can do.

"You cannot give up your title and place," Father says while Mother continues to remain silent.

"I have no place," I say in a smaller voice.

"You do," Father says. "And a more important one than ever."

"I don't want it." Rage still roils around in me, causing deep bitterness. I've never been needed, and when I am, it's the last thing I want to do.

"Fia." I hear the exasperation in Father's voice. He's stern and mad, but he's also worn. Fynn's disappearance weighs on him, and while Father won't make the mistake of having me run away, he also doesn't want to alienate me. "What can I give you? What do you want?"

I groan, loudly. I'm not going to give in, but I need to know what the stakes are. "Who am I supposed to have these children with?"

A small smile starts to grow on Father's face. It's a smile which makes my stomach seize.

"You'll be getting married," Father says with a tone of finality. "I have reached an agreement with someone. He will marry you and you'll have children together."

Now, more than ever, I need to find Fynn and bring him home. He's the only one who can save me. Fynn is the heir to the throne, and I am only a commodity. My father is selling me to the highest bidder.

CHAPTER FOUR

EMERIC

"You wish to barter me off?" My face flushes with heat. The castle workers have served my breakfast and leave us alone. I can now question my family privately. "In exchange for new trade routes?"

"No, of course not." Mother reaches for her cup of tea with honey. "The duke's daughter is visiting on her father's behalf. We'll entertain Lady Oria and listen to the proposal, but we would never force you to marry."

"You almost did," I remind my parents. "About six weeks ago. You were at the wedding."

"True." My father strokes the sides of his chin where he has a short goatee. "But it was a wedding to end a war."

My father, Prince Carmichael, married my mother without knowing about the dragon decree and what it entailed. After learning the Swen secret, he's done everything he can to protect us, but there's only so much you can do when fairies are involved.

"You betrothed me to Princess Snow and never told me about it," I counter. "How can I trust you won't sign my life away again?" The bitterness I've been trying to rid myself of starts to bubble up again. I know my parents thought they were protecting me by betrothing me to a girl whose blood could potentially dilute mine and allow our children to not attract dragons.

Fortunately, in a story worthy of a fairytale, Princess Snow or Eira, as she prefers to be called, ended up being Leo's true love. She saved his life with true love's kiss before she could recite her marriage vows to me.

"I understand why you might be upset, Emeric," Mother says. "But we've learned our lesson. Who you marry will be your choice, but we can entertain the options."

"Perhaps I won't marry." I pick up a piece of toast slathered with butter and honey from the plate in front of me. "I'm not having children to subject them to what I had to go through with a dragon."

"Leo and Eira are searching for a way to end the decree," Adette says. "Would you marry and have children if the decree ends?"

"And then what?" Toast crumbs scatter as I wave the bread in my hand. "Our blood still attracts dragons. Without the decree, we set Swendale up for the same devastation which caused our ancestors to sign the decree."

We don't know why Swen blood attracts dragons. The power of our blood and the decree are secrets kept within our family. A person with dragon attracting blood could be wielded as a powerful weapon. The kingdom is unaware for our safety. All they know is a fairy visits a Swen male on their eighteenth birthday to grant a quest. They have no idea we march off to our death to ensure their safety.

"Leo was able to offer a sacrifice," Adette says. Nearly daily I'm reminded of what my younger brother was able to do. I'm reminded how I fell short. I tear into the toast with my teeth, much like a dragon devouring a meal.

"Just because he did it, doesn't mean my children will be able to." I don't want my children to be failures like me. They don't need to have their insides eaten with deep guilt. "Only the sovereign's heirs need to fulfill the decree. If I don't have children, it doesn't need to be fulfilled until the next sovereign has children."

"You're planning to let Leo and Eira's children take the throne after you?" Adette taps her fingers on the table. If she doesn't have something in her hand to draw or write with, her fingers are moving as if she does.

"I have not made that a secret," I say. "You assume their children won't attract dragons because of Eira's blood, but we don't know for sure. We do know our children will attract dragons and will never be able to leave Swendale." I point at Adette and then myself. "I won't have children to subject them to a lifetime of danger."

Adette doesn't have to offer a sacrifice to a dragon when she turns eighteen in over a year, but she still can't leave the boundaries of Swendale because she would attract a dragon. None of us can leave. Besides Father, who doesn't have Swen blood, Leo and I are the only current royals to have crossed the borders of Swendale. We were covered in head-to-toe armor to prevent dragons from scenting our blood.

Even now, even traveling with Eira who may be able to grant him some protection against dragons, Leo must wear the protective armor. It's not the most comfortable attire to wear.

"Things are changing," Mother says. "Leo may return home with new information."

"When is he expected?" I hastily take another bite of toast.

"The last message he sent was nearly a month ago. It said they arrived in Somniara to locate someone they met when Leo was on his quest. They were going to attempt to gain access to the famed library to find information to help us," Mother replies.

"It may be a fool's errand," Father says. "Somniara was across the bay from Lanark, and stories ran wild about the palace being covered in thorns and devouring anyone who came near it. Leo and Eira may not even get into the palace to access the library."

Father is from the kingdom of Lanark at the southern end of the Greater World. His blood does not attract dragons, and his blood did not dilute his children's ability to attract dragons.

"Leo was the first to fulfill the dragon sacrifice," Adette says. "He could be the first to enter the palace."

I narrow my eyes at Adette. "You like to rub it in, don't you?"

"You were always first in everything, Em," Adette says with a roll of her eyes. "It's Leo's turn. And all the girls showing up here aren't for him, they're here to see you. You're still the heir."

"At least I'm still the devastatingly handsome one." I toss the last bit of toast into my mouth. I'm tired of my failures being thrown in my face. I'm tired of so many things and need a change.

"You're the most eligible and sought after young bachelor," Adette says. "While Leo is going to marry Eira."

"I'm perfectly happy to remain single," I say. "No one else needs to be let in on our family's secrets and misfortune."

"Not many women realize you want to be single," Adette says. "I can't believe how many of them throw themselves at you."

"You'll find this outrageous," I say, letting my guard down. "But I'm getting tired of it."

CHAPTER FIVE

FIA

"It's outrageous!" I storm out of the throne room.

Reimund is on my heels the moment I exit. With the fabric of my cloak pinched in tight fists, I stomp down the hallway and toward the back exit to the stables. Reimund's feet keep time with mine, but he remains silent and says nothing. I'm not going to be able to lose him, and I don't care. I only need to let this anger dissipate and come up with a plan to escape.

With the fabric of the cloak billowing behind me, I look stronger than a fierce wind, and the stable hands know to clear out of my way. I shove open an empty stall and throw myself down on a fresh hay bale.

Reimund isn't far behind, and while others might be afraid to enter the stall after me, he isn't. He stands at attention in the open door of a stall while I drop to a fresh hay bale.

My guard approaches me as if I'm a lonely and scared stray. He holds out the two kittens, one in each hand. "Here."

Though I want to hurl things or squeeze something between my hands to help lessen the anger raging through me, I gently take the kittens from Reimund's outstretched hands. I let them settle in my lap and my fingers trail over their heads, their tiny ears, and down their soft necks to the spine under their fur.

"They expect me to marry," I say softly.

My grandmother and Fynn are the only ones I normally have personal conversations with, as I don't have any close friends. But Fynn is missing and Grandmother left the day after my birthday to travel. Reimund is all I have left, though I may as well talk to myself or the kittens.

"Marriage is not a bad thing." Reimund steps near a wall of the stall.

"Then why aren't you married?" My voice is a little snarkier than I mean it to be and I notice Reimund flinch. "You're older than me."

"I'm the sole provider for my family," Reimund replies. "When they are well provided for, then I can marry, assuming I find a girl I love, and she wants to marry me."

I spend more time thinking about ways to outmaneuver my guards, when perhaps I should spend time trying to get to know them. I had no idea Reimund was the sole provider for his family.

"Who do you support?" I ask.

"My mother and my younger sister," Reimund replies. "My mother has taken ill, and my sister is only sixteen. I won't have her married off to cover our expenses."

I jerk my chin up, letting my gaze drift from the kittens in my lap to Reimund. He leans against the wall made of wooden boards.

"If you don't mind me asking, what happened to your father?"

"You wish to talk, Princess?" Reimund kicks a foot up against a board and crosses his arms over his chest.

"You well know I'm not one for conversation or social outings, but at times I can talk when needed." I shrug my shoulders. "Or yell."

"Very well." Reimund nods his head with a small smirk. He must have heard my shouts from the throne room. "My father is presumed lost at sea. He was in a fishing boat and ventured beyond the safety zone. He ignored the warning of danger, and a storm came up."

"I'm sorry for your loss." My palms run over the kittens' backs, and I can't tell if I'm warming them or they're warming me.

Reimund shrugs. "He made the choice to ignore the warning. Now I must pay for it."

"Did you have a choice to work or not?" I tilt my chin Reimund's way. Before he was my guard, he was assigned to Fynn.

"I must work, but I had a choice in what kind of work. I didn't want to be a fisherman like my father," Reimund replies.

The village below the castle mostly relies on the fish from the ocean for their livelihood. Ryutoa tends to be a self-sufficient kingdom providing for its own needs. I also prefer to be self-sufficient.

"What's your sister's name?" I ask.

"Miette," Reimund replies, and before I can ask another question he continues. "And I'm sorry for your loss. It must be difficult with your brother gone."

"He's not dead," I shoot back sharply, the course of the conversation veering away from what I want, but at the same time I need this conversation to get to my goal. My goal is to escape and find Fynn.

"I never said he was," Reimund replies. "Like my father, he is presumed missing."

"Fynn isn't dead," I repeat. I know he isn't. He's my twin and I feel it in my bones. If he were dead, I would know. But something's happened to him. "You accompanied him on his travels to Montagnia. You must have learned something. What do you think happened to him?"

Reimund was one of the five guards assigned to Fynn when he traveled for a month. Fynn told our father he was looking for a bride elsewhere, but in truth he was seeking his true love. The seer told him to travel to Montagnia, or she foresaw deaths occurring. He traveled there, failed to wake a sleeping princess, and returned home before leaving undercover to Somniara.

Reimund is now assigned to me, and we have not openly talked about Fynn.

"It does not matter what I think," Reimund says. "Only the truth matters, and Prince Fynntan is the one who knows the truth."

"Did Fynn tell you the real reason for traveling to Montagnia?" I keep my eyes on Reimund, alert for any change in his behavior.

"I'm not sure whether you're testing me, as Prince Fynntan swore his guards to secrecy and allegiance. We also swore allegiance to King Kenneth, but revealing your brother's desire to the king would result in harsh consequences."

"There is no test. I know my brother and while he wouldn't tell Father the real reason for his travel, he would likely tell you," I say.

"He did tell us something," Reimund says, maintaining allegiance to Fynn.

"Fynn told you he was looking for his true love, and I respect your decision to not tell my father or me. It was my idea for Fynn to run away after the trip to Montagnia. I know you helped devise Jarrod's escape from the dungeon so he could travel with Camille and Fynn."

Reimund kicks a boot against the wooden stall. "I could lose my position if word gets out."

"You won't lose it because of me," I say. "I'm happy you helped Fynn."

"Fynn revealed the truth of his true love out of desperation, and I wouldn't have believed it, except I witnessed it with my own eyes. Prince Fynntan said his true love was a princess in an enchanted sleep."

"And he found a sleeping princess in Montagnia," I say.

"But she was awakened by another with true love's kiss," Reimund fills in, telling me the story my brother revealed to me. "Prince Fynntan wanted to travel to find the story-book princess in Somniara, but fate led him home."

"He didn't elope with Camille," I say, speaking the truth. I don't trust many people, but something tells me

I can trust Reimund. "He went to find his true love in Somniara."

"Do you think he found her?" Reimund asks me.

I pick up a kitten and hold it to my chest. Its tiny claws stick in the lace bodice as strongly as I stick to my faith in my brother.

"I think he did," I say, "but I don't know the outcome of the situation. I don't know whether he's married or transformed, and with Fynn's absence my father is forcing me to marry. Would your mother marry off your sister if you disappeared?"

"You're a princess," Reimund starts. "Royals and nobility do not have the same practices and customs as commoners."

"Which makes me ripe to be sold to the highest bidder." My words are steely, backed by all the anger I felt when my father told me I'm expected to marry.

"Surely that will not happen," Reimund says, a look of disgust on his normally stoic face. "But you are royal and perhaps you need a marriage to rule in your brother's absence."

"I cannot rule," I say and focus on gently petting the kittens instead of letting my anger flow through my fingers. "But I can be married off to provide an heir to the throne."

"Oh." Reimund's eyes widen with realization. "Oh."

"Would you see your sister married off only to be a carrier of children?"

"I only wish for her to bear children if it is her desire someday," Reimund replies. "Children should not be used for gain. They're a blessing."

"In my family they're a bargaining chip, a vessel to carry on a cursed bloodline." I grind my teeth together and blink my eyes.

"I'm sorry, Princess." Reimund looks down at his black boots.

"Miette is lucky she's not a princess." I take my hands off the kittens and clench my fists. One kitten clings to my chest and another lies in my lap. "Because I've been sold to the highest bidder. To a man older than my father. And I'm required to bear an heir."

CHAPTER SIX

EMERIC

"I have no intention of marrying," I tell Mother as we walk the halls after breakfast. We're headed to her study to review new trade contracts with Montagnia's northern mines. "I won't marry, and I definitely won't have children to put them through what Leo and I went through."

"I understand." Mother pinches her lips together. While she didn't have to encounter a dragon, the worry and extreme anguish for her sons changed her. Deep grooves pepper the sides of her eyes and worry lines reside permanently between her eyes. Each glance at her face reminds me it's all my fault. "I also never wanted to have children, but then I married your father, and well..." Mother's hands flutter with long, pointed fingers in my direction.

Mother has told me she was reluctant to have children and put her sons through the dragon decree. Her older brother never returned from attempting a sacrifice to a dragon, leaving her as heir. When my grandmother passed on, Mother became queen. Adette would have been in the same position if Leo hadn't made a sacrifice which saved us all. Swendale continues to have protection from dragons until the next male Swen is born to a ruler.

And that child won't be mine.

"If children come with marriage," I say, "I won't marry."

"It's nice to have someone rule at your side with you." Mother's shoes make tapping noises on the stone floor as we walk the dark hallway. "Your father is invaluable in his help."

"I know." Father's home country of Lanark is known for their military and navy, and Father's advice helped our castle immensely when it was put under siege. "But I'll have an alliance with Leo and Eira as they rule Montagnia and Adette will be here. She'll help."

"If she remains here," Mother says.

"I'm counting on it." I push open the door to Mother's office and let her walk in. "She has Swen blood. She'll be here."

"Things in the Greater World are changing," Mother says. "Your generation is developing more bonds across kingdom borders and trying to figure out the mysteries fairies left behind when they retreated to the Mystic Lands after the Great Divide. Perhaps Eira and Leo will discover a way to protect you and any other Swen children from dragons if they choose to venture out of our borders."

"But there is no ending the decree," I state. Ending the decree risks the lives of all who live in Swendale, not only my family's lives.

Mother sighs as she sinks into a chair behind her large desk in the study. We often work in the banquet hall, but when more private conversations need to be held without excusing castle workers, we find ourselves in this secluded and small room.

"The decree was made for a reason. Our kingdom was devastated when dragons sensed Swen blood. It put people at risk of injury and death. The decree ensures a barrier keeps dragons out of Swendale." Mother taps her fingertips on the wooden desktop. "We have been over this at your eighteenth birthday and at Leo's. I have no more answers than I did before."

"I'm sorry." I grit my teeth and sit in a chair across the desk from Mother.

Leo and I didn't discover the secret of our family's blood or learn about the decree and what it meant until our eighteenth birthdays. Adette knows, though she isn't supposed to learn about it until she turns eighteen. Eira and her father learned our family's secret, but we also keep their secret about Eira's blood.

"Your father and I have done what we can to protect all of you, but aside from changing the blood in our veins, there's nothing else we can do." Mother runs the palm of her hand over a large, round marble paperweight on her desk.

"Could it have been a curse which causes our blood to attract dragons?" I run a hand through my curls to push them out of my face.

Mother's eyes pinch shut. "You know as much as I do. I don't know the reason for our blood, nor why it exists. We have it and it's a secret our family must bear."

"I understand." I once questioned why we kept our dragon attracting blood a secret, but the recent siege on our castle gave me firsthand experience as to why it's important to keep the secret of our blood hidden from the rest of the Greater World. Evil people could wield us as weapons.

I hate to think of someone kidnapping Adette and using her as bait to attract a dragon.

"You will be the first king to rule Swendale in a very long time." Mother continues to run her palm over the marble paperweight, as if she's some sort of fortune teller gazing into a glass ball to see the future.

"I hope it's many more years until I'm crowned. I have much to learn from you."

A small smile rises on Mother's weary face. She's endured much the past couple of years, and while I placed much blame on her for my fortune in life, I now know it was misplaced.

"Your confidence never fails you," Mother says, though she doesn't know what fears I hide from her. "I know you will do what is best for Swendale."

"We can't change our blood, nor can we rid the world of dragons." I'm not one to smile since my quest, though I realize it's something I should do. But what do I have to smile about? "We'd best focus on what we can do and what we can change."

Mother places her hands in her lap, lifts her chin, and smiles at me. "Spoken like a true ruler. Shall we get to work?"

I nod and kick out my legs, crossing one ankle over the other, ready to get to work.

The work of a ruler never seems to end. Even if it is only a prince making a choice between pea soup and stew.

CHAPTER SEVEN

FIA

I kick at my sheets with my feet, wishing I wasn't a princess. On my side in bed, I look through the tiny window slit and spot stars twinkling in the dark sky. They seem so close and yet so far. I wait for a shooting star to pass so I can make a wish on it.

I don't care if it's a legend about wishes on shooting stars coming true, I'm desperate. True love is supposed to be a legend, and yet - I kick at my sheets with my feet again - I have a true love somewhere. If I'm to marry the man my father chooses for me, true love won't matter.

The stars keep twinkling in the black canvas, but none shoot across the sky. There will be no wish for me. Very little magic remains in the Greater World since fairies and all magical beings retreated to the Mystic Lands over a hundred years ago. Fairies rarely set foot in the human world, and if there is any magic left, I must have used up my allotment.

I wish I had never slept with the rosemary under my pillow and dreamt of my true love. If I close my eyes – he's there – as if he were in front of me. Dark eyes stare at me. Dark curls drape around a face which looks chiseled out of stone. A shadow of facial scruff coats his face as if he can't be bothered to shave. His look is vacant, as if he's trapped and only his –

No.

I can't think of him. Can't dream of him. Can't believe he's real.

What's real is this nightmare I'm trapped in. There's no wish strong enough to help me now.

"Fia?" The door to my room cracks open. "Fia?"

I know the quiet, hesitant voice. It's my mother. She rarely visits me in my tower room, preferring to have me visit in her room. A nighttime visit is extremely unusual but not concerning enough for me to turn her way.

"What do you want?"

Quiet footsteps traverse across my floor and the mattress on my bed sinks as Mother sits on it.

"I couldn't sleep and wanted to check on you." Mother reaches out a hand and places it on my back.

Not one for physical touch, my back muscles tense and I squirm away. I love my mother, but I don't think she understands me. She never quite knows how to respond to me and perhaps I'm not quite the daughter she expected. I'm never what anyone expects.

Undeterred by my squirminess, Mother sets her palm on my back as I face away from her. She rubs her hand in a small circular pattern.

"I know today was not what you wanted," Mother says.

"How could you agree to this?" My words are bitter, strangled by emotion.

"You know I have no say in matters of the kingdom," Mother says in her quiet voice, but her hand puts a little more pressure on my back as if she wishes her hand mattered.

"I am not a matter," I say, the bitterness still tinging the edge of every word. "I am your daughter."

"You are." Mother's voice is again soft, and her hand moves in a circular pattern on my back. "But you're also royal and of your father's blood."

"Tanin blood." I say it like it's a curse word. "Does Grandmother know Father's plan?"

My father's mother married into this madness and understands what the curse does to Tanin men. She watched it take the life of her husband and father-in-law, and I know she's fierce about protecting the rest of her family.

"No." Mother shakes her head. "But I will get word to her. She won't be happy, but she'll know there's not much she can do to change your father's mind. Ryutoa is a man's world. A Tanin man's world."

"Grandmother told Fynn and me what happens to Tanin men after they marry. The curse still has a hold on them, even if they don't turn into a dragon. They no longer love."

"The Tanin men have always had a thirst for power, for riches, for a hold on the kingdom." Mother's hand is still on my back, and I wait for her to speak more. "Your father's true love is the might of his blood, even if it's cursed."

I hold my breath under Mother's frozen hand. I may have Tanin blood, but my true love is not what lies in my blood. My true love is a man somewhere in the Greater World. A man who can ignite my blood, and one I want to smother out.

"But the curse isn't on me," I say after I finally take a breath and banish thoughts of the man I never intend to meet. "I didn't turn into a dragon, nor did I have to marry by eighteen."

"And the curse may not be on your children," Mother says.

My breath stills in my chest again. I'm always thinking, always planning, and yet – I never thought of this. Why did it never dawn on me?

"There's never been a male heir from a Tanin princess," I say, my voice devoid of any emotion.

"Your child, your son, could be the answer. Your son may not be cursed," Mother says.

"We cannot know that for sure," I say. "A child of mine may still be cursed. Other Tanin princesses may not have had children to prevent the curse from being carried on."

"Perhaps it's only the heirs of Tanin men who the curse has a hold on," Mother says. "As a female Tanin, your male child may not be cursed."

"That's wishful thinking." I choke on a sob. "My child could still be cursed, and I don't want them to be subjected to this. I'll never have children."

"Oh, Fia." Mother sighs.

"And Fynn is heir, not me," I whisper. "He could still return. But he is most likely still cursed. His male children will still be cursed."

"Fynn." Mother's hand starts to rub my back again. "I know he's out there, but I don't know if he'll come back. He may be-"

"A dragon," I interrupt. "Which sounds a lot better than getting married and passing on a curse."

"Your father is working under the assumption Fynn won't be back."

"Fynn wanted to find his true love. He might have found her. He might be married and making his way back here as we speak," I say. "Why is Father making me get married so soon? What difference will five more years make?"

"He does not want to wait," Mother says. "He waited with Fynn and won't make the same mistake again."

"What about adoption?" I ask, my voice brightening with a thought. It's a simple thought, but one I haven't entertained before. "If you adopt a baby, would they be held under the curse?"

"They would not be." Mother sighs. "They wouldn't be of the same blood as the Tanin's."

"Adopt!" I roll over to face my mother and she tucks her hands into her lap.

In the darkness I can't see her expression, but I can sense it. A sadness, stronger than her usual one, drags her posture down.

"I wanted to," Mother says.

"Then why didn't you?" I don't know why I ask when I already know the answer.

"I would have loved to give you and Fynn more broth-ers and sisters, but my fate is bittersweet. I married into this family and while I have all the privileges of it, I have no real power. My only duty is to provide a male off-spring to keep the line going. For Tanin's, it's all about the blood."

"I know that all too well," I say. "Duty and sacrifice. But this time it's not for the kingdom, it's for the Tanin family."

"It's for the kingdom," Mother says. "Your father arranged this marriage to benefit the kingdom."

"Why do I have to marry a man I don't know?" I clench my hands into fists. Would I say the same thing about my true love? "Why make me marry a man older than you?"

Mother closes her eyes and when she opens them, they shine in the meager light with moisture.

"I fought for you and failed," Mother says. "I'm sorry. I tried every point and every excuse, even down to sug-gesting you marry the guard you can't run from."

"Reimund?" I'm surprised Mother fought for me and also surprised at her suggestion.

"You need to run," Mother says in a voice so soft I almost don't hear. "Just like Fynn."

"Run?" I repeat, startled and confused. Mother wants me to run away to avoid being married?

"I know you helped Fynn to run away," Mother says in a quiet voice, "and you need to do the same for yourself."

"How?" I wrinkle my nose. "How do you know I helped Fynn?"

"I discover things the same way you do," Mother says. "By being quiet and unseen. I know far more than anyone realizes."

I always thought Mother was different enough from me to not understand me, but perhaps I'm more like her than I know.

"Thank you." I place my hand over Mother's.

She bends down and places a tender kiss near my hairline. "I love you, Fia. You need to do the same for yourself. Devise a plan and run. It's time for new blood in Ryutoa. Blood without the Tanin curse."

Mother leaves, and I remain awake. I often don't sleep well, and this evening is no exception. In the darkness of night, my mind starts to devise plans.

Chapter Eight

EMERIC

It's black with darkness in my room when I hear the door slowly open. I hold my breath and remain still. It must be after midnight. There should be no one coming to my room while I'm asleep.

"Prince Emeric?" a quiet, but sultry sounding voice asks into the dark.

I recognize the voice, and I can nearly picture the young woman who works in the castle, but I don't remember her name. I don't want to answer her, but I fear if I don't, she'll make her way to my bed.

"Please leave," I say, scolding myself for not locking the door. In the past I may have left it unlocked for a girl like this, but things are different now. I no longer have a deadline for a date with death.

"You don't wish for company?" The young woman attempts a seductive voice, but it only repels me, and I grimace.

"No," I reply in a gruff voice. It's the same tone I'd use with Leo when I was trying to train him for his eighteenth birthday quest. The same voice I'd use when he would fail at the task I put before him. Now I'm the one failing.

Clenching the edge of a blanket in my fists, I remain quiet and wait. The girl stands at the door, and there's heavy silence between us. She waits and hopes I'll change my mind, and I only wait for her to leave.

Finally, the door closes with a click. Frustrated, I shove off the blankets and heave myself out of bed. My footsteps are heavy on the floor as I brusquely walk to the door. I slide the lock into place when a loud knock sounds.

With a huff of annoyance, I shove the lock aside and jerk the door open.

"I thought I told you-" I stop short.

Adette stands in front of my door in a robe and holds a candle. The flame flutters in the draft created with opening the door.

"I apologize." I shake my head. "I thought you were someone else."

"The girl leaving?" Adette tips her chin down the hall the way the girl probably left.

"Yes." My chin drops.

"Back to your old ways?" Adette asks with a lift of her eyebrows.

"No." I quickly shake my head. "Nothing happened. She came here hoping something would, but I turned her away."

"Wonders will never cease." Adette tosses long, loose waves of hair over her shoulder. During the day she wears her hair in fancy braids and styles, but now it lies un-adorned. It gives her the look of the young Adette I remember. The young girl who would follow me around the private royal garden and beg for me to play with her.

I grip the edge of the door in my hand. "Do you need something?"

"I can't sleep." Adette puts a hand on my chest and pushes me out of the way to walk in my room. "Let's talk."

"Okay." I'm unsure where this is leading as Adette and I haven't talked much in the last two years.

She idolized me when she was younger and followed me everywhere. After my eighteenth birthday quest, when I learned of our family's secret, I pushed everyone away, especially Adette. Looking at her only reminded me I was heading toward death, and she would take my place as heir.

"Sit." Adette pats the cushion on the bench in front of the fireplace where she settles herself.

Perhaps now I can start making up for the last two years or alienate my younger sister even more.

"What do you want to talk about?" I take a seat next to Adette.

"We're stuck here, aren't we?" Adette blows out her candle and sets the candlestick on the floor.

"What do you mean?" I watch the small flames dance in the fireplace. When I first returned from my failed quest to offer a sacrifice to a dragon, I wouldn't allow a fire for the longest time. I couldn't stand to see flames because it reminded me of the dragon I encountered.

"You and I." Adette points at me and then herself with a slender, pale finger. "We can't leave Swendale because we'll attract dragons. Leo at least has Eira, and if she can talk to the dragons, she can protect him."

"We don't yet know if she can talk to dragons, and Leo must be fully covered in armor when he crosses the border. We could cross the border if we were covered in armor."

I have no desire to put the boiled leather armor on again. To leave Swendale and lessen the chance of a dragon smelling me during my quest, I wore a full suit of leather armor, along with gloves, boots, and a full-face headpiece. My face, neck, and wrists were coated in beeswax to prevent any scent from escaping where my clothing pieces met. It was extremely uncomfortable.

"If Leo and Eira have kids, there's a chance their blood may not attract dragons." Adette's fingers tap on her thighs.

"Or because Eira has some dragon blood, the scent of their blood might be even stronger."

"I doubt it." Adette seems sure of herself. "Hopefully Leo's children don't have the same blood as us and there will be no need for his sons to go on a quest to sacrifice."

"You won't have children?" I know Adette is only sixteen, but it seems a big decision to make quite young. I'm nearly five years older.

"I don't know. Maybe if things change, but I don't need to provide an heir. I also don't want to subject my children to what you and Leo went through, if it comes to that." Adette twists her long hair into a bun at the base of her neck. "I thought a fairy would visit me on my eighteenth birthday and grant me a quest, just like you and Leo, and it turns out only males get a fairy visit to fulfill some ancient decree. I'm not sure if I'm relieved to not be a male and have to face a dragon, or if I'm disappointed I'm not important enough to help my family and kingdom."

"You're important. Important enough to keep alive. The men are the ones who get sent to their deaths."

"Em." Adette scolds. "Why do you always have to be such a-"

"I'm sorry," I interrupt. I've never spoken the words to her, even if I try to do things to make it up to her. "I know we kept secrets from you, and nothing has been easy the last couple of years."

"I know more than you all let on," Adette says. "I may even know things you don't."

My eyebrows lift high on my forehead. I'm afraid to ask what she does know.

"We're safe now," I say. "There's no threat of war and no other eighteen-year-old males to go on a quest."

"But we can't leave Swendale unless we want to risk attracting a dragon." Adette looks at the small flames in the fireplace. She has no firsthand experience with how massive the flames from a dragon's mouth can be.

"We can't change our blood." I sound like Mother. All the time I spend with her is rubbing off on me.

Adette's fingers flutter as if she's directing a silent chorus. "What if magic could change our blood?"

"All magic has a price." My hands rub the fabric of my linen trousers on my thighs. "Fairy magic protects our borders at a price."

"At the cost of you and Leo!" There's a passion behind Adette's voice, and she sounds like Leo and me when we discovered the cost of our blood. It's heartwarming she cares this much, but she won't have to honor the decree unless she must send a male child to sacrifice to a dragon.

My shoulders drop. There's nothing to say. I failed. When I learned the sacrifice was my life, I ran.

"I'm thankful the cost didn't take you." Adette presses her lips together.

"You probably wished it did after I returned."

"You were awful." Adette manages a small grin. "But I'd never wish death or being a slave to the High Fae on you."

"I wouldn't blame you if you did," I say. "I was quite bitter."

Some of that bitterness still lingers, much like ash remains after a fire.

"What if a magic wand could alter our blood?" Adette won't look at me.

"Don't even think of it." I know she's wondering about a magical item locked in the royal vault.

"Just because I think it, doesn't mean I'll do it." Adette's fingers flutter in motion again as she thinks.

"Promise me you'll never touch that wand." I once again sound like a big brother, but Adette doesn't acknowledge me as she's lost in thought. "Adette!"

Adette jerks her attention back to me, her eyes now focusing. "There must be some way."

"Everyone in our family for the past few centuries has pondered the same thing we do." I look away from the flames of the fire, as I try to tamp down the small rise of panic in me. This talk of our family's dragon attracting blood is causing memories to resurface. I won't sleep tonight. "We're lucky Leo was able to offer a sacrifice and we're lucky we have protection from dragons."

"I know we're protected from dragons because of the decree with the High Fae King, but do you ever think there's another way the fairies could help us?" Adette's eyelashes flutter. "Something besides requiring a sacrifice to a dragon?"

"Fairies are not humans," I tell Adette. "Their ways are not our ways."

"The fairy who delivered your quest and Leo's quest was not a full fairy." Adette has been infatuated with fairies since she was a young child. She studies and draws them as if she's going to be tested. "He's a faeling. Part human and part fairy."

"He was only a messenger fairy. He's not High Fae or even fully fairy," I say. "He can't change the decree, nor can he help us."

"But what if there's a fairy who can help us?" Adette's face brightens, or it might be the light of the fire dancing off her skin.

"We don't have fairy godparents, nor do we have a genie in a lamp to make wishes." There are stories of fairy godparents and genies in lamps granting wishes, but the only fairies who visit Swendale since the Great Divide are the fairy messengers.

"We don't need wishes," Adette says. "What if we married fairies and had children? Would a faeling be required to fulfill the decree? Or maybe they would have magic which would help?"

For a moment, I feel nothing. It's as if my body shuts down because my mind doesn't want to comprehend Adette's suggestion.

"Emeric?" Adette squints at me as I blankly stare, and I'm not looking at her, but rather through her. I have a habit of staring into space since I returned from my quest.

"No." I vehemently shake my head. "I'll have nothing to do with the kind who forced me to sacrifice to a dragon."

"You don't have to," Adette backtracks fast. "Especially if you're not going to have children."

"I don't want to marry a princess either." I press my lips together and shake my head. "No royals, especially ones with curses, tainted blood or decrees, or anything having to do with fairies."

"Em." Adette pats my knee with a hand. "I understand your hesitation with fairies, but they can't all be bad. Fairies can be quite magnificent. Even benevolent."

"Adette?" My sister has a dreamy look on her face. I hope her infatuation with fairies has not led her to thinking she can fall in love and marry one. Fairies in the Greater World are rare unless sent by a High Fae, like the messenger sent on my eighteenth birthday. Fairies are not free to wander among humans as they used to. Fairies tired of humans manipulating and using them, just as humans tired of fairies meddling in their lives. I never want to see a fairy again as long as I live.

"My children may not have to fulfill the decree with a sacrifice even if I sit on the throne." Adette's voice is soft, as if she doesn't mean for me to hear her dream.

"You don't know what you're talking about." I suddenly feel cold and small bumps emerge on the skin of my arms. "It's dangerous to fall in love with a fairy or have one fall in love with you."

"But it can happen. Faelings exist." A small smile rises on Adette's face.

The only hope I find in this situation is Adette can't easily leave Swendale, nor can she get to the Mystic Lands, and fairy visits to the Greater World are rare.

She's as likely to fall in love and marry a fairy as I am to find my true love and have children.

CHAPTER NINE

FIA

"I don't want children." I cross my arms over my chest and narrow my eyes at the man who agreed to be my husband.

Yesterday I was told I am to marry and bear an heir. Now I'm face to face with the man I've been bartered off to. His name is Gordon, he's from Ilzchen, and he owns merchant ships. There is nothing impressive about him. In a strange twist of fate I won't reveal to anyone, it was one of Gordon's ships I found passage on for Fynn, Camille, and Jarrod to escape to Somniara.

The unremarkable man turns to my father. "You told me children are a required expectation of this union."

"They are." Father turns a serious gaze at me before returning a diplomatic one to the guest I consider uninvited. "My daughter knows what's required of her."

"She'll be ready," Mother pipes in, which astonishes me. She often remains a quiet token when she's allowed to be at Father's side. "Princess Fia only needs time to adjust to the news of this union. She was taken by surprise."

Surprise is an understatement.

Mother shoots me a quick pleading look. I twist a lock of hair around my finger as I start to narrow my eyes. I can play this in many ways. I can be a defiant princess and outright disobey my father and king, which every bone in my body leans toward. I can play the perfect princess and acquiesce to all the demands put on me, which I have done before, but none of the previous demands were this life altering. Or I can fall somewhere on the vast line between those two.

My best play now is to be a proper princess with a small bit of defiance. I have no intention of marrying this man, but I need Father to think I will, but I also need to give Father enough defiance to believe me. He'll be suspicious if I fully give in without a fight, because I'm known to be defiant. Father can plan a marriage, but I plan to run away and find Fynn before any union can take place.

"It's not that I don't want children, rather…" I start, not quite sure how to finish the sentence, for I really don't want children, and it would be a lie to say I do. I only need something to placate my father and this man before me. The poor man has no idea what he's getting himself into. My father shoulders most of the blame for this situation, but Gordon agreed to marry me.

"Rather," my mother jumps in, again astonishing me. "Princess Fia would like to be assured she will have assistance with any royal children. She will need nannies and governesses. She should be given an allowance for any royal child she bears, and a stipend from the crown if she bears a male."

I pinch a smile from forming. My mother has learned some negotiation skills in her years of sitting quietly by Father's side. While these stipulations won't need to come into play, I'm happy she's on my side.

"I-" Father starts to object at the same time Gordon speaks up.

"Of course." From where he sits across the table from my family, Gordon rapidly nods his head. "The princess may have whatever she wants and I'm capable of supplying."

I feel sorry for Gordon. He must think fortune is on his side to be engaged to a princess, but he'll find there's more fortune in not being shackled to me. In a surprising turn of events, my father found a rich man who is simple and kind. I expected a cruel husband. Gordon's actions and words don't lend him to be overbearing or harsh, and he will make a noble husband for someone. But he's not for me, and I'm not for him.

"And a stipend from the crown for a male?" Mother's voice has an edge as she looks at Father. If she's ever countered Father or spoken up to him, it's only when I haven't witnessed it. I'm quite impressed.

"I'll add it," Father reluctantly agrees. "As long as the wedding is in a month."

"That won't work." I look up at Gordon.

He's a forgettable man. There's nothing about him which stands out. Gordon is older than my parents, and while his hair is not turning grey, he is most definitely losing it. His figure is slightly rounded, and I can look at him eye to eye as we are the same height. While he is not appalling, he is also not appealing to me. He needs someone who will love him for who he is.

Gordon's riches, his merchant ships, and his affiliation with kingdoms on the western coast of the Greater World make him appealing to my father. Father loves what Gordon can do for Ryutoa. Father could have done worse and betrothed me to a scoundrel like the one Camille's father intended her to marry before Fynn rescued her.

Fynn has a habit of rescuing maidens, but I don't expect him or any other prince to come to my rescue. This princess is going to need to rescue herself, with some help from her mother.

"Princess Fia would prefer the wedding be placed at least six weeks out," Mother once again interjects. "The timing would be more optimal in producing an heir."

Oh, no.

I know Mother is making an excuse to give me time to plan and run away, but the implication of her excuse still brings a blush to my cheeks.

"Of course, of course," Gordon stammers, his face turning a bright shade of red.

I feel sorry for the poor man. He must have had a difficult time with the ladies when he was younger, and even now with a successful family business to run, he can only find a wife through negotiation. When I'm long gone, I hope he finds a woman who will make him happy and doesn't control him. I sense Gordon will do whatever he can to make his wife happy, and he doesn't need a controlling one to imprison him. Marrying me would be a prison of a different kind.

"We shall have a wedding in six weeks," Father confirms, brushing aside any talk of womanly reasons for delaying.

After another hour of playing princess, I'm released to the custody of my guard as the men finish the negotiations of my betrothal.

"Stable?" Reimund questions when I let my shoulders drop after the throne room doors close behind me.

"Please." I take a deep breath as Reimund takes up a slow pace next to my side. He knows I need to pet some kittens to release the tension in me.

I'm grateful when Reimund clears the workers out of the stable to give me some privacy. The two kittens I rescued are alert and playful, their near brush with death forgotten. They bat at the ties of my dress while I sit on a hay bale.

"I'll be outside if you need me," Reimund says.

"You can stay." I place the larger kitten on the ground at my feet, while I clutch the smaller one to my chest.

"Okay," Reimund says in an unsure voice and steps into the stall with me.

He's not the only one surprised. I'm quite surprised by my invitation.

"The wedding is in six weeks." My voice is quiet.

"Oh." Reimund leans against the wooden slats of the empty horse stall. "What are your plans?"

"There won't be a wedding," I reply in a low voice.

"You'll go the way of your brother?" Reimund picks up the kitten batting at the laces on his boots.

"I promised Fynn I would come find him a month after his birthday," I say. "I'll push the timeline up depending on when I can escape."

"Princess Fia, I'll do whatever I can to help you." Reimund dips his chin in reverence to me.

"Thank you." I avert my eyes to the kitten I hold. "But I don't want to jeopardize your job. I know you need to support your family."

"I would be honored to help you," Reimund says as the kitten wriggles in his large hands. "I understand Ryutoa has a tradition of male rulers, but keeping up tradition for the sake of tradition is not always the right thing to do. If my sister were in your place, I would be helping her to escape. I'll do the same for you. I'll help you run away."

Chapter Ten

EMERIC

"She can't run away." Father assures me as we head to the dungeon for a check of the prisoner after lunch. "She's behind an iron door and thick stone walls in a castle with a moat. Plus, there's always a guard on duty."

"She may not be able to run away, but someone could help her escape," I tell Father as we walk down the set of stone stairs leading to the only entrance of the dungeon.

"Fortunately, Morella is the only one in the dungeon at the moment." Father acknowledges the lone guard at the station.

Before us lies a corridor with cells on both sides. It ends at a stone wall. The Swendale Castle dungeon isn't often used, but ever since my non-wedding to Eira, her wicked stepmother has been imprisoned here. Morella ruled Montagnia as regent while Eira and her father were in hiding.

Morella killed Eira's mother after Eira's birth, used magic to charm Eira's father and marry him, and plotted to kill Eira and King Gareth to rule Montagnia on her own. In a chain of events at our wedding, Morella was subdued after drinking a fairy potion which should have turned her into a dragon. Morella wasn't aware of the decree not allowing dragons in Swendale, and her failure to transform allowed us to capture her.

"Morella has more enemies than she does friends," Father assures me.

"But even enemies work together at times." The stale and unmistakable scent of the dungeon wafts our way as we walk down the wide corridor. Damp and ripe with the smell of mildew and a stagnant moat, the dungeon is not a pleasant place. It becomes less pleasant the further you walk in, and Morella is in the furthest cell. "What happens when the potion she drank wears off?" I ask, wrinkling my nose.

As we near Morella's cell, the sound of iron tapping on the stone floor sounds. Because Morella drank a potion containing fairy blood, magical iron boots meant to subdue fairies and prevent magic, were able to entomb her feet. Iron burns fairies, but because Morella is human, the boots only heat up her feet. She continually moves her feet to distract from the intense warmth.

"It sounds as if it hasn't worn off yet," Father says. "When the sound fades, we'll know the potion has worn off."

"What happens if she can remove the boots before we can get to her? Will she be able to do magic or spells?" I ask.

"She'll still be locked behind bars." Father sounds confident, but I don't feel it. How can a stone cell and an iron door stop a woman who inflicted so much pain on others?

"Then we'll send her back to Montagnia?" I ask.

If the potion is still active in her bloodstream, it's safer to keep her in Swendale. Once outside our borders, the potion will likely cause her to turn into a dragon, and we would be unleashing great evil and wickedness into the Greater World.

"If the potion wears off, and if it's feasible to move her safely, we'll send her back to Montagnia," Father replies. "King Gareth assures me they have a secure place for her in their dungeons."

"I'm not sure what it is," I say. "But I have a bad feeling about keeping her here."

The tapping noise grows louder as we approach the far end of the dungeon. Guards continually change shifts to keep Morella under constant supervision. Her feet are encased in iron and her magic wand is locked deep in the royal vault. She should not be able to harm us.

"Ahh." Morella's voice is muffled through the thick iron door. "To what do I owe this visit? Have you come to beg my forgiveness and release me? My kingdom awaits its queen."

Morella continues to call herself Queen of Montagnia, as she is still married to the king, and treats everyone as if they are beneath her. The people of Montagnia were suffering under her rule, and King Gareth and Eira are trying to restore peace, prosperity, and security to their kingdom. But it won't happen overnight.

"You have no right to rule." Father slides open a panel in the door at face height.

I shouldn't be startled because I've looked at her face before, but Morella's image peering back through the opening startles me. I expect a witch to be terrifying, like a dragon, but Morella is beautiful to gaze upon. But it's a dark beauty, and I look at the door rather than her face staring through the opening.

"I can rule, but many kingdoms have the outdated tradition of passing the throne to a blood heir," Morella says.

"Your blood is tainted," I say with an edge to my voice, but I fear I sound more like a cowering child in Morella's presence.

"Ahh. You're one to speak. How is the little heir?" Morella's chuckle sounds evil. "Are you looking for a wife, Prince Emeric?"

"That's not your concern." I'm not sure what we accomplish with these visits to Morella, other than making sure she's still locked up tight. Morella seems to accomplish more by getting under our skin somehow.

"If I weren't already married, you could have my hand." Morella laughs. "I should have killed Gareth when I had the chance, and that little brat of his. Never give a job to someone else when you can do it better."

"Is there anything we can get you?" Father asks.

He treats Morella far better than she deserves.

"Seeing as you don't fulfill my usual requests," Morella says, "I could use another blanket. It gets a little drafty down here. I could conjure up some warmth if you'd let me have my wand."

"An extra blanket you shall have," Father replies.

"How is my wand?" Morella asks, her small hazel eyes glaring through the slot. "You haven't tried to destroy it, have you?"

We were warned not to destroy the wand, which is why it remains in the vault. Witch's often have their wands protected, and to destroy it could mean something bad. All magic has a reaction.

"Is there anything else?" Father never answers about the wand, as he doesn't want Morella to know it's stored nearby.

"I'm awfully tired of pea soup," Morella says in a voice which seems light and airy but contains notes of bitterness. "I'll never understand why royals have such an attachment to peas."

I roll my eyes and grimace. It's as if she's mocking me with her pea soup declaration, but there's no way she could have overheard me settling the quarrel in the kitchen yesterday.

"Prince Emeric." Morella again addresses me, and I tense. "Do you prefer sweet or bitter? Sweet peas? Bitter peas? Sweet women? Bitter women?"

I glance at Father for guidance, and he only presses his lips together.

"My advice is to look for a woman with some bitterness. Too much sweetness isn't good for you. But I hear you've been able to sample a lot of flavors." Morella laughs as I clench my teeth together.

I'm not proud of the past couple of years, but it's hard to shake a reputation.

"My life should be none of your concern." There's a harsh clip to my voice.

"Ah, but you were to marry my stepdaughter." Morella clicks her tongue. "And how did that work out?"

"You were the one to wreck the wedding," I say.

"Such a pity." Morella shakes her head, her dark blonde hair catching the light from the sconces on the wall in the corridor. "Now she's going to marry your younger brother. What a twisted and sad tale."

I'm glad Eira is marrying Leo. I was only marrying her out of duty because our marriage would have allowed Eira to take the throne of Montagnia and end Morella's reign as regent and the siege she put on our castle.

"You interrupting the wedding was the best thing to happen," I say. "Because now Leo can marry Eira, and you're stuck here."

I slam the panel shut.

"When I'm free," Morella yells, "I'll finish the job I started, and you'd better run!"

CHAPTER ELEVEN

FIA

"Run!" Reimund yells at me as he draws his sword.

"You didn't plan this?" I whip my head around, assessing our attackers. "This is not my escape?"

Three days have passed since my meeting with Gordon, and I haven't had time to fully arrange an escape, but perhaps Reimund has.

"I'm sorry, Your Highness, this is not the plan." Reimund puts himself in a defensive position. "This is real. We are under attack. You need to run."

"No." I shake my head as Reimund places himself between me and our attackers. "I won't leave you."

It's not supposed to be like this. I'm supposed to run away when Reimund isn't with me. I'm not supposed to be attacked when he's with me. I'm not supposed to be attacked at all.

During the lunch hour, news arrived of a batch of puppies without a mother and I headed on a desolate path with Reimund to retrieve them. The early summer day is like any other in Ryutoa. Cool ocean breezes blow in and cause the grass stalks to ripple like waves on the ocean. Because of past dragon attacks, the land surrounding the castle is barren of trees, with only grasses and shrubs growing. It's been sixty years since a dragon attack, but the trees still refuse to grow.

I should have been alert, but my mind was elsewhere. I was planning an escape, but not one like this. Thugs or bandits suddenly materialized out of the tall grass, and they now block any escape. Three men on horses slowly circle. I should have run when Reimund told me to, but now it's too late. The men surround us and start to hem us in, coming slowly together. We're outnumbered and they have us trapped.

In the distance there is a horseless cart with a driver. I noticed it earlier, but didn't pay any attention to it. Now I know it belongs to these thugs, and they were hiding behind it in ambush. I regret not being more suspicious.

"What do you want?" I yell.

"You, Princess," the largest man replies.

He's in front of Reimund and me and nudges his horse closer to us, as the men at our sides and rear do the same. The large man is obviously the leader of the bunch. He draws a sword from behind his back.

"Give us the princess and you're free to go," the leader tells Reimund.

The leader is on a horse, but on the ground he would tower over Reimund, who isn't short. The bandit leader is almost twice the bulk of my guard and more muscular. A dark tattoo pokes out of the top of his worn shirt, and both his biceps have tattoos, but I can't tell what they are.

"Never!" Reimund yells back.

My eyes nervously glance around assessing our opponents. The leader is armed with a sword, has a dagger on a strap across his chest, and most likely has daggers in his boots. The two men with him point swords our direction. Reimund has his sword drawn and mine is still hidden beneath my cloak. If I knew there was a chance we could best the attackers, I would draw my sword. But it's unlikely Reimund and I can take down all these men, especially when they're on horses. Keeping my sword hidden for now may be to my advantage.

"Give me to them," I tell Reimund. "You can go free."

"It's my duty to protect you." Reimund's hand tightens on his sword, and he protectively shields me with an arm, but I twist into a defensive position with my back to his. Reimund faces the leader, and I face one of the henchmen. The third hems us from a different side.

"You should not have to die for me." My heart beats erratically in my chest and I try to steady my breathing. This looks bleak for us.

"The princess or your life!" the large man yells. "It's your choice. Either way, we take the princess."

"You can go free," I tell Reimund. "Leave me."

Reimund's back presses against mine and we both tighten our leg muscles to brace our feet against the ground.

"I've seen them," he says in a hushed whisper. "You really think they'll let me run back to the castle? They don't want witnesses."

I inhale a sharp breath. If these men want me, they won't let Reimund live. But the big question is – why do they want me?

"Hand her over now!" the leader again declares.

"You'll have to kill me!" Reimund lashes back.

I clench my jaw at Reimund's exclamation. No one is going to get killed because of me.

"It wasn't in the job description, but since you added it, gladly," the man says with a vicious grin. He advances his horse forward and points his sword.

Reimund assumes a defensive position and my heart rate soars as dust rises into the air.

"Wait!" I step out from behind Reimund with my hands held up. "I'll go."

Everyone stops their motion to look at me.

"Your Highness," Reimund nearly growls. "You can't do this."

"I can." I narrow my eyes at him as I step to his side.

"Come forward, Princess." The large man beckons to me with a bend of his fingers.

I start to walk forward when Reimund grabs my wrist. "Please, Fia," he says, not using my title for the first time. "Don't do this."

"I see no other way," I say with a sad glance at him before the large man yells again.

"Princess! Move!"

I don't move and instead stare hard at the big brute. "I'll come if you promise you will not harm my guard. We leave and let him be. Can you give me your word?"

The large man nods once. "I give you my word. I will not attack if he doesn't attack."

I shake my hand out of Reimund's grip, as he doesn't want to let go. "Please," he begs.

For a moment, I think of running. Reimund would fight all these men to give me a chance to run. But then I think of his sister, Miette, and his mother. If I run, Reimund will surely be cut down and he needs a chance to live.

My father said being royal means sacrifice and duty, and I'm doing it.

"Take me." I hold my hands, palms out, in front of me.

A devilish grin covers the large brute's face. He jumps from his horse and darts toward me at the same time another man uses his horse to block me from Reimund. Large arms harshly wrap around me when I hear the clash of metal. It's the sound of swords hitting each other.

"Reimund!" I shout and try to twist in my captor's arms, but the hold is too tight. Knowing Reimund, he lashed out at the attackers and is now fighting them, but I can't see what's happening.

I thrash with all the energy I have and attempt to bite the arm holding me. The sword under my cloak is seized and pulled away from me. I have nothing left to defend myself.

"Help!" I scream. Fear swamps my body, and it's heavier than I thought it would be. The weight is daunting and unlike anything I've ever felt in my life. It crushes me, but not enough I can't still thrash against my captor and yell. "Help!"

"You'll stop screaming and fighting, Princess," the rough voice says, "unless you want to be the reason for the death of your guard."

A whimper escapes me as my body sags. I'll still have a chance to escape if I'm alive, and I can't do it dead. And Reimund needs a chance.

Quickly, my hands are bound, and I'm dragged toward the waiting covered cart. My captors let me see the carnage left behind.

The long grass is stomped down and stained red in places. Red with blood. A body lies on the ground. A body clad in the uniform of a Ryutoan royal guard.

"You gave me your word." A single tear rolls down my cheek as I look away from Reimund's body lying prone in the grass.

"I did. I said I wouldn't harm him." The large man shoves me into a corner of the cart. "But your guard attacked my men, who are defending something valuable. And you are valuable. I gave my word I would capture you. And I have."

"Hel-" My scream is cut short when a damp rag is placed over my mouth and nose.

I try not to breathe, but my chest tightens, and my head begins to feel as if it's in a fog. I gasp for a breath, and everything goes black.

Chapter Twelve

EMERIC

Black.

I see nothing, but infinite blackness, and it tears me through the heart.

It's not a still blackness, but one which instills fear. One which I don't want to be drawn further into, but I am. The call of duty draws me close, though everything in me wants to turn and run.

No.

My lips flutter with the movement of the word leaving my mouth.

Then the darkness explodes. It's a brilliant flash of light. An enormous head with multiple horns. A snakelike body with scales the color of frozen water. Talons with claws the size of a man's leg. Frightening eyes glowing an ice blue. Whiskers which can kill with a single touch.

The terrifying beast fully emerges from the depths of the vast lake, it inhales, readying to blast me with a stream of fire.

I turn to run, but –

My eyes fly open. My heart beats hard and heavy in my chest, and my body is slick with sweat. It dampens the linen shirt and trousers I wear. The blankets which wrapped around me earlier in the evening no longer cover me or my bed.

It was only a dream. A reoccurring nightmare.

Except at one time, it wasn't a nightmare. I lived it. And now I relive it in my dreams.

I clench my fists together and start to shiver as the coldness of my room and the remnants of fear wash over me. If anyone knows of the nightmares which trouble me, they have not said anything. I suffer in silence and darkness, keeping guilt and fear locked deep inside.

I change out of my damp night clothes and quietly walk into the hallway. Leaving the confines of my room helps me to separate myself from the spirits which haunt me.

The water dragon.

I thought it was a myth until I encountered it. Legends say water dragons are benevolent creatures. They're supposed to bring luck and prosperity to those who honor them. But the one I encountered was malevolent and I knew the moment I saw it the sacrifice it wanted was my life.

It nearly undid me, but I remain here.

Instead of offering my life, I ran, leaving the burden to my younger brother when he turned eighteen. Even though Leo survived, the guilt still eats me. The nightmares of the water dragon bring to the surface every guilt and failure trapped in the shell of what remains of me. I wasn't willing to die to save my family and kingdom. And I'll never forgive myself for it.

I'm the heir, but also a spare. Heir to the throne, but the spare when it comes to saving my family and kingdom. How can I rule a kingdom if I couldn't even save it?

As if led by a spirit, I walk the halls and run my hands along the thick stone walls. Swendale Castle was built as a stone keep for defense. The castle contains a large court-yard with buildings, and everything is surrounded by high stone walls. A moat surrounds the walls and the only access to the castle grounds is over a drawbridge with an entrance protected by an iron gate. While stone keeps are built as defense from invaders and enemies, Swendale Castle was built to protect people from dragons.

Before the decree, Swen family members would hide in secret tunnels under the castle to contain their scent. I now find myself in the secret tunnels. These tunnels lead to the safe room my family hid in when the castle was under siege by Morella's army. But instead of heading to the safe room, I find my way to the royal treasury.

Mother and Father have entrusted me with the secret to gaining entrance. The key is a polished piece of granite, which only looks as if it's a pretty rock someone would place on a shelf. A wooden door leads to what looks like a small storage room, and it is within the storage room where a hidden keyhole resides. I must thread my hand through a hole in the stone wall and insert the key to open the heavy door to the vault.

Adette will someday need to learn the secret to the vault, and I will pass it on to her, but not yet. I fear what she will do if she can enter. There are valuables and jewelry, crowns and tiaras, but it is the homeliest looking object which needs to be protected.

Morella's wand.

I close the door of the vault behind me, and the dark room is only lit with the lantern in my hand. I set the lantern on an empty table in the center of the room. Along the west wall lies a chest of drawers, and in the middle drawer lies the wand.

Without a thought, or maybe it's a suppressed urge I can't control, my fingers grab the knob of the drawer and pull it open.

On a velvet liner, the wand rests. It looks like a twisty branch from a tree, worn smooth at the base from the touch of a hand. The color is a faded brown mixed with gray, but it almost shines in the meager light.

My shadow rests dark on the chest of drawers, as if it's the evil part of me and it wants to pick up the wand. It wants me to see if I can wield it.

What would I do with the wand if I could use it to make magic? Would I rid myself of nightmares? Rid myself of the memory of my quest? Rid my blood of whatever attracts dragons to it?

What would be the price for using such magic?

My hand hovers over the wand, but I don't touch it. Such a simple object, no more than a glorified stick, but Morella can use it to channel her evil magic and cast her spells.

I don't know what lies within a witch to cause them to have magic, but I hope Leo and Eira can find a way to rid ourselves of Morella and her wand. I fear keeping Morella here will only bring more despair upon my family. If I couldn't beat her before, I can't beat her again.

My body involuntarily shudders at the memory of the spell Morella put on me. After she shot Leo, I reacted. I went after Morella with my sword drawn, determined to not fail my family again and to save my brother. Morella aimed her wand at me, and in only a moment I was magically bound, and the sword fell from my hand. Invisible ropes tightened around me, squeezing another failure out of me. The wand caused me to fail again.

I let my hand hover over the wand. It can't hurt to touch it.

"Meow."

Startled, I look down to find a cat rubbing its neck and head against my leg.

"Where did you come from?" I bend down and hold my hand out as an offering.

The black cat immediately rubs its head into my hand and I scratch its chin. It twists its tail in a circle.

"How did you get here?" I ask the cat, looking around the room in the glow of the lantern. "You're like a shadow."

The door is closed, and I can only surmise the cat quietly followed me into the tunnels and into the vault.

"Come on, kitty." I stand. "We need to get you out of here."

"Meow," the cat answers, though I have no idea if it's agreeing or disagreeing with me. It rubs the side of its belly against my leg.

I pull open the door and the cat follows me out. It continues to rub against me and purr as I seal the vault.

"Where did you come from?" I hold the lantern above the cat.

As if it knows I'm talking to it, the cat lifts its chin and continues to purr loudly.

"Hungry?" I keep my eyes on the feline.

"Meow."

It's a good enough answer for me. I head to the kitchen and the cat follows me closer than a shadow the entire way. I thought it would head off in another direction, but it didn't. The head cook wouldn't like me bringing a cat in the kitchen, but no one is here and the cat followed me of its own will.

I find a saucer and pour the cat some thick cream. It eagerly laps it up while I snack on a leftover crusty roll from dinner which I slather in salted butter.

"Meow." The cat looks up at me after it finishes the cream.

"More?" The cat doesn't look skinny, but it does look hungry, and I pour some more cream into the saucer.

Noises of pleasure leave the cat as I watch it lap up the milk and I finish my roll. I need to start taking pleasure in the simple things of life again. The taste of salted butter on a roll, the feel of a cool breeze on a hot day, the sweet smell of a flower, and a night of dreamless sleep.

"Alright," I say to myself and stand. "I'll see you out before I return to bed."

A door in the kitchen leads outside to the courtyard of the castle. I push it open a crack. The cat walks over but doesn't venture out the crack into the night air. It sits on its back legs and looks up at me.

"Meow."

"Fine." I sigh. I swear it understands me and responds. "Your choice, but I'm going back to bed."

I close the door and head out of the kitchen. When I turn back to look, the cat saunters behind me. It follows me through the hall and up the stairs to the private royal quarters. The cat even follows me into my room, and I close the door. It really is a shadow.

"You're stuck until morning," I tell the black feline.

The cat only replies by rubbing against my leg and purring again.

"Fine." I sigh again.

Blankets lie on the floor, tossed aside during my night terror, and I throw them back on the bed.

The cat sits next to my feet and its eyes follow my hands as I toss the blankets.

"Are you spying on me?" I take a closer look at the cat. It's mysterious, almost mystical looking, but that could be because it's a black cat.

The cat's response is to rub its head against my leg and purr.

Animals are used for a variety of tasks in many kingdoms, but cats – they're of the independent and solitary variety. Perhaps even strong willed. Cats are kept in castles and villages to help control vermin populations, but you can't command a cat as you would a dog. The cats do as they please, and kill the vermin when they want to, not when they're told to.

"Meow." The cat tips its angular chin up.

This cat is different from the usual castle cats. The cats which roam the castle grounds stay out of sight, much like this black one, but while the castle cats cower around people and shy away, this one wants to make itself known to me.

But why?

"Meow." The cat again tries to get my attention with a loud sound. It lifts its chin as if asking permission.

"You want on the bed?" I lift my eyebrows as the cat rubs my leg again with the side of its face.

I pat the bed, giving the feline permission to join me. The cat responds by gracefully leaping to the top of the mattress.

"Don't be a bed hog." I climb into bed, not too eager to sleep after my nightmare.

I lie on my back, my head on a soft pillow, and pull a blanket up to my chin.

The cat starts to knead its front paws into the blanket and mattress, as if trying to find the best spot to lie down.

"What do I call you?" I ask the cat, who clearly won't answer me with more than a meow.

"Boy or girl?" I reach over and snuff out the lantern on the bedside table.

"Meow," the cat replies.

"I'm going to call you Max." I run a hand over the cat's head, and it leans into my palm.

Max kneads the mattress some more and then settles down with his belly on the bed. He leans his side into me, and the vibration of his purring tickles me.

"This is nice." I no longer want someone next to me in bed, but it's comforting to have a warm body, and Max will do quite nicely. I almost want to smile.

I place my hand on the cat and his form vibrates with pleasure. He's as happy with the situation as I am.

"Night, Max."

The cat contentedly closes his eyes, as I expect to remain awake, fighting off nightmares and reliving them in my thoughts.

But somehow, I fall into a dreamless sleep with a black cat by my side.

CHAPTER THIRTEEN

FIA

I wish I was dreaming.

"How is she worth so much?"

I'm on my side as I emerge from a forced sleep. Even though I'm groggy, I'm alert enough to hear. I keep my eyes shut and remain motionless while I still feign sleep. I hear men's voices, and they talk as if I can't hear them.

"Are you holding her for ransom?" the same voice asks. "Or selling her to the highest bidder?"

"All you need to know is you'll be paid after we deliver her." I recognize the voice of the man who demanded I come with him.

"But what if we can get a higher price for her elsewhere?" the other voice asks.

"We do the job as promised." The voice is stern and unwilling to answer further.

Job?

Someone paid to have me kidnapped?

Carefully I lift one eye to peek through my eyelashes. I'm alone on the floor of the covered wagon. The two men talking are separated from me by a thick canvas cover. They must be riding on the bench of the cart behind the horses.

The noises of other horses come to me as I strain to listen. There were three men on horses when Reimund and I were attacked. There must be at least four in the group, and two ride up front in the cart.

And Reimund. Poor Reimund. I grit my teeth together. These people will pay for what they did to my guard.

My hands are bound in front of me and rest against my chest. If there's a way I can loosen the bonds, I might be able to get free and make a run for it, especially if we're not out in the open and I can find a place to hide. It feels as if the cart is traveling over uneven terrain, and the kidnappers must be avoiding common roads and paths.

I start wiggling my hands back and forth to loosen the bond. It's still too tight to slip out a hand and I start to chew on the coarse rope to help.

There's the loud sound of canvas being roughly pushed aside and a brush of air across my face.

"I wouldn't do that if I were you," the lead captor's rough voice says.

It's too late for me to feign sleep again. He's seen me awake and I stare hard at him with narrow eyes.

"Where are you taking me?" I demand.

"Drive." The lead captor shoves the shoulder of the man next to him and climbs over the backrest of the driving bench to crawl into the cart with me. He sits on a bench above me.

I don't want to act scared, but I also want to slide away from this man. There isn't much room for me to move, and I don't have the use of my hands to push myself up easily. The man stomps a dirty boot down on the hem of my long overcoat, his sign to let me know I can't go anywhere.

"Where are you taking me?" I demand.

"That's not your concern, Princess." The man grins, his pink lips turning up between his black beard and mustache.

"Who's paying you?" Anger starts to overtake my fear. I squirm backwards and try to maneuver my body into a sitting position, but I can't get the right angle, especially since the man has his foot on my clothing.

"We have a long trip, Princess." The man examines his dirty fingernails. "We can either make it comfortable for you, or not at all." He grounds his foot into my overcoat leaving dirt marks on the fabric.

"Where are you taking me?" My voice is more menacing than before. I kick my foot at his boot and his bulk barely moves. I knew he was large, but with being close to him he appears to be the long-lost relative of a giant.

"I only have to deliver you alive. I wasn't told in what condition." The man now picks at a fingernail. "I can make it easy and drug you again, or you can make it easy and do as you're told. The choice is yours."

A huff of air blasts out of my nostrils. "I can't trust you. Your word means nothing. And I'm never given choices."

"Ahh." The man clicks his tongue. "You're a fast learner. But this time you do have a choice, Princess. What will it be? Cooperation or suppression?"

"I'll cooperate," I gruffly reply.

I stand a better chance of escaping if I'm alert. My head still feels like it's in a fog from whatever they drugged me with, and I don't feel inclined to have another forced sleep.

"That's a girl." The man now rubs his beard with the fingers of one hand. "Now I'll give you another choice. Would you like to sit on the bench or remain on the floor?"

My body is stiff and sore from bouncing on the hard wooden planks of the wagon.

"I'll take the bench." Sitting may allow me a position to get a glimpse of where we travel.

The man grasps me by my shoulders, hoists me up, and roughly sets me on the bench. "There you go, Princess Fia."

"You know my name, but I'm at a disadvantage not knowing yours." My bound hands rest in my lap, and I hope to get a chance to try to loosen them if there's a moment I'm not watched.

"I'm known as Ido," the man says.

"Either you're brave and stupid enough to give me your real name, or that's a fake name," I say.

"Nobody knows." Ido's voice is deep, a bass sound I haven't heard before but will now never forget.

"I need a stop to relieve myself," I say.

Ido's deep laugh is a chilling sound. He pulls a bucket out of the corner. "We're prepared."

I grimace at the sight of the dirty metal bucket.

"How long will we be traveling?" I ask.

Ido sets the bucket in front of me and his bulky body sways with the movements of the wagon as he attempts to stand. "Longer than you can hold it."

I lift my bound hands. "Will you release my hands?"

"I'm not stupid, Princess." Ido nudges the bucket with the toe of his boot. "I've been in this business a long time. Your hands will remain bound."

"You're in the business of kidnapping?" I stare hard at the large man, trying to memorize details to describe him if I make it out of here.

The tattoo I glimpsed from a distance peeking out of his shirt is a dragon. Its head runs along Ido's sternum and the wings stretch across his chest and collarbone. The tattoo on his left arm is a sword with an intricate handle. The right arm appears to have a tattoo of a snake.

Bent over because of his height, Ido continues to sway on his feet with the wagon's movements. If he becomes more unbalanced, I could shove him with my feet. But if Ido shouts, the others will be alerted to my attempt to escape.

"I'm in the business of doing what others won't for a high price." Ido sits down next to me, limiting my options to kick him. "Do you need help, Princess?"

"Would you take a higher price from me?" I wriggle my wrists. The bonds are tight, and I haven't found a way to loosen them yet. "I'll pay more for you to free me."

"Ah, Princess." Ido's chuckle is hoarse. "I can respect the need for freedom, but I'm afraid you can't meet the price on your head. While you might not respect me, I have a reputation for doing the job I'm hired to do, which is why my price is high. Now do you need help with relieving yourself?"

I warily eye the bucket. This is going to be a very unpleasant trip.

"I don't need your help, but I would appreciate privacy." I usually sound slightly irritated when I answer people, but now the irritation is real and at a high level.

"I cover my bases." Ido then looks forward. "Stop the wagon!"

I tighten my body and jerk as I try to remain seated when the wagon is slowed. Ido gets up and pokes his head out between the thick canvas covering at the back of the wagon.

"Eike! Come here!"

A minute later, a slender person climbs into the wagon and stands before me.

"Eike shall help you," Ido tells me.

I thought all the bandits or thugs were men, but up close, and with the hood of her cloak removed, Eike is obviously a young woman. She's near my age, and very similar in stature, but extremely beautiful. Her creamy brown skin is flawless as if it's painted on her. A dark beauty mark resides on her left collarbone as I note identifying marks. Full arching eyebrows lie over eyes which are two-toned. They have the blue of an ocean which surrounds a tan the color of sand on a beach. I can't see her hair as it's kept under a tan wrap. But her eyes – they're mesmerizing. Her eyes are not something I'll easily forget as she fixes me with a hard stare.

"Don't mess with her. Eike's skilled with a sword," Ido says. "She knows how to kill, but also how to wound without killing."

In turn, Eike pulls a familiar sword out of a sheath at her side. It's my sword and she swings it around as if testing its weight. It's meant to be an intimidating move, and it nearly works on me. I can tell she's skilled by the way she holds the sword.

"You can leave." I nod my chin at Ido.

"Don't think about trying to escape, Princess." Ido starts to climb out. "You're only surrounded by men who are loyal to me, and we're nowhere near a place where anyone can hear your screams. And screaming means we knock you out again."

The canvas falls shut and Eike grins, but it's not a nice one.

"Your Highness." Eike's curtsey is a mocking one.

I've never been one for making friends, but it might be time to start. If it's the difference between life and death, I'll make a friend.

CHAPTER FOURTEEN

EMERIC

"You don't have many friends, do you?"

The sound of the iron boots hitting the stone floor is loud, but it's Morella's voice which makes me cringe.

"I'm not here for small talk," I say.

I shouldn't be here alone, but something from my midnight wandering last night keeps nagging me.

What if I could wield Morella's wand? What if it could be used for good?

"I doubt you have any friends," I say loudly.

I don't dare open the sliding panel to look at Morella, it's enough to hear her voice muffled through the door. Typically, I'm confident and self-assured around women, but I'm a trembling ball of fear with Morella. It's as if being near her pulls out every hidden insecurity, of which I have many.

"I look for people who are useful, not people who want to be friends." Morella's voice sounds as if she's sneering. "Which are you? Useful or a friend?"

"I need you to be useful to me," I say.

Morella is the prisoner and I'm the one in the position of authority, though it feels much the opposite.

"Ahh." Morella cackles and I can only imagine the delight on her face. "You need me."

"I don't need you," I reiterate. "I have some questions for you."

"Ahh, dearie." I hear Morella's lips smack. Her voice is now sickly sweet. "You remind me of myself. Beautiful, cunning, clever, and devious."

"I'm not devious!" I know I shouldn't react, because Morella is trying to get under my skin, as she usually does. But her comment pricks at me like tiny irritating nettles.

"You're here on your own," Morella says. "You don't want anyone to know of our conversation. That is devious."

"No!" I stammer. "It's for security."

"I too was an heir, upstaged by my younger sibling," Morella says.

I step back and lean against the cool stone wall for support. No one has ever mentioned Morella's family. Was she royal or heir to a family fortune? Morella could be lying, but the clenching of my belly tells me she isn't. I wait for her to say more, but she doesn't. There's only the sound of her iron boots hitting the floor, tapping out an eerie tune.

My curiosity gets the best of me. "What were you heir of?"

"Ahh." Morella's lips smack again. "The young prince needs a story?"

"I don't need a story," I spit out, mad at myself. I'm straying from the reason I came here. Discovering Morella's past isn't necessary. "I need to know if anyone can wield your wand or if only you can?"

"Ahh. Do you want to try it? Bring it to me and I'll show you." There's a dare in Morella's voice, but also a command.

A command I shouldn't follow.

"I cannot bring it to you."

"Just like you couldn't save your family?" Morella laughs.

"You know nothing of what I had to do." Anger starts to rise in me. This is a fruitless quest, just like my quest to sacrifice to a dragon. I turn and storm off, my feet slapping hard against the ground.

"Poor bitter prince." Morella's echoing voice follows me. "I understand what you need. You'll be back here."

Chapter Fifteen

FIA

"Here." Ido shoves a crusty biscuit into my bound hands.

As far as I know, it's been two days since I was taken.

I stare at the food, wishing it was a dagger. I lift my hands, still bound at my wrists and bring the biscuit to my mouth. It smells of rosemary.

I close my eyes and the image which always appears behind my eyes is there. I've learned to block out or ignore the ever-present vision, but the scent of the rosemary only amplifies it.

The image behind my eyes is my true love, imprinted in my mind because of the rosemary induced dream. I see him whenever I close my eyes. But just because I see an image of him doesn't mean I'll ever find him or see him in real life. I know he exists, but I don't know who he is or where he lives. All I know is I have a true love, and I don't want to find him.

Love doesn't exist for those born into my family.

"Better eat up, Princess." Ido's voice jerks me back to the present.

I still hold the rosemary biscuit in front of my mouth. I'm not sure I can stomach taking a bite of it with the overpowering scent.

"I can't eat this." I lower my hands.

Ido grunts and lifts his eyebrows. "You think we poison your food?"

I didn't think it until this moment. Ido reaches forward and pinches off a piece of the biscuit in my hand with his dirty fingertips. He tosses the piece into his mouth.

"See?" He exaggeratedly chews and then swallows. "Would I poison myself?"

"Anything's possible," I sneer.

If I can dream of my true love, it's possible for Ido to eat a poisoned biscuit without a problem. Ido might be immune to the effects of poison, and he seems to be immune to any sort of bribery. For a thief and kidnapper, he's loyal.

"Where are we headed?" I ask.

I've asked the question enough times, no one bothers to reply.

"How much farther?" I ask.

I still get no reply.

I lift the biscuit to my mouth, wrinkle my nose, and take a tiny nibble. The rosemary is overpowering, but I don't close my eyes to see the vision of my true love. He's so thoroughly imprinted in my mind, I can draw up his image without even closing my eyes.

I don't want a true love.

Sometimes I wish my family's curse fell to the women. I wouldn't marry and would turn into a dragon. Then I would launch fire at these thugs, rather than being kidnapped. Life is quite unfair.

"Who's paying you?" I try again, knowing it's useless. "I bet someone would pay you more."

I'll attempt to wear down my captors with questions.

"Is it the man I'm to marry? My father? Someone who wants to hold me hostage?" I ask.

It's quite possible I've become valuable being the only known living Tanin who can bear an heir. Someone could hold me hostage hoping my father would pay to recover me. Which makes me wonder – would my father pay to get me back? What am I worth to him?

"What happens if I escape?" I ask.

"You won't escape," Ido finally replies to one of my questions.

"Will you not get paid if I escape?" It's my turn to flip the table. "I hope you were smart enough to take half up front."

"You cannot escape." Ido leans forward. A sprig of rosemary is stuck between his stained front teeth. At least the rosemary sweetens his foul breath a bit. "And even if you did, you would be the one running, because I would hunt you down faster than you can count to ten."

"You can count to ten?" I feign surprise. "I didn't know kidnappers could count that high."

"Ah, Princess." Ido smirks. "You'd be surprised how high I can count, especially when it comes to what I'm being paid to deliver you."

I curl my lips down. "You kidnapped me."

"I prefer to think I acquired the package I need to deliver." Ido picks at his teeth with a dirty fingernail.

"How many princesses have you kidnapped?" I ask. "Any princes? Other royalty?"

Ido starts to chew on the nail and I cringe. I hate to think where those nails have been with how dirty they are. Or what the fingers attached to those nails have done. My only source of comfort is knowing Ido won't kill me because he's supposed to deliver me alive.

"You haven't taken any of my things. Why?" A royal ring with the crest of Ryutoa is on my finger, marking me as a princess. I even wear a gold chain attached to a beautiful blue piece of lapis lazuli, a gift from my grandmother for my seventeenth birthday.

The superstition in Ryutoa is lapis lazuli will protect you from dragons. But I know the truth – it doesn't. It's only a pretty stone. The one from my grandmother held sentimental value to her because my grandfather gifted it to her when she was seventeen and won his hand in a competition to marry him. They were married before he turned eighteen, to prevent the curse transforming him into a dragon. But the curse still took hold, making it so he never truly loved her. The necklace now resides around my neck, a reminder I don't want love.

Ido grunts. "I'm not a thief."

"Isn't stealing a person thievery?"

"Do you always talk this much?"

"No." I shake my head. "At home I rarely talk to people I don't know, unless I'm forced to. When my parents have banquets and balls, I'm forced to socialize and act like a princess." I straighten my legs and kick my bound feet out. "This whole kidnapping thing is quite the holiday for me. Are you sure it wasn't me who paid you to kidnap me?"

"Quite sure," Ido replies, but the twitch of his lips means he has a doubt.

"You're not sure who hired you," I say, watching for another reaction from Ido. There's another small twitch of his lips which moves the rough whiskers of his mustache.

"It doesn't matter who hired me, I only know I have a job I was hired to do."

"Where are you taking me?" I ask.

"Eat up, Princess." Ido tosses me a hunk of aged cheese. "I'll let you know when we're there."

I still have no clue where I'm headed, but I surmise we're still in Ryutoa or near the border. The canvas drapes are always kept closed on the cart and I haven't been able to glimpse the terrain or assess the sun in the sky to give me an idea of what direction we travel.

I'm headed to the unknown.

CHAPTER SIXTEEN

EMERIC

"I would like you to travel with the new guards to the watchtower at the border," Mother tells me. "They will relieve the other guards posted there."

"That's not a quick journey," I say, recalling the watchtower guard who rushed to the castle to bring news Morella's army was spotted in the mountain pass.

"You'll have company," Mother says, leaving no option for dispute. "The time away will be good. You haven't left the castle since..." Her voice trails off.

I haven't left the castle since the siege. I haven't even ventured into the nearby village. Even before the siege, I never ventured further than the village after returning from my failed quest.

It's not a secret Swen's don't leave Swendale until their eighteenth birthday when they're presented with a quest from a fairy. Inhabitants of Swendale think it's tradition.

It's our family's tradition to lie to our people and not let them know the real reason we can't leave, nor why eighteen-year-olds must go on a quest.

Before my eighteenth birthday and before learning of the decree, I dreamed of all the places I would go when I could leave the confining borders. I wanted to scale mountains, feel the spray of the ocean, swim in a large lake, stick my feet in the sands of a desert, taste foods from different kingdoms, and meet people and princesses from other countries. I wanted to be fully immersed in new and different places.

But then I found out what it means to be a Swen male and how leaving Swendale erases any protection from my dragon attracting blood. I traveled on my quest, but it was fraught with danger. After consultation with Father, we decided my best path was to journey east toward the Great Lake to find a water dragon, as we believed the stories of benevolence. But I found a different story, and a reason to fear travel.

"You want me to travel to the border?" It's the border Leo traveled to during his quest, but he avoided the pass and watchtower because of the invading army.

Mother tries to keep from frowning. I'm not sure if it's because she's disappointed in my lack of enthusiasm or because she now realizes what she's asking me to do.

"You don't have to cross the border," Mother says in a voice which is supposed to be reassuring. "And you'll have guards with you the entire time. You can even take a friend with you, if you'd like."

Mother hasn't been paying attention. I don't have any real friends. People clamor to be my friend, but only because they want to be close to a prince or use my position for their benefit.

"Take Jude," Mother finally says when I don't say anything.

"Jude?" I lift my eyebrows. Jude is Leo's best friend. I haven't been the greatest big brother to Leo the past two years, and Jude won't side with me.

"He's anxiously awaiting Leo's return so he and Amelie can marry," Mother says. "It'll do him good to get away for a bit, and he has experience traveling with members of our family."

What Mother doesn't speak in words is Jude knows our secret.

"Okay." I respond with a lack of emotion. "I can at least ask him."

"You want me?" Jude points at himself with his eyes wide. "You want me to go with you to the Knoller Mountain pass watchtower?"

Why did I even ask? Jude would never want to go with me and probably resents me for the way I treated Leo after I returned from my quest. He's also witnessed other mistreatments of my brother. Jude was six years old, and Leo was five when I pushed Leo in the moat. Jude pulled him out and they've been best friends since. Jude followed Leo on part of his quest. I didn't have one friend or acquaintance follow me on mine.

"Don't feel obligated to go." I scuff the toe of my boot in the dirt of the courtyard of our castle. "You don't have to. My mother-"

"I want to go! I can get someone to cover for me at the inn." Jude breaks into a huge grin. If I have a lack of smiles, he has an abundance of them. "I haven't been on an adventure since I went with Leo on his..." Jude grimaces. "I mean, I'm honored you asked me. I'd be happy to go."

I exhale. I'm not sure if it's in relief, but part of me is glad Jude is going.

"Great." I nod once. "We'll set off tomorrow with the new guards."

"Any word from Leo?" Jude flicks his head to move the wavy brown hair from his eyes.

"Not lately, "I reply, "but we expect him home soon. I know he doesn't want to miss your wedding."

"No wedding plans for you?" Jude tilts his head to the side. He looks younger than his age, and I can't believe he's getting married at nearly twenty, but I know he and his fiancé have been together for a few years.

"No." I shake my head. "It'll take a girl falling out of the sky and me catching her before that happens."

"Your true love then?" Jude smirks.

"That's rare," I say. "Leo got his. It's not likely for anyone else here, especially me."

"Emeric." Jude leans closer to me. He's close to my family and doesn't need to use our titles. "You don't have to-"

"Prince Emeric." A girl from the nearby village inter-rupts. She bats her eyelashes and throws me a flirty smile. "I could use a strong man to help me."

"I apologize, but I have plans to make with this young man." I slap Jude on the shoulder before I call a guard over. "Richard will assist you."

With a frown, the girl leads the guard away.

"That wasn't subtle," Jude says and cocks his head at me in surprise. "She was throwing herself at you and you let her go."

"I'm turning over a new leaf." I slap Jude on the shoul-der again. "I told you. I'm not looking for love. If it wants to find me, it's going to have to do something big."

Chapter Seventeen

FIA

Something big will have to happen if I'm to escape.

The days and nights start to run together. I think it's been five days since I was taken. Five days is plenty of time to leave the borders of Ryutoa. I sense we travel near mountains, which means the kidnappers didn't head north. They must have headed east or south.

Raindrops hit the canvas with a plunk, soft at first and then the intensity picks up. I hear muffled voices from the front and Eike grimaces at the little we can decipher. It sounds like Ido and his younger brother, Rivo, can't agree on a route to take.

I've gotten to know the kidnappers through observations, overhearing their conversations, and what little they tell me. Ido is in charge, while Rivo likes to think he's second in command. Keil is a wisp of a man compared to Ido and stays quiet most of the time. Eike is the only female, and she sits with me in the covered cart.

"Sounds like a bad storm is approaching," Eike says with a tilt of her chin to angle her ear to the heavy canvas.

Wind starts to lash and the fabric thwacks against the sides of the wooden cart. There's a rumble of thunder in the distance.

"It's getting close fast," I say.

Storms would blow in from the ocean and thunder would shake the castle at home. I'm familiar with the rumble of thunder and how it grows louder and closer to the lightning strikes as a storm approaches.

It's not long before the storm worsens, and there's no staying dry, even in the covered cart. Lightning flashes all around, thunder explodes overhead, and rain is pushed through the canvas with the lashing wind. Wrapped tightly in a damp blanket, I sit in a huddled position to conserve as much warmth as I can.

Eike shivers, her arms bare. Ido and Rivo sit on the driving bench at the front of the cart while Keil must be on a horse. This weather is miserable for all of us. It isn't long before all motion ceases, and the cart is brought to a stop.

I watch everything, waiting to see if the storm will provide a means of escape, but it doesn't. My hands and feet are still bound, and someone constantly watches over me. I contemplate grabbing the sword from Eike, hoping she'll be too cold to react, but she steers clear of me, as if she knows my intentions.

From outside I hear a rush of water, which can't be the storm. We must be near a river, but which river?

"Hit the hay, ladies." Ido peeks through the wet canvas. "We're bedding down for the night."

"Without supper?" If I have anything nice to say about my kidnappers, it's that they feed me.

"Too wet," Ido replies as Eike grunts. "You'll survive until breakfast."

It's a damp and cold night's sleep. In the early hours of morning, Eike leaves me alone when she attends to emptying my bucket. As usual, I listen carefully for any clues. I catch the crackle of a fire in between the noise of rapids.

"The rivers too high," I hear Ido say.

"We should have ventured north instead of south," I hear Rivo say. "Then we wouldn't be dealing with mountain fed rivers swollen with rain."

"That would have taken longer," Ido says, his voice more disgruntled than usual. "Time is money. We'll find a way to cross near here. It can't be this swollen everywhere."

"We could venture downriver to the crossing," Keil says. "It's not far out of the way."

"There's a bridge at the pass," Rivo says. "We can cross there."

"Think!" Ido bursts out. "There are guards at the watchtower. They'll search our cart. They might have heard of a missing princess."

"There can't be notices of a missing princess yet," Rivo says.

"I don't take chances. We cross away from the bridge." Ido's voice remains gruff.

I strain to listen, curious with questions. Are my parents looking for me? Did Reimund survive? Is anyone looking for me? I'm not sure if anyone will be coming to rescue me, which is why I need to do it myself.

"Here." Eike tosses me a rosemary biscuit when she returns to the cart.

"I'm getting sick of these things," I mutter before tearing off a piece with my teeth. The biscuits have grown drier and harder in our days of traveling. But it's not the texture or taste which bothers me, it's the scent. It brings my true love back to the forefront of my mind, when I so desperately try to push him away.

Why?

Why do I have to have a true love? I don't want one, when there are others who do.

"Get comfortable," Eike tells me after she settles herself on the bench. "We're going to be here a while."

"Can I at least go outside?" I ask. "Why keep me hidden in here if there's no one around?"

Eike picks at her biscuit, mentally weighing my request. "We need to scout a river crossing. Once the area is secure, I'll see if Ido will let you out."

"Thank you," I say.

Eike's not so bad sometimes. I have some respect for a woman who can hold her own with a band of male thugs, but she could be putting her talents to a better use.

"Why work for bandits?" I ask. "You could head up a royal guard, be a constable in a village, even be a spy in another kingdom. Yet you resort to a life of crime."

"But crime..." Eike leans forward and takes my bound hands in hers. She looks at the royal ring on my finger. "Crime is so much more fun than sitting around waiting for something to happen. And it pays well."

Eike pulls the ring off my finger and slips it on hers while I frown.

"You plan on selling it?" I ask.

"Nah." Eike holds her hand up and examines the gold ring. It has a tiny crest of Ryutoa. It's a shield with flames flanked by a crown and swords. "I'm only going to borrow it for a bit. If you think I can be in the royal guard, then I'll pretend I'm a princess. Same difference."

"You could do bigger things. Better things." I lift my thick eyebrows up. "You could lead a royal guard. You could steal back from criminals and help the poor."

"You have a rather fantastical view of the world, Princess." Eike crosses one ankle over the other and continues to look at my ring on her finger. "I bet you read lots of books."

I grunt. I do read a lot of books. Most of the time they're better than real-life and a wonderful place to escape to.

"You could do so much more," I tell Eike. "Be a woman general, lead troops, fight crime."

"This is amusing coming from a princess who can't rule her own country." Eike snorts. "Why don't you do more than be someone who has to pump out heirs?"

"I would try if I wasn't kidnapped," I retort back. "I had planned on running away."

"Oh, Princess." Eike chuckles and flashes white teeth with her grin. "Running away is what led me to this life."

"What did you run from?"

"We're not that different, you and I." Eike closes her eyes and leans her head against a frame of the cart. I know she didn't sleep much last night. "We're far more alike than you may think. I too was put in an impossible situation with my family and ran away."

"How'd you end up with Ido?"

"All you need to know is I owe him my life." Eike's lips press together for a moment, and she keeps her eyes shut. "I'm freer with him than I am without him. I owe him a debt before I can venture out on my own."

"To a life of crime?"

"To a life of freedom." Eike's chin bobs once. I can't tell if it's because she likes her thoughts or because she's nearly falling asleep.

I keep my questions to myself for the moment, hoping Eike will fall asleep while the others are scouting. This could be my chance to escape.

"Eike!" Keil bangs on the wood frame of the cart from outside. "We need you."

Eike jerks up and her eyes flick open. "What about the girl?"

"Boss says to leave her."

Eike looks at me with narrow eyes before responding to Keil. "We won't be able to see her if we leave her in here. We should shackle her to the outside of the cart to keep an eye on her."

"Lemme check."

Eike has a hint of a grin as we hear footsteps retreat, and I also have one.

It's not long before Keil returns and bangs on the cart again. "Hurry. We can tie her up. We need to test some places to cross the river."

"Looks like you get your wish, Princess." Eike performs a mocking curtsey, but I don't care. I finally get to leave this stinking cart and hopefully find out where I am and where I'm being taken.

Eike leaves Keil to tie me to the outside of the cart. Keil never smiles and always has a slightly frightened look, as if he's seen himself on wanted posters and is afraid of getting caught. He usually hides his pale skin under long sleeves and a hood, as any sun would cause him to burn. Keil is a grunt worker, stealing into small places, and running tasks the others won't do. Either Eike is helping me, or she doesn't know how incompetent Keil is. A child from the fishing village near my home could tie better knots.

"Don't go anywhere." Keil tugs one more time on the knot securing me to a metal ring attached to the outside of the cart.

"It's not like I can." I lift my fingers to show Keil I'm still bound at the wrists.

My ankles are also bound with a length of rope. I'll have to free my hands before I'm able to bend over to unbind my feet. With the way I'm tied to the cart, it's not possible for my hands to reach my feet.

"Keil, hurry up!" Ido yells. "I need you to scout upstream before another storm rolls in. We need to get the cart across."

Keil hurries off and I get my first chance to look around.

A raging river is on one side with forests and fields beyond it. To the other side are foothills of mountains. The terrain doesn't give me a clue as to what country we're in. My options for escape are to head to the mountains or cross the river and hide in the forest. Or to run in whatever direction I can.

Eike guides a horse into the river. The large beast seems hesitant but follows Eike's command. The water is deep enough it reaches above the bottom of Eike's boots. The cart will take on some water if we cross here. Rivo follows Eike on another horse while Ido yells directives from the bank. Keil heads further upriver on foot.

While keeping my eye on Ido, I start to wiggle my bound wrists. Keil tied loose knots and didn't examine what he tied me to. The metal ring is anchored into the wood of the cart, but it's not tight. The wood of the cart has dried with age, and water has damaged the hold the anchor has on the cart. I start to wiggle my bound wrists, trying to move the metal ring. It doesn't move much at first, and this might be a fruitless operation, but I have nothing better to do.

The clouds overhead are dark and there's a sudden chill in the air. Goosebumps rise on the exposed flesh of my arm. I keep moving my wrist back and forth, as the ring now moves slightly in the wood. If I can pull the ring out, I'll be free to move and untie my legs.

Ido's head swivels and I stop all movements. He glances over his shoulder at me, and once satisfied I'm still here, he returns to yelling at Eike and Rivo.

I bite my lower lip, trying to think of my next move. Even if I manage to free my ankles from their bonds, I'm not going to be able to run far. Ido has a horse nearby and can chase me down. There aren't many places to hide near this open riverbank.

But I'm not deterred by my lack of options, and I keep trying to free the metal ring from the wood.

"Hail!" Eike yells.

Small, pea-sized balls of ice start to rain from the sky as I pull the ring free from the cart. The commotion keeps Ido from looking at me.

"Yes." I mumble excitedly to myself and keep my wrists near where the ring used to reside while I scan for my captors.

"Can you keep going?" Ido yells at Eike.

Eike is nearly across the river and Rivo isn't far behind. The hail is cold and bounces off my skin. It's annoying, but it's not big enough, nor is there a vast amount of it to cause a problem.

"It won't be easy," Eike yells back. "But I think we'll be able to get the cart across here. Let me finish getting across."

It won't be long before they turn around to come back for the cart. My time frame for escape is dwindling. It's going to take more than a wish to save me now. Eike is across the river and Rivo leads his horse up the riverbank when the pea-sized hail suddenly grows. Forgetting to check Ido and Keil, I throw myself under the cart for protection. The hail is at least as large as my fist.

Across the river, Eike gallops toward a lone tree to shelter. Rivo falls and crumbles to the ground while his horse takes off after Eike. Rivo must have been hit by the hail.

"Princess!" Ido yells. "Where's the princess?"

Quickly, with trembling fingers, I try to untie my ankles. A large ball of hail hits the cart with a thud, and

I'm thankful I'm sheltered underneath. I hear footsteps running toward the cart and I roll on my belly. It's Ido's feet. I don't know whether he's coming for shelter or to grab me, but I can't let him get his hands on me.

But my hands won't work. They're cold and numb, and the knots on the rope holding my ankles together are tight.

"Princess!" Ido yells, closer to the cart now.

"Please, please, please," I desperately whisper as I try to wedge my fingernails under a knot to loosen it.

The knot loosens and I quickly untie the rope around my ankles.

"Princess!" Ido yells again.

Horse feet stamp right next to the cart where I cower beneath it. Grimacing, I wait for Ido to bend down and look for me. When he does, I'll have to take a chance and run. Dodging the large hail will be my next obstacle.

There's a loud grunt, a large ball of hail bounces off the grass, and then a body falls on the ground next to the cart, causing me to reflexively jump.

Ido lies on his side, his cheek in the dirt, and his face turned in my direction. He looks my way, except his eyes are closed. A large bump starts to swell on his temple. My eyes widen at the prone man on the ground. It's a wish come true.

The large piece of hail knocked Ido out, and other than Keil, I'm left alone on this side of the river.

CHAPTER EIGHTEEN

EMERIC

The river lies to our left as Jude and I travel with the guards relieved of their duty at the watchtower. Mother wanted me to include a visit to the nearest village on this journey.

"The river is flowing a lot stronger than the last time I was here," Jude comments.

"Must be more snow melt and there's some dark clouds further ahead." I point in front of me, though it's not hard to miss the growing black clouds. We'll be lucky if we miss the storm.

"The last time I was by this river-" Jude starts, but he doesn't finish.

"You were with Leo on his quest." I lean forward and gently pat my horse's neck. "You can tell me about it if you want to."

"It won't upset you to hear about his quest?" Jude purses his lips.

We've traveled together at a leisurely pace for a couple days now, but we haven't broached subjects more serious than the weather and Jude's job at his fiancé's family's inn.

"I don't mind," I say. "Leo only told me a few things, and I'd like to hear your version."

Hearing Jude's tale might take my mind off my own memories. I haven't slept well on this trip for fear I'll have a night terror in front of someone.

"Thankfully we don't have to cross the river," Jude says. "The last time I saw a huge bear across it. Not far from here."

"There are black bears in Montagnia, and even Swendale." I'm surprised Jude has never seen one in his travels.

"I've seen black bears," Jude says without any of the sharpness I would use in my voice. "But this bear was different. It was massive, not a normal bear. It reminded me of those legends of shapeshifters."

I groan. "Fairies! I hope it's not true."

Legends say fairies put curses on humans to turn into animals and some can even shift from humans to animals and back. All problems lead back to fairies.

"I don't know whether the legends are true, but I can't forget that bear. I hope I never see it again," Jude says.

"What else did you see?" I look ahead. Sheets of rain fall from the black clouds, and one lone crack of thunder sounds in the distance.

"I almost forgot!" Jude laughs loud. "Leo fell in the river when he pulled a golden ball from the mud."

"Golden ball?" I jerk my head Jude's direction. "What golden ball?"

"He didn't tell you?"

I shake my head.

"I guess I never asked him what he did with it. He talked about using it as a sacrifice for…" Jude clears his throat. "You know."

"He was going to offer it to a dragon," I say. Dragons are known to hoard treasure, but a golden ball wouldn't have been an acceptable sacrifice for the decree.

"I'm not sure what he did with it. I never asked," Jude says. "He commanded me to return home after we met Eira."

"Do you wonder what would have happened if you stayed with Leo?" I ask.

"Wondering how to change the past only leads you the wrong way," Jude replies. "What happened has happened. You can't change it."

Jude has a chipper outlook on things. He doesn't look like a guy you'd pick first for your team because he's unassuming and scrawny, but I understand why Leo trusts him wholeheartedly.

"I often wonder what would have happened if I made the sacrifice," I say, just loud enough for Jude to hear.

There's silence, as if my revelation isn't a normal comment for me and it startles Jude. Then he inhales a long breath.

"Leo wouldn't have met Eira, and your family would have been heartbroken to lose you."

"But Swendale would have been saved," I say.

"No." Jude forcefully shakes his head. "The castle still would have been put under siege. Swendale would have been lost because Leo would never have run into Eira. She was a key piece in saving the kingdom."

"Oh." I clench my jaw. I never thought of it that way.

"Leo wouldn't have missed all your badgering and training, but he would have missed you," Jude adds.

"He has every right to hate me. I was cruel, unkind, and bitter. And I nearly married his true love." I cringe at how I flaunted Eira marrying me over Leo.

"It all worked out," Jude says.

"Because I failed," I say dismally.

"Your failure led to Leo's success; therefore you played a part. You did what a big brother should."

"When did you get so smart?" Talking to Jude is easy. "I thought you were just the kid stealing your grandmother's biscuits from the castle kitchen."

"I still steal her biscuits." Jude turns a wide grin on me, and I get an idea.

"I have a proposition for you, but I don't want to steal you from Leo if he has plans for you," I say, testing the water.

"What's the proposition?" Jude's eyebrows lift under his hair which blows in the breeze. The wind is starting to pick up.

"I haven't hired a personal assistant yet, and I'd like to offer you the position. Someday, if I become king, it would mean you'd be one of my advisors. But if Leo wants you, I don't want to get in the way."

Maybe this is a bad idea. Leo might resent me for trying to steal his best friend, but Jude knows our family secret and he can be trusted.

"I told Leo I can't accompany him to Montagnia when he goes there with Eira. Amelie and I plan to stay in Swendale, and I'm honored to be asked."

"You're free to do whatever you want," I say. "If it will cause problems with Leo, you don't have to accept."

"I don't foresee any problems," Jude replies. "While I would like to accept, I do need to talk to Amelie because it would mean I couldn't help at the inn. But please hold the position for me until I give you a firm answer."

CHAPTER NINETEEN

FIA

I'm free!

It's as if I received an answer to my wish and I'm presented with a means of escape. My captors left me alone and
a random hailstorm knocked them out. I was protected
from the hail, the storm subsided, and now I'm able to take
a horse and run.

I urge the horse into a gallop and head downriver. I'm
not far from the cart, but the ground is no longer littered
with the large hail balls. It seems the life-saving hailstones
only fell where my captors were. This must be a good sign.
Something is going to work in my favor.

I push the horse to run harder. Rivo mentioned a bridge
over the river, and Ido mentioned a watchtower. There
must be people nearby. Someone must be able to help me.
But the question is – who can I trust?

Right now, my only focus is putting a greater distance
between me and my captors. While the hail has ceased, the
rain hasn't. I glance over my shoulder, and no one follows
me.

"We can do this." I lean over the horse and rub a hand on its neck.

I don't know what it is about animals, but they calm me. I think I understand animals better than I do people.

Suddenly, a thought comes to me, and I slow the horse. My captors will expect me to ride toward the bridge.

"What do you think?" I ask the horse, bringing her to a stop.

The horse tilts her head toward the river. It's slower moving and not as deep. Keil went the wrong way. Little did Ido know, he wasn't far from a better crossing.

"The river?" I ask. "You think we should cross here and avoid the bridge?"

I look across the rock-strewn water. It's still raining, and I'm now soaked through to the skin. My teeth start to chatter. My captors will assume I use the bridge or stay on this side of the river. I'm going to cross.

"Let's go." I gently tug on the reins, and the horse follows my lead again. The crossing is easy, and I hope our tracks will wash away in the rain.

I ride the horse away from the river, and across land where sheep graze. There are wooden boxes dotting some fields, which I assume are beehives. As we venture further from the river, the ground becomes more saturated, as if a heavy downpour of rain passed through here. The horse can't run as fast on the soggy ground, and I slow her.

I keep glancing over my shoulder to make sure I'm not being followed. It's one of those moments when I look back and not forward when the horse stumbles. Whether its foot lands in a gopher hole or the ground gives way under her, the horse falls to the ground.

Because I'm looking back, my reaction time isn't what it would be if I was watching the terrain.

"Ow." A sharp cry escapes me as I land on my side in mud.

A fall into mud might have been okay, except the horse lands on top of me, while my leg is still in the stirrup. A painful sensation rips through my lower left leg, and I whimper.

I muffle a scream as the horse rapidly shuffles its legs and manages to right itself. But I'm not going to be able to right myself. My hands slip in the mud as I try to push my body up. I gnash my teeth together as any little movement of my left leg makes me want to cry out in pain.

"No." I whimper.

This can't happen. I escaped only to fall and break my leg. This will allow my captors to more easily catch up with me. I glance around, careful not to move my leg any more than I need to. A dirt road lies ahead. It's unfair how close level ground is, and now I'm immobile in a muddy field.

The horse stands to the side of me, munching on wet grass. The rain subsides to drizzle, but it's still cold. I shiver, but I'm not sure if it's because I'm cold or because I might be shocked from my injury. I want to save myself. I don't want to yell for help, but I see no other choice. I'll have to risk yelling for help and hope my captors don't hear me.

"Help!" My first attempt is feeble, because I'm not quite sure if this is the right thing to do.

I hate I need help. There must be a way for me to rescue myself.

I try to roll to my belly, but a pain wracks my leg when I move. Next, I try to dig my palms into the soft ground and push myself backwards. It works, except I'm not going towards the road, but away from it. And turning my body in another direction is going to be quite painful.

I groan loudly. I'm not going to get anywhere fast and my teeth chatter more.

"Help!" I let loose with the loudest scream I can.

Off in the distance, in the midst of the foggy haze, I see some dark shapes. I could be mistaken because of delirium, but I think it's riders on horses.

"Help!" I yell and grit my teeth as pain again courses through me.

The riders are getting closer, but I'm not sure they hear me. I squint, trying to identify them as my captors, but they're still too far away for me to tell.

"Help!" I yell, but this time my voice is weak.

The riders can't be Ido or the other bandits. They wouldn't be approaching from this direction. I need these unknown people to hear me. I need them to help me. Each shiver of my body causes waves of pain, and I let my head drop to the ground. I'm going into shock. My body is doing what it thinks it needs to do to keep me alive.

"Please," I whisper hoarsely, not sure if I'm pleading with myself, my body, or someone else to come and rescue me.

I can't give up. I need to escape. I need to find Fynn. Fynn must have found his true love.

True love.
I muster everything I have for one final call.
"Help!"
Then everything goes black.

CHAPTER TWENTY

EMERIC

"Help!"

I twist my head, angling my ear for the faint sound.

"Did you hear that?" I ask Jude.

We're on the dirt road to the nearest village and it can't be far now. The two guards direct the cart while Jude and I ride horses.

"Hear what?" Jude tugs on his hood and drapes it further over his face. The worst of the storm skirted around us, but we ride through lingering remnants. The rain has lightened, but it's now foggy and cool. A mist clings to everything, shrouding the landscape in a haze.

"It sounded like someone yelling for help," I reply and strain to listen.

"It's probably just a sheep," Jude says. "Being out here will play with your mind. This fog makes everything look mystical."

"Perhaps." I still strain to listen in case I hear it again. I'm sure it was someone yelling for help.

"Do you think this fog is like the fog that surrounds the barrier to the Mystic Lands?" Jude asks.

"No," I say in a gruff voice, not too eager to talk about anything having to do with fairies and the land they live in. "I imagine you can't see through it."

"I wonder if Leo-"

"Shush!" I wave a hand at Jude to have him shut up. I know Jude is wondering if Leo will see the fog barrier between the human Greater World and the Mystic Land of fairies and magical beings, but that's not why I want him to be quiet. "I heard someone yell for help again."

I pull my horse to a stop and Jude does the same. On both sides of the road are fields where sheep graze and beehives are kept. The landscape is void of any humans besides our traveling party, probably because of the weather. I squint at an area off to my left, wondering if my eyes are playing tricks on me. There seems to be a horse in the field.

"Help."

It's softer this time, but I know I heard the cry.

"Did you hear it?" I ask Jude. "I don't think it's a sheep."

"I heard it that time." Jude's hood falls off as he swivels his head around. "Where did it come from?"

I point in the direction of the horse in the field. "I think it came from there."

I nudge my horse off the road in the direction of the cry.

A riderless horse seems to be standing over something. Or rather, over someone.

"Help." It's a soft female voice.

I jump off my horse and run. The ground is soggy, and my feet sink in the uneven ground. If I'm not careful, I could sprain an ankle, but I rush to the prone figure in the mud.

"It's a girl," I shout to Jude. I kneel next to the young woman. She's pretty, and while not the most beautiful woman I've ever seen, there's something intriguing about her I can't quite place.

Jude is off his horse and holds the reins of mine. "Is she okay?"

My fingers glide over the cool skin of her neck. There's an energy pulsing between my finger and her skin, which startles me. It must be from the complete surprise of this situation. A pulse beats weakly against my fingers, and I exhale in relief. Then I place my hand near her nose, where a shallow brush of warm air hits my skin.

"She's alive and breathing," I tell Jude. "Only unconscious."

Jude approaches the lone horse. He rubs his hands over it and tries to calm the anxious beast. "If I had to guess, it seems the horse fell, and she went down with it." Jude points to the horse, who has mud splattered on its left side.

"Alright. We shouldn't move her until we know the extent of her injuries," I say.

"Can you figure out if anything is wrong?" Jude asks.

"I'll see what I can do."

I've had training in field medicine, which was intended for me to use when I was on my quest. I've not had much use for it until now, even when the castle was under siege.

The girl doesn't look as if she's lying on the ground the way she fell. She seems to have pulled herself into a position to be comfortable, though I fear she's unconscious because of shock.

"There's no saddle bag on the horse. Do you think she's from around here?" Jude asks.

"I'm not sure." The girl doesn't wear anything to mark who she is or where she's from. She wears a long overcoat covering a rather plain and unadorned blouse over leggings, which are all coated in mud. "But she's cold."

My jacket is wet, but it's better than nothing and I take it off to drape over the girl.

"We should probably get her to the cart and then to the village to see if anyone can identify her," Jude says.

"Yeah," I agree. "Just give me a minute."

I visually scan her and no wounds stand out. She has no obvious head injury, but that doesn't mean she didn't hit her head when she fell from the horse. Her shoulders and elbows aren't dislocated, and her breathing doesn't indicate a cracked rib or punctured lung.

The young woman hasn't given me her consent to touch her, but as she's unconscious and I'm going to have to move her, I gingerly touch her stomach to check for any reaction to pain or internal injuries.

Nothing.

My fingers graze over her legs. There aren't any obvious broken bones, but when my fingers run over her left shin, a small whimper escapes.

"I think her lower left leg is broken," I tell Jude. "It's an internal fracture. The pain and shock probably caused her to lose consciousness."

"Can we move her?" Jude asks.

The young woman must be near our age. Her face is round with a square chin. Dark blonde hair hangs to her shoulders and I use a finger to brush some away from her soft cheek. There's something about this girl I can't quite place. Do I know her?

"Maybe it's good she's unconscious, because she'll be in pain with movement, but I don't think we'll do any other damage to her," I say.

"Any other damage?" Jude repeats. He grips the horses' reins and leans in. "Maybe we shouldn't move her?"

I lift my chin and look at Jude. "Should we leave her here instead? Where she'll probably die from exposure?"

"We can't leave her." Jude exhales and his warm breath looks like dragon steam in the cold air. I look away. "I can't believe she's out alone in this weather."

"She must have a good reason," I say. But what?

"I'll take our horses back and get the cart to come to the closest point on the road. I'll come back for the extra horse while you carry her to the cart," Jude says.

"Sounds like a good plan." I get to be the rescuer and carry the girl. I would have insisted I carry her if Jude offered. For some reason, I feel the need to rescue this girl.

Carefully, I wedge my arms under the girl's neck and her knees. I know it can't be comfortable for her broken leg to be in this position, but it's the best I can do.

The walk isn't far, but carrying a girl with a broken leg over soggy ground makes my arms burn, but this burn is far better than the one from a dragon.

CHAPTER TWENTY-ONE

FIA

A deep groan escapes between my lips.

I lie on something hard. I'm no longer on the ground.

Are my eyes open or closed?

"I think-"

I'm not sure if I speak the words or someone else does, but then everything goes black again.

CHAPTER TWENTY-TWO

EMERIC

"She might be from the village," I tell Jude. "Hopefully someone knows who she is."

"And what if they don't?" Jude drives the cart but turns his head over his shoulder to look at me. He has a curious grin. "What if this is a girl who's fallen from the sky into your arms?"

"Things like that don't happen. She must be from around here." But as I sit on the floor of the cart with the prone girl in my lap, I can't help but wonder about her. What is her story?

"We're not too far now," Jude says, keeping the horses at a pace which doesn't jostle the cart too much.

"She's freezing cold." The back of my hand rests against the girl's cheek. Her skin is pale and flecked with mud. She has thick, dark eyebrows and plump lips. She has a simple and understated beauty, which gives her an innocent look.

"Here." Jude removes his coat and tosses it back. "Use my coat too."

"Thanks." My coat is around the girl, and I add Jude's damp one on top.

"Too bad I don't have the red cloak Eira gave me," Jude says. "I bet that would keep her warm."

"What cloak?" I don't take my eyes off the unconscious girl. What is it about her that has me mesmerized? It's not as if she's the first girl I've ever seen.

"I met Eira at the secret entrance to the tunnels before she met you." Jude reveals another story I have not yet heard. He knows a lot of my family's secrets and can be trusted. "She handed me a red cloak and said to pass it on to someone in need. She said it could protect someone from whatever hunted them."

"Do you think someone or something is hunting this girl?" I ask.

The girl's eyelids twitch, but they don't open. My hand hovers near her nose, making sure I can feel the warmth of her breath.

"Probably not. She's likely a farm girl who got stuck in the storm." Jude shrugs as he follows the guards on the horses ahead of us into the village. "The cloak is nice, but not quite my style. It would have kept this girl warm."

"Do you still have the cloak?"

"I gave it to Amelie for now," Jude replies. "We'll pass it on when the need arises. Though I hope no one ever has a need to hide."

Jude brings the cart to a stop.

I brace the girl tightly, so she doesn't move much with the swaying of the cart. "Would you mind finding a healer or someone to help identify this girl?"

"I'll be back soon." Jude jumps from the cart and ties up the horses.

Something about this girl reminds me of Max. The black cat disappears during the day, but at night finds his way to my room. It's as if we both need each other to sleep. Max nestles next to me on my bed and the vibration of his body as he purrs lulls me to sleep. Everyone seems to know about my former trysts with girls, but no one knows a feline currently occupies my bed. I wonder what Max is doing while I'm away.

With my fingers, I brush some strands of damp hair away from the girl's forehead. I continue to wonder what her story is. She fell into my lap much the same way Max did, with little explanation. They're both a mystery.

"I won't let any harm come to you," I whisper to the girl.

A gold chain hangs from her neck and is tucked under the front of her blouse. Carefully, I pull on the chain to discover if anything is attached to it to help identify the girl. Hanging from the chain is a brilliant blue stone, no bigger than the nail of my smallest finger. It's a charming blue run through with lines of gold and white. It's smooth to the touch, but there are no engravings or anything to give an indication of origin.

Something or someone bangs hard against the side of the cart, and I hold the girl steady.

"Oh. Ay." A large round head pokes up and looks over the side of the cart. My gut clenches.

I let the stone attached to the golden chain fall into the girl's hair to conceal it from this stranger. I don't have a good feeling about this man.

"Who are you?" I demand of the round face with a scruffy beard and stringy hair.

"Ay." The man's bleary eyes narrow on the girl resting in my lap. "I heard you have an unidentified girl."

"What concern is it of yours?"

The man is obviously drunk, and sways while he stands outside the cart. He leers at the girl, and I'm disgusted. Disgusted with the man and disgusted with my past self. Did I once look like this man? Drunk and leering?

"She." A stubby finger juts out and points at the girl in my lap. "She is mine."

I clench my jaw. "What is her name?"

"She is, ah..." the man blinks repeatedly. "She is Amy."

I highly doubt she's Amy. "Tell me what is on Amy's gold chain?"

"She has a gold chain?" The man's eyes widen. "I mean, yes, she does."

"Be gone!" I raise my voice.

"She is mine!" The man starts to climb in the cart.

I can't move much as I don't want to injure the girl, but neither can I let this man touch her. My sword lies next to me, and I quickly pick it up and aim the point at the man's chest as he climbs in.

"You will not enter!"

The man lifts his chin and looks at the point of my sword.

"Ay." The man nods, not so drunk he'll try to fight me. "I won't enter, but you'll give me my girl."

"I will do no such thing." My voice is harsh. I keep the sword at the ready, the point mere inches from the man with ill intentions. "I don't believe she is yours."

"Barley!" A shrill voice rises from behind the man. I hear a slapping sound. "You get away from here and leave this instant!"

"Madge!" The drunk man falls backwards. "I was doin' nothin'."

"Don't you lie to me! Now you get!" the shrill voice yells.

I protectively keep the sword in my hand and watch Jude help the man move away. I now view a small woman, who swats at Barley again.

"You go on home, Barley," she scolds. She's about a third of his size, but commands Barley as if she's three times his size.

"This is the town healer, Prince Emeric," Jude says with a reverent dip of his chin. In private he calls me Emeric, but he's respectful enough to use my title when around others.

"Thank you." I set the sword to the side. "Will you keep watch while she examines the girl?"

Jude nods and turns his back to the cart as the small woman climbs in.

"I'm sorry, Your Highness. Barley has a penchant for ale, and we do our best to keep him out of trouble, but alas, when he's had a touch of the drink, he's not right." The tiny woman sets a canvas bag down and throws a blanket over the girl in my lap. "I'm Madge. I'm the town healer.

Mostly deliver the babies and treat regular ailments, but I'll see what I can do."

"We found this girl in a field, unconscious. I think she has a broken leg," I say.

"Ah." Madge carefully kneels at the side of the girl and against me. "Excuse me for touching you, Your Highness. But we're in close quarters and I need to examine her. You can leave if you wish."

"I wish to stay." I'm not leaving this girl alone.

"As you wish." Madge runs her palms over the girl's forehead and cheeks. She carefully checks the girl's neck, arms, chest, and belly before moving to her legs. All the while the woman makes little noises like a mother cat examining her kittens.

"Curious she's not waking up." Madge starts to dig in her large canvas bag. "Must have been through quite an ordeal, but if she stays this way for some time, we must make sure she can take food and drink."

"Of course." I nod in agreement.

"Boy." The woman beckons to Jude from the open cart. "Go to the wood smith and tell him Madge needs two boards for a lower leg. He'll know what I need."

Jude hurries off and I keep my eyes on the young woman.

"She's a petite little thing, isn't she?" Madge's eyes rove over the girl. "Reminds me of a drowned kitten."

Funny Madge should make that comment after the girl reminded me of Max.

"Is she from around here?" I ask. "Do you recognize her?"

Madge's head shakes. "I don't recognize her. I've delivered most of the babies in this area for coming up on three decades. This girl would have been one of them. Makes you wonder what happened."

"It does," I reply in agreement. "Do you think she can be transported safely?"

"Once I bind up her leg, she can be, though if she wakes up, she'll feel pain. If you prefer, I can keep her here, Your Highness," Madge says. "She will be well cared for."

I think of Barley, and even if Madge promises to keep this girl safe, I don't trust leaving her where Barley can get his hands on her. I didn't like the way he was leering at her. I'm going to cut the visit to the village short and head for home immediately.

"I appreciate what you have done, and I'll gladly pay for your services, but I'll bring this girl back to the castle," I reply.

"I understand." Madge nods. "If anyone comes looking for a missing girl, I'll send them to the castle."

CHAPTER TWENTY-THREE

FIA

Castle.

My body moves. My leg hurts. My head hurts.

Someone speaks of a castle.

Am I home?

I'm so tired.

I keep my eyes closed and let the darkness enrobe me again.

Chapter Twenty-Four

EMERIC

It's late when Jude and I arrive at Swendale Castle. Darkness shrouds everything, hiding our arrival. I feel a sense of relief, but also a distressing sadness I can't explain.

"Thank you," I say softly as Jude collects his bag when we're in the courtyard.

"Hmm?" He jerks his head back to me.

"I appreciate you accompanying me." I keep my eyes on the girl. She still lies on the floor of the cart and her lips are turned slightly downward. She looks how I feel, as if there's a hidden sadness, but it only comes out in a small frown, which someone could mistake as apathy or even bitterness. "You'll think about my offer?"

"I will." Jude slaps a hand on my shoulder and smirks. "You're not as bad as Leo says."

"Maybe you could tell him that." I've had more time with Jude than I've had with Leo since he returned from his quest. I regret how I treated Leo for the past couple of years, but regrets don't change anything. I'll need actions to make any headway with my younger brother.

"Would you like some help with the girl?" Jude asks as he adjusts the bag on his shoulder.

"Help me get her out of the cart and I'll carry her to the healer," I say.

"You traveled with her unconscious for over a day?" Liora, the castle healer, looks at me aghast. Like the healer in the village, she's a tiny woman, not even five feet tall. But the vivid expressions on her slender face give away every emotion.

"Yes," I nod, not sure if it's the correct answer.

"And you fed her and gave her water?"

"I tried my best," I say, feeling as if I did everything wrong. I held the girl against my chest to keep her upright as I tried to spoon small amounts of water and a rich broth into her mouth to give her some nourishment. I even spoon fed her small amounts of honey, as Swendale honey from the Abella bee is known for its healing properties.

"You attended to her other needs?" Liora stares hard at me, as if accusing me of something.

I lift my hands up in a surrendering position. "I promise I was a gentleman, and I did my best to care for her. I had the help of a healer in a village."

Liora nods her head at me with a soft smile and then runs her hands over the girl's face and neck. "I'm quite impressed, Your Highness. You've taken good care of her."

"Do you think she'll wake?" I ask.

Liora has been the castle healer since before I was born. She attended to my mother for my birth and the births of my siblings. She tended to Leo the many times he was injured while training with me and when he was struck by an arrow. She mended my broken arm when I was younger. I trust her judgement.

"Yes." Liora gives a firm nod. She always keeps her hair covered in a wrap and her brown eyes crinkle at the corners. "I'm not sure when she will wake, but the life breath in her is strong. Her body is only protecting her for the moment. When it's ready, she'll wake."

"Is there anything I can do?" I ask, not quite ready to leave the girl who's been a silent presence next to me. I have a desire to hear her voice.

"You're free to go, Your Highness," Liora says. "I'll refresh her, change the braces and binding on her leg, and attend to her."

"I'll remain here until you get your supplies and start." I settle into a chair next to the bed where the mystery girl lies.

Liora nods in agreement. "I shall return soon."

Liora leaves the door to the small windowless room open after she leaves. This part of the castle is quiet. The cozy room is lit with a lantern, and it smells of soap and herbs. My eyes linger on the girl in the bed, and I have no idea why I'm drawn to her. Plenty of young women flirt with me, though lately I have no interest in the ones who pay attention to me. But this mystery girl – I know nothing about her, and she intrigues me beyond explanation.

"Meow." A noise comes from the hallway.

"Max!" I find the black cat rubbing the side of his body against the door frame.

My family hasn't greeted me yet, but the stray cat is here.

"How have you been?" I bend over and scratch the cat behind the ears. As he usually does, he nuzzles his head into my palm and purrs loudly. "I'm guessing you found food and a place to sleep while I was gone."

"Meow." Max seems to nod in agreement and rubs the side of his belly against my leg before lifting his chin to peer at the girl.

"I've acquired another stray. Do you want to see her?" I ask the cat. Max looks as if he wants to jump up on the bed but isn't quite sure if he should.

I gently pick Max up and set him on the mattress near the girl's chest. The cat leans in to sniff at the girl's neck and chest before rubbing his cheek and chin against the girl's chin. A loud purring emanates from Max.

"Do you like her?" I reach out and run a hand down Max's spine as he starts to knead his paws into the mattress near the girl's arm.

It's not long before the black cat settles next to the girl's body.

"You do like her," I say, hoping Liora doesn't walk in to find me talking to a cat. It will counter the insensitive personality I garner among castle staff.

Max tilts his head to look at me and slowly blinks, as if he's wondering why I would question him.

"Okay, okay," I say. "I get it. You're a good judge of character. But if you like me, what does it mean about the character of this girl?"

I have a reputation for being charismatic, arrogant, and quite cold and ruthless. But Max seems to think otherwise, or he doesn't care. Much like I don't care what most people think of me.

Max only continues to purr and settles his head down. With my elbows on my knees, I lean forward to better watch the cat and girl, the two strays I picked up. Or maybe they picked me up as the stray.

"Ahh." Liora walks into the room with a contented sigh. "I see the mystery girl has already found a companion."

"Oh." I jump from the chair and reach for Max. "I can take him out with me."

Max bares his teeth and hisses at me, which makes me step backward. He's never acted aggressively before.

"I don't think he wants to leave the girl," Liora says.

"He?" I look down at Max, my suspicions about him confirmed. No wonder he's taking a liking to the mystery girl. I'm not sure why he likes me. I tend to repel other males.

"I haven't seen him around." Liora sets some supplies on a table as she nods her head at the feline.

"I'm not sure where he's from," I reply. "But he likes to follow me around."

"It seems he's taken a fancy to this mystery girl." Liora's eyes linger on the unconscious girl for a moment and then on me, as if she's reassessing her judgement of me. "Hmm. I assume you don't know the girl's name, but does the cat have a name?"

"Max."

"That's a fine name." Liora walks to the bedside and reaches a hand toward Max. The cat responds with a slight hiss. "Alright, Max." Liora smiles. "I know you're protecting her, and I'll leave you be, but you have to let me attend to the girl."

Liora turns her stare to me. "Your Highness?"

"Oh." My face reddens. "Yes. I'm leaving. Please let me know if there's anything I can do."

I step out of the small room and walk the back hallways toward the private royal quarters of the castle. A strange sensation of loneliness lingers over me. Usually, Max follows me when I'm alone in the castle and spends evenings with me, but now he's with the girl. I've spent the past few days traveling with Jude, and the remainder of the trip with the mystery girl in my arms. Now I have nothing and no one.

I enter my vast, quiet room. I drop onto the cushioned bench in front of the fireplace. A castle worker has stoked the fire and the flames dance high in colors of a vivid sunset. I close my eyes against the sight of the nightmare inducing flames and a calming image appears in my mind.

It's the girl.

CHAPTER TWENTY-FIVE

FIA

"What do we do about this girl?"

I suddenly hear a woman's voice. One moment I'm out of it, and the next I'm thrust back into the world of the living. It's a jarring feeling, as if I was out of my body, and suddenly I'm plunged back into it. I remain immobile, unsure what's happening around me.

"We could try the pea." This voice is younger, also a female.

"Not until she's awake and recovering," the other woman says. "But I don't think she's a candidate for it."

I remain with eyes closed, feigning sleep, as I don't recognize the voices. How long have I been out? Where am I? Where are the kidnappers? Who are these people?

I'm flat on my back, most likely on a bed, because it feels soft under my body. It's not the hard floor of a cart or wagon. My head rests gently on a comfortable pillow. Blankets cover me, keeping me warm with a safe feeling.

"She could be a princess," the younger voice says. The feeling of safety dissipates, and my heart starts to beat faster.

"I doubt it," the older female voice says. Neither voice belongs to Eike. "I need to go, but you can stay with the poor girl until the healer returns."

Healer?

My mind starts to assess what's wrong with my body. My leg doesn't have the pain it used to, but I can tell it's bound. It must be broken.

The room grows quiet, except for the scrape of a chair on the floor. Then I hear someone turn a page in a book. I lie still, trying to mimic the same breathing style and motionlessness my body had before I woke, but I'm not entirely sure I'm doing it correctly. My heart thumps against my chest and if the person in the room looks at me, I'm sure they'll see the blanket over me moving up and down in time with the rapid beats.

I try to gauge where I am, but I have no idea. The room smells fresh, of herbs, soap, and flowers, with only a slight medicinal tinge. I don't hear the rushing water of a river, nor the large thump of wheels on a dirt path. There aren't many sounds, and I would guess I'm in a building with thick walls.

I couldn't have escaped only to be recaptured. Someone else must have rescued me. I slowly peel my eyes open.

"You're awake!" A girl next to me exclaims and I startle.

My eyes are fully open and rest on a girl who smiles at me. Her smile is not one of the vicious smiles of my captors. She seems genuinely happy to see me. Blue eyes sparkle out of wide eyes and the girl's golden-brown hair is woven into an intricate braid piled on top of her head.

"How?" I blink in the light of a lamp next to the bed. My throat is dry. "How long have I been, uh…" I close my eyes trying to remember. My last memory is of lying on the ground in a muddy field.

"As far as we know, you've been unconscious a few days," the girl replies, leaning in close to me. She holds out a glass of water.

"Where am I?" I take the glass and sip while looking around the basic room. Stone walls with no window, stone floor, and a wooden door, but the room doesn't appear to be a dungeon cell. I'm in a comfortable bed and the girl sits nearby in a wooden chair. There's a table next to my head and a lamp sits on it. I set the glass on the table.

"You're in the Swendale Castle," the girl says.

"Castle?" My voice squeaks. What am I doing in a castle? "How did I get here?"

"My brother found you unconscious and injured in a field. No one in the closest village could identify you and he brought you here." The girl beams at me and leans forward. "Do you have a name?"

"Fia," I quickly reply and then still. I have no idea if I'm safe. My kidnappers could be nearby. "What happened?"

"You broke your leg." The girl points to my leg. "You're here to heal until you can go home. Where are you from?"

I reach out and bend over to touch my leg. It's bound and aches, but it's not the excruciating pain of when I was first injured. To the girl it appears I examine my leg while my brain quickly runs through scenarios of my situation.

"I don't know where I'm from," I finally respond as the girl curiously eyes me. She has a sweet doe-like appearance, as if she's always on alert and inquisitive. "Do you know who I am?"

"No." The girl shakes her head. "Other than you told me your name is Fia."

"I..." I need to come up with a plan. "I'm not sure Fia is my name."

"You don't know where your home is?" The girl's finger taps against her skirt covered legs in quick motions.

"I..." I shouldn't have given her my name, but it'll have to do. I can still change the course of this. "I..." I press my lips together and furrow my brows in an act. "I can't remember. I don't know my name or where I'm from."

I clasp my hands to my head and start to breathe quickly, feigning panic. It will be in my favor to pretend I have amnesia until I have more details.

"I...I...I can't remember anything." I look up at the girl with crazed eyes. "Who am I? Where am I from? Why am I here?"

"Don't panic." The girl stands up from her chair and grabs my hands in hers. "It's going to be okay. We'll figure this out. My brother said it looked like you fell from a horse, and you must have hit your head."

"My memory!" I pinch my lips together and fake holding back a sob. "I can't remember anything."

"I'm sure your memory loss is only temporary," the girl kindly assures me. She pats my hands. "Someone must be looking for you."

That's what worries me.

"Am I safe here?" The tension in my voice is now real.

"I won't let anything happen to you." The girl's smile is gentle, and I want to believe her.

"Okay. Thank you." I profusely nod my head as she lets go of my hands.

"Is it okay if I call you Fia until we figure out who you are?" The girl seems eager to talk and once again sits.

"Yes," I reply. It'll be easier to go by my name, and I don't have to risk forgetting I have an alias.

"Do you remember anything?" the girl asks.

"I..." I'm not sure what I should be able to remember. I remember everything up until I was lying in the mud, but I'll pretend I remember less. "I remember...nothing. I mean, I remember things, like how to read and write, but I can't recall any memories or people or even who I am."

"Interesting." The girl presses her lips together. "Strange my brother didn't leave you where he found you."

"Where was I found?" I don't know the terrain of – where did she say I'm at? Swendale?

"Over a day journey from here. Just north of the southern border of Swendale," the girl replies. "I'm surprised my brother risked bringing you all the way back to the castle."

"Your brother?" I don't recall a rescuer, but at least I'm not in the hands of my captors. I'm now a different kind of captive, but I'm not sure who's keeping me. "Who are you?"

The girl smiles again. She seems warm and welcoming, nothing like the harsh and cold attitudes of my kidnappers. "You can call me Adette."

"Adette," I repeat, which elicits a smile from the girl. She is near my age or within a couple years of me. I would guess she's a little younger, but I've never been a great judge of ages. Although I could tell the man my father wanted me to marry was older than my parents.

"Don't worry," Adette says with a sweet upturn of her lips. "We'll do our best to help you."

"Do you work here?" I look around the small, but clean room. It must be an infirmary room of some sort.

"In a way," Adette replies with a curious smile. "I've been sitting with you when I can. You piqued my curiosity."

"How?" I don't want to be fueling anyone's curiosity. I want to stay hidden in the background. I can't have anyone discovering who I really am.

Adette giggles. "My brother tends to hide girls in the castle, not bring them from someplace else. I mean, he used to hide girls." Adette waves her hands. "Oh, never mind. I'm happy to see you awake, though hopefully you recover your memory. I'm sure it's only a matter of time."

Adette is quite friendly and likes to talk. She might be helpful in answering my questions and helping me to hide or leave.

"Do I need to leave now that I'm awake?" I grasp the chain around my neck. There must be some way I can get out of here.

"Oh, no! You have a broken leg." Adette bounds up from the chair. "I should get the healer to check you and it's nearly afternoon teatime. I'll get you some real food, if you think your stomach can handle it. We've been try-ing to feed you a rich broth and honey."

"You've been feeding me?" I may be faking amnesia, but there are obviously some things I don't remember from when I was unconscious.

"Me, my brother, the healer, the apprentices." Adette smiles. "I'll be back soon."

"Thank you."

The moment after Adette leaves, I throw off the blankets covering my body and try to swing my leg over the bed. Stiff boards brace the leg, and linen strips are wrapped tightly around them to keep my leg in place.

"Ow." I grunt. I won't be going anywhere easily for quite some time with my leg broken and bound.

I'm not sure if this is a stroke of fortune or quite un-lucky. I wouldn't even know where to go. An infirmary room in Swendale Castle may be the safest place for the time being. Adette doesn't seem to have evil intentions. If I keep my royal identity hidden and fake amnesia, hiding here is the best plan until I'm able to leave on my own.

I cover my legs with the blankets again and settle back on to the feather pillow and sigh. I need to find Fynn. I promised I'd come after him. There's no time to wait, even with a broken leg.

I once again lurch up and throw off the blankets. If I can acquire a horse and a crutch, I may be able to make my way to Somniara. I swing my right leg off the bed and gently follow with my left to test weight on my broken leg.

"You shouldn't do that yet," a voice behind me says. "You won't be walking on it quite yet or going anywhere real soon."

CHAPTER TWENTY-SIX

EMERIC

The mystery girl is awake and trying to get out of bed when I get to her infirmary room. I've tried to imagine what this girl is like, and it appears she's a determined one. Who tries to get out of bed with a broken leg?

"I can do it." I hear the stubbornness in the girl's voice.

From my position in the doorway, the girl's back is to me, and I can't see her face. Nor can she see me.

"You may be able to," I say and step into the room, "but it isn't a wise choice."

"I think I know what is wise for me," the girl says.

"You don't want to risk further damage," I remind her.

"It's already broken." The girl's body tenses as she tries to lean forward and put weight on her bad leg.

"You shouldn't do that," I warn. I want to reach out and gently pull her back in bed, but I have a feeling she'll react like a scared cat and claw me. "It's best if you put your leg back up and rest it."

"Are you the healer?"

"No," I reply as the girl starts to shift on the bed and tries to turn my direction. "I'm-"

"You!" The girl's eyes widen when she first sets her eyes on me, and then they narrow. She pulls her leg back up on the bed and flops her head to the pillow. She mumbles something under her breath, which I can't hear.

"Do you recognize me?" A slight smile rises on my lips. I'm often recognized by young women.

"No." The girl presses her lips together and fiercely shakes her head.

I now furrow my brows. It's not often a young woman doesn't know of Prince Emeric. "You don't know who I am?"

"No." It's a quick answer. "Am I supposed to know who you are?"

"Well..." I push back some of the dark curls hanging over my face. Mother is always after me to shave and cut my hair shorter, thinking it's not becoming of a prince, but no one else seems to mind. Most girls like it. "I guess there's not a reason you should know who I am."

Except I'm a prince and heir to this kingdom.

"Are you the one who brought me here?" The girl avoids making eye contact with me, but she quickly lifts her eyes to mine for a brief second. Her eyes are bluish gray and remind me of the sky before rain.

"I rescued you." I nod once and can't help the small smile starting to curl my lips up. I didn't save my kingdom or my own life, but I was able to save someone else's life. For once, I don't feel like a complete failure. I step closer to the bed.

"Of course." The girl huffs. "Of course you would be the one to rescue me."

She sounds angry, but it's probably because she's in pain. Girls are usually delighted when they first meet me, except my feeling of success at this girl's rescue is starting to dwindle. It sounds like she didn't want to be rescued.

"Most girls don't complain when a prince rescues them," I say, keeping the usual air of confidence to my voice, even if it's really lacking.

"You're a prince?" The girl pushes her head back into the pillow and frowns. She sounds disappointed, rather than astonished. I get the one girl who isn't happy a prince rescued her.

"Would you rather I wasn't a prince?" I used to often wish I wasn't, especially when I found out what being a prince of Swendale means.

"It doesn't matter if you're a prince or not." The girl tugs the blankets back up. "But of course you have to be one. Please don't tell me you have a white horse."

It seems a prince is the last person mystery girl would like to have rescue her.

"He's actually brown." I can't help smiling at the mystery girl.

She only makes a grunting noise.

"You're lucky I found you." I'm not quite sure what to do with this girl, but I don't want our conversation to end. There's something about her which makes me smile and I haven't smiled much in a long time. Rather than me charming her, she's charming me without even trying. "You could have died out there."

"Just my luck." The girl starts to twist a lock of hair around her finger. "Out of the frying pan and into the fire."

I only wrinkle my nose in confusion. "I'm Prince Emeric."

"I met your sister." The girl's eyes narrow slightly. "But she didn't tell me she was a princess. Why did you bring me here?"

"Was I supposed to leave you unconscious in a muddy sheep field?" I ask. This isn't the reaction I thought I would get from this girl when she woke. I imagined a little more gratitude and fawning over me. Oddly enough, it's refreshing to not have a girl fall all over me. "What were you doing in the field?"

"I don't know." The girl shrugs, seemingly not having a care about much. "I can't remember anything."

"Nothing?" Curious about this mysterious girl, I slide into the wooden chair next to the bed. "Not even your name?"

"Nope." The girl presses her lips together and shakes her head. "I guess you can call me Fia until we find out what it is."

"Fia," I say, enjoying how the short name rolls off my tongue. "It's better then what I've been calling you."

The girl lifts her bushy eyebrows high on her forehead in a questioning gesture. It's a rather cute look on her. "And what have you been calling me?"

"Mystery girl," I reply. "But I like Fia better."

Fia.

Why does her name stir my soul?

CHAPTER TWENTY-SEVEN

FIA

Oh, no. Why is he sitting? Why is he saying my name?

"Fia," Prince Emeric says again.

I wish he wouldn't say my name like that. Like it's the air he breathes, like it sets him free.

Does he know he's my true love?

Of course, my true love would have to be a prince, and of course, he would have to be the one to rescue me.

Fate is playing a joke on me and laughing hard.

I may not be cursed like my brother, but it seems I am. I don't want a true love, nor did I want to be rescued by him. There's no denying this man before me is the one from my rosemary induced dream. The features are the same – the long nose, full lips, dark eyes, chiseled cheek bones. And the dimple. Oh, the dimple. Right in the center of his chin. The dimple is present in the image in my mind and it's right in front of my open eyes.

The image seared into my brain is now flesh before me. It makes me want to throw up. If fate is making sure I can't ignore or avoid my true love, I'll show fate a thing or two.

"Is there anything I can get you, Fia?" Prince Emeric asks.

My belly clenches. Why does he have to say my name again?

"No, thank you," I spit out, not sounding thankful. "You've done enough. I'm sure you have royal duties or something to attend to."

"Eventually." Prince Emeric's lips rise into a slow smile and a feeling I want to be rid of spreads ever as slowly across my belly.

I look away, furious at my body for reacting to this guy's smile. It should not react at all. I need to be immune to his charm. I twist a lock of hair furiously around with my finger.

"I'm curious about the girl I rescued," Prince Emeric continues, "and I'd like to know more about you."

If I can help it, this man before me will never discover the truth about me.

"As I can't remember anything, there isn't much to learn about me."

"No idea where you're from?" Prince Emeric leans forward and places his elbows on his knees. He's close enough I can smell the soap on him. Notes of honey and something woodsy like sandalwood permeate the air around him. His face takes on a serious look. "Any family? Friends?"

I twist the edge of the blanket in a fist. "I told you I don't remember anything."

Family has me thinking of Fynn again. And Reimund. So much tragedy has happened, and I can't let anything further take place. I need to get to Fynn and not let anyone else get hurt.

My eyes flick back to Prince Emeric's face. I'm drawn to stare into his eyes, but I can't. I can fight true love. I lower my eyes once again, but they flutter back up. If anyone discovered I was rescued by my true love, they'd be writing sonnets and ballads. I must keep this quiet, if I can.

"Do you know anyone named Morella?" Prince Emeric's gaze is more piercing than when I throw a dagger at a target.

I wrinkle my nose. It's a strange question. Even though I fake amnesia, I don't know anyone named Morella. "No. I don't recognize the name."

"She's not a spy or some evil henchman." Adette walks in with a small tray and sets it on the table. She gives me a gracious smile before turning back to her brother.

"We can never be too careful," Prince Emeric says. "We don't know who Fia is."

Nor do I fully know who these people are. I recall studying Swendale, but my recollection of the current royals is hazy. I do know Swendale is an absolute monarchy, like Ryutoa. Swendale has more free enterprise than my kingdom. It's also known dragons don't cross into Swendale, and if Fynn is a dragon, my chance of running into him here is slim.

Though, I thought my chance of finding my true love was slim. And he's before me with a smile on his face.

Ugh. I need to find a way to get to Fynn and away from this prince.

"She could be a princess," Adette says with a tip of her head to me.

"I'm sure lots of people would be looking for her if she were a missing princess," Prince Emeric says.

I try to remain placid and keep a calm look on my face. If they only knew how close they are to the truth. Unfortunately, my kidnappers are likely the closest ones looking for me. I want to believe my parents have searchers out looking for me, but they never sent anyone after Fynn.

"Do you have any identifying marks?" Prince Emeric keeps his gaze on me, his eyes searching for something, but I'm not quite sure what. "Scars, tattoos, or anything of that sort? Something someone could use to identify you by."

"Ah." What am I supposed to say? "Yes, I have a large tattoo of a dragon across my back."

"Really?" Prince Emeric's eyes widen to an astonishing circumference. I'm not sure if the mention of a dragon is fascinating or causes him fear.

"No," I reply. "I don't remember anything, but I don't think I have any identifying marks."

I extend my arms out and twist my hands around as if looking for tattoos or birthmarks.

The prince lifts his eyebrows under his dark locks of hair. "Do you need someone to help-"

"Emeric!" Adette exclaims and throws a biscuit at her brother.

In a quick action, Emeric's hand launches up and he catches the biscuit before it hits his face. He brings it to his mouth and takes a bite, while I watch the entire time, as if

I'm mesmerized. And maybe I am, though I don't want to be.

"She doesn't need help." Adette gives her brother one of those knowing looks between siblings. "Especially not from you."

Emeric brushes his lips with the back of his hand, and I still find my eyes on his lips. "Just a thought. We don't know when she'll get her memory back."

"Don't you worry. I'm sure you'll regain your memory soon or we'll discover where you belong," Adette tells me as she prepares a cup of tea. "Is my brother bothering you?"

"He...ah..." I close my eyes and pop them back open. "He-"

The prince before me is identical to the vision I see when I close my eyes. This is quite unsettling.

"She's speechless in my presence." Prince Emeric grins, but it's directed at his sister.

"She's hungry." Adette shakes her head, and I detect an eyeroll. Emeric and Adette act like my brother and me. "Don't mistake being famished for falling all over you. I sense this one's smart and won't fall for your charm."

"True." I nod eagerly, maybe a little too eagerly because my head bobs like a puppet on a string.

"Excuse my brother." Adette gives Emeric a side eye. "He can act like a rake sometimes."

"I have no use for rakes," I say. "I'm much better at burying things with a shovel."

Adette chuckles. "I like this one. She has a sense of hu-mor." She holds up a small pitcher. "Cream or honey?"

"Both, please."

Prince Emeric pulls his elbows off his knees and pushes himself out of the chair. He's tall and lean with obvious developed muscles.

I close my eyes again to rid myself of the sight of him, but he's right behind my eyes too.

"Well..." Prince Emeric brushes his hands together. "Welcome to Swendale Castle. I hope you have a pleasant stay. And please, if you need anything, anything at-"

"No!" Adette nearly shouts and glares at her brother before pointing at the door. "Out."

Adette hands me the cup of tea and takes the chair her brother left. "I'm sorry about him." She smiles and I can tell while she may be annoyed by her older brother, she has a soft spot for him. "He has a way with the ladies and knows it."

"Don't worry about me." I take a small sip of the hot liquid, and the slight sweetness is soothing. When I have tea in Ryutoa with my grandmother, I add a sugar cube, but the addition of honey is a nice change. "It takes more than a handsome face to move me."

"You don't remember if you have a boyfriend or a husband?" Adette takes a cup of tea she prepared for herself from the tray.

"No." I set the teacup back on the table and pick up a biscuit. "I could be married."

I lift the biscuit to my mouth and Adette points at my hand. "You aren't wearing a ring, nothing to indicate you're married."

I nearly choke on the bite of biscuit. My ring! I examine my hands. Eike must still have my royal ring. It's a mystery to me as to what happened to Eike and the other kidnappers, and I fear they're looking for me.

Chapter Twenty-Eight

EMERIC

"The mystery girl is awake?" Mother looks over the table at me with her blue eyes.

"Fia," I clarify and set down my spoon.

Father has already left the table to attend to a matter and I'm rather eager for supper to end. I want to pay Fia another visit. Mother has kept me busy, and I haven't been able to return to the infirmary to further question the mysterious girl.

"She doesn't remember anything," I say.

"Emeric thinks she's a spy." Adette twirls a spoon in her hand.

"I only questioned it," I say flatly and lift a teacup. "But I don't think she is."

While I once always had a glass of wine at dinner to numb my emotions and memories, I've switched to tea. I don't enjoy reliving my nightmares, but numbing them with alcohol wasn't helping anyone, especially me. It was a crutch which hasn't been easy to get rid of, but I no longer need it.

"Being suspicious of strangers is necessary when you're in our position." Mother lifts a goblet to her mouth and steals a glance at Adette.

"Are you suspicious of Fia?" My eyes dart between my mother and younger sister. They're not telling me something.

"We're merely curious," Mother replies. "We don't know anything about her."

"She has amnesia," I say in defense of the mystery girl.

I keep surprising myself. I'm not easy to be friends with, but I'm acting as if this young woman is my best friend.

"There are ways of figuring certain things out. Will you let me try?" Adette's eyes widen with anticipation, but I'm clueless as to what she's talking about. She's mysterious herself.

"No," Mother answers. "I don't think there's a reason to try."

"Try what?" I jerk back from blankly staring to question Mother.

"Emeric." Mother focuses her attention on me but doesn't answer my question. "Why don't you check on Fia right now? Please make sure she's been given some supper and is comfortable. Adette will check on her before she retires for the evening."

"Of course." I'm already standing. When Mother mentioned I could check on Fia, I was out of my chair faster than if -

I hate to think it, but faster than if a dragon was after me.

Dragon.

Will I ever be rid of thoughts of a dragon and the nightmares caged within me?

As I walk to the infirmary, it feels as if the walls are closing in on me. The dark hallway lit by small sconces makes me feel as if I'm in the path of the dragon's fire. The roar of the water dragon I encountered during my quest echoes through my mind, causing my body to tremble in fear.

"Fia." I softly say the name the mystery girl gave me, and a strange calmness sweeps over me.

Images of the dragon fade, giving way to thoughts of the mystery girl. The corners of my mouth start to tip up at the memory of the stubborn girl trying to get out of bed with a broken leg.

I knock on the wooden door. "Fia?"

All I hear is an exasperated groan. It's a displeased sound which causes me to smile, and I push the door open. Fia reclines in bed in an upright position, pillows supporting her back. She twists a lock of hair around her finger, her lips are pressed together, and her cheeks are flushed pink. Her dark blonde hair shines in the glow of the lamp near her. Fia looks sweet and innocent, but there's more to her. We both need to figure out who she is and what strength she has.

"You've had supper?" I pull my shoulders back and point to the tray on the table near Fia. No need to dive into emotions when we can start by scratching at the surface.

"You're prince of the obvious." Fia glances at the remnants of her meal.

"Thanks for noticing." I smirk and settle myself into the chair next to the bed, much to Fia's utter dismay.

"Don't make yourself comfortable." Fia balks and tugs the blanket up to her chest. "You don't need to stay."

"What have I done to make you dislike me so?" I straight out ask.

I'll start digging beneath the surface. I'm fascinated by her reaction to me. It's rare for young women to be repelled by me, and Fia isn't shy in showing me she'd rather be with anyone else.

"How could I possibly dislike you after you rescued me?" Fia exaggeratedly rolls her eyes.

Pleasantly startled by the action of Fia rolling her eyes, I nearly laugh, but keep it pinched in. There aren't many women who would dare roll their eyes at me, and the only ones who roll their eyes at me are my siblings.

"You dislike me because I saved you?" I watch Fia twist a strand of hair around her finger.

"I could have saved myself." Fia's voice has an edge. She's either slightly unsure or merely confident, or like me, she's one and faking the other.

"Your leg was broken, you were lying in a muddy field, and you were unconscious." I squint at Fia. She's amusing. "It seemed the right thing to rescue you."

"Do you have some sort of savior complex?" Fia's upper lip curls. I have a sudden reaction to want to relax it in a way she might disapprove of right now. "You get some sort of high off rescuing girls?"

"Where do you get that idea?" I'm mesmerized by the action of Fia twisting the lock of hair.

It seems as if she has an absent look on her face as she twists her hair, but there's something deeper. There's a depth to Fia, one I can't quite see because it's hiding or unknown, but I want to dig deep to discover what she's thinking. Because she's thinking, and apparently, it's not very nice thoughts about me.

For some reason, I have a strong urge to change her mind, no matter what kind of wall she puts up. The higher she builds the wall, the higher I'll climb. I haven't been motivated to try something in a long while. My life has been walking the line of duty, and now I want to fight for something.

"I know your type." Disgruntled, Fia crosses her arms over her chest.

"You do?" I mockingly drop my jaw, intrigued by what Fia is going to say.

"The type who gets off on making himself seem bigger than he is. You'll call out failures of others while not admitting your own many failures. You get ahead with your charisma and charm, but your personality overcompensates for your inadequacies."

"Whoa." I let out a slow breath as if recovering from a gut punch. Because this is a gut punch. Fia is digging into me before I can dig into her. "You may not have your memory but you're very perceptive."

"Is the prince admitting to having a savior complex?" The corner of Fia's lips twitch.

"Can you keep a secret?" I feel I could bare my soul to this woman.

"Who am I going to tell?" Fia's hand flies up as she shrugs. "I don't know anyone."

"If anything, I have more of a failure complex," I say in a soft voice. Maybe I tell Fia because she doesn't know who she is or even who I am. The truth is I keep my failures buried under a fake savior complex. A personality I over exaggerate to compensate for my inadequacies. Just like Fia said.

"Right," Fia scoffs, taking my admission as a joke.

"Meow."

At the noise, Fia and I both turn our attention to the door.

"Max," I say, relieved for the interruption. There's only so much soul baring I can take at one time. "Come on in."

"Who's this?" Fia's face immediately softens.

The cat takes Fia's question as an invitation and immediately jumps on her bed. Fia's face melts into bliss, and I realize Max might be my way into this girl's heart.

Not that I want to get into her heart, but I'm perplexed as to why Fia dislikes me so, and I want her to like me.

"This is Max." I watch the cat step closer to Fia's hand, which she holds out for him to examine. "He's been keeping you company at night."

Max brings his head to Fia's hand in acknowledgement. Fia kneads her fingers into Max's chin which starts Max's motor running. "He's a sweetie."

A sudden pinch of jealousy surprises me and my body twitches. Why do I want to trade places with Max and have Fia's fingers gently stroking my chin?

"Max is a traitor. He usually stays in my room, but has abandoned me since you arrived," I say, eager for a reaction from Fia.

"I would say he chose the right side." There's a slight smile on Fia's face as the palm of her hand slides down Max's back to his tail.

Max meows.

"Great," I say in a sarcastic tone and direct my attention to the cat. "You're agreeing with Fia after all I've done for you. What has she done for you?"

Max kneads the mattress with his paws and then settles on to his side next to Fia.

Fia chuckles, which is one of the loveliest sounds I've heard lately. Much better than the roar of a water dragon or petty arguments over pea soup.

"Cats are a good judge of character." Fia's face glows as she watches Max, and my heart warms. Could I ever have a woman look at me like that? One full of sweetness rather than bitter desire?

"I've heard," I reply with a lift of my eyebrows.

"Obviously, I must have a better character than you." Fia tilts her head back.

"You're definitely some kind of character." Now I'm the one who is chuckling. "You can't remember who you are."

"I'm pretty sure I like animals," Fia says as she continues to pet Max. "They're easy to love."

Max's purring fills the small room like a breath of fresh air. It's a sweet song of contentment. Once again, I'm mesmerized by Fia and watching her hand stroke over the fur of the cat. I'm jealous of a cat. He's easy to love, and I'm not. I'm a prince and heir to a throne, and I'm jealous of a stray.

"Good night, Lady Fia." I abruptly push out of the chair and dip my chin to the young woman petting the cat. "I wish you a pleasant night's sleep."

I'm not sure if Fia tells me good night as I quickly leave. Once in the quiet hall, I lean against the wall and shake off the building emotions. I'm only confused because I have yet to get a good night's sleep.

CHAPTER TWENTY-NINE

FIA

"How did you sleep?" A bright and chipper face asks immediately after I open my eyes.

"Oh." I blink my eyes and start to push myself to a sitting position. I'm not used to waking with someone in my face. At home I don't have a lady-in-waiting or attendants. "Princess Adette. What're you doing here?"

"You can call me Adette." She grins. "I wanted to check on you. I brought you breakfast."

A tray of food lies on the table next to the bed. Adette eagerly looks me over with sensitive and warm eyes.

"Did you sleep well?" she asks, her concern once again genuine.

"Uh." I reach a hand to where the black cat was when I fell asleep. I know I slept some, but it felt as if I was awake most of the night contemplating too many things.

How can I avoid Emeric? How can I leave as quickly as possible? How can I get to Fynn with a broken leg? How can I neglect true love?

"Yes. Thank you," I finally reply. "For being unconscious for so long, I slept like I was unconscious again."

My hand pats the space at my side. Max is gone. Did I dream the cat stayed the night with me? Did he abandon me for the cocky prince? The only remnants of the cat being with me are some strands of black fur on top of the blanket.

"Do you remember anything?" Adette settles herself into the chair her brother occupied last night. She leans forward, elbows on her knees, and chin cupped in her hands. She looks like an eager child awaiting a favorite fairytale.

"No," I lie, remembering everything except for Emeric rescuing me and bringing me here.

When I slept last night, Emeric infiltrated my dreams, which I never asked for. Rosemary may give me visions of my true love when I close my eyes, but it's not supposed to make me continually dream of him.

"Any idea how old you are?" Adette questions.

"Um." I shrug my shoulders. I hate deceiving this sweet girl but telling her the truth could endanger us. "Seventeen, eighteen? That sounds familiar."

"I'm sixteen. I'll be seventeen in a couple of months," Adette says. "We must be close in age."

"How old is your brother?" I hope I don't sound too eager. I shouldn't be interested in anything about Emeric.

"I have two brothers," Adette replies. "Emeric is twenty, but his birthday is next month. Leo turned eighteen not long ago."

Twenty.

I try not to tense and clench my jaw. Instead, I pull on the chain around my neck. At least my true love isn't as old as the man I was supposed to marry. Not that it matters, because I need to get as far away from Emeric as soon as I can.

"That's a pretty necklace." Adette thankfully changes the course of the conversation on her own and waggles a finger in the general direction of my chest where I absently finger the token connected to the gold chain.

I tilt my chin down and look at the blue stone in my fingers.

"Oh." I wrap the stone in my palm and try to hide it from view.

"It reminds me of a blue dragon pendant Leo received from his former tutor for his birthday," Adette says. "It's some sort of blue stone said to protect people from dragons."

"Really?" I try to act surprised. I know full well what she speaks of, as the superstition is from Ryutoa. I can't have Adette relating the lapis lazuli stone on my chain to my kingdom. "I don't remember hearing anything about that."

"Maybe you're from the kingdom where the stone was mined?" Adette leans in even closer. She smells of honey and lavender.

"Or..." I tuck the stone back under the soft, linen blouse I wear, my dirty clothes now discarded. "Just as your brother's pendant was a gift, this necklace could have been a gift from someone."

"We need to discover the mystery of who you are." Adette leans back in the chair as if settling herself in for a long visit.

"I can assure you I'm not important enough," I reply.

"Someone must be looking for you."

That's the problem. I don't want to be found.

"Good morning."

The one person I never wanted to find, who found me, pokes his head in the door. He looks too good for this early in the morning.

"Em!" Adette quickly rises out of the chair at the sight of her older brother. Her eyes dart between him and me. "We have a mystery to solve."

"This mystery better not be what we talked about that one night." Emeric's reply is curt.

"No!" Adette balks. "I'm talking about figuring out who Fia is and where she belongs."

Even if I do have my memory, Adette hits on the truth. I need to figure out where I belong, because I don't know. I can't go home, and I can't stay here.

"I would love to quiz Fia on things she doesn't remember." Emeric angles his chin my way and slightly lifts his eyebrows, to which I only frown. "But I'm needed to prepare for the arrival of the noble party traveling from Verdelle."

"Oh." Adette's voice has a tone I recognize. It's a good-natured sibling teasing tone. "Lady Oria is coming, and you have to dine and dazzle her."

"I don't have to dine and dazzle anyone." Emeric's voice has a slight gruffness to it, and my belly twitches, but not in hunger at the breakfast platter lying untouched next to me. "I'm not looking to make the kind of alliance parents hope for. It's strictly kingdom to kingdom business."

"Don't blame me." Adette lifts her hands. "I know perfectly well how you feel. I would never force you to marry."

"Are you being forced to marry?" I can't help but pipe up with the question. After avoiding eye contact, my eyes meet Emeric's. This topic is a little too close for comfort, and I can sympathize with him.

"Not forced." Emeric sighs. "But highly encouraged."

"It's more of a suggestion," Adette clarifies. "Mother doesn't want him to rule alone."

"I won't be alone," Emeric snaps. "I'll have you."

I hold my breath. Emeric looks at me as he says it, but he's talking to Adette.

Chapter Thirty

EMERIC

I find myself alone with the mystery girl.

Fia.

We're not sure if it's her real name, but it feels right.

"You don't need to stay." Fia pointedly looks at me. She makes eye contact but also avoids it. "You can follow your sister to your breakfast."

"Did Max leave?" I need something to ask, if only to stay for a minute more.

"He was gone when I woke," Fia replies.

"I can bring him back this evening if you enjoy his company." I long for her to enjoy my company.

"It's nice to have company," Fia says, and while I know she's indicating Max, I have some hope she may be talking about me too.

"Excuse me." A young woman with dark brown hair wound into a bun at the base of her neck and tendrils of hair hanging in curls next to her cheeks peeks her head in the room. "Oh, Prince Emeric."

The young woman immediately smiles and dips into a curtsey.

"Please, come in." I gesture for the apprentice healer to enter. I recognize her and from the blush crossing her cheeks, it's obvious she's one of the girls to cross my path. My gut clenches in regret, because I don't remember her name.

"I need to change the patient's bindings." The apprentice focuses on me rather than Fia, and I sense Fia's annoyance. But Fia is annoyed with me, rather than the apprentice.

"I can leave." I step toward the door.

"Please, Your Highness." There's a sweet pleading tone to the apprentice's voice. "This task is easier with someone and I'm alone this morning. Will you stay and assist me?"

Fia lifts her eyebrows at me, as if challenging my response. She seems to think I'll stay with the flirty apprentice, which makes me want to leave. But I also have a desire to stay with Fia. The choice isn't easy, but staying with Fia and annoying hers wins out.

"I can help," I reply with a slight smile. But my smile is directed at Fia and not the apprentice.

"I'm sure you have better things to do." Fia gives the response I expect.

"I assure you I'm well trained in dealing with injuries." I hold my hands loosely behind my back, knowing it accentuates some of my best features.

Fia rolls her eyes in response, making sure I see, which in turn causes me to smirk.

"Prince Emeric is quite skilled at many things." The apprentice bats her eyelashes at me. I completely understand where she's going, but I no longer want to go there with her, or any other castle worker.

"Oh, I'm sure he is." Fia scoffs. She's not shy about showing her distaste for me.

The apprentice is not shy about showing her affection for me.

"I need you to hold the brace here." The apprentice boldly takes my hand and places it on a wood piece against Fia's lower leg. She keeps her hand on mine longer than necessary, and all the while, Fia watches with a scowl and narrowed eyes.

I don't notice the way the apprentice glides her hand over mine or lets her fingertips linger on the back of my hand. I notice the coolness of Fia's skin under my palm. The tension in her body with my closeness to her. The way her breath hitches when I gently move my hand on the brace and my finger brushes the skin of her shin.

"Don't look," she hisses at me.

"It's a leg," I say, though I lift my eyes to hers and then pointedly look above her head. "It's not as if I haven't seen the bottom of a leg before."

"Not my leg." Fia's words are terse.

"You were unconscious in my arms for quite some time." I smirk but keep my eyesight above Fia's forehead. Some pieces of hair stick straight up from her night of sleep, and I have an urge to reach out and smooth them down.

"Oh." Fia gasps, as if realizing the implication of what it means.

"I assure you..." I smile at the memory of taking care of Fia. Now that she's awake, I sense she's the type who wants to take care of herself and being left vulnerable to a stranger is hard for her. Not many people would want to care for an injured and unconscious person, as it's not easy, but it was my honor to care for Fia. It made me feel useful and of some value. "Nothing unseemly happened, and you were well cared for."

"Ugh." Fia groans and I glance at her. She closes her eyes tight and then immediately opens them again. "You're still here."

I smile at her. "At your service."

"Your hands are very skilled, Prince Emeric." I forgot about the apprentice, even though she's doing the majority of the work to change and rebind Fia's bandages. "I need your hands here."

Again, the apprentice moves my hands in a way which means she's more than a little familiar with me. My body burns with regret and embarrassment, but I suck in a breath and maintain my usual confident composure, even if it's fake.

"When we're done here," the apprentice continues, her voice more sensual than it needs to be, "I'd appreciate your help with another matter."

There's no mistaking the apprentice's look and words. Even Fia understands. Fia rolls her eyes and gives me a look which says – you've got to be kidding me.

"I apologize," I say, though the apprentice most likely doesn't understand I'm apologizing for my past behavior. "I'm thoroughly occupied for the rest of the day. You'll need to find someone else to assist you."

"Of course, Your Highness." The apprentice brusquely dips her chin and hurriedly finishes Fia's bindings.

Fia winces as the apprentice ties the last bandage tight. I have a desire to reach out and grasp Fia's hand, which I know will only illicit a telling reaction from her. She'd pull her hand away.

"Aren't you occupied for the rest of the day?" Fia lifts her eyebrows at me after the apprentice hastily exits the room.

"I am." I settle into the chair near Fia's bed and lift one ankle up to my other knee to cross it over my leg.

"Then no need to make yourself comfortable." Fia continues to look at me with narrow eyes, pressed lips, and the cutest wrinkled nose.

"Perhaps you're what I'm occupied with." I throw Fia my most charming smile, which I know she'll reject. I don't typically like rejection as it amplifies my feelings of failure, but I look forward to Fia's rejection. It's a breath of fresh air.

"Please." Fia again scoffs and shakes her head. "It was as if I was invisible while she was in the room."

"I can assure you." I throw Fia a flirty smile, if only because it riles her up. "I saw you the entire time."

"Ugh." Fia exaggerates a shudder and crosses her arms over her chest. "You had better not be talking about when I was unconscious."

"Of course not." And it's the truth. "You can relax knowing I was a gentleman the entire time."

"Meaning you're not normally a gentleman?" The condescending look doesn't leave Fia's face.

I'm torn between trying to get her to change her face or leave it, because she's quite adorable.

"I'm a gentleman with you," I reply. "I want you to trust me."

The scowl leaves Fia's face, but neither does she smile.

"I like her," Adette tells me as we leave the banquet hall after a late supper with our parents. There were many details to go over for the arrival of the party from Verdelle. We were not told an arrival date, but it's best to be prepared.

"We know nothing about her," I say.

"There's just something about her," Adette says, which echoes how I feel about Fia.

I can't quite put my finger on why I like Fia, as she's different from any other woman I've known.

But maybe that's why I like her – because she's different.

Fia doesn't give into any charm, no matter how hard I press it. And now I only press it because I like how she reacts differently from other women I charm.

Fia makes me want to be different. I no longer want to charm others.

"I think she's a princess." Adette has declared this a few times without any evidence.

"Mother doesn't seem to think so," I say.

It's unlikely a foreign princess would show up in Swendale with amnesia and no one would be looking for her. Granted it's only been a few days, but there has been no news of a missing princess, or even of a missing young woman.

"What if I can prove it?" Adette does a little skip in the hall, as if she has a grand plan and it excites her.

"That's unlikely until we know who Fia really is." I sigh. What will happen when Fia regains her memory? What happens if someone comes for her?

While I want her to regain her memory, part of me doesn't want Fia to leave.

"Are you headed to bed?" Adette asks as we pause at the stairs leading to the private quarters.

"I-" I had planned to visit Fia one more time, but I'm not too keen on Adette knowing my plans. "Are you?"

"I'll pay Fia one more visit before I head to bed," Adette replies, a curious look on her face. Adette knows more than she's telling me. She often does, and I'm afraid to ask what she knows.

"What're you going to do?" I probe Adette with a curious big brother look.

"I'm only going to make sure Fia is set to sleep." Adette flicks her wrist in a quick wave before scampering down the hall toward the infirmary and away from the stairs to our quarters.

I silently pad my way up the stairs, hoping to not meet anyone lurking in the dark corners.

But I do meet someone.

"Max." I sigh in relief.

The cat rubs up against my leg and meows.

"I'd thought you'd be with Fia."

I gently pick up the cat, still not quite sure why he lets me hold him, but he does. Max nuzzles his face against mine. I haven't slept well the past couple of nights since Max has been sleeping in the infirmary. Night terrors once again plague me. The beast which emerged from the Great Lake on my quest now emerges in my dreams and rages against me. It quickens my pulse, freezes my insides, and instills a fear I can't rid myself of.

"I need you to sleep," I tell the furry feline.

His only response is to meow and again nuzzle the scruff on my chin with his own.

"But she might need you more."

With the cat in my arms, I wait in my room for Adette to return to hers. When I hear Adette's door close, I find my way to the infirmary with Max.

All is quiet and dark when I slowly open the door to Fia's room. The lamp near her bed has been doused and the only light which shines into the room is from the sconces in the hallway.

Fia appears to be sleeping, but I'm a master at faking sleep, and I know it when I see it. But I'll play along.

I set Max on the bed, and he immediately kneads the mattress near Fia's side before settling into the curve of her body.

"Sweet dreams," I say from the door, with one more look at the girl I wish would invade my dreams.

CHAPTER THIRTY-ONE

FIA

"How did you sleep?" The same bright and chipper face as the previous morning greets me again. I heard Adette come in earlier, but I pretended to be asleep.

"Oh." I blink my eyes and start to push myself to a sitting position, just like the previous morning. "Adette. Good morning. What're you doing here?"

"Bringing you your breakfast, of course." Adette grins from the chair next to the bed.

Like yesterday, a tray of food lies on the table next to the bed.

"Don't you have visitors to prepare for?" I recall the conversation about nobles traveling from Verdelle and Emeric needing to entertain a royal lady.

"We don't know when they're arriving, and Emeric is taking care of it. I'm more concerned about you. Did you sleep well?" Adette eagerly looks over me. She is quite inquisitive, and I'm afraid she'll see through my lies and deceit. I don't want to hurt her.

"Quite well, thank you," I reply through a smile faker than a dragon pretending to be a cat.

I didn't sleep at all, not even a wink during the entire night. I usually don't sleep well, but last night was the most miserable night of sleep ever. I had better sleep bouncing on the floor of the kidnappers' rickety wooden wagon.

"Really?" Adette's lips pucker and lines form between her brows. "You weren't uncomfortable?"

"Not at all," I reply. Everything up to this point has been a lie, and I might as well continue my slide down the slippery slope. "It was the most comfortable night's sleep I can remember."

"I thought you can't remember anything?" Adette continues to furrow her brows.

"That's correct," I say with a sly smile. "I remember sleep, and what it means to sleep well. And if I can't remember many nights, then last night must have been one of my most comfortable."

Adette returns my smile and then again purses her lips. "Did you have any trouble falling asleep or did you wake up during the night?"

"Not at all." I was awake when Emeric brought Max in. I was awake through the wee hours of the night. I was awake when Max jumped off the bed in the early hours of the morning. I was awake when Adette thought she was sneaking in.

"Hmm." Adette's chin drops, and she frowns. "I was positive you were a princess."

"What would make you think I'm a princess?" I keep my expression in check and try not to react.

How could Adette possibly know I'm a princess? Is there something which gives me away? Is it written on my forehead?

"It was a hunch." Adette lets out a sad sigh and her shoulders sag. "I thought you wouldn't sleep well because you're a princess. But I guess I was wrong."

She's not wrong, but I'm confused.

"What does not sleeping well have to do with being a princess?" I straighten up in bed, relieved I lied about my lack of sleep.

Adette leans toward me. "You can't tell anyone."

She has a secret.

"I won't," I say. "I promise."

Even though everything about me is a lie, my promise is the truth.

"My mother is in possession of a magic pea," Adette tells me in a lowered voice. "When you place it under the mattress of a person, it reveals if they're royal or not."

"A pea does that?" It sounds absurd, but anything with magic is quite unbelievable. "How does it work?"

"It's magic. The pea causes royals to not sleep, and it causes nonroyals to sleep," Adette replies.

"Ohh." My exhale is a long sound as I realize something. My lie about sleeping proved my lie. If I had said I didn't sleep well, Adette would know I'm royal. I can't have the Swen's knowing I'm royal and jeopardizing their safety and mine. "I slept meaning I'm not royal."

"I guess you're not." Adette shrugs. "My intuition is usually correct, but not this time."

"Do you use the pea often?"

"I've only seen it used once before, not long ago after my mother shared the secret with me." Adette's hands twist as if painting on an invisible canvas. "It's a secret passed within the Swen females."

"Oh." I'm being let in on a big secret, and I'm not sure whether to be honored or worried. "How did it work last time?"

"She was royal," Adette says. "She stayed in the room next to mine and I put the pea under her mattress. I could tell she didn't sleep, even though she tried to tell me she rested well."

"Who was the girl?" There's an unusual twinge in my body, and I don't want to admit it's a bit of jealousy. Royal women seem to parade through Swendale.

"She's the princess of Montagnia." Adette claps her hands together. "Everyone thought she was dead, and she reappeared here."

"That's quite the story." I slide forward, eager for more. I have vague recollections of hearing of a princess near my age who died young. "You used the pea to determine who she was?"

"We already suspected she was the princess because she visited here when she was young, and she had a ring matching one we have here, but we needed to be sure, and my mother and I used the pea."

I'm eager to ask many questions, but I need to start with one.

"Why did she show up here and not in Montagnia?"

Adette bites her lips and it's a moment before she answers. "Because she was betrothed to Emeric and needed to marry him to take the throne of Montagnia from her evil stepmother."

I have even more questions, but only one pops out of my mouth.

"Emeric is betrothed?" I grab the chain around my neck. My true love is betrothed to another princess – this might be for the best.

"Eira and Emeric were nearly married," Adette continues, "but Emeric couldn't marry Eira when she was in love with Leo."

"She loves your other brother?"

I'm riveted by this story. It sounds like it's out of a book.

"Leo met her on his travels, not knowing she was betrothed to Emeric, and they fell in love. They're off traveling right now."

"Wow." I settle back against the pillows. Emeric isn't betrothed, and he gave her up for his younger brother. Is his heart broken?

"Was Princess Eira able to take her throne?" I'm in awe of kingdoms who let women rule.

"Someday she will," Adette replies. "For now, her father has returned, and he rules. Now are you positive you slept last night?" Adette stares hard at my face, and I feel as if the dark circles under my eyes are declaring my lie.

"Positive," I reply. "It was a far better sleep than I deserve."

I don't deserve how kind the Swen's are to me. They don't need the danger I would place them in if my royal lineage were discovered. Emeric might like the danger, and therefore, I don't need to place him in it and help stoke his ego.

"Sleep didn't bring back any of your memory?" Adette continues to look at me.

"We know I'm not royal," I reply with a nonchalant shrug of my shoulders as I reach for the cup of tea. "But I don't remember anything else yet."

I swear Adette can tell I'm lying, but I won't admit to having my memory yet. I need a change of subject.

"Where did you get a magic pea?" I ask. "Magic isn't used without someone paying a price."

Adette's lips pinch together. "I've already told you far more than I should. Please keep the pea a secret. Not even Emeric or Leo knows of its existence."

"I give you my word I won't tell anyone about the pea," I say. "I'll treat the secret as if I'm your sister."

"Do you have a sister?" Adette asks.

I'm not sure if she's trying to jog my memory or trap me in a lie, but she's quite clever.

"I don't know," I say, which is the answer I'm going to give to most questions. "And this magic pea. It's under my mattress right now?"

Adette nods. "Do you mind if I reach under and get it?"

"Not at all." I set the tea on the table and slide to the side of the bed while Adette reaches a hand under to retrieve the pea.

She places it in the palm of her hand and holds it out. "Do you want to look at it?"

I take the pea between two fingers. It's an ordinary dried and wrinkled pea. The green color is muted. There's nothing to mark it as having some sort of royal determining power. I wouldn't believe it was magical except for the fact I didn't sleep a wink last night and Adette claims when this pea is under a mattress it keeps a royal from sleeping. Or it's a rare coincidence I had the worst night of sleep in my life while lying on top of a tiny dry pea.

"What is that?" a voice asks.

Adette and I look up to find Emeric in the door and he points at my hand.

"A pea," I answer. "A green pea."

"Why are you holding a pea?" Emeric lifts his eyebrows.

"It's-" Adette starts.

"It's part of my breakfast," I interrupt and slam my palm toward my mouth.

I mean for the pea to stay clasped in my hand. I don't mean for it to enter my mouth, but it does.

And I swallow.

CHAPTER THIRTY-TWO

EMERIC

Fia swallows hard. "Yum."

Her full lips pinch together while Adette's mouth falls open.

"You didn't really eat it, did you?" Adette gawks at Fia as if she's a fairy granting curses.

Fia sucks her lips in and slowly nods. "I'm sorry," she squeaks. "I didn't mean to."

"It's just a pea." My eyes bounce between my sister and Fia. They're acting strange. "I hope you eat more than one pea for your breakfast." An untouched tray of food lies on the table next to the bed.

"It wasn't just a pea!" Adette's voice rises.

"I'm so sorry," Fia says. "Maybe I can find you another one?"

"It was one of a kind," Adette says with a sad shake of her head.

"Again," I say, fearing one of these girls may near hysteria. "It's a pea. I'm sure you can find more in the garden."

"Are you okay?" Adette grabs Fia's hand in a friendly gesture. "Upset stomach, burning throat, feeling funny, anything?"

"I'm fine, truly," Fia replies with an imploring look at Adette.

"It was a pea." I may as well stare into space for how they ignore me.

Adette acts like Fia swallowed a jewel or some magical charm, and Fia – she looks a little pale.

"Whoa." Fia starts to sway and brings the hand Adette isn't holding to her head.

"Oh, my goodness!" Adette smacks my upper arm hard with the back of her other hand. "She's going to faint. Emeric, help her."

Fia's face pales even more and it does look as if she's going to pass out.

"What am I supposed to do? She's already in bed." I quickly step near the bed and grasp Fia's shoulders to help her recline on the pillow.

Fia puts her free hand over mine. Suddenly I feel light-headed as if I'm hypersensitive to her touch, in a good way.

"No, no." Fia suddenly shakes off Adette's hand and slaps at me. "Don't touch me! Just let me be for a moment."

Both Adette and I step away from Fia, startled at her outburst. I know she's not fond of me, but this is quite a change in demeanor. Fia arches and leans her head over her legs. She takes slow breaths.

"Are you okay?" Adette asks.

"Can I get you anything?" I ask at the same time.

"I'm sorry." Fia slowly straightens and exhales. "Maybe the pea did something to me."

"It was a pea," I say again.

"A very old and special pea," Adette counters.

"An old pea could make her sick." I nudge Adette. "Why did you bring her an old pea?"

"I didn't mean for her to eat it." Adette scowls at me.

I'm off to a great start this morning. I already have two young women who don't care to see me.

"I'm so sorry." Fia starts her habit of twisting a strand of hair around her finger. "I think – wait." She holds out her left hand in front of her and twists it at the wrist.

"What is it?" Adette asks, concern covering her face.

Fia's hand has a slight shake. "Can I touch your hand?"

"Of course." Adette holds out her hand.

I watch, slightly confused as Fia presses some fingers on the back of Adette's hand and then pulls her hand back.

"I'm feeling a little odd," Fia says.

"You're acting a little odd," I say and earn a look of disgust from both Fia and Adette. I'm on a roll with them this morning.

"Emeric, would you mind finding Liora for me?" Fia asks and then stares hard at my sister. "Adette, would you help me with something requiring a more feminine touch?"

Adette grins. "I'd be delighted to."

"I don't know what's going on between you two, but I have things to do," I say, and straighten the waistcoat I wear. "I'll get Liora."

"I won't stand in your way," Fia says. "You're free to leave."

"You can't stand." I point at Fia's leg.

Fia's facial muscles tighten in a pout, while mine tighten to try to hide a smile.

Fia points at the door. "Go get Liora!"

"Of course, Your Highness." I perform a mock bow. "Do you require anything else?" I now look at my sister.

"Just go." Adette smirks at me as I leave.

CHAPTER THIRTY-THREE

FIA

"I'm so sorry I swallowed the pea." I profusely apologize to Adette once Emeric leaves and closes the door behind him. She's only ever been nice to me, and I swallow her magical royal determining pea.

The Great Divide didn't get rid of all magic in the Greater World, and I'm now helping. Except magic has a price, and I think I've discovered the price of swallowing the pea. Or I'm about to.

"What happened?" Adette returns to the chair next to me. "The pea did something to you, didn't it?"

I hold my left hand out. It looks ordinary, unchanged and unremarkable, but something is different.

"When you and then Emeric touched me-" My body shudders involuntarily at the memory of my hands on them. The sensation with Emeric was particularly strong. "I felt something."

"Are you telling me you can tell if someone is royal by touch?" Adette's face flushes and she shimmies in the chair.

"Yes. No." My head bobbles and I twirl a finger in my hair. "I don't know."

"We need to test it," Adette immediately says, which is what I was thinking. "Do you want to try touching me?"

Adette bounds out of the chair and drops to sit on the edge of the bed. She holds her hand out to me with her palm up.

I place my fingers into her warm palm and an odd sensation occurs. A vibration travels up from my fingertips to the palms of my hand and remains there.

"Yep," I say and pull my hand away. The vibration ceases. "I feel something when I touch you."

"Try touching my arm," Adette says. "And then my neck or shoulder, just to make sure."

I hesitantly reach out and place my fingertips on Adette's forearm. The same sensation occurs.

"This is so strange." I pull my hand away and the vibration immediately stops. I shake my hand.

"I've seen stranger things," Adette says. "You wouldn't believe half the stuff I could tell if I was allowed to."

"You mean there's more than the pea?"

Adette only nods. "Now try my neck."

Adette wouldn't believe half the things I could tell her if I didn't have a case of losing my memory. Adette's hair is braided in a crown around her head, and her neck is exposed. I touch the skin on one side.

"Same thing," I say.

"You felt it with Emeric, too?" Adette settles back in the chair.

"Yes," I reply, not wanting to explain exactly what I feel with Emeric. I don't even want to think about it. "Now you should touch me to see if it works in reverse."

Adette leans forward and places a hand on my arm. "Anything?"

"No." I breathe a sigh of relief. This new magical power could be quite irritating if every touch caused a sensation. Emeric's touch causes an intense feeling, but that bit of information will remain as locked up as everything else about me.

"Let me try your hand." Adette places her fingers on mine and again I feel the strange sensation.

"It comes from my hands." I pull my hand away from Adette. "Whether you touch my hand or I touch my hand to you, that's when I feel it."

"I wonder how long it will last." Adette stares at my hands.

"I'm not sure," I reply. "I need to touch someone who's not royal to see if this works the way we think it does. Maybe I just have a magical tingling touch."

"I'm certain you have a royal touch." Adette nods with a smile on her face. "If Emeric did as you asked, Liora should be here soon, and you can test it on her. But you can't tell her about this."

"I'll keep it a secret," I say. "I promise."

I keep my promises, even if my life is full of lies.

"Good morning, Fia." Liora walks in a few minutes later. "How are you feeling today?"

I look at Adette who gives me a slight nod. "Wonderful," I reply, piling on the lies thick. "But I'm getting quite tired of lying in bed."

"Let me check your leg and bindings and I think fairly soon we'll have you up and putting some light weight on it."

Liora proceeds to examine my leg, and I feel nothing with her touch. It's ironic. I'm not a fan of hugs and touch, and now I'm imbued with some sort of magic touch.

Adette gives me a slight nod of her head to encourage me in my next task.

"Thank you." I reach out my hand and place it over Liora's before she finishes her tasks. "I appreciate all you've done for me."

"It's my pleasure, Miss." Liora dips her head to me and curtseys to Princess Adette before leaving.

The door is barely closed before Adette bursts out with her expected question. "Did you feel anything?"

"Nothing," I reply.

"We need to test on one more person." Adette squirms in the chair. She reminds me of a famished kitten eating.

Adette cajoles a castle worker to clear the tray of food after I quickly eat a biscuit and gulp tea. When the girl reaches for the tray on the table, I manage to brush my hand across her hand.

Adette widens her eyes, and I gently shake my head as the girl heads to the door.

"Thank you, Sara. You've been helpful." Adette pushes the castle worker out of the room as quickly as she pulled her in.

"Nothing," I clarify. "I didn't feel a thing."

"I thought you eating the pea was a tragedy, but this is a fortunate turn of events!" Adette flutters around the room with so much motion I nearly get dizzy. Or it's because of the added predicament I now have. I keep creating catastrophes for myself.

"I'm not sure I would call this fortunate." I lift my hands up and turn them over. They don't look any different than normal, but the pea did something to me.

"It's completely fascinating." Adette claps her hands together. "This is even better than the pea, and so much easier."

"Easier?" I question. "I have to touch people, and we don't know how long this lasts."

"Now you have a reason to stay indefinitely," Adette says.

"Indefinitely?" I swallow hard. I need to get to Fynn and away from Emeric as soon as possible.

"Your leg is still healing, and your memory hasn't returned," Adette says, "so you really ought to stay. You can even stay in my room. Now you can assist Mother and me in determining if visitors are indeed royal."

"Why would you want to know?"

Adette's skirt fluffs out as she again drops into the chair. It won't be long before she jumps out again. "I want to know if they're lying. Mother wants to check certain women as prospects for Emeric. Like Lady Oria, she'll be visiting soon."

"For Emeric?" I swallow hard again. I'm supposed to determine if someone is royal so they can court Emeric?

How in all the soggy hay do I get myself into these situations? "I need to touch girls for Emeric?"

"Shh." Adette waves her hands at me, though I'm sure there's no way Emeric can overhear us. He's nowhere near here. "Emeric doesn't want to get married, but Mother thinks if he finds the right woman, he will. She'd prefer someone royal, though in my opinion it doesn't matter much. Honestly, I think he'd be better off with a commoner, or someone like you."

"No." An immediate rush of heat starts to flood my cheeks. "Not someone like me."

"I think I'd like to marry a fairy." Adette gets a dreamy look on her face. She's obviously a dreamer, because that will never happen, and while I don't mind bursting people's bubbles, I won't do it to Adette.

"That's not something you hear every day," I say. "Have you ever seen a fairy?"

"One always shows up for a Swen's eighteenth birthday," Adette replies.

"Is that how you're in possession of a magical royal determining pea?" I ask.

"Oh!" Adette jumps to her feet. "I need to tell Mother about the change of events. Only the three of us know about this. Can you keep the secret?"

"Of course." I don't want to go around announcing I have a magical pea power.

Stupid Emeric.

I ate the pea because of him. What is it about him?

CHAPTER THIRTY-FOUR

EMERIC

What is it about her?

Something about Fia causes me to turn and head in the direction of the infirmary again. I should head to breakfast, but Fia and Adette were acting odd.

The door is closed when I return, and I hear muffled voices. I pick out Adette's voice, excited about something, and Fia's voice. What is it about her voice that hypnotizes me? It's sweet with more than a touch of irritation, which makes it magical.

I knock on the door and before I can say anything, it flies open and Adette is in my face. She pulls me into the tiny room.

"Emeric! Perfect!" Adette bounces on her toes, nearly as excited as the two times she's seen a real fairy. "You can help."

"What do you need help with now?" I cross my arms over my chest and look at Fia. She's not nearly as excited as Adette, she still looks pale and petrified.

"We're moving Fia to my room!" Adette exclaims.

I know my sister can easily get excited about things, especially anything to do with fairies, but why is she excited about Fia staying in her room? Fia's only been here a few days and we know nothing about her.

"Adette, I need to speak to you outside." I exit the room, knowing Adette will follow. She should follow.

But she doesn't.

"Adette!" I holler my sister's name.

She takes her sweet time coming out to meet me. "Emeric." She presses her lips together in a thin smile.

"Do you really think it's a wise idea to move Fia to your room? She's perfectly fine here where Liora can check on her."

While having Fia down the hall from me is appealing, it's also not a wise idea considering we know next to nothing about Fia.

"She'll be more comfortable upstairs," Adette says.

"But in your room?" I run my finger over the stubble on my chin, sure Mother will remark on it when she sees me, unless she has something to say about moving Fia first.

"It's not exactly my room," Adette says with a small shrug. "It's the room connected to mine."

"The one Eira used when she was here?" The small room is an old servant's room, used when our ancestors wanted attendants nearby.

"Yes." Adette nods. "Until we know who Fia is or where she's from, she's going to be here while she heals."

"Exactly." I stare hard at my sister. "We don't know where Fia's from or who she is. She could be a spy from another kingdom. What if she's here to free Morella?"

"Really, Em?" Adette crosses her arms over her chest. "You're the one who found her and brought her back here. You really think she's a spy?"

"What about a princess in hiding?" I could come up with some more things. Fia seems crafty enough to be anything.

"I can guarantee she's not a princess," Adette replies.

"Then why are you having her stay in the room connected to yours when you've only known her a couple days?" I ask.

"I only knew Eira for a couple hours when I invited her to stay in my room. And Leo brought her here." Adette presses a finger to my chest to make her point. "It's nearly the same with Fia. You brought her here, and I'm inviting her to stay in my room."

"Eira was my betrothed when you invited her. Fia is not." I gently brush Adette's hand away.

"Fia is still quite useful, even if she's not here to marry you."

"How is she useful?" I now cross my arms over my chest and mimic Adette. "She doesn't remember anything. What value does she bring?"

"She's priceless," Adette replies. "Someday you'll see, but until then, just know, Mother and I have a use for her."

"Mother agrees with Fia staying with you?" I rake my hand through my hair.

"She will," Adette says.

I would like to prove Adette wrong, but with my luck, this is not going to work in my favor.

"If this goes bad, you can't blame me," I tell Adette. No one can accuse me of wanting Fia down the hall, though it's what I secretly want.

"It's not going to go bad." Adette gives me a reassuring smile. "This will work out better than you ever imagined."

"I don't even know what to imagine," I say as I hold open the door to Fia's room for her.

But when I lay eyes on Fia, I do know what to imagine.

"Are you ready?" I ask Fia.

"Ready for what?" Fia pulls a teacup away from her lips.

Her lips are moist with tea, and I can't keep from looking at them. I don't know what makes Fia so mesmerizing to me, but there's something about her or in her, and I can't keep from feeling as if I'm drawn to her.

"Ready for me to sweep you off your feet?" I give her a charming smile, and even if Fia can't see it, there's more sweetness to it than the one I used to give other women.

"Too late." Fia lifts her good leg up and down. "I'm already off my feet."

"If you're looking for volunteers," a voice says, "I'll let you sweep me off my feet."

Simultaneously, I witness Adette and Fia roll their eyes before I turn to another young woman standing in the doorway of Fia's room. It's starting to get a little crowded here, and unfortunately, it's not the same apprentice who was flirting with me yesterday.

"How can I be your damsel in distress?" The castle worker runs a finger down my arm from shoulder to elbow, and I'm quite taken aback at how bold she is in front of my sister and Fia. Mostly because I don't want Fia to get the wrong idea about me. But from her snips and attitude toward me, she already has the wrong idea.

But to be fair, the boldness of this castle worker isn't very different from how I used to be, and whatever Fia is thinking, it probably has a ring of truth to it.

I step away from yet another girl whose name I can't remember and bump into the end of the bed. "I'm not-"

"Emeric isn't looking for a damsel." Adette gives me a quick glare, when I feel it should be directed at the castle worker, but I'm thankful for her interruption. The poor castle worker scurries away immediately.

"Now where were we?" I quickly recover and focus on Fia.

CHAPTER THIRTY-FIVE

FIA

Emeric is carrying me. Full on – in his arms – carrying me.

With my new royal touch and this true love thing, which I'm trying to forget, I keep my bare hands away from his skin. My hands are linked together behind his neck. Emeric has one arm around my back and under my arms, and his other arm is under my knees, which isn't the most pleasant with a broken leg. Except, I feel all sorts of things besides the pain of my broken leg. Pleasant things.

I need a kitten to hold, not this man holding me.

"Don't drop me." Hopefully Emeric doesn't mistake the hesitation in my voice as meaning more than it does.

"Fear not, my lady. I will carry you as if you are the most precious thing in all the Greater World."

"Does this flattery work on other girls?" I ask and behind us Adette snorts.

"Unfortunately, it does." Adette snorts again. "It's embarrassing, but girls fall for lines like that as if it was their last drop of water."

"I'm not thirsty and you don't have to worry about me falling for any lines."

"You just fall from horses?" Emeric grins at me.

I might be in danger of falling off more than a horse, but I'll keep myself from going over the edge. Just because my true love is carrying me doesn't mean there needs to be anything more between us. True love does not always mean romantic love.

Except I need to convince my mind and body of that. They're traitors.

"I don't think I tend to fall often," I say. "I don't remember any other falls from a horse."

"You don't remember much." Emeric starts to carry me up a set of stairs. "How do you know you haven't fallen off a horse before?"

"I..." I'm completely distracted by Emeric carrying me up the stairs. Our faces are close together and Emeric doesn't seem to be winded from carrying me, but I can feel the warmth of his breath on my cheek. His strong chest muscles press against my side and his biceps are taut under my body.

What were we talking about? I shift my back a bit and try to move my hands away from touching the skin of Emeric's neck.

"Are you doing alright?" Emeric tilts his chin toward me as he continues to climb the stairs with ease. "Do I need to set you down to rest for a moment?"

"Only if this task is too difficult for you," I comment.

This nearness to Emeric is a difficult task for me. No one ever tells you how hard it is to resist your true love. But I must. For I didn't ask for one.

"I could do this all day." Emeric takes another stair and smirks.

"Emeric trains hard." Adette's voice comes from behind her brother. "He pushes others to train just as hard, but sometimes he pushes them too hard."

"For a good reason," Emeric replies to his sister, though I hear the note of bitterness. "Maybe he didn't fail because I pushed him too hard."

It's not hard to miss the bitterness in Emeric's statement, though I don't know what it means.

"Em. The past is in the past." Adette's voice has as much sweetness as Emeric's bitterness. They cancel each other out.

"If only more people would realize that," Emeric says under his breath. I hear him, but I'm not sure if his sister does.

"These are the private royal quarters," Adette says as Emeric steps into a hallway.

"This is my room." Emeric nods his head to a door on the right.

"She has no need to know where your room is." Adette pushes past us in the wide hallway.

"You never know." Emeric's hands tighten on my leg. "She might need rescuing again."

"You rescued me when I was unconscious. I doubt I'll find my way to your room when I'm unconscious and need rescuing again," I quip.

Adette laughs and points to a door on the left. "This is my room." She then pushes open a door one down from hers. "And this will be your room. There's also a door inside between our rooms."

"Where should I deposit your new pet?" Emeric asks with a lift of his eyebrows.

"Pet?" I lift my bushy eyebrows.

"I mean it in the most endearing way, like a nickname." Emeric again smirks. "I could call you my pet."

"That will never do," I say. "Unless you want me calling you a smug pretender?"

Emeric grunts. "How about I call you sweet pea? Since you ate Adette's special pea?"

"The bed?" Adette interrupts.

I nearly forgot she was here and look where Adette points. The room is much larger than the infirmary room, but it's small for a royal. It was obviously the room of a servant but is now used for guests of Adette. A bed is pushed against the far wall. A small fireplace is on the wall to my right while a door is on the wall to the left. A chaise lounge resides in front of the fire and a small wardrobe is near the door we enter.

"Oh." I shake my head to clear thoughts of banter with Emeric. "Yes, the bed is fine. Please put me there."

"With pleasure." Emeric winks.

That wink. Why did he have to wink and amplify that dimple in his chin? It's a good thing I don't usually act on intrusive thoughts. I sometimes speak them, but there's no way I'm speaking what is going through my head now as Emeric gingerly sets me on the bed as if...

Ugh. I need to kick out these intrusive inner thoughts.

As soon as Emeric's hands leave me, I exhale and grip the edge of the mattress I sit on.

"I don't know what it is about you," Adette says after Emeric leaves. "But he acts quite strange around you."

She flutters near me, adjusting the blankets on the bed and fluffing a pillow.

"He acts strange?" My heart starts to pitter patter in my chest. I don't want him acting any different around me than he does with other girls. There's no reason he needs to act strange around me – at least, that's what I can tell myself. "Perhaps it's my new magical royal touch?"

Adette laughs again and it makes me smile. "Not strange, but more like his true self. It reminds me of what he used to be like. Not some stuck up prince who thinks all girls should fall all over him. He's smiling again. I haven't seen him smile for real in years."

The smile falls off my face.

"I fall in mud, and not all over young men. You don't need to worry about me."

"But Emeric is the young man who pulled you from the mud." Adette continues to laugh and it's the sweetest sound I've heard in a while.

"I didn't ask him to." Emeric's smiles cannot be because of me.

"I'm glad he did," Adette says. "I think he found you for a reason."

Fate is again laughing hard in my face.

A chorus of nerves runs through me. I'm in the castle of my true love, and I want to run, but I don't want to. I'd feel safer if someone locked me in a dungeon and threw away the key.

CHAPTER THIRTY-SIX

EMERIC

I find myself heading to the dungeon with Father after breakfast.

"Is it necessary to do these checks this often?" I don't relish the visits to Morella. She gets under my skin like a worming parasite which can't be killed nor eradicated. It's as if the magic she used on me at my wedding lingers under my skin. It's there, waiting to turn into a poison which can kill.

It's ironic I find it necessary to check on Fia every single day, even though Adette assures me the mysterious girl isn't a spy. I prefer my checks on Fia over checking Morella.

"With an evil witch like Morella in our dungeon, it is, especially with noble guests on the way," Father replies. "She tried to take over Swendale and kill all of you. Checking to make sure she's still locked up is the least I can do."

The ever-present sound of iron boots tapping on stone travels down the dungeon hall. I strain to listen, unsure if the beat of the taps is different than normal. Is there more time between each beat?

"Ahh." Morella's haunting voice travels toward us. "My subjects are paying me another visit."

Father and I glance at each other with resigned looks. Father shakes his head with his lips pinched together. Morella's statement doesn't surprise us. She can't see us, but other than guards, we're the only ones to visit her.

"What will you do for me today?" Morella asks when we stand outside her cell door. "Have you brought me any news about my stepdaughter's next wedding? Has she returned?"

"Leo and Eira make the plans." Father pushes aside the sliding panel to reveal Morella's cold face. "They may decide to hold the wedding in Montagnia."

"I'll need to return for that." Morella clicks her tongue, as if it's a forgone conclusion, though she must know she's not getting out of this dungeon for a long time. "What about you, Prince Emeric? With your younger brother marrying my stepdaughter, your former betrothed, will you choose a new bride?"

"That is not your concern." I try to keep my voice even, and more on the harsh side. If you give Morella a handle, she'll tug it hard.

"I'd say it is my concern," Morella replies. "I have a concern for anyone who will rule a kingdom, especially one bordering my own. You're heir to the throne of Swendale, an unlikely heir, yet you are. Your bride will be your co-ruler."

"Emeric is quite capable of ruling on his own." Father's voice is harsh toward Morella, but I hear the fatherly pride behind it, and it gives me a rush of confidence.

"I don't foresee my parents stepping down from their thrones for a very long time," I add.

"Is there a special someone, Prince Emeric?" Morella's voice becomes sickly sweet. "Someone who tickles your fancy, makes you think fanciful thoughts, gets you to smile?"

"I..." I pause, for there's no need to answer Morella's question. But there is someone tickling the edges of my thoughts right now. Someone who makes me smile.

"You should have seen Gareth when he first fell in love with me." Morella gives an exaggerated sigh. "He was so unlike himself. Such a fool in love. Always smiling."

"Because you tricked him," I say, and Father gives me a stern look for responding. But it's the truth.

We know Morella used a potion on Eira's father to make King Gareth fall in love with her, after she had killed Eira's mother following Eira's birth. Morella then worked on taking over the kingdom.

"It's hard to know who to trust when you're in a position of authority." Morella clicks her tongue again. Shadows dance off the hard lines of her face and the tapping of the iron boots adds an air of danger to every word. "Everyone is always out to steal something from you."

Immediately I think of Fia. I was speaking in jest about her being a spy, but could she want something from my family? She has already worked her way into a princess's room.

"You were out to steal King Gareth and Eira's throne," I shoot back. Morella is the one who can't be trusted. "And you haven't succeeded."

"I would have if it weren't for your family." Morella's voice takes on a more vicious tone and her eyes narrow. "I was supposed to turn into a dragon, but something prevented me from doing it. Your family has something to do with it."

"Our kingdom is fortunate in being protected from dragons," Father says, not explaining why we're protected from dragons. "Being royal means knowing who to trust and knowing who you're dealing with. You did not learn enough about us."

"I plan to remedy that," Morella says, the tapping of her boots still sounding their eerie tune as my mind circles back to Fia.

We know nothing about Fia and don't know how to learn more about her. Can we trust her?

CHAPTER THIRTY-SEVEN

FIA

I shouldn't trust anyone, but I completely trust this girl standing next to me. She's the one who should be wary of trusting me. I'm a bad omen.

"Ahh." I sigh and look at my gloved hands. It's such sweet relief.

"What is it with girls coming to Swendale from other countries and needing to wear gloves around my family?" Adette tosses another pair of gloves on top of me as I sit in bed.

A bed that has been given to me to use. A bed in a castle. In the royal wing. How did I get here?

"Maybe I'm from Swendale," I say and pick up the next pair. "I can't remember."

"I have a feeling you're not." Adette holds out a hand to take a discarded glove from me, and I tug at a long satin glove.

"Other girls have had to wear gloves?" I ask.

When I think my family has strange customs and curses, it seems others do too.

"Eira, Leo's fiancé, she feels something when she touches members of my family. When she was first with us, it was so strong she needed to wear gloves to not feel it. But she was getting better at touching us without gloves when they left to travel."

"Does she have a magic touch?" I ask.

"Not quite." Adette averts her eyes from me and it's obvious she doesn't want to go into detail.

"Where are they traveling?" I hand Adette the second satin glove and ask a question to change the subject. I pull on a pair of short, lace gloves as we're experimenting with different gloves to see what I feel.

"They traveled to Montagnia with Eira's father and the last we heard they were going to Somniara, but we have no news if they made it."

"Somniara?" I immediately break into a sweat. Somniara is where Fynn traveled. "When will they return?"

"We expect them any day now." Adette pairs gloves together, oblivious to my keen interest.

I adjust the gloves on my hands. Fate may be playing a joke on me but also keeping me here for a reason. Leo and Eira might be a great help in guiding me to Fynn.

"Ready?" Adette holds her hand out to me.

"Let's try the lace gloves." I reach my hand out and wrap it around Adette's.

"Anything?" she asks.

I pinch my eyes closed, to concentrate on the feel of my hand, but what I see is a hazy image of my true love.

Emeric.

The image is dimmer than it used to be, and I hope it's because I no longer have a true love, but it's more likely because I've seen him with my actual eyes. Unlike my brother who went looking for his true love, I never intended to find mine. I hope Fynn found his true love. It would be a cruel world in which the one searching for his true love doesn't find her and the one not looking for her true love finds him.

My brother deserves to find his true love, and while I might be something of a cynic, I choose to believe fate can't be that cruel or bitter.

"I feel a tiny tingle." I press my lips together.

"It must be the spaces in the lace," Adette says. "It allows some skin-to-skin contact."

"It's better than fully touching you without anything," I say.

"Is it an unpleasant feeling?" Adette sets the pair of satin gloves on the table near the bed.

"I wouldn't call it unpleasant," I say. "My broken leg is most unpleasant. The bruises on my body are most unpleasant, but the pea feeling is more of a tingle, but it doesn't cease while I touch someone. It's rather disconcerting to have it go on for a long time."

"Pea tingle." Adette chuckles. "It's your super royal sense."

"I'd rather have the touch of something else." I lean back into the pillows which were placed behind me. They're soft and comfortable, much like my ones at home. From what I saw of the castle as Emeric carried me here, it's a similar design to the one we have in Ryutoa. It was built for defense. While ours was built for defense from dragons, I assume this castle was built for defense from invaders.

"If you could have a magic touch, what would it be?" Adette asks.

"You mean, like if I touch things, they turn to gold?" I ask. I like the way Adette's mind thinks.

"Like that, yes." Adette nods.

"A golden touch would be more annoying than a royal touch," I say. "How would you eat anything?"

"Have someone feed you?" Adette grins.

"I wouldn't mind touching certain people and having them transported somewhere else," I say.

"Do you remember anyone you would want to transport somewhere else?" Adette stands and starts to straighten things around the bed.

"No," I say, though the people who kidnapped me would be at the top of the list. "I have a sense there are people who annoy me."

"I'm pretty sure Emeric wouldn't mind having that power," Adette replies. "He gets a general sense of annoyance with people too."

"Hmm." I pretend to examine my hands. It seems Emeric is brought back to me many times, whether through conversation or seeing him. "Everyone thinks he's charming and yet he's annoyed by everyone?"

"He's a contradiction," Adette replies. "Which makes it funny that he seems to prefer to annoy you rather than charm you."

"I thought he was trying to charm me." I start to twist a tendril of hair with my finger.

"If he is, it's different." Adette grabs a blanket and throws it over me. "But you know not to fall for him."

"Right," I say.

I can't fall for my true love.

"Do you mind if I leave you here on your own for a while?" Adette asks. "I need to have a conversation with my mother about the pea."

"Again," I say. "I'm truly sorry."

Adette sighs. "Perhaps it's the price I'm to pay. My mother told me not to put it under your mattress. She didn't think you were a princess, and I disobeyed her."

"Oh." I try not to act surprised. I'm not sure why Adette would think I'm a princess and her mother wouldn't.

"Don't worry." Adette waves a hand at me. "I think Mother will appreciate the turn of events and will be pleased to keep you on for a bit, especially since some guests are to be arriving soon. Can I get you anything before I leave?"

"Perhaps a book, or something to read?" Asking for a kitten or a puppy might be too much. Max is a nocturnal visitor, and I never see him during the day. I wonder if he'll find me in my new room.

"Any subjects which interest you?" Adette walks toward the door between our rooms.

"I'm not sure." I give my new typical answer. "I'll try anything."

"I'll be right back." Adette disappears into her room and it's not long before she's back with a stack of books in her arms. "There's a little variety here. They're mostly books from my tutor. You might find royal etiquette or the history of Swendale more fascinating than I find it."

"Thank you," I say as Adette places the books on the table near me.

Once she leaves, I pick up the Swendale history book. I might as well learn about the place I'm staying.

CHAPTER THIRTY-EIGHT

EMERIC

Once again, I'm drawn to Fia. Whether it's the talk with Morella which has me questioning Fia's motives or it's my own deep curiosity, I find myself outside Fia's room before lunch.

Fia's room.

It may be connected to Adette's room, but this mystery girl has a room in the royal wing of the castle. A room not far from mine.

I stand in front of the wooden door, waiting for a sign. It's quiet in the room, and I know Fia is alone. She could be napping, reading, or plotting.

But plotting what?

I bang my knuckles on the door and open it a crack without waiting for an answer.

"Fia?" I stick my head through the opening. "May I come in?"

"Oh." Fia looks up from a book in her lap, a startled look on her face. She wasn't expecting me, but it doesn't look like she's plotting my death. "Yes?"

She pulls on a pair of long, satin gloves as I make my way across the room.

"I see you're doing a little light reading." I gesture to the thick book in Fia's lap.

"It's quite fascinating." Fia's gaze tilts toward the words on the page. I recognize the book as the history of Swendale. One that isn't quite as accurate as Fia might think. "I noticed Swendale has a long line of female rulers."

"Umhmm." My lips press into a thin line.

If I had been a more astute learner, I would have questioned the same thing Fia notes. But I never noticed, or perhaps I did, but my question was shoved aside.

"The book doesn't say anything about succession." Fia's eyes widen, and she looks at me with awe building. "How does succession work in Swendale? Is Adette in line for the throne?"

"She is," I reply, realizing the pain my parents must have felt when they were questioned on the same things. They couldn't reveal why females were the only rulers until Leo and I each turned eighteen. "She's in line after me and Leo. Swendale leaves the throne to the eldest living heir."

Living being the operative word. Females are the only ones who have lived far beyond eighteen, until Leo and me.

"Not to be morbid, but if something happened to you and your brother, Adette could be queen?" Fia's eyes sparkle as her gloved fingers turn a page in the book.

I swallow hard. Fia's curiosity is a little unnerving.

"Yes. She could rule on her own as queen," I reply. "Just as my mother is queen now."

"It's fascinating." Fia's face brightens. "I wish more kingdoms would allow female rulers."

"There are plenty," I say. "Montagnia will one day be ruled by my brother's betrothed, as she is heir to the throne."

"I'm sure there are kingdoms where only men rule and women are exempt from the succession." Fia closes the heavy tome on her lap. "What if twins are born, one female and one male, and the female is the oldest? Who do you think should be first in line for the throne?"

"The female," I reply. "That's what would happen here."

I came here to test Fia, and she's the one testing me with her questions, but it seems I pass. Fia's face cracks into a huge smile. Her smile is like finding a hidden key and unlocking a treasure chest. I have a feeling it's a rare thing.

"Your kingdom gives everyone a fair chance," Fia says.

"In a way." I again press my lips into a thin line. "The men in my kingdom are unlucky, as we've always had queens."

"If you want to talk about bad luck," Fia says. "Take a seat. Bad luck is my middle name."

It's hard not to chuckle and I settle into the chair near the bed. It's a good sign she's inviting me to stay.

"You don't know your name." A small grin builds on my face, and for some reason, Fia looks pleased.

"I know." She shrugs and tries to keep a smile concealed with a press of her lips together. "But I'm obviously bad luck."

"Too soon to tell." I grab a book from the table and make a scoffing noise. "Royal etiquette for a princess?"

"You've read that one?"

"I understand the need for etiquette, protocol, politeness, and respect for others' customs, but I don't know." I shrug my shoulders and replace the book on the table. "Sometimes there's more to life, and Adette hasn't been given the chance to live a life outside these walls. I don't think she's gone past the nearest village. She can ride a horse, but she hasn't learned archery or how to wield a sword or dagger."

"Have you learned all those things?" Fia pushes the heavy book on her lap off to the side.

"I have."

I was taught skills to prepare me for my quest. When I failed and returned, I did all I could to train Leo for his quest. As Adette will never have to attempt a quest, there was no point in teaching her.

"Why don't you teach your sister?" Fia asks. "Isn't important she have the same skills as you?"

"I..." I pause. Adette may never have to encounter a dragon, but I suppose it isn't reason enough to prevent her from learning other skills. "You're right. I spent a lot of time training Leo, but I never thought to include Adette."

"My brother," Fia starts and then shakes her head. "I mean, if I have a brother, I think I wouldn't mind learning things alongside him."

"Are your hands cold?" I wiggle a finger at Fia's glove covered hands.

"Oh." She lifts her hands and twists them at the wrists. "Yes. Adette gave me some of her gloves to wear."

"Did you need a fire?" I start to stand to check on the fireplace along the wall, even though the thought of stoking flames incites fear in me. But I would do it for her.

"No, no." Fia rapidly shakes her head as I exhale in relief. "I'm fine, but you still haven't told me the reason for your visit."

"Ah." I stop at the end of the bed. Do I have a reason for this visit? I'm not sure it's wise to tell Fia I'm here only to see her. "I was coming to check to see if you were comfortable in your new room."

"I am, thank you." Fia tugs the gloves, looking rather uncomfortable. Does she want me to leave? "Your sister is too kind to let me stay with her and she's been enormously helpful. I don't think I can ever repay all she's done. All you've-"

Fia clenches her jaw, as if thanking me is more painful than breaking her leg.

"All I've..." I lean forward, anticipating the next words from Fia's mouth.

She has the most perfectly shaped mouth, with full pink lips centered above the gentle dip of her chin. Does she know she sometimes quirks up one side of her upper lip when she's listening? I want to-

"Meow."

A noise interrupts my thoughts. Fia and I look to the black feline on the floor at the end of the bed. Max either has the worst timing or the best timing.

"Come here, boy." I move to pick up the cat while Fia's eyes follow me with a hint of a smile. Her eyes are on the cat, but I prefer to think they're on me.

I place Max on the bed next to Fia, and immediately the cat starts to purr under her gentle touch.

"You haven't fallen under Emeric's charm too, have you?" Fia tickles the cat's chin while a hint of a smirk covers her face.

"Does that mean you have?" I throw a charming smile Fia's way, and she makes a scoffing noise.

"No." Fia's fingers twist around Max's ear in the same way she twists her hair. "I mean, we're the only two in the castle who probably won't."

"If that's the case..." I lean close to Fia and Max. I'm close enough I can smell honey and tea on Fia's breath. "I'm only motivated to try harder."

I put my fingertips on top of Max's head and caress his face with gentle strokes. Max's purring becomes louder.

"Traitor." Fia narrows her eyes at the cat.

We both continue to pet the cat, and without intending it, my fingers glide over Fia's glove covered fingers. I hear a sharp inhale of breath from Fia and lift my eyes to hers.

She meets my gaze with an intense look. I'm not sure whether she wants me to kiss her or wants to pull a knife from beneath the sheets and stab me.

"Don't move," I say, my voice low.

"You need to move." Fia's voice is low and commanding. "I can't because I have a broken leg."

"Don't move." I lean closer to Fia, extending my hand toward her neck. "Because there's a spider on you."

My fingers touch the side of Fia's neck near the collar-bone when there's a gasp.

CHAPTER THIRTY-NINE

FIA

"Ahem."

Emeric's mother walks in at the same moment he's supposedly getting a spider off my neck, and I realize the timing of this looks bad. Even though nothing is happening between us, the position looks a little compromising. Emeric leans over me, and his fingers are on my neck.

I'm not sure if there really is a spider on my neck. But why would Emeric lie?

"There." Emeric stands straight and brushes his hands together. "Spider gone. Hello, Mother."

"Emeric." Queen Adelinde lifts her eyebrows at her son. "I need you to check and make sure the rooms are ready for Lady Oria and her party while I talk with our mystery girl."

"Fia," Emeric says, and I feel a small sense of pride at what seems his defense of me.

Queen Adelinde nods at her son. "Fia and I need to talk."

I press my lips together as Emeric obeys his mother and leaves. Even Max leaves, following Emeric like a shadow. I wish the cat stayed. I need to do something with my hands and petting the cat would keep them busy.

I'm not making the best first impression in front of the queen, and I know what happens when someone makes a bad first impression in front of my father.

"I would curtsey," I say, "But-"

"There's no need to curtsey." Queen Adelinde lifts her large skirt with both hands and takes a seat in the chair Emeric vacated. "I understand you have a special skill."

"I'm truly, truly sorry, Your Majesty. I never intended to eat the pea and cause you misfortune." I look forward and tilt my chin toward the regal looking queen. While my mother tends to shrink into her throne chair and leaves all eyes on my father, Queen Adelinde commands notice even in a regular chair. With straight posture, her shoulders back, chest forward, and her eyes closely examining me – I can already tell Queen Adelinde is a formidable ruler.

"My daughter seems to think fate placed you here for a reason, and you eating the pea is a stroke of good fortune," Queen Adelinde says, her eyes still not leaving me. "I'm not quite sure what fortune we have yet."

I don't want to talk about fate, but I'm quite sure I'm bad fortune, and I'm not about to tell it to the queen.

"I will do whatever is within my abilities to make it up to you for losing your magic pea."

"I understand you now have a magic touch." Queen Adelinde lifts her arching eyebrows. She's an older version of Adette with wavy golden-brown hair and blue eyes. But

I see where Emeric gets his cheekbones from. "Will you touch me and tell me if I'm royal?"

"I'll try," I reply, slightly nervous.

If I feel nothing, I'll tell her the truth. I tug off the gloves and set them to the side.

Queen Adelinde extends a hand with her palm facing up. Very gently, I place my fingertips in her palm. The sensation immediately comes alive in me, and I can't deny Queen Adelinde's royalty.

"I see." Queen Adelinde pulls her hand away before I remove my fingertips. "You felt something."

"You are royal." I lift my eyes to hers.

"What makes a person royal?" Queen Adelinde asks.

This is a question which people continually debate. My brother loves to debate, especially with our father, and this is a question which would spark an argument.

"Certain people would say blood," I reply. "Many royal families are descended from bloodlines, but others would argue there is more to being royal than blood."

"Very true." Queen Adelinde runs the fingers of her left hand over the veins on the back of her right hand. "My family has long been rulers of Swendale, and something runs in our blood. But to be royal means sacrifice. We rule, but for the benefit of our people and not ourselves."

"That is very royal." I remark, respecting the wisdom in this woman before me. If I were ever to rule someday, which I won't, I would want to learn under her.

"What is it you sense in a royal?" Queen Adelinde asks.

"I'm not sure," I reply. "It's magic."

"Of course." Queen Adelinde nods once. "And magic is a give and take."

"There's always a price to pay for using magic."

I always thought it was a myth, but many of the things I believed to be myths and legends are being shoved in my face.

Emeric is one of them.

"I'm not sure what the price is, but I see the benefit of your magical touch," Queen Adelinde says. "It's much more convenient than trying to place a pea under the mattress of a sleeping person. I had rare occasions to use the pea in the past, but it seems we may have more reasons to in the future, which is why I'm here."

"How can I help?" I ask the question, because it seems the polite thing to do, though I know where this conversation is going. Whether it's good luck or bad luck, fate wants to keep me stuck with my true love.

"I have need of you here," Queen Adelinde replies. "We're expecting visitors, and I would like you to determine if they are indeed royal."

"You need me to touch them?" I swallow hard. Touching royals involves being around people and exposing myself to others.

"Yes." Queen Adelinde's nod is decisive. "As you don't know where your home is or even who you are, I propose we house, clothe, take care of your injury, and feed you in exchange for your service."

"For the service of a magic touch?" I ask, not sure how this will work.

"Your royal touch is needed," Queen Adelinde replies. "But as I kept the nature of the pea secret, we will need to keep the nature of your touch secret. For your protection and ours."

"Yes." I swallow hard again. "I would like to keep this a secret too."

A magic touch is a rare and valuable tool. I've already been kidnapped once, but there are others who would kidnap me to utilize this magical skill. Having this magic touch could be dangerous if others find out about it.

"The use of your secret skill will require you to parade through the castle and attend certain meetings. You will need a different title, and some additional skill sets to accommodate this. We need to keep your magic touch a secret but also have a way to explain your presence in the castle." The corners of Queen Adelinde's lips rise. "I have the perfect job for you."

"What job?" I ask, fearing I've destined myself to cleaning the moat or toilet chambers.

"You don't appear to be much older than Adette. You're articulate, polite, knowledgeable as far as I can tell, and seem adept at picking up new skills." A small crease forms between Queen Adelinde's eyebrows as she looks at me. "As Adette is getting older, it's time she had a lady-in-waiting."

I try to keep my eyes from widening. "You would like me to be Princess Adette's lady-in-waiting?"

"Yes." Queen Adelinde gives a firm nod. "You'll provide Adette companionship, assist in her daily routines, accompany her on outings, help manage any correspondence and schedule changes, and assist Adette where needed, including using the magic touch when it is required. Can you handle this?"

"Of course." I quickly nod, relieved. While being a lady-in-waiting sounds like a lot of work, it can't be much different than my life as a princess in Ryutoa. It might allow me more freedom. "I won't let you down. Thank you."

"I see you're reading history and etiquette, which will benefit Adette." Queen Adelinde looks at the stack of books. "Her head is often elsewhere, and she could use some friendly prodding from someone who isn't family to take a little more interest in those subjects."

"I'll do my best," I tell Queen Adelinde. "I'm grateful to you for the opportunity."

"Adette has requested you stay in this connected room, and while I have some reservations about leaving a stranger with my daughter, I'm going to trust her judgement on this." Queen Adelinde fixes me with a stern look.

"I promise I won't let you down," I say.

Queen Adelinde stands and straightens the long skirt of her dress before looking down at me. "There's one other thing."

"Yes?" I eagerly await her directive. Everything so far has been wonderfully pleasant, and I can't imagine anything worse.

"I would appreciate you keeping your distance from my son, Prince Emeric." Queen Adelinde's eyes darken, whether she's lost in her thoughts because of Emeric or because of me, I'm not sure. "He has or rather, he had a reputation around the palace. He may think I don't know, but nothing gets by me in the castle, especially when it concerns my family. His life hasn't been easy the past couple of years, and he sought refuge where he shouldn't have, and perhaps I'm at fault for not stopping things, but we all have regrets."

Queen Adelinde takes a quick breath.

"Ah..." I'm not sure if I'm supposed to say anything and I have my fair share of regrets. I regret using rosemary.

"You seem like a sweet girl," Queen Adelinde says. "I would hate for you to get hurt. Don't fall for Emeric's charm. Stay out of his arms and his bed. I would warn you not to get into his heart, but it's more likely he would break yours first."

"There's no need to worry," I assure Queen Adelinde, and I hope I sound sincere. "I'm not looking for love."

Emeric was already seared in my head, and I can't let him in my heart.

CHAPTER FORTY

EMERIC

My heart pounds.

I clasp my chest and my eyes fly open. I feel the thump, thump, thump of my heart against the palm of my hand.

I'm alive.

My heart used to be reckless, beating only because it had to in order to keep me alive. But it didn't feel.

From the time I encountered the water dragon until Leo saved us all, I was a hard shell with an unfeeling heart. My heart stopped beating with the rhythm of life the day I met the water dragon. After that time, I kept trying to fill the emptiness and the void with earthly pleasures. But nothing satisfied me. Nothing made my heart beat with the rhythm of life.

Until now.

The hard shell is melting, like beeswax under a flame. I'm being filled up and it's causing my heart to beat.

And it scares me.

Not like fire scares me. Nor my nightmares.

It's a fear of feeling. A fear I'm not enough.

Because I don't deserve love. I don't deserve to love anyone, nor have anyone love me.

In frustration, a loud grunt leaves me, and I throw off what blankets remain on me. Another nightmare has caused me to thrash about and throw off the covers.

I'm not going to be afraid. I'm not going to fear.

I set my bare feet on the cold stone floor and let the frigid sensation fill me. Being able to feel, even something painful, is something to be savored.

I clasp my palm over my chest again and inhale a deep breath.

Something is melting my hard shell, filling me up, and causing my heart to start to beat with life again.

And her name is Fia.

A nightmare may have pushed me out of bed, but it's the thought of Fia which causes me to wander the halls tonight.

Silently, while my family sleeps and the castle is quiet, I slowly walk along the hallway of the royal private quarters. Leo's room is unoccupied, and I slip past Adette's closed door. I'm drawn to another room, and I don't understand why. Why does she have me feeling as if I've been rescued by her when I was the one to pull her from the mud?

I stop outside Fia's door, which is left open a crack.

I'm not sure what to think of the news of Fia being named a lady-in-waiting to Adette. It's wonderous, but also worrisome. I'll be able to keep a closer eye on Fia while she's with Adette, but why do I want to keep an eye on her? I know there's more to Fia than I see, but I have yet to discover what it is. It's the thought of what it could be which keeps me close to her.

Morella would say to keep your enemies closer than your friends.

Fia is so close. Only steps away.

I could enter any girl's room, and they would welcome me with open arms, but not Fia. A small smile creeps up my face at the thought of how she would react to me coming into her room in the middle of the night.

Would she throw a pillow at me?

Only hiss for me to leave, like a cat?

Or tell me she can't stand me?

"Max?" I whisper the cat's name from the hall. "Max?"

It's not long before a stealthy shadow silently slips through the door on four paws, and I let out a relieved sigh.

Maybe now I can sleep.

"Do you want to come with me?" I lead the way down the hall to my room, only to have Max venture past my door.

"Max?" I question the cat and his ears swivel at my call.

He turns his head to look back at me and his tail curls gracefully in the air above his back. It's as if he's painting secrets in the air.

"Where are you going?"

"Meow." Max walks a few steps, stops, and then looks back at me again. He repeats the motion as I curiously watch. "Meow?"

"You want me to follow you?" I wrinkle my nose. Max is usually the one who follows me.

"Meow."

It sounds like a yes to me.

"Alright, let's do some midnight wandering," I tell Max and set off behind him like his shadow.

Max leads me on a series of twists and turns, and I fully expect him to take me to the kitchen. He might be craving a saucer of cream, and I wouldn't mind a midnight snack. But he saunters right on by the kitchen.

"Max?" There's a prickle at the base of my neck, a slight worry, and I try to brush it away.

"Meow." Max lets out a slow sound and turns back to look at me, as if he's comforting me and reassuring me to continue to follow him.

"Where are you taking me?" Why do I have a feeling Max knows more about things going on in the castle than I do? "Do you go visiting the ladies at night?"

Max doesn't answer me this time but keeps walking with sure steps. His ears twist slightly, listening to sounds I can't hear. I'm immersed in watching his body movements, and before I realize it, we're at the entrance to the secret tunnels under the castle.

"You want to go in here?" I ask the cat who sits at my feet and looks up at me with his piercing green eyes.

I swear Max bobs his head as a sign for yes, and as soon as I open the secret entrance, he dodges through faster than if a dog were after him. Max waits in the darkness while I get a lantern before entering the dark tunnels.

These tunnels aren't exactly peaceful to me. They were made for the Swen royals of the past as a place to shelter from dragons, and later as a place to hide from enemies.

My family hid in the tunnels when Morella put our castle under siege. Now I stand a broken man in front of a vault which holds the wand of an imprisoned witch.

"Really, Max?"

The cat looks up at me, as if he knows I want to go in the vault.

I do. And I don't.

"Do you have a thing for jewels?" I lift my eyebrows while staring at the cat.

"Meow." Max rubs against my leg and leads the way into the vault.

"You want to pick out a pretty thing for one of your girlfriends?"

All the jewels, crowns, tiaras, and anything of value are stored here. I lift the lantern to a case with glass doors. Sitting on a velvet pillow is the king's crown. It hasn't been worn in over two centuries, not since King Aberthol Swen. He was the ancestor who signed the decree with the High Fae to have Swendale protected from dragons.

I'll be the first since King Aberthol to wear the king's crown, if I make it to that point. I'm aware there are plenty of things in the Greater World which could take me out before my mother leaves the throne for me.

"What do you know of magic?" I ask Max as I set the lantern on the stand in the center of the vault. It shines in the dark space, lending a soft warm light to the dark corners.

Max stands in front of the chest which holds Morella's wand in a drawer.

"Meow."

I pull the drawer open. The last time I was in the vault I looked at the wand and met Max for the first time.

"You aren't Morella's pet, are you?"

There's a twitch to Max's face, almost as if he's shaking his head no. But it could only be my hopeful wish. There are many superstitions and myths about black cats, but they're just that – stories. Max is only a cat who happens to be black. He's not a harbinger of bad luck or a fairy creature bringing blessings or mischief, nor is he an accomplice to a witch. He's a cat. Only a cat.

Max sits on his haunches on the floor. I stare at the cat, and he stares back at me. Max's green eyes reflect the light, and I blink before he does.

"I don't need any more magic, curses, decrees, witches, or anything having to do with fairies entering my life. Okay?"

"Meow." Max answers as if he understands.

"What would happen if I break it?"

The wand looks like an old branch of a tree, worn smooth by time and use. The branch swirls around itself in three places before it tapers to a tip. It's fascinating how an ordinary object can be the thing which harnesses and directs a witch's magic. The one thing which can cause havoc and change a person's life.

"What do you think, Max?"

Suddenly, Max jumps up and lands in the velvet lined drawer. He lowers his nose to the wand and sniffs it. His tail extends out like a branch and the fur on his back rises. He hisses and then lunges for the wand.

"No!" I yell.

CHAPTER FORTY-ONE

FIA

I heard him.

I heard Emeric during the night.

No one here knows I don't sleep well, and not because of the magical pea. It's my nature. Fynn, being a brother, used to joke my surly attitude is because I don't sleep. But we both know it's the way I am. Perhaps my mind is too active to sleep, or my body doesn't need much, but I've never slept well. Even Mother has said I didn't sleep much as a baby.

But unlike me, Emeric needs his sleep, and he hasn't been getting it.

"Breakfast?" Emeric stands in the open door with a tray. The dark circles under his eyes announce his lack of sleep.

"Why are you here?" I ask when I really want to question him on why he wasn't sleeping last night. Plus, I'm aware I'm supposed to keep my distance from Emeric, but he apparently didn't get the same message from his mother. "Aren't you one of those princes who sleeps late?"

"You read too many books. Princes only do that in stories." Emeric sets the tray of food on the stack of books occupying the table near the bed. "It's about time you did something besides read."

"On that note, Liora cleared me to put some weight on my leg and use crutches, which is good, because I'm tired of lying in bed."

"Oh." Emeric brings a hand to his chest as if he's hurt. "How will I ever be the gallant prince if I can't carry you everywhere?"

"It seems you have no lack of girls willing to let you carry them. I'm sure you'll survive." I look at the tray of food Emeric brought me as an intoxicating scent draws me to it.

A small vase of flowers sits next to the plate of food and teacup. The sweet scent, a mixture of honey and citrus, is uplifting and reminds me of Emeric. Pastel pink flowers resemble delicate butterfly wings on slender, climbing stems. I hate to think about it, but the flowers give a rather ordinary breakfast tray a romantic appeal. It's a sweet gesture.

I need to rid myself of these sickeningly sweet thoughts, but they're like seeds planted in me. They keep popping through every time Emeric appears.

"What kind of flowers are those?" I ask.

"Sweet peas." Emeric lifts his eyebrows as if some inside story about the flowers resides between us.

Sweet pea.

I hate pet nicknames, but one from a flower as pretty as these can't be so bad.

"I bet you give all the girls in the castle flowers." It's not hard to imagine Emeric whipping out a handpicked bouquet of flowers from behind his back to present to some blushing girl. He seems the type to have someone else pick the flowers while he uses them to flatter a girl to do his bidding.

Emeric's cheeks start to blush with the pink shade of the flowers. "I brought them for Max. Have you seen him?"

"Not since last night when you put him on my bed. He was gone this morning, like usual."

I heard Emeric wandering the halls. I heard him call Max. The cat was on my bed, and I set him on the floor so he could go to Emeric. I could sense Emeric needed Max to sleep.

"He tends to disappear, and I'm not sure where." Emeric reaches out to arrange the delicate flowers in the vase. "I put some catnip in the flowers for him."

I smell it as Emeric brushes his fingers over the leaves of the aromatic plant. It's crisp and mint like and offers an enticing balance to the sweet pea flowers. It's a sweet and bitter balance which melds nicely together, a strange pairing I never would have thought of.

"Perhaps he's found a quiet place to rest," I suggest.

"After listening to your snoring all night, he must need a quiet place." Emeric settles into the chair next to my bed as if he's going to take up residence here.

"I do not snore!" I smack my fists into the mattress at my sides. "And how would you know?"

"I can hear you from down the hall." Emeric smirks.

"You hear no such thing, you liar." I hastily reach out and grab a biscuit slathered in butter and honey. These have become my favorite thing to eat here.

"True." Emeric's smirk settles into a smile. "You're as quiet as a mouse, but I like to see you riled up."

I make a grumbling noise and take a bite of the biscuit. The soft texture with the slight crisp edges nearly makes me melt in delight. Quite like Emeric's touch can.

Biscuit. Biscuit. Biscuit.

I need to focus on things besides Emeric. Why does he insist on visiting quite often?

"Now you're cleared to move around, would you like to visit the garden where these flowers came from?" Emeric keeps smiling.

Why does his smile with the dimple in his chin have to be so charming?

"I can't be at your beck and call." I shoot Emeric a fierce look. "I do have a princess to attend to."

I try to think of what I'm doing with Adette today, versus thinking about what I shouldn't be doing with Emeric. He needs to do something to make me loathe him, not bring flowers and food.

"What if I said I outrank her?" The smirk reappears on Emeric's face as does my tendency toward a surly attitude.

"Your mother outranks you," I say. "She warned me to stay away from you."

"Did she?" Emeric kicks his feet up and places his boots on my bed, as if he's challenging the order.

I grimace and swat his feet off.

"You can go attempt to charm an apprentice or someone who will appreciate it," I say. "Do you need your ego stoked daily?"

"If I did, why am I here?" Emeric licks his bottom lip and the dimple on his chin gets deeper.

"Why are you here?" I blurt out. My heart starts to pound, fearful he knows the truth and he's toying with me like a cat plays with a mouse.

"I don't know." Emeric now bites his lower lip. "Perhaps I like a good mystery."

I sigh. I'm a mystery to most people, even when they know me, but I tend to rub people the wrong way and they give up on whatever mystery I present.

Emeric has not given up yet.

"Or you enjoy being annoying," I comment.

"There's a fine line between annoyance and acceptance." Emeric pushes himself out of the chair. "One of us will cross the line."

"Or dive further from it." I take a bite of the biscuit I nearly forgot about.

"As always, it's been a pleasure, Lady Fia." Emeric tips his chin to me. "I'll let you finish your breakfast and attend to Adette."

I watch Emeric's backside as he strides to the door.

"Emeric. Wait," I say, surprising myself.

"Yes?" Emeric turns back with such a hopeful look.

"Do you have time after the lunch hour?" I ask and Emeric's eyes light up even more.

"For you, I do."

"Wonderful. Adette has an opening in her schedule, and I would like you to train her. She needs some self-defense skills."

"I-" Emeric blinks and his shoulders drop for moment before he stands tall. "If it pleases you, I'll do it."

CHAPTER FORTY-TWO

EMERIC

For a moment I thought Fia wanted to do something with me. Last night, I thought for a moment Max was going to put the wand in his mouth and run off with it. But he didn't, and Fia only wants me to train Adette.

Adette is dining at breakfast with Mother and Father when I arrive.

"Have you spoken to your lady-in-waiting this morning?" I ask Fia.

"Not yet," Adette replies. "I left her with Liora and will bring her breakfast soon."

"No need," I say. "She's already been served and is scheduling your day."

"Oh?" Adette's lips purse and she turns to me, keenly interested. "You've already spoken to Fia?"

Mother's teacup clatters as she sets it on the saucer.

"Emeric." Mother sets a stern gaze on me and I know what's coming. "Lady Fia is not your concern. I don't want you scaring her off."

"I don't believe Adette's lady-in-waiting is scared of much." I dig a spoon into the bowl of biscuits and gravy set in front of me. "She's quite keen on self-protection and wants me to train Adette."

"Me?" Adette's bright face lights up even more, but then her eyes slightly narrow. "You're going to train me?"

"I'll try," I reply. "What sort of weapon would you like to start with?"

"Oh!" Adette starts to squirm in her seat. "Bow and arrow. No, dagger. Oh! Maybe a short sword."

"Adette. Emeric." Mother places her palms on the table. "We need to talk about this."

"Dear." Father places a large palm over the back of Mother's tense hand. "I think it's a good idea if Emeric trains Adette, considering what we've been through. I blame myself for not thinking of this sooner. Adette should be able to handle a weapon if the need arises to protect herself."

"I don't want the need to arise." Mother bangs her other fist on the table before bringing it up to cover her mouth, but not before I catch her lip quiver. "I knew the boys would need skills with weapons, but I never wanted to imagine more than fulfilling the decree."

"There's always the risk someone could kidnap Adette," I say, with a soft glance at my sister. Someone would have to get by me first. "She should be able to protect herself."

"Kidnap me!" Adette exclaims. "Why would anyone kidnap me?"

"Our blood," I say softly after glancing around to make sure I can't be overheard. "If our secret gets out, we'll be in danger. Not to mention we have a witch in the dungeon who put our castle under siege. Plus, you'll have young men knocking on the door to attempt to win your hand, and you should be able to protect yourself."

Adette lowers her eyes and blushes. "It would be nice to learn. Plenty of young women learn to use weapons."

"I think it's a great idea," Father says. "I would recommend starting with daggers. They're easy to conceal."

"Eira always has one hidden on her!" Adette grins while Mother grimaces.

"We'll start with the dagger," I agree.

After lunch, I arrange daggers on a table while an attendant stands nearby in the training arena. The last time I was here was the day of Leo's birthday when I took him down in ten seconds with a sword. My eyes pinch at the memory, and I take a deep breath. I brandished a sword at the water dragon, which I now know from Eira, was the wrong thing to do. Swords make dragons attack.

"Em!" Adette's joyous voice pierces through my dark memories and I open my eyes to find her at the entrance.

"You changed," I comment. Adette no longer wears an embellished dress, but leggings with a plain linen blouse.

"Fia said I would be more comfortable in this," Adette explains. "She said it would be easier in the beginning."

"She can learn the movements first and then train later in her usual clothing." Fia hobbles out from behind

Adette, a crutch under her left arm. "I don't want her hindered by corsets, ties, and flowing garments until she's familiar with what you're teaching her."

"It's a…" I can't take my eyes off Fia. I haven't seen her standing much and she's a sight to behold. "A wonderful idea. And it's nice to see you about, Lady Fia."

"It's nice to be out of bed," Fia comments and my mind goes where it shouldn't at her comment.

I clear my throat and turn my focus to my sister.

"Ready to begin?" I ask.

"Show me what to do," Adette says and joins me at the table.

"We'll start with throwing," I say, "and then move to some self-defense moves when an attacker is close."

"I know where to kick if I need to." Adette picks up a small dagger.

I groan. "That's not what I'm talking about."

"You could be attacked be a female." Fia limps with her crutch to stand next to the table.

Adette grimaces. "Then teach me."

Fia leans against the stone wall to the side of Adette and me. Adette and I throw at a target, but I find myself looking out of the corner of my eye to Fia. She intently watches us but remains silent. She doesn't offer any tips, remarks, or opinions.

When Adette starts to tire, I hold a dagger out to Fia. "Would you like to throw?"

"I shouldn't," Fia replies. "This lesson is for your sister."

"Please try, Fia." Adette skips over. "Do it for me. You never know if you might need to use a dagger."

"I'll try." With a determined face, Fia uses the crutch under her left arm to limp out and position herself in line with the target.

"Shall I help you hold it and guide your throw?" I give Fia a smoldering look for good measure, knowing exactly how she'll respond.

"No, thank you." She clenches her jaw and takes the dagger from my hand.

"You might want to remove your gloves for better control," I advise.

Fia eyes the target with narrowed eyes. "I think I'll be fine."

"Now you want to-"

Thwack.

In a matter of a split second, the dagger leaves Fia's hand and now resides in the target.

I look up in astonishment. The dagger is in the dead center.

"Fia!" Adette jumps up and down and claps.

"How?" I need to pick my jaw off the sawdust covered ground.

"Beginner's luck." Fia leans back on the crutch under her left arm.

"No." I shake my head in disbelief. I know she threw with her nondominant arm. "That is not beginner's luck."

"What else can you do?" Adette excitedly asks and I get an idea.

I hurry over to the rack of training swords and grab two. The dull edged swords won't slice, pierce, or kill, but they can leave a nasty bruise.

"Here." I hold a sword out to Fia, and she warily eyes it. "Take it."

"I don't know." Fia's lips press together.

"Take it." I push the sword at her again. I know she wants it as I see the gleam in her eye.

With a huff, Fia finally takes the sword from my hand. She starts to test the balance of it before she realizes how close I watch her. She lets the tip drop to the ground and lightly holds the handle in her right hand.

"What do you want me to do?" Fia's eyes bore into me as if challenging me.

I plan to challenge her. I take a step back and lift the sword in my hand.

"Emeric! No!" Adette yells when she realizes what I'm doing.

I lunge at Fia, holding back a little, which she would hate to know. As I suspect, Fia skillfully blocks my attempt. The swords clash together, and the sound reverberates loud in my ear.

"I thought you were going to hit her." Adette exhales a shaky breath as I lower my sword.

"She knows what she's doing." I nod my head toward Fia who still holds the sword in a defensive position.

"You were going to hit me!" Fia points the dull tip of the sword at my chest, but it doesn't reach me where I stand away from her.

"But I didn't," I say. "You blocked it like someone who's trained with a sword. Like someone who knows what they're doing."

"It was instinct. It doesn't mean I know how to use a sword." Fia's right fingers flex and unflex around the sword handle. She's left-handed.

"You threw a dagger at a target and blocked my sword with your nondominant hand." I watch a small breeze pick up the tendrils of hair at the sides of Fia's face and they flutter into her eyes. She swipes them away with the fist wrapped around the sword. "You've trained with weapons before. Who are you?"

"I don't know." Fia leans on her crutch and runs the tip of the sword through the sawdust at her feet.

"Maybe you were a bodyguard and don't remember." Adette sidles up to Fia's side.

"Or an assassin." I take another look at the dagger lodged deep in the target. Fia would have no problem throwing a dagger into someone's chest. I don't doubt she knows exactly how to hurt or kill an attacker.

"It looks like I know how to throw a dagger and keep myself from being hit by a sword," Fia says. "It still doesn't mean I know who I am or where I'm from."

"What else can you do?" Adette's excitement is rising.

"I-" Fia pales and I feel a need to rescue her.

"I think that's enough for today," I interrupt. "You're going to be sore tomorrow, Adette."

"You have a lesson with your tutor soon." Fia holds the sword out to me.

"We can train again tomorrow," I say, my eyes on Fia as I reach for the sword in her gloved hand.

"You're to train your sister, not try to figure me out," Fia whispers. She keeps a grip on the sword. My hand is right above hers and a warmth radiates from it.

"I like a mystery, and maybe I've already figured you out," I say softly.

"No, you haven't." Fia pushes the sword at me, and even with a crutch, I can tell she's storming away.

I smile at her retreating form. Fia is becoming more intriguing with each passing day. I can't help but wonder if she knows hand to hand combat.

CHAPTER FORTY-THREE

FIA

Liora's hands gently tighten the wraps holding the braces on my leg.

"You're a lucky girl," Liora says. "You're healing fast. I would say in a few months' time you won't even know which leg you broke."

"If I'm lucky, it's because you're the one taking care of me." I adjust the skirt over my legs and stand straight.

"Prince Emeric is the one who found you." Liora winks. "Who's the lucky one then?"

I keep a groan locked inside of me and only force a small smile as I thank Liora. I use the crutch under my left arm and hobble into the hallway, thoughts of Emeric once again infiltrating my mind. Adette has trained with her brother for the past few days, and I do my best to avoid any interaction with Emeric or letting him put another weapon into my hands. I thought Emeric would push me to use a weapon, but he hasn't. He only cautiously eyes me as if he's not sure I might be a trained assassin or a bandit for hire. Little does he know I was the one taken by bandits. My sword couldn't save me or my guard.

Reimund.

Thoughts of him are painful. It's all my fault. Lost in my haze of guilt, I'm not completely aware of my surroundings as I make my way to the stairs to the royal quarters. I'm meeting Adette in her room for her tutoring session. As if a dark spirit passes by, the hairs on my arms rise and I suddenly turn around and focus down the hallway.

No.

No, no, no.

This can't happen.

I have the worst luck.

Desperate, I look around for a place to hide, but I'm in a wide hallway which leads to the banquet hall. There's no escape. I can only turn and walk away, and hope no one notices me.

"Fia."

My name is called from both in front of me and behind me. I quickly turn away from the ones I don't want to see and bump into the hard chest of my rescuer.

"Emeric." I keep my voice low. "Hide me. Please."

Whether it's the desperation in my voice or my use of please, Emeric immediately reacts. With a quick look over my shoulder at the visitors, he puts an arm around my waist and pulls me with him. We don't walk very far before we round a corner, but I still don't foresee how I'll manage to get away.

"Fia!"

A shout of my name comes from behind us.

"Here." With a quick flick of his hand, Emeric pushes aside a heavy curtain.

"What're you doing?" I hiss.

"I'm hiding you." Emeric lifts his eyebrows. "Get in."

There's a small rounded out alcove behind the curtain, with enough space for me to stand and hide. With a relieved sigh, I quickly dodge in and wait for Emeric to drop the curtain to cover me. Instead, he follows me in and lets the curtain fall behind him.

"What're you doing?" I hiss again.

"Hiding with you," Emeric whispers. "They saw me with you."

I try to wriggle further in, but my back is pressed to the curved stone wall. And Emeric's chest is pressed against mine. There's barely enough room for both of us. I'm acutely aware of his body touching me. His strong chest is pressed against mine as it rises and falls with shallow breaths.

"Who are we hiding from?" Emeric's warmth breath, lightly scented with mint, washes over me. I lock my knees.

"I..." I'm not supposed to remember anything. "I'm not sure. I have a feeling about those people."

"Do you get feelings about people often?" Emeric's voice has an amused lilt.

I'm getting some sort of feeling now, and it's not a bad one.

It's dark in the alcove, but I can sense Emeric looking down at me. His face is near mine, so close to me I can feel the stubble on his chin brush against my temple. His right hand moves to rest on the curve of my waist in a light touch. I brace my palms against the cool stone wall and resist the urge to touch Emeric. I don't have gloves on.

"I have a feeling they're bad," I whisper, trying to keep my voice even. I find it a little hard to breathe in this tight area. Emeric's chest rises and falls next to mine.

Emeric slowly twists his chin, and his mouth moves near my ear. The stubble of his chin catches my hair, and a cascade of tingles shoots through every nerve ending in my scalp. I have to stifle a gasp.

"What feeling do you have about me?" Emeric whispers in my ear.

"I have a feeling you've been in here with many girls." I tighten my body, refusing to feel anything. I don't need to be captive to any feelings. I'm strong enough to brush them aside.

"Your feelings are accurate." Emeric lets his other hand also rest on my waist and I don't brush him off. "But I haven't been in here in a while."

"Why?" My question comes out breathy sounding, and I inwardly cringe.

"Because there hasn't been anyone I want to be with."

Now he's in here with me. I find myself holding my breath as Emeric's hands tighten on my waist, as if he's pulling himself closer to me.

"Shh." Emeric's whisper in my ear causes another cascade of tingles through me. "They're right outside."

My heart races, pulsing hard against my chest. Emeric has to feel it.

"I saw her," a voice says. "She couldn't have gone far."

"She's here," another voice says. "We'll find her."

I suck my lips in and pinch them in my teeth. The voices are the ones I've heard before. Both Emeric and I remain still, the only movement the gentle press of his fingers into my waist in a soothing gesture.

"They seem to know you," Emeric says when the footsteps and voices have trailed off. "Why are you scared of them?"

"I'm not sure, but I feel like I have a reason to fear them." I take a shaky breath and tilt my chin up toward Emeric. "Please don't let them take me."

Emeric's hands lift off my waist and he brings them to my face. His fingers gently cradle my neck, and his thumbs run along my jawline. It's hard not to think how many girls he's done this with as his touch ignites something in me. It would be so easy to extend on my tiptoes and bring my lips to his. Perhaps this is the move he does, and that's how girls respond. But I won't.

Even if his touch is stoking something in my soul, he can't win me this easily.

"I won't let anyone take you," Emeric whispers. "I promise."

But his words might win me over, because at them, my heart starts to crack.

CHAPTER FORTY-FOUR

EMERIC

She didn't kiss me.

Fia didn't kiss me.

I rub a hand across my forehead, still recalling the nearness to her. I don't know how many times I've had a girl behind the curtain in the alcove outside the banquet hall, how many times I've caressed a girl's face, how many times I whispered sweet nothings, and they were the ones to initiate the kiss. They always did.

But not Fia.

Maybe it's because my words weren't whispered nothings. They meant something.

"Prince Emeric." A royal guard stands before me. "There are guests in the banquet hall who would like to speak to you about a missing girl."

"Of course," I reply. "I'll head there straight away. Thank you."

With Fia sequestered in Adette's room, I now get to meet the people who set her shaking like a scared puppy. Always so strong-willed and confident, I haven't seen

Fia be so vulnerable until today. She didn't even make a disparaging comment about me holding her close. I knew inside Fia must be hiding something, and even if she can't remember what it is, it's there in her soul. It's a part of her.

I won't let anyone take her without a good reason.

A royal guard opens the door to the banquet hall for me, and another accompanies me across the room to where a group of three sit at a table. The walk to the other side of the room gives me a chance to assess the strangers. They turn in their chairs to assess me as I walk towards them. It's the same group which sets Fia on edge.

A young woman, probably around my age, elegantly dressed in a gown of dark red velvet, smiles slightly at me. My stomach clenches. She had better not be another princess set on winning the hand of the most eligible bachelor in the Greater World. Flanked by two young men, one quite scrawny and the other brawny, both dressed in a mismatched assortment of trousers, shirts, and waistcoats, they make an interesting looking group.

As I approach the table, the two men stand and bow, only after the young woman they sit with jabs them both in the sides with her elbows.

The young woman doesn't stand, but extends a hand to me, purposely showing a ring on her finger which resembles a royal crest. "I don't believe we've ever had the pleasure of meeting." The young woman flutters her eyelashes at me in a flirtatious move I'm quite familiar with. "I'm Princess Fia of Ryutoa."

Fia?

Is it a coincidence this young woman has the same name as the feisty woman currently hiding in Adette's room?

The young woman before me doesn't resemble the Fia I know. This woman has a more angular face and long nose, darker skin, and eyes that are two toned blue and brown. I can't tell the color of her hair as it's covered with a silk wrap.

I take the young woman's hand in mine and quickly kiss the back of it. I give her the same charming smile I give all beautiful women I meet. Sweet and shy women tend to be fascinated, yet wary of me. Bitter and bold women are drawn to me. I shall see what this Princess Fia is, as my Lady Fia is neither.

"I'm pleased to meet you," I say. "I'm Prince Emeric of Swendale."

The young woman nods her head and clasps her hands in her lap. "I've been told there's an injured young woman in the castle who was discovered in a field south of here."

I round the table and take a chair across from the group. "That's correct."

"I'm hoping the young woman is my missing lady-in-waiting," Princess Fia says. "We encountered a storm near your southern border. Large hail hit us near the river. In the chaos of the harsh weather, my traveling party got separated. Fia was lost to us. It took us all some time to recover from injuries and regain our property before we could start searching for Fia. I'm relieved to hear you rescued her and she's been well cared for."

Under the cover of the table I clench the sides of my chair with my hands. The terrain and conditions match when and where I found Fia. It's plausible it took time for them to recover before setting out to find Fia, but something doesn't add up.

"Your lady-in-waiting has the same name as you?" I remark.

"Fia is a common name in Ryutoa," the princess replies with a sly smile. "Especially after I was born."

"Fia, the young woman here, has no memory," I say. "She doesn't remember family or where she's from."

"Oh." The princess gasps and brings a hand to her mouth. "Poor thing. Does she remember anything?"

"Nothing," I reply. "She has no memory. She wasn't even sure of her name."

"Oh, the poor dear." The princess keeps her hand over her mouth in shock, but the curve of her lips seems to indicate this news isn't at all disappointing.

"Are you aware she broke her leg?" My eyes narrow, and I wait for reactions.

"I only know she was injured," Princess Fia replies, her face relaxed. "Is she ready for travel?"

"I'm not sure it would be advised for her to travel yet." I'm purposely stalling for Fia's sake. "We would need to check with the healer."

"But you managed to move her here?" Princess Fia lifts her full, arching eyebrows.

"At great risk," I reply. "She was unconscious."

"I'm already delayed in my travels because of our unfortunate incident, and I cannot bear to be without Fia for a day more," the princess says. "I request she join us at once."

"She will not have any memory of you." Whatever feeling Fia had about these people is starting to infiltrate me. Something is not right.

"Even if she doesn't remember us, she's best off with people who know her and care for her," Princess Fia says, her eyes now narrowing and challenging mine.

"How do I know she belongs with you?" I ask. They should have been here much earlier if they cared about Fia. It would not have taken me this long to find Fia if she disappeared from my sight.

"Aside from the fact we're the only ones who have shown up to claim her, I can describe her." The visiting princess gives me another lazy smile. "She's left-handed, has dark blonde hair, blue gray eyes, and she wears a chain around her neck with a blue stone. Would you like me to continue?"

I know it all to be true, which is a disappointment.

"It sounds like she may be the same girl," I say with a sinking feeling in my stomach. "But we'll need to test the legitimacy of it somehow."

I need to discover the legitimacy of this royal in front of me. Is there truly a Princess Fia of Ryutoa?

Mother would know, but she's not here. She and Father left this morning to travel to a northern village for a summer festival. They'll be gone for two nights. As if this is a test and trial run, I have been left in charge of all matters in the castle. And this is a castle matter.

"Please have Fia brought to us." The princess may say please, but it's a command.

"Of course." I push out of my chair and stand. "I will retrieve her myself."

I clench my jaw. This isn't looking good for Fia, or for me.

With tense movements, I exit and then rush to the private quarters of the castle. I told Fia I wouldn't let anyone take her, and I don't know how I'm going to keep the promise.

FIA

"You promised."

I can't believe what I'm hearing.

"I know," Emeric reassures me with a wave of his hand. "All I'm asking is for you to meet them and see if any memories return. They seem to know who you are. They were able to describe you and even detail the necklace you wear."

"No." I shake my head and grasp at the chain around my neck. I don't want to see the people who harmed Reimund and kidnapped me.

"Emeric?" Adette breezes through the door from her room.

When Emeric came into Adette's room saying he needed to talk to me privately, I knew what it was about. Adette obviously was curious and left us alone for half a minute before returning.

She catches sight of Emeric's tense pose and my distraught face. "What's happened?"

"There are people claiming to know Fia and they want to take her," Emeric replies.

"No." Adette rushes over to the bed where I sit with my leg up and plops down on an edge. "Truly? You're leaving?"

"No." I shake my head. "I don't want to. I don't know them."

"A young woman says she's Princess Fia of Ryutoa and has two men with her. She claims Fia is her lady-in-waiting."

"No. Wait." My head starts spinning. I can reveal I'm the true Princess of Ryutoa and expose my lie, or I can somehow expose Eike without giving myself away. "Has anyone in your family met the Princess of Ryutoa before?"

"No." Emeric's answer is confident.

"Are you certain the woman is a real princess?" I ask.

"She has a royal ring," Emeric replies.

"What if she's lying?"

Adette's eyes widen at my question. She knows what I'm referring to. She jerks her head to her brother. "We need to be sure she's a real princess."

"Mother would be able to tell us if she were here," Emeric replies. "She might know of the Ryutoan royals."

"I need to meet her," Adette says. "I'll determine if she's truly a princess."

"You?" Emeric lifts his eyes while Adette gives me a sly look.

"I've been learning about royals in my lessons. Let me meet her and Fia can accompany me."

"Me?" It comes out as a squeak.

"You can test her," Adette says in a low whisper, "but you'll need to meet her."

"I'll go with you." I exhale sharply. I don't want to see Eike, but I don't have a way to avoid meeting her without giving up my lie.

"They seem to know you and seeing them might bring your memory back," Emeric adds.

"You want to get rid of me." I mean it to sound like a typical joking remark, but it doesn't come out that way. I sound rather sad.

"I don't want you to leave." Adette places a hand over mine. I wear gloves to shield myself from the tingle of the royal touch. "But you should meet with these people and see what happens."

"I didn't have a good feeling when I spotted them in the hallway, and I still don't have a good feeling about them."

All the memories of the kidnapping came flooding back to me when I saw Eike, Rivo, and Keil in the hallway.

Reimund.

I stifle a small sob and blink back the smallest sting of tears. I'm not one to get emotional, but at times, I can no longer hold them back. The emotions and feelings come at me like one of the tidal waves on the ocean. I'm the rocky cliff which withstands the strong wave, but even small bits of rock can be removed by the biggest wave.

And poor Reimund.

I've been able to keep him in the recesses of my mind, but it's hard to ignore what happened to him when his attackers are in my presence. I want to grab a sword and show them what they deserve.

"Fia, please." Emeric's eyes pour into me, and I must avert my own to look at my gloved hands. The magic still flows through me. "If you still have a bad feeling after meeting these people, we'll come up with some excuse to keep you here. We can say your leg needs longer to heal."

"They've already seen me walking with a crutch," I say. "They know I can be mobile."

"It doesn't matter." Emeric presses his lips together. "If you want to stay here, we'll work something out."

"First we need to discover if this Princess Fia is truly a princess." Adette taps my hand, a secret signal I need to use my magic touch. "And if she isn't, we'll lock her in the dungeon."

"That might not be the best choice," Emeric says, "but it sounds good to me."

I'm once again in Emeric's arms, and I hate to admit it, but it's even more pleasant this time. My gloved hands are wrapped around Emeric's neck as he carries me. He and Adette decided Emeric carrying me would give the illusion I'm not ready to travel.

When I travel, it won't be with Eike. I'll leave of my own freewill when I set off to find my brother.

Heat travels from Emeric's skin through the gloves to my palms, but the magic touch isn't strong with the gloves. It's something else I feel with Emeric, and it's both bitter and sweet.

Bitter because I don't want to feel this, but sweet because it's an all-encompassing warmth, like a kitten cuddling next to you.

"Are we making this a habit?" Emeric asks.

"What habit?" I'm slightly distracted. Distracted by being in Emeric's arms, distracted by what awaits me, and distracted by the task I still need to complete with finding my brother.

"Carrying you?" Emeric smirks.

"It seems you need to have your ego stoked daily, and what better way than carrying a girl with a broken leg," I quip.

"You shouldn't be surprised if more girls in the castle find themselves with broken legs," Emeric jokes.

"Oh, please." I scoff. "I didn't break my leg to have you rescue and carry me. And if some girl breaks her leg for you, then she really needs to set her priorities straight."

"I would never want a girl to break her leg for me." Emeric's hands grip me more firmly, causing my belly to tighten. "But breaking your leg was fate."

"Because it led you to me?" I lift my eyebrows. "Quite presumptuous, aren't you?"

"It led us to something." Emeric's voice is low, barely a breath in my ear. His words stir me to my core. I want to banish this feeling but also hold on to it and have it cover all my other bad feelings.

"I'm being led to meet people claiming to know me, and I have a bad feeling about them." My fingers absently twist Emeric's hair, rather than my own. "Is that fate?"

"I won't let them take you if you feel something is off," Emeric reassures me.

And I believe him.

But I don't believe what I feel when I'm seated in the banquet hall.

This isn't possible.

No.

It can't be.

I try to remain placid and still. I can't let anyone see my shock, and I can't jerk my bare hand away from Eike. My heart pounds in my chest in huge rhythmic beats. They're like the drumbeats of the royal guard marching in line.

How is this possible?

"Do I truly know you?" I keep my palm over the back of Eike's hand. There's no denying the sensation I feel. The tingle rippling through my hand is as strong as when I touched Queen Adelinde and her children.

Eike is royal. Really royal.

"Yes." Eike smiles and fixes her eyes on me. It's hard to tear my eyes away from her mesmerizing ones. They're not easily forgettable. "I'm so delighted to find you alive and well. Now we can continue our journey."

"I'm sorry." I pull my hand back into my lap. "I don't remember you."

Adette is on the edge of her chair. She leans far forward and waits for a sign from me.

I give a slight shake of my head to Adette. Eike may be royal, but she's not Princess Fia from Ryutoa.

"Dear Fia! You know me!" Eike leans toward me and clasps my hand. It takes everything in me to not pull my bare hand away from her tight grip. There's no denying the magic sensation coursing through Eike to me. She is royal. And she wears my ring on her finger. "I've been in such distress thinking we lost you. I'm relieved to see you again. You must come with me."

Eike is a brilliant actress. She even has a tiny tear in the corner of her eye. But I know her to be strong willed and bordering on ruthless. She may have a drop of compassion in her, and she displayed it once before, but I know her motives for being here. She wants to deliver me and collect her payment. She wants to pay her debt to Ido, except I have yet to see Ido. Did he send his crew to collect me?

"I have no memory of you." I tear my hand away from hers and continue with my amnesia ruse. It's safer this way. "How do I know it's safe to leave with you?"

The question is addressed to Eike, but my eyes are on Emeric.

"You're among strangers here." Eike's eyes rove between Emeric and me, sensing something. "You're safer with those who know you."

"I have no memory of you." I try to keep my voice even. "I know these people have cared for me."

"I propose-" Eike starts, but she's interrupted by Emeric.

"I propose Fia is examined by the healer one more time, to see if she's able to travel. Then we'll proceed from there. It may mean leaving your lady-in-waiting here a little longer while you travel, Princess Fia, and returning for her later. Or perhaps she'll be ready to travel with you. Is that agreeable?"

"If it must be so." The fake princess nods her head. "I would like to accompany Fia to the healer."

"I would prefer Princess Adette to accompany me," I say. "She's the one who has been overseeing my care since I arrived and I'm her lady-in-waiting."

Eike's jaw tightens and I know inside she's seething at this delay. But I have information which might work in my favor now.

"I insist I come along," Eike says. "You're my lady-in-waiting."

"It won't take long," Adette says with a gracious smile. "You can enjoy tea, and we shall return shortly."

"I should like to speak to your healer," Eike says in a voice displaying her displeasure.

"Of course." Adette dips her chin and looks at her brother. "Emeric, carefully transport Fia to the infirmary."

The tiny infirmary room I used to occupy is a safe place for a meeting away from the eyes and ears of Eike and the band of ruffians.

"She's lying," I say. "She's not Princess Fia of Ryutoa."

I'm not exactly lying. It's the truth Eike is not Princess Fia, but she is royal.

"What do we do?" Adette asks. "They obviously know you and you must be from Ryutoa, but how do we discover the truth?"

"I'm not sure where I'm from. Does it matter if I don't remember?" I twist a strand of hair around my finger, trying to figure out how I can play this. It's not ideal to have Adette and Emeric know I'm from Ryutoa. "I don't want to go with them. She's not a princess and doesn't seem to be family."

"We won't let them take you." Emeric pinches his chin between his fingers making his dimple stand out. "If you don't want to go with them, we'll come up with a way to detain them or have them leave without you."

"Arrest them." Adette gives a sure nod as if this is the only way. "She's not Princess Fia, and if you had the royals from Ryutoa here, you could prove it. I know she's not a Ryutoan royal."

"How do you know she's not royal?" Emeric crosses his arms over his chest and directs his narrowed gaze at Adette. "How are you so sure she's not Princess Fia of Ryutoa?"

"Please, Emeric." Adette looks at her brother with wide eyes. "She's not royal. You know I know things. Put them in the dungeon. When they realize they've been caught in a lie, they'll leave."

Emeric blows air out pursed lips. "This is not exactly a diplomatic way to handle this. You want me to put someone in the dungeon based on a feeling of a girl with no memory?"

"If Fia says the girl isn't royal..." Adette grips her brother's forearm, "then she isn't royal. The girl in the banquet hall is not Princess Fia. I guarantee it."

I flinch in surprise. Adette is strongly in my corner.

"Mother isn't going to be happy about this," Emeric says. "Nor Father."

"They're not here and you're in charge," Adette says firmly.

"I don't want to make the wrong choice." Emeric's voice is so soft, as if he can't believe what he says. He exudes such an air of confidence, it's hard to believe he's worried about making the wrong choice.

But I understand his hesitation. I hate making wrong choices.

"You're not making the wrong choice." I give Emeric a small smile of encouragement.

"Mother will agree," Adette says. "She'll believe Fia about this fake royal."

"Fine." Emeric huffs a large breath out of his nostrils. "We'll have to take guards and surprise them. And hope with all we have we're not arresting real royals from Ryutoa, or we might be instigating another war."

"Trust me," I say. "There won't be a war."

CHAPTER FORTY-SIX

EMERIC

"Trust me!" The girl claiming to be Princess Fia shouts as she's gripped between two of my guards. "I'll bring war to your doorstep for arresting me."

"You'll regret this." The largest man escorting the fake princess growls. He jerks in the arms of two of Swendale's largest guards.

"This is only temporary," I tell the three people who are now my captives. "When someone arrives to identify you, then you're free to go. If you're Princess Fia, then you'll have my deepest apologies."

"Prince Emeric?" Adette addresses me and continues with a plan we quickly devised to fish out who these strangers are. "Are you sending someone to Ryutoa to verify these guests as quickly as possible?"

"I have a rider on the way," I reply.

I don't. We aren't sending anyone to Ryutoa. *Yet.*

But the reaction I get from the fake princess is enough to know this isn't what she wishes. She doesn't protest, but the deep intake of air and the widening of her eyes lets me know she's lying. She glances at the largest of the men who accompany her, and he gives her a slight nod.

"I'm sure we can work something out," the fake princess says, her voice dripping with sweetness, which is just as fake as her.

"Are you aware of the punishment for impersonating a royal?" I lean forward toward the beautiful girl but keep my distance. Why would she be pretending to be a princess?

"Death," Adette replies with a decisive nod.

"Wait!" the smaller man cries out until he's fixed with a stare from the larger man and clamps his mouth shut. He's close to admitting their ploy, and it only strengthens my trust in Fia. She's right about this group. But it still begs the question – how do they know Fia?

"Fortunately..." I focus my stare on the fake princess. "We're merciful in Swendale, and imprisonment is the consequence. If Ryutoa agrees with our claims and you're found guilty, you'll be transported back to where you came from."

"Lock us up then." The fake princess's voice is demanding. "No matter the outcome, you'll regret this."

I really hope Adette and I aren't being reckless with this.

"Take them away," I tell the guards.

"You have a real princess in your midst!" The fake princess yells as a guard escorts her away. "You do not know what you're doing!"

"Well..." Adette brushes her hands together as if dusting off dirt from travel. "That was quite fun. I think we handled that well."

"Did we?" I ask. "We're trusting Fia, and she has no memory. What if the young woman we sent to the dungeon is the real princess of Ryutoa?"

"You don't believe she is, do you?" Adette smooths the front of her skirt.

"No." I sigh. For some reason, I completely trust Fia.

"Is this what it will be like someday?" Adette grins, pleased with our little charade.

"What do you mean?" I'm not quite as pleased. Something feels off, but it's not Fia.

"Someday you'll be ruling Swendale and have to make decisions like this," Adette says, swishing the fabric of her skirt back and forth with her hands.

"We'll be ruling Swendale together."

"You and me?" Adette grins.

"Leo will be in Montagnia," I reply. "I'm going to need some help, and who better than a real princess?"

Adette performs a perfect curtsey. "Why, thank you, brother. I'd be happy to help you until the day I leave Swendale."

"We can't leave," I remind Adette.

"Wishes can come true," Adette says and lifts her skirt. "I'm off to get assistance from my lady-in-waiting and tell her the news."

"Wait." I grasp Adette's arm. I don't know why I didn't think of this before. "Fia must be from Ryutoa. Do we send someone there to see if anyone matching Fia's description is missing?"

"Ryutoa is a large kingdom," Adette replies. "Sending one rider there is like looking for a lost button in a plowed field. It's not going to be easy. Plus, Fia wants to stay here."

"The woman pretending to be the princess of Ryutoa seems to know our Fia. What if they are Fia's only connection to what she knows? What if we're keeping Fia from those who love her?"

"Fia seems genuinely scared of those people and that's not love," Adette says. "Even if she knows these people and can't remember them, something in her subconscious tells her to keep a distance."

"Who do you think Fia is?"

Adette shrugs her shoulders. "I don't know what to think. Fia is a mystery, but one I would prefer to keep here."

CHAPTER FORTY-SEVEN

FIA

I can't stay here.

As usual, I don't sleep well, and not because of a pea under my bed or a magic tingle. I limp out of my room while Max catnaps on my bed and Adette is asleep next door. I traverse the quiet halls to the dungeon, hoping tonight isn't one of the nights Emeric will do his midnight wandering.

I devise excuse after excuse and story after story in my head to tell the guard, but he only lets me through with a nod of his head. He must have heard the people occupying the dungeon know me.

The dungeon is below ground with one long corridor and cells on either side. It's a familiar design, as much of the Swendale Castle is similar in construction to the castle I grew up in.

I limp past Rivo and Keil, who appear to be sleeping in their shared cell. The cells after them are empty and I find Eike in a cell at the end of the corridor. The distance from the men will be useful, as Eike is the one I want to talk to. She resides in a cell with iron bars. Across from her is a sealed cell with a thick, solid iron door. A small sliding panel covers a window at head height but can be opened from my side. No noise of any kind comes from the opposite cell and either it's unoccupied or the occupant is asleep. It doesn't seem the dungeon here is used often, quite unlike the dungeon in my family's castle.

"I've been waiting for you." Eike immediately sits up when she spots me and swings her legs off the cot she was lying on. "I thought you might show up. It's your fault we're here, isn't it? You have your memory."

"Eike." My whisper is harsh. "You said we're not that much different, you and I."

"You're lying to everyone here." Eike narrows her eyes. I can't look away. "They think you lost your memory, but you haven't. What will happen if I share that bit of news with the Swendale royals?"

"You're lying too," I say.

Eike took a risk coming to Swendale Castle to retrieve me, knowing I won't willingly go with her. She must have thought her fortune changed when she learned I lost my memory, only to discover I have it. I'm taking as equal of a risk by coming down to the dungeon to talk to Eike, but it's a risk I'm willing to take because I think it will play in my favor. It's time luck was on my side.

"Obviously I'm not Princess Fia." Eike flicks a hand at me. A hand adorned with my royal ring. "But it was a way to get in here and retrieve you."

"I don't want to be retrieved," I say. "You kidnapped me."

"You're a job," Eike says. "Nothing more, nothing less. A job I need to finish."

"I don't think so," I say. "Where's Ido?"

"No one knows," Eike says, a hesitation in her voice. I'm not sure whether to believe her.

"Then why are you here?"

"You're valuable!" Eike's voice rises and then she quickly lowers it. "And I need the money."

"Who's paying you?" Behind bars, Eike might now be in a position to give me the information I desire.

"I don't know," Eike admits. "I don't know all the details of the job. But it doesn't matter. Someone will pay, especially when you're the only living heir to the throne of Ryutoa."

"You know I'm not in line for the throne," I hiss under my breath.

"But your male children are." Eike's grin is vicious. "That makes you valuable."

"I will not be married off and forced to produce an heir." Bitterness seethes through me at what my father planned for me.

"That's not the only reason you're valuable." Eike clicks her tongue and shakes her head. "Haven't you figured it out?"

I'm smart. I have figured it out, but if I don't speak it, it might not be true.

"I'm as valuable dead or gone." My voice is monotone. "With no other heirs, when my father dies, someone else could take over Ryutoa."

"I don't envy you, Princess." Eike unties the wrap around her head and shakes out her hair. "I'm not sure of the reason we were hired to kidnap you, but you can be assured we're to deliver you alive."

"You're doing this without Ido?" I lift my eyebrows, my eyes on Eike's hair. It's a color I haven't seen before, an unusual mix of black and blonde making her hair look like the sand on a beach.

"He's not around and there's a contract to fulfill."

"What if Ido returns and finds out what you're doing?" Ido doesn't seem like one who would let a job go undone, nor one who would let someone else take the money for a job he was supposed to complete.

"We don't know if Ido is alive or dead," Eike says. "If he hasn't come to find you, then it's likely he won't. The boys and I agreed to finish the job."

"Then I'll make a deal with you." I cross my arms over my chest.

"You want to make a deal with me?" Eike makes a scoffing noise. "Are you going to pay me?"

"I'll make a deal to get you out of here," I reply.

"Ha!" Eike's single laugh is sharp. "We'll be out of here before you can blink and you'll be coming with us."

"I will not be going with you," I say. "Not willingly and not as your captive."

"What happens when the royals here find out they've been unknowingly housing the princess of Ryutoa?" Eike leans forward and puts her elbows on her knees to stare at me. "What happens when they find out you have your memory?"

"Nothing," I say. "Because they won't find out."

Eike clicks her tongue and starts to examine her nails. "Too bad I know."

"I know something about you too." I grip an iron bar with my bare hand. "I'll keep your secret if you keep mine."

Eike's eyes jerk up from her fingers to me. In the dim light of the lanterns hanging on the wall outside her cell I see an edge of fear written in the slight lines of her face. "What do you know?"

"You're royal," I say.

"You can't know that." Eike's hands carve through the wavy hair that lies to her shoulders.

I recall the bits and pieces Eike told me about her life. "You weren't kidnapped, but I'm guessing you ran away. Princess."

Eike's eyes widen at my last enunciated word. "It's not possible," she whispers.

"I know you're royal." I press my lips together and nod my chin quickly.

"You have no proof." Eike's eyes narrow.

"I have proof," I say, "and the royals of Swendale will believe me. I wonder what the payment is for the return to your kingdom. Will your fellow kidnappers turn you in if they can get a big reward?"

"How do you know that?" Eike hisses in a low tone.

I guessed the last part, but my risk is paying off. Eike is ready to break.

"Make a deal with me." I narrow my gaze at Eike and resemble my father when he's making deals. "I'll keep your secret, and you keep mine. I get you out of the dungeon and you run off to wherever you want without another thought of me or the job you were to do. If I ever see you again, or if I'm ever kidnapped again, even if it's not by you, word will get out about you."

"You have a deal." Eike's eyes drop. She's reluctant to agree, but she knows the information I hold is too valuable to risk getting out. "I need you to let me out."

CHAPTER FORTY-EIGHT

EMERIC

"I need you!"

I hear a female voice, and someone shakes my arm as I lie in bed. Sleep has been elusive and right as it comes, this person shakes me as if I'm cream that needs to be butter.

"Prince Emeric, wake up!"

"Please leave," I mumble to my midnight visitor. The only visitors I want in my bed are Max and -

"Please, Emeric!"

My eyes fly open as my brain registers the owner of the voice.

"Fia!" I sit up fast, blinking my eyes in the meager light of a candle next to my bed. I try to focus on the body standing next to me. "Are you alright? What's going on?"

"I need you."

Well, this is a strange turn of events. I pat the mattress next to me and plaster on one of my teasing smiles. "I'm here for you."

Fia grunts and punches me in the arm with her fist. "Get up. I made a deal with the people in the dungeon, and I need your help."

"You made a deal with them?" I blink again.

"Yes." Fia answers as if she's the royal in the castle and the one who makes the decisions. "You need to let them out."

"Wait." I shake my head trying to clear the remnants of sleep. My brain is not working fast. "You're letting them go?"

"Wasn't that the plan?" Fia pulls on my arm with a gloved hand, but I don't budge. "We know she's not a real royal and she's agreed to leave and never come back if we let her go now."

"You talked to her? Without me?" I run a hand through the mess of curls sitting on top of my head.

"I went to see her again. To see if I could remember anything." Fia bites her lower lip.

"And did you?"

"No, and she didn't give me much more information." Fia starts to twist her hair.

"Can't this wait until the morning?" I wonder where Max is if he isn't with me and Fia isn't in bed.

"No." Fia reaches out to tug on me again. "Let's take care of this now. They give me a bad feeling, and I want them gone. I owe you for this."

I throw off the blankets, more in a rush of bitterness than the usual feelings I have for Fia. "You should not use those words with me."

"This is a huge favor," Fia says. "You've already done so much for me and I'm asking one more thing. I owe you."

I grab a coat lying over a chair and quickly stuff my arms into it. "Never be in anyone's debt. It leads to problems."

My family's decree is a debt, and it led to problems. I owed a dragon a sacrifice and I failed. And I owe my life to Leo. There's no way I can repay him.

"You misunderstand me." Fia tries to keep up with me on her crutch as I head to the door. "I only mean-"

"And you don't understand me! No one does!" Even if Leo endured a quest like mine, our endings were different. Leo found his true love, and I'm alone. "You don't owe me. I know you don't want to owe me anything."

The girls who feel like they owe me something are only empty bits I've used to try and fill up my self-loathing shell.

"I-" Fia starts to speak but thinks better of it and clamps her mouth closed.

We head down the stairs before she speaks again.

"You're cranky if you don't get your beauty sleep," she says.

Whether it's a release from bitterness or an inappropriate response to the situation, a loud laugh leaves me. I should continue to be mad, but for some stupid reason, I can't stay mad at Fia. She's right. We need to get these uninvited guests out of the castle before my parents return. Whatever deal Fia made with them is better than any idea I would have.

"You're saying I'm normally a joy to be around?" I can't help trying to rile Fia up.

"I wouldn't say a joy." Fia snorts. "You don't sleep well most nights."

"How do you know that?" I pause at the bottom stair without warning and Fia runs into my back.

"Girl with broken leg," she huffs. "Stop getting in my way."

I turn and hold out an arm for Fia to grip. "How do you know I don't sleep well?"

"While others only notice your handsomeness, I see the bags under your eyes." Fia reluctantly takes my arm with the one not holding her crutch. "And I hear you in the halls."

"You hear me?" I must sound shocked, as if my most precious secret has been revealed and Fia picks up on it.

"Don't worry." Fia squeezes my arm with her hand. "I won't tell anyone. It'll be our secret, along with letting these prisoners out."

"You know..." I look down at Fia and lift my eyebrows. "There's intimacy in sharing secrets."

"Secrets are also a weapon." The end of Fia's crutch hits the ground with a loud sound. "It all depends on the person using them."

"What kind of person are you?" I should have a moment of hesitation. We still don't know much about Fia, and she could wield my secrets as a weapon, but something tells me she won't.

"It's to be determined," Fia replies. "I still don't know who I am."

But we know the woman and two men I let out of their cells are not royal. I give the guard on duty a break and a simple excuse as to why I'm releasing the prisoners. He asks no questions and happily takes a break.

"Normally, I'd have guards escort them out of the kingdom," I tell Fia as we walk to the cells.

"I guarantee they'll leave Swendale and never return," Fia says. "In exchange for their freedom, they'll never come back."

"It doesn't seem wise to release prisoners without guards or help." My mind runs through all the scenarios of every way this could go.

I could release the prisoners, and they remove hidden weapons from their boots and kill us. Or they could use surprise and force and overtake us. There are a million ways this could go bad.

"We have swords," Fia reminds me.

I would only enter the dungeon if Fia agreed we could arm ourselves.

"Like you're going to do much with a crutch in one hand and a sword in the other," I say.

"You've seen what I can do." Fia hides a smile as we near the end of the dungeon corridor.

"If I have to find myself at the end of anyone's sword, I'd only want it to be you." I turn and give Fia the charming smile she seems to both hate and like.

As expected, she curls her lips down and grunts. "I-"

"Or he'll find himself at the end of mine," comes a voice from not far away.

The endless tapping of iron boots on stone now hits my ears. Did I hear it when we first entered the dungeon or was I thinking too much about everything which could go wrong? I didn't factor in Morella, and she could add a decidedly evil mix to any trouble.

"There's someone in that cell?" Startled, Fia points to Morella's cell.

"The person responsible for putting our castle under siege not long ago." My jaw clenches. Fia doesn't need to know the entire saga.

"You were attacked?" Fia's right hand tightens on the sword in her hand.

"Ahh." The fake princess rises from a cot in her cell and steps to the bars separating us. "My saviors approach. Am I to be at the end of your swords or will you be at the end of mine?"

"There will be no need for violence," I say, on alert for anything which could happen. Morella's cell looks like it usually does, and the fake princess has her hands out in front of her. She doesn't appear ready to grasp for a hidden weapon, but I'll be ready. "We're letting you go, and you'll leave this kingdom immediately."

"And I was just getting acquainted with the lovely woman in the cell across from me. Oh, dear." The fake princess gives a dramatic sigh. "So many stories we have yet to tell, but alas, it's time to make another one."

"We have a deal," Fia interjects before I can question what this woman talked to Morella about.

"Maybe this isn't a good idea." I glance at Morella's cell. If the fake princess has been talking with Morella, we may have a problem.

"We have a deal." The fake princess grabs the bars with her hands and sticks her face between them. "We leave in the dead of night, never to bother your little Fia ever again."

"Please." Fia's face is a mix of want, need, and fear. "I want to stay here."

I can't deny Fia this, even if everything about letting this fake princess leave the dungeon seems wrong. I want Fia to stay. I need Fia to stay. I fear what will happen if Fia leaves.

"Prince Emeric," comes a saccharine voice from the secure cell. "I have a need to talk to you when you've finished your task."

"It can wait until the morning." I'm tired, though the nerves coursing through me will keep me from sleeping. As usual.

"No," Morella replies with a scoff. "This is a matter of life and death."

"Everything with you is." I exhale as Fia looks curiously at me. "I shall return when we're done here."

Perhaps Morella will reveal what she was talking to the fake princess about, or it will be another pointless conversation with pointed remarks and demands to be released.

CHAPTER FORTY-NINE

FIA

Eike is gone. The last I see of her, Rivo, and Keil are their backs blending into the dark night as they walk across the bridge over the moat.

Emeric is silent as we walk under the large iron gate, through the entrance to the castle courtyard, across the empty courtyard and into the quiet castle. I also don't speak. It's as if tonight drew a line in the sand, and we're on the same side. But I'm not sure what is on the other side.

"You should head back to bed." Emeric holds a door open for me into the main part of the castle.

"Okay." I use my crutch and carefully step through. Emeric can't see my stubborn face. "Thank you and good night."

I'm not letting Emeric off easy after what I heard in the dungeon. I'm not sure what the woman in the dungeon wants with Emeric, but I'm going to find out, especially since it seems I was mentioned.

I head toward the entrance to the private quarters and once out of view, I wait. I give Emeric a head start to the dungeon and then follow. Luck is with me when I discover the guard Emeric sent away is still gone. Luck doesn't seem to be on my side lately, and perhaps it's not a good thing I'm sneaking after Emeric and spying on his conversation with the prisoner.

A repeated tapping sound echoes softly in the dungeon. If I'm not careful, Emeric will be able to spot me in the faint light of the lanterns lighting the corridor between cells. I slide into the empty guard station, and strain to listen.

I can't hear every word, but I can manage to listen for any trouble and poke my head out to keep my eyes on Emeric.

"You have something of value in your castle," the woman prisoner says.

"If this is about your wand you already know you can't have it," I hear Emeric say over the incessant tapping.

Wand? I crinkle my nose. Is the woman in the cell a witch?

"Oh." The woman's cackle is loud and echoes. "I'm not talking about my wand. You have no idea what you have in your midst."

My eyes widen. She must be talking about me, especially if she overheard Eike and me. What if she gives me away?

"Meow."

Startled, in more than one way, I look down where Max rubs his side against my leg. The cat always shows up at the strangest of times. I hope Emeric didn't hear him.

"I want to talk to-"

I strain to listen, but I miss what Emeric says and the witch's response. What did she say?

"I'll see what I can do," I hear Emeric say.

"What if I were to make a deal with you?" The witch sounds like she's taunting Emeric. "You unlock my cell, and I leave."

"Never to return to Montagnia or Swendale again?" Emeric sounds suspicious.

"I can't promise that." The witch chuckles. "You can't keep me from my stepdaughter."

Stepdaughter? Who is the woman in the cell?

"...exactly what we're trying..." I hear only some of what Emeric says.

"...regret not making a deal..."

"...chance I'll..."

"...can't protect...you love..." I strain to hear, but I only catch some of the witch's words.

I press my back against the stone wall at the far recesses of the guard station. My leg throbs. I've been on it a lot today, and I need to elevate and rest it, but it's going to have to wait a little longer.

"We're done," I hear Emeric say.

"Poor Prince. I may be the one in a cell, but you're in a prison of a different kind. What would you give to be released from it? I can help." The witch's loud call follows Emeric down the hall. "You know I have the ability to help."

What does Emeric need help with?

I hold my breath and wonder what I'll do if Emeric spots me. But he's in such a hurry he rushes by without a look. After I hear him exit the dungeon, I make my way to the prisoner's cell and stand outside of it. Max lingers somewhere nearby in the shadows.

"Hello, dearie." The voice is smooth and confident sounding, nothing at all like I would expect from a witch. Even Sibylla, a seer and not a witch, had the ancient voice I would expect of one who uses magic and spells.

Humans do not have the magic of fairies. Humans can't wield magic when and where they want but instead have to be thoughtful and plan their spells and magic acts. Witches usually need something to help them direct their magic, such as a wand. While most witches tend to do good magic, there are evil witches.

I remain still and silent, though every breath I take sounds like a whistle of wind through a barren wasteland. The tapping sound coming from the cell starts to subside.

"I know you're out there," the witch says in a voice which lures me in.

"Are you a witch?" I ask.

"I am Queen Morella of Montagnia," she replies, and I furrow my brows.

"You're royal?" There's a way I can test it, but I'm not sure how I can touch her.

"I've had two kingdoms taken from me." Morella's voice drips with bitterness. "I'm sure you've been told lies about who is currently in charge of Montagnia and why I'm incarcerated here. I hope you're wise enough to draw your own conclusions."

"I don't have enough evidence to draw a conclusion," I say.

"I'll give you time, Princess." Morella sounds like one of my tutors waiting for me to finish an assignment, but I haven't been given the directions.

"I'm not a princess," I say.

"Don't bother lying to me." Morella laughs, but it's more a cackle, the noise I expect from a witch. "I heard you myself. And I want to make a deal."

"I'm not in a position to make deals with you."

"Oh, but you are." Morella's voice sounds sure. "I haven't shared your secret with the Swen's. If you want to remain unknown, you'll be kind enough to do one simple thing for me."

"Meow." Max rubs against my leg and purrs. It feels like he's encouraging me to listen to this woman. I glance down the corridor. It won't be long before a guard returns.

"You can tell my secrets," I say as my heart rate increases. "They'll come out eventually."

I won't let her use my secrets as a weapon against me, even though I'm not ready for them to come into the light yet.

"You'll make a trade with me." Morella's voice doesn't indicate she's disappointed with my answer. "I have something of yours. Open the panel."

I don't know why I obey without question, but I do. As if my hand isn't my own, it slides the panel open to reveal a small window. Through the opening something shiny appears. Held between two fingertips it glints in the meager light and with a drop of my stomach, I immediately know what it is.

"My ring!" I exclaim and try to reach for it.

Instantly, the ring disappears into the cell. "The lovely woman across the way gave it to me."

"It was not hers to give away," I say in a seething tone.

I should have taken the ring from Eike before she left here. It was an oversight on my part as I fought the fear seeing my kidnappers instilled in me.

"But now I have it," Morella says. "She gave it to me in return for a promise and I'll give it to you in return for a promise."

I press my lips together and watch Max as he continues to rub his side against me. I don't know what to do. I want my ring, but it's never a good idea to make a deal with a witch.

But Morella is in a secure cell.

"What do you want?" I ask, hating to think what Morella would do with a royal ring which isn't hers. The need to have my ring is strong.

"My wand," Morella replies. She keeps her face out of view. "Just as your ring was taken from you, my wand was taken from me."

"You want your wand?" I ask, doubtful it's even something I can do.

"Of course I want my wand." Morella scoffs. "It's important to me."

"Because you'll be able to use your magic?" What will I be unleashing if I return a witch her wand?

"There's no need to worry about me being able to perform magic if you return my wand. These iron boots prevent me from performing any magic. Ask your boyfriend, his family put me in the boots and in here."

"He's not my boyfriend." Something in me electrifies at the word.

Boyfriend.

"Ah." The clicking of a tongue sounds from behind the door. "You know who I'm talking about."

I grind my teeth together. I was too quick to respond about Emeric. "Why do you want your wand?"

"It has sentimental value to me." Now I hear a longing sigh. "It's all I have left from my family and our ancestral home."

"What does the wand look like?" My interest is increasing, and it may be mixed with a bit of compassion. I want my ring, and she wants her wand.

Max settles on his haunches and looks at the door, as if he's interested in this information too.

"It's beautiful. It's from the branch of a twisted juniper tree and the wood swirls in three places as it tapers up to the end. I carried the branch with me as a child. It was the only thing I could take with me when we were run out."

"Where was this?" I ask.

"It's better if you don't know," Morella replies leaving an air of mystery. "But I would appreciate the only bit of my history I have left."

"I'll need my ring first."

"I'm to trust a lying princess will get me my wand if I give her the ring first?" Morella mocks me with her tone, and I react.

"I promise!" I reply strongly as if I were talking to my father. "When I make a promise, I do it."

"Alright, alright." Morella switches to a placating tone. "I'll trust you. Perhaps we'll even become friends."

I'm about to retort when the tips of two fingers glide into view through the opening. They rest on the iron. Small, neatly filed and arched fingernails tip slender fingers and between those fingertips are my ring. Quickly I reach out to grab the ring and my fingertips touch Morella's skin.

There's a tingle. A faint one, but it's there. I jerk my hand back.

Morella is royal.

I heard she claimed to be a queen, but she's not only a royal through marriage, but a legitimate royal through blood. Does Emeric know?

"Meow." Max looks up at me with his eerie green eyes.

I stare at the cat and clutch the ring in my palm. What am I doing?

"We have a deal then." Morella's fingers disappear from the slot.

'It could take me some time to get information on your wand," I say with a glance down at Max. Is he understanding this conversation? He stands on four feet, his tail twitching in the air in agitation.

"All I have is time, dearie," Morella replies in the sickly-sweet voice I heard her use with Emeric. "Until one of us is gone."

CHAPTER FIFTY

EMERIC

"She's gone." Adette's face is drawn tight when she walks into the training arena for our daily lesson.

"Who?"

Mother's still gone with Father and not expected to return until tomorrow. The fake princess has left in the dark of night. Morella is safely locked away in her cell, with only her words and empty threats to taunt me. She claims she can give me all I want if I get her wand but threatened those I love if I don't.

"I couldn't find Fia."

"She can't be gone." The dagger in my hand clatters to the table. My stomach clenches at Morella's threat to harm someone I love. "She can't get far with a crutch."

"When did you last see her?" Adette looks at me with innocent round eyes, except she's probing me.

"Well..." I swallow hard and scuff a boot into the sawdust. I'm going to have to tell Adette at some point. "We let the fake princess leave last night."

Now Adette's eyes start to blaze with anger. "Why?"

I hate to bring Fia down with me, but I'm going to tie her to me. "Fia made a deal with them. We'd let them go if they never return."

"You let them go?" Adette shoves a hand on my chest. It doesn't move me much, but I can tell she's getting stronger, which gives me a small sense of pride. That pride is quickly wiped out by the anger on my sister's face. "And you didn't let me help?"

"It was late." I lift my hands up in a surrendering position. "Fia seemed in a hurry to do it."

"Where is Fia now?" Adette exaggeratedly looks around the training arena. The only other person here is the attendant who assists.

"I don't know," I answer honestly. "The last I saw her was when she was headed to her room after letting them go."

"What if they came back for her?" Adette reaches for a dagger and clenches the handle in her small hand. "What if they followed Fia and kidnapped her? What were you thinking?"

I warily eye Adette's hand on the dagger. It's as if she's stabbing me with it, though she hasn't made a movement. Adette has taken a liking to daggers and is getting proficient at throwing them. For her inefficiency with a sword, she wields a dagger like she does a drawing pen. Fluid, talented, and careful with the details. Adette is starting to hit the target as well as Fia. I don't want to get on either of their bad sides and make myself their target. When they're armed with daggers, they could be a secret weapon.

"I wasn't thinking," I stammer, a sudden jolt of fear hitting me at the thought I've made things far worse and put Fia in danger. "I was only trying to help Fia."

"How are you helping her by releasing the people she's scared of?" Adette demands.

"Oh, no," I whisper to myself. Pressure builds in my chest, squeezing me tight enough it hurts to breathe. I slump against the table. "What have I done?"

Morella could have planned this. She made a deal with the fake princess to come back for Fia. They're likely holding Fia hostage until I do what Morella wants. Until I give back her wand.

"I need to go." I shove my hands against the edge of the table to push myself away from it. My movements are unusually clumsy as I reach for a dagger and then stumble toward the door.

"Where are you going?" Adette calls after me.

"I need to check something." My mouth feels dry, and I rub my lips together. I need to get to the dungeon. "Stay here."

"I don't think so," Adette says, and I hear the thunk of a dagger in a target.

I look over my shoulder and see Adette has thrown the dagger. It landed just outside of the center.

"Lucky shot," I say. It's the closest she's come to the center.

"You'll let me come unless you want me using you for target practice." Adette storms up to my side. While I like to win, this is one fight I won't attempt. All I care about is finding out what happened to Fia.

"Are you feeling alright?" Adette grips my left forearm. "You're pale and clammy."

"I will be." I clench the dagger in my other hand. This will find its mark if Morella doesn't give me what I want.

"Em." Adette's voice gets a further note of worry as she clings to me, and we enter the dim hallway. "Where are you going?"

"I need to do something." I blink at the change from the bright training arena to the dim hall, and a shadowy form emerges ahead.

"Fia?" Adette questions the image limping toward us.

I blink my eyes repeatedly. It's her. It's Fia.

Fia is beaming. Her face is lit up like the sun rising in the morning after a much-needed rainstorm. She literally glows with joy as she ambles her way toward us.

"Where have you been?" The relief in me is palpable. If I was pale before, the blood is rushing back and filling every crevice. The thought something happened to Fia scared me, and now that she's before me – I never want to let her out of my sight again.

I can't help staring at Fia. She looks so happy. So filled with joy.

"I've been with the puppies." Fia can't stop smiling.

"What puppies?" Adette's eyes crinkle as she starts to soak in Fia's joy.

"Max led me to a dog in the stables. She must have come in from one of the fields and was about to have puppies."

"Max led you to a dog?"

"Come on." Fia reaches for my hand but stops short of grabbing it. "Why are you holding a dagger?"

"Oh." I lift the dagger. The weapon I imagined plunging into Morella when I thought she had something to do with Fia's disappearance. A slight shade of pink starts to blush my cheeks, and I tilt my chin to try to have my hair hide it. "Adette and I were training, and you weren't there. We were coming to look for you."

"Em was worried something happened to you." Adette lifts her eyebrows at me and tosses me a sly smile.

"I'm fine." Fia tilts her chin up at me and smiles. "I promise."

Fia may not be holding my hand with hers, but a similar warmth spreads across me as if she's touching me. She directed that smile at me, and now she looks away just as quick. A pink blush spreads across her cheeks.

"Puppies," I say, more to distract from this moment and having Adette witness it. "Are you going to show us?"

If Fia looks this happy talking about puppies, I can't wait to see how she looks holding one.

"Follow me," Fia excitedly says.

CHAPTER FIFTY-ONE

FIA

"You want me to follow you?" I hesitate in bed as Max's ears twitch. He stands next to the bed and turns his head toward the door.

I hear it too.

It's Emeric.

But he's not wandering the halls or standing outside my door this time. He's crying out. He sounds terrified and in pain, or as if something terrible is causing him pain. It wracks my heart with each piercing cry.

"Meow!" Max saunters over to the door and it looks as if a shadow stares back at me in the dark. "Meow?"

"You want me to come?" I ask the cat. "What am I supposed to do?"

"Meow," Max's voice answers in the dark.

I light the candle next to my bed and throw my legs over the side. As much as I'd like to stay in bed, my chest pinches in pain with each call of Emeric. My stupid traitorous heart can't stand to hear Emeric in pain and if I don't find out what's causing his terror, I might cry out in pain from the sheer clenching of my heart. I'm selfishly going to Emeric to only soothe my own ache.

Leaving the crutch behind, I carefully limp to the door and into the hall where Max waits for me.

"Why doesn't Adette wake up and do anything?" I ask as Max stealthily slips past her door.

I'm not as stealthy, and I wouldn't mind if Adette woke up and handled the situation. She knows her brother better than I do. I know Emeric wanders the halls at night, but I haven't heard him cry out like this.

Another cry sounds as my chest pinches again.

"I'm coming," I huff as Max twists his head to look back at me. "Girl with broken leg."

This is the farthest I've hobbled without my crutch, and while my leg can do it, it's not quite comfortable. I'm afraid to put too much weight on the leg I broke and cause more injury or pain. I'm nervous to try walking normally.

I clench my jaw at a quick pinch of pain. This one isn't because of my leg. It's because another cry comes from Emeric.

Max sits outside Emeric's door and I finally make my way there. I look down at the cat. "I don't know what to do."

Sometimes I wish I could understand animals as Max stares at me, his eyes an unnerving green in the candlelight.

"Do you want me to knock, open the door, or what?" I place a hand on the cool wood. "What if it's locked?"

Except, as if answering my question, the door creaks open under my touch.

"Emeric?" I call through the crack. "Are you alright?"

A groan, one filled with pain, is the answer I get. I push the door open wide enough to enter. The room is similar to Adette's. On my left side the embers of a fire glow a dark red in a fireplace. To my right side I can make out a four-poster bed and someone thrashing under the blankets.

"No! No! No!" Emeric lashes out in his sleep.

"Emeric." I push his door closed, not sure where Max is, and rush toward the bed. "Emeric."

"Don't! I need to save her!" A heart wrenching sob leaves Emeric.

I set the candlestick on the table next to the bed and wonder who he's trying to save. In the lowlight I can tell Emeric is perspiring. His hair is damp, and his face is slick. Every muscle is drawn tight in his face, neck, and shoulders. My eyes dip to his bare chest which is exposed. My eyes follow his muscular torso down to where the blankets lie over his waist.

"No!" Emeric yells, startling me.

I need to get him out of this night terror.

"Emeric." I try a soothing voice, not sure I should touch him. "Wake up. You're only dreaming."

"No!" he yells and turns on his side to face me, his eyes pinched tight.

"Emeric," I say again and sit down on the edge of the bed.

Whether it's the movement of the bed or Emeric hears me call his name, his eyes fly open. In a burst of movement, he reaches up and grabs me and pulls me down to the bed. I'm on my back, my feet still hanging over the side and

Emeric hovers over me, his damp hair hanging around his face and over mine.

"No. No. I need to keep you safe," he pants.

He's still dreaming and somehow, I'm now in his dream world.

"Emeric," I say gently, acutely aware of his naked torso over my chest. I'm only wearing a thin nightgown, not one I would wear at home, but it's what was given to me. I feel rather naked in it. "You're dreaming."

"Shh." Emeric places a hand over my mouth. He's not gentle, not rough, but wants me to know I'm supposed to stay quiet. "You can't let it hear you. It can smell me."

I can smell him. Fear, perspiration, the honeyed soap, it's all mingling in my nose as his hand stays on top of my mouth and his arm across my chest. Emeric brings his face close, the stubble of his cheek rubbing against my skin and sending a torrent of nerves electrifying throughout my body.

I don't want to feel things and I bite my lip, tasting my blood and the salt of Emeric's sweat.

"Emeric," I try to say as his hand still covers my mouth.

"I won't let anything happen to you." Emeric's words softly and sweetly melt into my ear.

It's as if my royal touch is consuming me from the inside out and I haven't even placed my hands on Emeric yet. But I need to. I don't have gloves on, but I need to touch him.

I grip his shoulders, feeling the tingle of the magic royal touch and so much more.

"Emeric." I squeeze his shoulders. "I'm safe. Nothing has happened to me. You're dreaming."

"No." The word softly leaves Emeric, and he removes his hand from my mouth. He still leans over me, looking at the hand he touched me with. He twists it and examines it as if it doesn't belong to him.

"You're dreaming." I now pull my legs up on the bed to get in a more comfortable position and try to adjust my nightgown, but Emeric is still leaning over me.

"Fia?" Emeric blinks. He looks at the candle on the table and then at me, his eyes wet with moisture. "You're here?"

"I'm here," I reply. "I heard you crying out. You were having a bad dream."

"It seemed so real." Emeric lets out a breath and his chest presses into mine.

"Maybe you should lie down and go back to bed." With my hands on Emeric's shoulder, I try to guide him off me to lie back on the bed.

"Fia." Instead, Emeric engulfs me in a hug and my arms fall to my sides as I lie on my back.

Like a startled rabbit, I freeze as Emeric holds me, but the longer he holds me, the more his breathing settles. As the rhythm of his heart and respiration decreases, so does mine. The pain in my chest dissipates and I find myself sinking into the feel of Emeric's hug.

I'm about to wrap my arms around Emeric when he suddenly sits up.

"Sorry." Emeric looks around wildly, more awake and alert, as if he's finally realizing where he is and what's happening. "I'm so sorry."

"Do you remember what you were dreaming about?" I push up on my elbows.

"I was dreaming?" Emeric shivers and pulls at a blanket but can't seem to find the end.

"You were having a nightmare and yelling." I grab the end of the blanket and pull it up toward Emeric.

"It was a dream?" Emeric sits, blinking his eyelids over glassy eyes. The low light of the embers creates a pale glow in the room. Shadows dance on Emeric's face, making him look as if he's from a dream.

"It was only a dream." I gently nudge Emeric down and pull the blanket over him. "You should go back to sleep."

I take one last look, one longing look, knowing I should go. I slide my body over to the side of the bed when a hand grasps my wrist.

"Please don't go," Emeric whispers. "I don't want to be alone."

"Max was with me," I say, glancing around the dark room. Max is a shadow, sometimes obviously following like a shadow on a sunny day and sometimes lurking in dark corners as when a shadow disappears with a cloud. "Max?"

"I want you to stay." Emeric is so quiet, I barely hear him. His eyes are once again closed, but there's some rigidness in his face. He isn't fully relaxed.

I should go. I can't stay. But Emeric's hand doesn't leave my wrist, and I settle back on the bed. His grip will lessen when he falls asleep. I'll stay until Emeric sleeps and then I can slip away. I don't sleep well, so I'll wait.

CHAPTER FIFTY-TWO

EMERIC

I slowly awaken, my eyes blinking in the bit of sunlight streaming through the slender window. My body is relaxed, and I haven't felt this calm in a long time. On my back, I inhale, fill my chest with air and slowly let it out.

Then I hear a dainty exhale which is not mine.

I turn my chin to my left and find Fia facing me. She's on her side and asleep, her cheek lying on my pillow, her curling eyelashes pressed together, her lips plump and smooth, her nose intaking air with the tiniest of a whistle. She's beautiful.

And she's in my bed.

My heart starts to thump in my chest as my mind spins, trying to remember the night. I thought Fia being here was a dream. I don't move; fearful I'll wake her.

She stayed. Fia stayed the night with me.

I'm nervous.

I never get nervous. No, that's a lie. I get nervous, but I never show it. I remember being nervous on Leo's eighteenth birthday, the day the iron gate of the castle was dedicated. As the prince and heir, I gave a speech, but inside I was dreading what was to come. I thought it was the deadline of my existence, and my heart raced as if it was making up for the beats it would no longer accomplish if I died.

And yet, my heart still beats. I'm still here. I'm nervous, but it's a different kind. Rather than the dread of a future I'm not promised, it's nervousness from what could be. What if this is how I could always sleep and always wake? I slept even better with Fia than I did with Max. But then something sharp pierces my toe under the blankets.

"Ow." I kick my foot and the movement jostles Fia awake.

"What?" Her eyes fly open, but she doesn't move. She seems to think if she stays still, I won't see her. She doesn't look at me.

"Sorry I woke you." I nudge my toe at the cat who is now batting at my feet under the blankets. He's a troublemaker. "Max bit me."

I act as if it's not a huge deal for Fia to be waking in my bed, when really - this is not something tiny or insignificant.

"I fell asleep," Fia mumbles.

"That's usually what happens in bed at night." I sit up and move over to give Fia some room, though I already miss the closeness to her. And the warmth of her near me.

"You were dreaming, and I came in," Fia says, still on her back. Her fists clutch the blankets, and she holds them at her neck.

"Thank you," I say, not quite ready to relive my night terror. "For helping me, and well, we should probably keep this to ourselves. My nightmares and you being here."

"Oh." Fia's eyes widen. "If your mother catches me in here, you'll be in so much trouble."

"Me?" I clasp a hand to my bare chest. "What about you? I'm more worried about Adette finding us together."

"Nothing happened!" Fia shoots up straight.

"I know." I chuckle at Fia's alarmed state. "But Adette's teasing will make you wish something happened to make it worth it."

"Really?" Fia huffs and slides off my bed. She straightens the nightgown she wears and crosses her arms over her chest. "I hope you slept well."

"I did, thank you." I pat the mattress. "Anytime you want to help me sleep, you're more than welcome."

I can't help myself. Even with Fia, I'm covering whatever I'm feeling with stupid remarks. But I do enjoy how they make her cheeks flush pink.

"Em?" There's a loud knock on my closed door. "You awake?"

The door starts to crack open and Fia's eyes widen in terror. I don't exactly want my sister catching her night-gown clad lady-in-waiting in my room, even though nothing happened between us.

Except something did.

"Don't open the door!" I yell.

"You don't have someone in there, do you?" Adette's voice has a ring of accusation to it. Fia's look at me matches Adette's voice and I shrug at her.

"No!" I scramble out of bed. "I'm changing. I'll be down to breakfast soon."

"You haven't seen Fia, have you?" Adette asks through the door.

"No." I rush past a stunned Fia and lean against the door to prevent Adette from coming in. "I just woke up."

"Any idea where she might be?" Adette asks.

I glance at Fia who barely shrugs, she's frozen in place.

"Maybe checking on the puppies," I say and grimace. It sounds like something Fia would do. Her being in my room is definitely out of character.

"Hurry up and get ready," Adette says. "There's a lot to do today. Mother and Father are returning, and it seems Lady Oria's party will be arriving this evening. The banquet is to be tomorrow, and we need to organize things."

"Give me a couple minutes," I say in a direct voice and wait until I hear Adette walk off.

I think Fia's been holding her breath the entire time because she lets out an audible whoosh of air from her lungs. "Thank you," she says in a breathy voice. "I don't want your sister to misunderstand anything or think any less of me."

"Because being seen with me isn't a good thing?" I'll admit the statement is like a dagger nicking my skin, but there's a ring of truth to it.

"You do have a reputation, I've been told." Fia looks down at the flimsy nightgown she wears and blows air out her cheeks. "But you were a gentleman and haven't shown me any less. I'll give you that. Thank you for, um, for..."

Fia gives a tiny flick with her wrist, as if to encompass everything between us which is unspoken.

"I'd say you owe me..." I brush my hair back from my face with a hand and lift my eyebrows. Fia's trying not to look at me, and I can't help but smirk. "But we're not doing the owing each other thing. Thank you for what you did last night. For pulling me out of a nightmare." I pull the door open and Adette isn't to be seen. "You're clear to go."

Fia limps toward me, and I notice she doesn't have her crutch.

"Shall I carry you?" I aim a sultry look at Fia, only because I want to break the awkwardness of this moment and see the cute quirk of her lips as she scoffs at me.

And she doesn't disappoint.

Fia's lips curl in disapproval, but they're trying to hide a grin. "I think you're still dreaming."

CHAPTER FIFTY-THREE

FIA

Last night must have been a dream. Did I really fall asleep next to Emeric in his bed?

For once I was lucky, and no one caught me doing the walk of shame leaving Emeric's room in the morning. Except, I'm not ashamed. He was having a night terror, and I helped him out of it. But what is Emeric so afraid of in his sleep?

I tighten the belt on the long overcoat I wear. It covers a blouse and loose trousers which hide my leg braces. This outfit is much more akin to what I would wear at home versus the dresses Adette has been giving me. I'm hiding in the toilet chamber after leaving Emeric's room. I don't want to leave yet, but the scent is getting to me.

I wrinkle my nose, but not because it's an awful stench. It's one with a reminder. Dried rosemary hangs from a hook to mask scents and there's a vase of sweet peas. The scent reminds me I have a true love. A true love who can never know he exists but keeps trying to crack open my heart as if he does know.

"I can do this," I whisper to myself. I can be strong and keep him out.

But the way Emeric softly smiles at me when I arrive at breakfast, hiding it behind a teacup he brings to his lips, taps at the shell I keep taut around my heart. He licks his lips as if we share a sweetly delicious secret.

If only he knew what secret I keep trapped within the depths of me.

"Good morning," I say as I take a seat next to Adette and act as if this is as normal as any morning I've had since arriving. "What tasks await us today?"

Adette stops slathering a biscuit with honey and gives me her wide-eyed curious look. "How are the puppies?"

Oh. That was the excuse where I was, but I don't want to lie.

"You should come check them with me later," I say and grab a biscuit from the basket on the table. Emeric keeps his lips hidden behind his teacup, because he's shielding a laugh. I can't look at him.

"Mother and Father return this afternoon," Adette says, "and we've received word Lady Oria and her party will arrive tonight. It's going to be a busy day."

Adette keeps rattling off the list of things to do today and I try to focus. I like plans and direction and executing things, but my biggest desire is to execute the feelings running rampant through me. They're getting out of control, and I like to be in control.

"Does that work for you, Fia?" Adette asks, jostling me from my inner world.

"Hmm? What was the last thing you said?"

"You'll help me escort Lady Oria to her room in the guest wing." Adette shoots me a knowing look. She wants me to use my magic touch on Lady Oria.

"Of course," I reply. "I'm looking forward to meeting her."

"Perhaps she'll recognize you," Adette says.

In another stroke of luck, I've never met Lady Oria or anyone from Montagnia or Verdelle. Even though Montagnia is the kingdom on Ryutoa's east border, we haven't had much contact with them. My father has kept Ryutoa a fiercely independent kingdom until lately, as he realizes the need for ties with other kingdoms. But he wants to control those ties and marrying me off to a merchant in another country is one way of handling it.

"We'll see," I say, "though her name brings no recognition to me."

"Are you remembering anything?" Emeric's eyes probe into me from across the table.

I remember last night.

"No." I shake my head. "Nothing yet."

I can't help remembering the previous night with Emeric as Adette and I escort Lady Oria to her quarters after her late arrival. Whether Emeric is avoiding me, or I'm avoiding him, we've had little contact today. With Lady Oria's arrival, I'll get to see Emeric interact with a visiting young woman, and I'm thankful for the attention it will take off me.

Lady Oria is beautiful, but not quite what I expect from someone with a title. Her infectious personality is one I could quickly tire of, but instead, I find myself smiling along with her. She's refined, yet rough around the edges. Polite, yet confident in her requests. In the short time Adette and I have escorted her into the castle, I've learned she is skilled with a bow and arrow, she's from Montagnia but has spent the past two years in Verdelle, and she aspires to run the duchy her father oversees. I quite admire a young woman being in charge.

Adette and I stand in the hallway outside a door to the room designated for Lady Oria. Her small traveling party of an older married couple has settled into a room next to her. A strap hangs over Oria's shoulder and holds a canvas bag at her side. The bag rustles with movement and then a large bleating sound comes from it.

Oria presses her lips together and clasps the top of the bag shut.

"What is in there?" Adette points at the bag as the sides of it press out. "It sounds like a baby lamb."

"It's my unfortunate sidekick I'm tasked with caring for." Oria gives a loud and very unladylike sigh as her shoulders slump. "He was supposed to remain quiet and still until we were in the room."

"What is it?" Adette's curious look returns.

I'm quite curious too, as it seems to be an animal of some sort.

"I don't want it to startle you, and I would leave him in the moat, but he insists on following me everywhere and would find his way here," Oria says.

Adette giggles. "Now I need to know what you have in the bag."

"I'll show you in the room."

Adette and I follow Oria into the room and I shut the door behind us. Whatever is in the bag doesn't need to escape this room.

"I don't want you to get the wrong impression," Oria says as she removes the bag from over her shoulder. She keeps a hand clasped over the top. "This is going to seem strange."

Adette and I stand on either side of Oria as she sets the bag on its side on the bed. She lifts the opening and out of it hops a large animal.

"It's a bullfrog!" I exclaim and lean closer to look at the amphibian.

He's large, and it would take both of my hands to hold him. Like a typical bullfrog, he has a bumpy olive-green body. He's quite bulky with an orange-colored throat, but there's something different about this bullfrog. I'm not quite sure what it is.

A deep guttural sound emerges from the frog's sizeable mouth.

"You have a pet frog!" Adette chuckles. "He's huge."

"Oh, he's not my pet." Oria eyes the frog on the bed. He seems to lift his eyes to her, and that's what's different about this bullfrog. His eyes. They're almost human like.

"He's not your pet?" I tilt my head to look at the massive amphibian.

"No. I'm only tasked with caring for him." Oria shakes her head at the frog. "He's rather annoying and I'm not fond of him at times, but he's persistent. He insists on coming with me and won't leave my side."

Adette now stares hard at me, encouraging me in the task Queen Adelinde has hired me to do, but I haven't found a way to touch Oria without it being unnatural.

"Does he let you hold him?" I ask.

"I only hold him when I have to move him where he can't easily get, like my bag," Oria replies, her eyes still on the frog who looks at her as if he's trying to speak to her through his eyes.

"Can I hold him?" I ask.

Oria's eyes flicker to me in surprise. "You want to hold him?"

"If you don't mind handing him over to me," I reply. "I've never seen a bullfrog quite this big, though I've read they can grow quite large."

Oria seems confused as to why I want to hold a large bullfrog, but she doesn't question me. Her slender hands pick the frog up from under his belly, and the frog doesn't protest. He's calm as Oria hands him over to me.

I don't get a good enough touch on Oria as she sets him in the palms of both of my hands. My magic touch is working, just not on Oria.

"If I didn't know bullfrogs could be this large, I would have thought he was an enchanted frog." I hold him out to Oria as a sign I'm done holding him.

Oria's shoulders drop, and she takes the frog from my hands. This time I'm able to touch her as she takes him. She is also royal, though the tingle is not strong.

"Thank you, Princess Adette and Lady Fia, for your hospitality," Oria says, signaling an end to our conversation. "I look forward to meeting with everyone tomorrow."

Adette immediately questions me when we get back to her room.

"And?"

"She's royal, or noble. There was a slight twinge when I touched her," I reply. "Not as strong as when I touch you, but it's there."

"Then it's confirmed." Adette decisively nods and starts to undo the braids in her hair.

"Here, let me help you." I limp my way over to Adette.

"No." Adette presses her hands on my shoulders. "You sit. I can undo my own hair. You've been on your feet long enough and you'll need to get your rest for tomorrow."

I sit on Adette's chaise as she unravels her braids.

"There's one more thing," I say, not sure how Adette will take this. It could be my magic touch is failing or something else. "When I touched the frog, I got the same tingle as when I touch a royal human."

"You're saying the frog is royal?" Adette's hands drop from her head.

"I think so, but it's hard to be sure," I say. "I didn't want to tell Oria because it would give away my magic touch. What do you think of the frog?"

"This is a surprise." Adette brings a hand to her open mouth. "He must be an enchanted royal. A fairy must have done it. The only way to break an enchantment is to fulfill the requirements or-"

"True love's kiss," I fill in with a heavy sigh.

If Emeric were enchanted into an animal, would I be willing to kiss him and change him back?

CHAPTER FIFTY-FOUR

EMERIC

"What do you think?" I ask the cat at my feet.

Max tilts his chin and looks into my eyes with his green ones. Sometimes I swear he's more human than cat.

"Meow." Max rubs his side against me.

I release a large sigh as I unlock the royal vault. I don't want to be down here, but I was asked to lock up something of value for Lady Oria while she is here. Whatever is in the small wooden box is heavy, and my guess is it contains gold, but it doesn't jingle like coins.

Everything in the vault is as I left it the last time. I tuck Lady Oria's box into a cabinet and lean back against it. While most of the secret tunnels are damp, cool, and musty, the vault is built for extra protection and is more pleasant to be in. All day I haven't been able to stop thinking about Fia.

It seemed natural to have her sleep in my bed. Her round face looked at peace as she slept soundly on my pillow. How I wanted to reach out and run my hand along the dip in her waist to the rise of her hips. I wanted to trace the bones of her face and run my fingers over her lips. I close my eyes imagining what it would feel like to have her lips press against mine.

But it's a dream.

Fia is no more interested in me than I am in Lady Oria.

"Meow." Max rubs his side against me again and my thoughts are drawn to what lies in the cabinet on the other side of the room.

Morella has offered me a deal. A deal which could protect all those I love. But Morella isn't trustworthy. I would have to make sure there's no way she can change, alter, or go back on a deal.

For the deal, I must bring her the wand.

I make my way over to the cabinet and pull out the drawer which contains the wand. It would be easier to seal the wand in the drawer and never visit Morella again.

I start to push the drawer back in when Max startles me by jumping in, like the last time we were here. But this time he picks up the wand in his mouth, jumps down to the floor, and scampers out the door I left open.

"Max!" I holler, quite stunned at the quick feat. He took the wand like a dog takes a stick.

This could mean huge trouble. A lump forms in my throat, my heart crashes into my stomach, and I run on adrenaline. I need to do damage control fast.

I hurriedly lock the vault and ask the guard at the dungeon if any cats entered. None have. The guard is baffled when I tell him to make sure no cats enter, but he gives a nod of agreement. I rush through the castle looking for either a traitorous or rather intelligent cat. When I can't find Max, I return to the royal quarters. Max has to turn up at some point.

And he does.

The black cat sits in the center of the hallway, right outside my room. His black tails swishes side to side against the floor in a mesmerizing arching motion.

"Where is it?" I rush up to the cat and he holds his position, not at all afraid of me. "Max!"

Adette's door opens, and she steps into the hallway.

"Are you feeling okay, Em?" Adette peers at my face.

I must have a sheen of perspiration covering me, and nerves run wild. I'm not sure if I should tell anyone about what happened with the wand. Who will believe a black cat stole a witch's wand? I need to find the wand on my own or hope it remains lost forever.

"I'm fine. Nothing a night of sleep can't fix," I reply, my eyes on Max. He continues to swish his tail back and forth. "I'll see you in the morning."

Adette heads toward the toilet chamber and Max follows me in my room. It's as if he can sense I'm not going to sleep well tonight and need him. He jumps up on the bed and starts to knead the mattress in his usual spot.

"Do you know what you did?" I ask the cat as I start to take off my waistcoat.

Max stops kneading for a moment to look at me. I take it as a reassuring look. It's as if the wand just vanished from the drawer on its own. It may never be seen again.

"I hoped you helped me rather than hurt me," I tell the cat.

Because if Max hadn't taken the wand, I was tempted to.

CHAPTER FIFTY-FIVE

FIA

"You're tempted to dance with me, aren't you?" Emeric extends a hand to me, and I disregard it.

I've only seen Emeric from afar today, but he looked out of sorts. I didn't hear him cry out in his sleep, but it's likely he didn't sleep well. He may be tired from the meetings with Lady Oria or the organization of the banquet and ball we now attend. Dinner is over and the floor has been cleared for dancing. I retreat to a far corner to rest my leg and watch from the sidelines. I prefer to hide during gatherings.

"I believe you are required to dance with Lady Oria." I lift my eyebrows at Emeric as I spot the castle visitor slowly making her way over to us.

"Has anyone told you how beautiful you look tonight?" Emeric gives me a dazzling smile, but I've strengthened the shield around my heart tonight. I won't let him break through.

"I'm sure you tell all the women that," I reply.

Adette was simply delighted I let her dress me for the evening. I wear a light blue ballgown with a corseted top which ties in the back. The skirt is overlayed with a silver sparkly material and the same fabric adds ruffles to the top of the dress and over my shoulders. While not something I would pick on my own, Adette knew it would suit me, and it does. She put my hair in a loose bun and topped it with a sparkly headband, leaving some tendrils hanging around my face. I currently twirl one of them in my gloved hand.

"Do I get the pleasure of dancing with you tonight?" Emeric keeps smiling.

I want to say something to wipe the smile off his face, but I also want it to stay.

"My leg is not quite ready for dancing." A quick glance at Queen Adelinde also shows she doesn't want me dancing with Emeric. There's a disapproving look on her face as she watches us talk and I'm going to need to get Emeric out on the dance floor with Lady Oria.

"I could support you," Emeric says, not giving up.

"Tonight is not the night," I say.

"Then you'll owe me a dance another time." Many women are eyeing Emeric, and they'll be shocked to know I'm denying him.

"I believe you told me to never owe anyone anything." I meet Emeric's gaze with my own pointed stare. I can throw his words back at him.

"True." Emeric nods. "Then when the opportunity to dance comes up another time, I hope you won't deny me."

"You're very sure of yourself." I force myself not to chuckle at his self-assuredness, which I know is mostly for show.

"You'll never find a better partner than me."

Now a lump forms in my throat. Fate seems to think the same thing, and I need to keep denying it. Luckily, an opportunity presents itself.

"Lady Oria." I call her as she approaches. "Prince Emeric would be most obliged if you would honor him with a dance."

"Of course." Lady Oria politely smiles, and I notice a hand protectively covering the bag hanging at her side.

"If you would like me to watch your possession, I'd be happy to." I point at Oria's bag, and she understands what I mean.

"That is most kind of you." Oria takes the strap off her shoulder and gently hands me what I know to be the bullfrog in a bag.

With one withering glance at me, Emeric leads Oria to the dance floor and I'm left blissfully alone in a corner. Except I have an enchanted frog with me. I set the bag on the table with the opening aimed at the dance floor. It's not long before the large mouth of the bullfrog pokes out and then his eyes emerge. He silently scans the room.

"She's dancing with Prince Emeric." I point to the handsome couple waltzing as if they've been dancing together their entire life.

The frog's eyes narrow. If I didn't know better, he's green with jealousy. Or he's just green.

"Are you under an enchantment?" I have nothing to lose by talking to a frog, even if he isn't an enchanted human. I'd rather talk to a frog than a human at a function.

The frog tilts his head my way and then nods.

"You understand me?" This isn't completely unexpected, but I'm still surprised when the frog nods.

"And you're royal?" I ask.

If a frog can look shocked, this one does. His eyes widen and he gives a small hop in surprise. The bag he's in moves up with his body and then settles again. The frog's head vigorously nods.

"Prince?" It's my best guess and the nodding frog confirms it.

"Enchantment?" I ask and the frog nods again.

"That's rough." I blow a stream of air out of pursed lips. "It's not easy being royal."

The frog pokes his mouth out and opens it a bit, a movement I can only surmise means one thing.

"You're looking for true love's kiss?" My hand starts to rapidly twirl the tendril of hair. Fate is laughing at me again. It's bringing up true love in the form of an enchanted frog. The frog continues to nod.

"Not to rain on your party," I say, "but I know you're not my true love."

"Who's your true love?" Adette lifts her ballgown skirt and drops into the chair next to me. How did I miss her approach in this dark corner?

"Um..." I need to cover this. "I was talking to the frog and he's looking for his true love. It's not me."

"Did you kiss him?" Adette is the only person who would not question why I'm talking to a large frog. While I don't want to tell her who my true love is, I can prove the frog isn't it.

"Watch." I lean over the table and plant a kiss on the top of the frog's head. His bumpy skin is a little tacky. He'll need to get in some water soon. I sit back up. "Nothing."

The frog blinks and then turns his gaze to Adette.

"Oh, no." She shakes her head. "I'm not kissing a frog."

"Not even an enchanted one?" I rub a finger over the frog's head. Poor guy. I wonder how long he's been a frog and how old he is. "You could be his true love."

"Ah." Adette squirms and makes a face. "I'm holding out for a different kind of true love."

"I understand," I say.

The frog and I return our attention to a certain couple on the dance floor. I'm holding out for neglecting my true love. The frog must be holding out to find his true love. It's a shame mine is right before me and I'm going to refuse him, and this enchanted prince next to me is stuck as a large bullfrog because he can't find his. Life is not fair.

CHAPTER FIFTY-SIX

EMERIC

Life is not fair.

Fia is kissing something, but not me. What is she pressing her lips to?

Oria is in my arms, waltzing with me, but her attention is also on the corner of the room.

"I'm going to ask a strange question," I say and Oria looks up at me. "What is in your bag that my sister's lady-in-waiting seems to have kissed?"

We both turn our heads back to the table where Fia sits with Adette.

"Oh, my." Oria presses her lips together. "My answer will be even stranger than your question."

"I've seen enough things in my life to nearly believe anything." I saw a cat steal the wand of a witch. I saw a water dragon try to kill me. I saw a fairy make a grand entrance on my birthday. I saw true love's kiss wake a man from the dead. I saw a young lady unconscious in a field with a broken leg.

"It's a bullfrog in my care," Oria replies as we make a turn. She keeps perfect time with my lead.

"Why would Lady Fia kiss a bullfrog in your bag?"

Oria presses her lips together as we move to the side. I sense there's much to this story, but I only want to know why Fia would kiss a frog.

"Perhaps the frog coaxed it out of her," Oria replies, as if someone kissing a bullfrog is an everyday occurrence. "Do you think your sister would kiss it?"

I'm jealous of a frog.

Green with envy.

I used to never have to coax a kiss from women, and while I'm no longer trying to coax a kiss from anyone, the one woman I want to kiss is more interested in kissing a frog.

"Why would a frog want a kiss?" I ask.

"Why does anyone want a kiss?" Oria replies holding her shoulders taut as I hold her arms out for the finish of the dance.

It's a question with many answers, none of which I'll speak. Kisses used to cover my pain, but now the lack of a kiss causes a heartache. But I'll gladly take heartache over covering pain.

Now that I know what is in the bag on the table, I see the frog's eyes watching Oria and me. If a frog's looks could kill, this one wants to throw a dagger at me. I gently lead Oria to where Fia sits with the frog and Adette.

"Did I spy you kissing a frog, Lady Fia?" I jut my chin towards her and smirk.

"Jealous?" Fia bats her eyelashes in a mocking way, but I see the blush rushing to her cheeks. She was hoping no one witnessed the kiss, except for Adette. "I'll kiss animals. Puppies, kittens, this frog, Max."

If only I were an animal.

"Did you kiss the frog, Princess Adette?" Oria inquires.

"No!" Adette shakes her head and shivers in disgust.

The frog looks up at Oria with its bronze eyes. Its mouth opens and a low, throaty croak emerges.

Oria gently tucks the frog into the bag and places it over her shoulder. "If you'll excuse me, I should retire for the evening as we're going to get an early start. I thank you very much for your hospitality and meeting with me."

"It's been a pleasure," I say, giving the back of Lady Oria's hand a kiss as I peek at Fia. She averts her eyes. "I'll have your box returned to you as you leave."

"Would you kiss a frog if it was an enchanted princess?" Adette asks me once Oria has left the banquet hall.

"Why would I be kissing an enchanted frog?" I ask.

"Because it's your true love," Adette says, "and you need to transform her to a human with a kiss."

I cough. Adette loves fairytales and fantasies, but this is far-fetched.

"If I had a true love, I doubt she's a frog." My eyes dart to Fia, who avoids eye contact. "What would a princess have to do to get herself enchanted into a frog? Could that even happen?"

"Strange things happen all the time," Adette replies. "But I can't imagine anyone wanting to be a frog."

"I might want to be," Fia says. "Sometimes animals are better than people."

"You would let yourself be enchanted?" Adette's lips turn down at her lady-in-waiting.

"No," Fia replies. "I wouldn't resort to magic or an enchantment to become a frog. There's always a price to pay for using magic."

"I would volunteer to kiss you if you were enchanted." I pucker my lips, making it seem like this is a joke.

"Good thing I'm not enchanted," Fia says, with a small quirk to her lips. "Your kiss is more likely to turn a princess into a frog."

"Good thing you're not a princess," I retort. "My kiss might do something else to you."

Fia looks like a princess tonight, especially with the pink blush blooming across her cheeks. Fia is a beautiful young woman and wears a beautiful gown, but she has a way about her which makes her seem more like a princess than some other royals I've met. Fia is stubborn, yet warmhearted and generous. She's a little bit defiant, yet kind. She's brave and quite skilled at many things, yet willing to learn.

"Seeing you two are the prince and princess." Fia gives Adette and me each a pointed look. "You'd better attend to your guests and your royal duties. You have spent far too long in this corner with me, and you don't want your mother coming over here to scold you."

"She's right," Adette says. "Mother is already giving us that look."

"Care to dance?" I hold a hand to Adette with a withering glance at Fia as I lead my sister away. There's really only one young lady I'd like to be dancing with.

CHAPTER FIFTY-SEVEN

FIA

"You have molded into castle life quite easily," Queen Adelinde says to me at breakfast a couple mornings after Oria and her party leave. "It leads me to believe you're quite familiar with it."

I swallow hard and the biscuit I chew lands like a rock in my stomach. I can't have the Swen's figuring out who I really am. "If I have molded easily, it's because everyone has been so welcoming and made things easy for me," I say.

"You have no memory yet?" Queen Adelinde lifts her teacup to her lips, but peers at me over it.

I quite admire her, but her scrutiny and earlier warning about Emeric makes me nervous. I don't want to disappoint her.

"No, Your Majesty," I reply.

"And there has been no news of anyone looking for you?" Queen Adelinde asks.

Adette, Emeric, and I are busy with our breakfast and avoid looking at each other. Somehow the release of Eike,

Rivo, and Keil has drifted away like dust in the breeze. Not even the few guards who witnessed it have spoken up.

"No news," Adette replies.

"If you feel the need for us to send messages out to farther reaches of Swendale or to other kingdoms, please be sure to let one of us know," Queen Adelinde tells me.

"I'm quite content at the moment, thank you," I reply, "but if any memory comes to me, I will let you know."

Queen Adelinde nods at me and turns to her children. "Adette and Emeric, I have need of you both to come to my office with me when we're done here. We have some matters to discuss. Fia, you may have the morning off to do as you please."

I know when I'm being excused and I quickly finish my breakfast, curious about the meeting the queen is having with her children. With the way she kept eyeing me, I'm slightly paranoid. I might be a topic of discussion, but I'm sure I'm not that important.

It's bittersweet seeing the Swen's together. While Fynn and I are close, or were close since we are no longer together, the relationship with our parents isn't what the Swen's have. While my family dined together and attended functions, everything was left at the surface level. Nothing was done out of love, though I now know my mother did things out of love when she was able to. There is an undercurrent of love in everything the Swen's do for each other, which they let me see and partake in. It will be hard to leave them when I set off to find Fynn.

I decide to spend my time away from Adette and duties in the private royal garden to read. It's a lovely day to be in the walled garden with a book and I find a chair in a hidden corner under a tree to enjoy the sun, breeze, and scent of flowers. I find myself fascinated with the large bees gathering pollen from nearby lavender. I know female bees do all the work in the hive, and these worker bees are infertile. Only the queen is responsible for laying eggs and regulating a bee colony's activities. Without a queen bee, the colony could collapse. My father wouldn't agree with how a beehive is run, but he could learn a thing or two from it. Without females, bloodlines will collapse and falter, except in the case of my family, I will never get to be queen.

A large bee drinks nectar from a lavender blossom and then moves to another one, its pollen baskets laden with pollen. I'm so immersed in the sights, scents, and sounds of the garden I miss someone else entering.

"When were you going to tell me the truth?"

"The truth?" I repeat. The words nearly get stuck in my throat as I tilt my chin up to Emeric. His face displays no emotions. No smile, no frown, not even a press of his lips.

"I know the truth about you," Emeric says, and now slight lines form between his eyes. "Were you ever going to tell me?"

"I..." I swallow hard, not sure what to tell Emeric. Worry and regret start to swell in the center of my belly. I've only kept secrets to protect myself and to protect this family who has opened their castle to me. Deflection is the only way around and I let my eyes meet Emeric's. "Are you ever going to tell me what causes your nightmares?"

"They're of a dragon I had to face. One which I couldn't conquer, but it nearly conquered me," Emeric replies in a flat voice. "It invades my dreams every night reminding me of what I couldn't do and how close I came to dying. How close everyone in my family came to dying because of me. You're now the only one who knows, but perhaps I should tell my family."

"Oh." I swallow another lump. I didn't expect Emeric to tell me and neither did I expect that answer. I look down at my hands and tug on one of the gloves sitting in my lap. What did Emeric go through? "Thank you for telling me." Is it my turn to lay myself bare before him in a quick and efficient manner?

"I know you have a magical ability to determine who is royal," Emeric says. "Adette and my mother told me."

"Oh." A relieved breath exits my lungs.

Emeric doesn't know I don't have amnesia. He doesn't know I'm a princess. He doesn't know he's my true love.

"Were you going to tell me?" Emeric exhales, seeming relieved to switch the subject off him.

"I couldn't," I reply, tugging on the second glove. "It's not only my secret, and I didn't want to betray your sister or mother's trust."

"They both know keeping secrets from family does not benefit anyone." Emeric's voice has a low grumble to it.

"Which is why they now told you," I say. "But it's a secret which could be dangerous if it gets out beyond your family."

"Because someone could kidnap you and try to use you for their benefit." Emeric's shoulders drop as if he understands my dilemma.

"I have no idea how long the magic touch will last. It could disappear at any time or stick around."

"Do you feel something when you touch me?" Emeric holds his hand out, palm up.

This is a very dangerous question, for I feel very strongly.

"I don't feel much with a glove." I lift a gloved hand and twist it at my wrist. "When I touched you without a glove I felt a tingle, indicating you're royal. I feel nothing when I touch someone who is not royal."

"You feel tingles when you touch me?" The corners of Emeric's lips start to rise. It's a smirk bordering on a smile.

"With you, your sister, your mother," I say, trying hard to not show any emotion. Touching Emeric gives me the tingles of the magic touch and feelings I'm trying to bury. I need to get out of this castle before they're unearthed.

"I need you to do something for me." Emeric pulls out a clipped stem of sweet pea flowers from behind his back and holds it out to me.

"Anything," I automatically respond as I look at the flowers he holds out to me. I quickly have to correct my response when Emeric starts to grin. I know what he'll say if I leave my one-word answer. "With certain stipulations."

"Do I get to suggest the stipulations or do you?" Emeric grins wide and twists the stem between his fingers.

"Let's start over." I try to pinch back a smile. "What do you need me to do?"

"I need your magic touch." Emeric leans forward and tucks the sprig of flowers into my hair behind my ear.

His touch is the one that is magic, because there is no way the smallest touch of someone's fingers should send such a pleasant sensation through my body.

"You're testing me?" I bite my lower lip and look at the hand Emeric has extended before me. We stand outside the double doors to the banquet hall.

"Yes." Emeric jiggles his hand before me. "Touch me to make sure your power is still working."

Power.

I hadn't thought of my magic touch as a power until Emeric said it. I have the power to declare someone royal or not, especially if their history is not known. This power could allow me to establish someone as royal and let them lead a kingdom. I can also declare someone not royal, as I did with Eike.

"Touch me," Emeric says one more time.

But for me, touching Emeric is different than touching anyone else. What he thinks is a simple task – one touch of my hand to his – is not so simple when my heart is trying to cry out from the box I've locked it in.

I tug the glove off my right hand and gently place my fingertips into Emeric's warm palm. A heated, tingling sensation spirals through my palm. But instead of residing there as the magic royal touch does, this sensation travels up my arm straight to my heart. I jerk my hand away from Emeric's.

"It still works," I say, releasing the breath I hold.

"I have four people you will touch and let me know if they're royal or not," Emeric says.

"They won't suspect anything or think this is strange if an unknown person is touching them?" I ask.

"Not if it's for me," Emeric answers and pushes open the door. "Just give a slight nod of your head if you sense they're royal."

I glance around the room quickly as we walk in. Four chairs are lined up and I see the backs of heads.

"Where are Adette and your mother?" I ask, sure they would be here.

"I didn't want any bias in this test," Emeric replies. "I can't have you nodding to them or exchanging looks."

This is the strangest test I've ever been presented with, and I'm not sure what it takes to pass or fail. Perhaps the people I'm touching are also being tested, and my answer determines if they pass.

Before me are four young people, two men and two women. There's nothing which makes them stand out, they look as if Emeric plucked them from the castle courtyard or from the nearby village. But I know one of them must be royal, if this is a test.

"This is Lady Fia, Adette's lady-in-waiting." Emeric introduces me to the young man with hair as dark as his, but much straighter. While Emeric is broad, this man is lanky.

"A pleasure to meet you, Lady Fia." The young man holds out his hand without giving his name. I shake his hand and the magic tingle is unmistakable. He is royal.

I give a slight nod to Emeric who stands next to me. With the tips of his fingers on the small of my back, Emeric gently guides me to take a step to the next person in line. The group of four are seated in chairs before us, as if on display.

"Lady Fia." A young woman smiles at me, her eyes bright as she reaches out to clasp my hand.

Nothing.

Her hand is warm, and slightly rough, but there's no tingle.

The second young man is next.

"Lady Fia." He gives me a small and curious smile, as if we're already acquainted. Like the woman before him, he takes my hand in his without a question.

Nothing.

He is also not royal.

One young woman remains, and I cannot guess if she's royal or not. My gut leans to not royal. Her black hair is jaggedly cut above her shoulders, and it's obvious she's been out in the sun as freckles dot the pale skin of her cheeks. It looks as if she spends more time outdoors than she does inside a castle.

"Lady Fia," the young woman says. "It's a pleasure to meet you."

We clasp hands and I inhale a breath.

Her hand is warm and slightly chaffed like the previous young woman, but there's a difference.

This young woman is royal. And something else. The tingle is strong, but different from Emeric or Adette.

I turn my head to Emeric and give him a quick nod along with a questioning look. Who is this young woman and what is different about her?

"Thank you," Emeric says to all of us.

As quickly as I'm ushered in by Emeric, he ushers me out.

"Who are they?" I ask after he closes the doors behind us.

"You'll find out soon enough," Emeric replies.

"The last girl." I shake my hand, as if the strange tingle she gave me still resides there. "There's something different about her."

"You sensed something different about her?" Emeric's eyebrows draw together, and I know I've hit on something.

"Who is she? Do I get to find out if I'm right or wrong?"

"I'm going to make you wait." Emeric's lips arch up into a smirk.

"I can wait." I narrow my eyes at Emeric as I try to stop my breaths from being shallow and rushed. I can wait. If anything, I can keep Emeric away forever.

"As long as you're waiting for me." Emeric arches his eyebrows, and I huff in response.

"Keep lying to yourself," I say. "But you'll only seek me when you need me."

Emeric's hand wraps around my arm in a gentle move, not a threatening one. He sidles up next to me, so close I can feel his breath on my ear. "You're the one who showed up in the middle of the night to help me when I wasn't seeking it. I may lie to myself and to other people, but you're the one who sees through me."

"Are we done? I have things to do." I'm desperate to get away. Desperate to shake these feelings off me before the box around my heart shatters like glass against the stone floor. Desperate to not see Emeric for who he really is. Someone I could love.

And I can't.

"For now." Emeric smirks again. "I can tell you're desperate to go check on the puppies and you do have the day off while I'm occupied with my family."

Chapter Fifty-Eight

EMERIC

Fia heads off, a slight limp in her step, while I return to the banquet hall.

"She was correct," my brother, Leo remarks. He stands and holds the hand of Eira, my former betrothed.

"She was." I nod. Fia correctly identified Leo and Eira as royal, and Jude and his bride-to-be, Amelie, as not royal.

Leo and Eira returned to the castle late last night, though no announcement has yet been made of their return to keep it from Morella. They were let in on Fia's secret, as were Jude and Amelie to assist in the test.

"She knows there's something different about Eira." I tilt my chin to the young woman whose blood may have the power to help alter my family's blood. But it won't be me she helps, it'll be Leo.

"But she doesn't know what," Eira says, confident her secret is still hidden.

The number of secrets contained in this castle could build or destroy whole kingdoms. The power or problems that lie in the blood of Eira, Leo, Adette, Fia, and me would make some people salivate with desire. But I only want to be rid of it.

"She didn't seem to recognize me," Jude adds.

"She was unconscious when you were with her," Amelie remarks. "But she seems sweet. We'll get to know her more when you start working for Emeric."

As if sensing potential conflict, Eira jumps right in.

"Amelie." Eira gently pulls the girl away from Jude. "You have wedding plans I can help you sort while the men sort their own things."

I'm not sure where Eira and Amelie head off to, but Jude and I follow Leo to his room. Jude tries to make small talk as we climb the stairs, but all I can think of is – what did Max do with the wand?

"You don't have any objections to me working for Emeric?" Jude asks as I close the door to Leo's room. He didn't wait long to bring it up.

Leo flops down on his bed and closes his eyes. "I love coming back to Swendale and not having to wear armor and beeswax."

Leo was a master at changing the subject when he would lose. I sense he thinks this is a fight for Jude, but I never intended it to be a fight.

"Jude already knows our secrets and isn't leaving Swendale." I start to lay out the facts as Jude and I stand at the end of Leo's bed. "He's-"

"You won't find anyone better than Jude." Leo's eyes pop open.

"I'm not trying to take him away from you." I look over at Jude as he stands with his hands clasped behind his back and his lips pressed flat.

"I'll always be your best friend," Jude tells Leo.

"Work together." Leo sits up. "It's fine. I should have been the one to suggest it, but-"

"But you didn't want him working for an arrogant guy who couldn't even take responsibility for his own family and kingdom," I interrupt. The bitterness in me starts to take on a sharp edge and it takes everything in me to tamp it back down.

Then I think of Fia. The smile on her face when she pets Max, the way she works through a broken leg and not having her memory, and the soft touch of her hand. She is stubborn and sweet at the same time.

"I'm sorry. For everything." It's the closest I've come to an apology, but I owe Leo so much more for the way I treated him and how harshly I trained him.

"At least I know Jude will quit or speak up if you're not treating him well," Leo says and then good naturedly slaps me on the arm when he stands. "Or he'll tell me and then I'll push you in the moat."

"I'd like to see you try." It sounds more like a joke than my past demands and threats.

"I think Fia would push him in the moat if she got the chance," Jude says.

"I think Emeric would like it." Leo grins at me. "What's going on between you two?"

"Nothing." I take a step back and shove my hands in the pockets of my trousers. "She's just a girl I found unconscious in a muddy sheep field and brought back to the castle."

"And Eira was just a girl I found unconscious on a mountain side and brought back to the castle," Leo parrots.

"At least Fia didn't walk into a castle under siege," Jude adds as my heart starts to tick up a notch.

What has Fia walked into? We have a witch in the dungeon and her wand is missing.

"Did you discover anything about Morella or her wand?" I can't help asking.

"Not much." Leo sadly shakes his head. "I'll tell you about it in the meeting with Father soon."

"What was your favorite place to visit?" I can turn the conversation to lighter things for the moment. There's going to be enough heavy stuff throughout the day, and I haven't decided if I need to break the news on the wand.

Leo's lips pucker. He sits on the edge of his bed and Jude joins him. "This is going to sound sappy, but anyplace I get to be with Eira is my favorite place. It could be standing in front of majestic mountains, drenched in rain on a dirt road, or even facing a dragon, and it's my favorite place if she's there."

My body flinches at the mention of a dragon.

"That's not sappy," Jude says. "That's the way it should be."

"It sounds...nice." I'm not sure what else to say. I've never been jealous of Leo, but what he has with Eira makes me envious. I'm glad I refused to marry Eira. Leo really does love her.

But it hurts.

It hurts to lose, even if it was something I was never going to win. Time is supposed to heal old wounds, but now something else is healing me.

I'm not ready to bear my soul to my brother. "Lots of things are different now," I say.

"Jude talked to me," Leo says, and I can't help but wonder how their conversation went. "I know you're different."

"This isn't about me." I slap Jude on his upper back and deflect. "This guy is getting married in a couple of days. We should be celebrating him."

"Next we'll celebrate Leo when he marries Eira." Jude's smile is wide. He's excited to marry Amelie.

"Then it will be Emeric's turn," Leo says. I can't tell if he's joking or serious.

"I don't think so." I frown. "I'm set on not marrying."

"If the right girl comes along, would you?" Jude asks. Both he and Leo look at me with interest.

"What kind of girl wants to marry a guy who doesn't want children, can't leave Swendale, and has a history he's not proud of?" I ask.

"The right girl for you," Leo replies.

CHAPTER FIFTY-NINE

FIA

Attending a wedding causes a surge of strange emotions. The examples of love and marriage I witnessed in Ryutoa only strengthened my desire to never marry, but it's different in Swendale. Even though Queen Adelinde is the head ruler, she rules in tandem with her husband. Both show each other adoration and don't shy from public displays of affection. Right now, they dance with smiles on their face at the wedding reception of Jude and Amelie.

I feel like an intruder in this special and intimate event, even though I was invited. The reception area is outside the nearest village in a grassy field. Dusk is approaching and lanterns and candles are being lit. The air is fragranced with the sweet scents of cut grass, sweet peas, and lavender. There's music and laughter, all kissed with a slight breeze. If I ever had a reception, not that I'm ever getting married, I would want it to be like this one.

As is my custom, I sit on the outskirts of the party, watching it all when there's a soft tap on my shoulder.

"I believe this is our chance to dance." Emeric glides around from behind me and holds out a hand.

I look at the palm of his hand in front of me. Lines are etched into it. When I visited the seer with my brother, she took our hands to help her see our dreams and paths. I jerked my hand away as soon as she saw my true love. But what if I had let her hold my hand longer? Would she have foreseen this path? And where does it lead from here? If the seer held Emeric's hand, what would she see?

"Do you intend to make me keep holding my hand out? Or should I get down on a knee?"

I realize I've been staring at Emeric's hand without answering him, and I finally look up to see him arching his eyebrows at me.

"Oh." I'm quite shaken, and my usual retorts are lost. "It might be more of a stand than a dance with my leg."

"I can't fix your leg, but I can help you to dance, or at least sway." Emeric throws me a grin, one I shouldn't let affect me, but it does.

My body is warm but grows even warmer as Emeric carefully assists me to where other couples are dancing to the tunes of the musicians.

"I can't," I say, my eyes on the coordinated movements of the couples as we stand on the edge.

"We don't have to do this dance." Emeric grins. "You only need to let me hold you as we sway to the music. That counts."

"Okay." I nod, more unsure than sure. But only because I'm not sure what it's going to feel like to be close to Emeric again. Each time I get close to him, something locks into place, and I can't get further attached. Being attached means pain when you're torn apart.

"May I put my hands around your waist to take some weight off your leg?" Emeric waits for my permission, and I nod. I will my body to not give anything away as Emeric's hands wrap around my waist. My hands find their way up to Emeric's neck.

I may not be swept up in Emeric's arms tonight, but it feels like it. My heart beats, my spirit soars, and my soul feels as if it's breathing while Emeric holds me in his arms.

I found my true love and I know with him I could touch the sky, if I only surrender to it.

But I can't.

I wasn't supposed to find my true love, and I need to find Fynn.

Emeric should have remained a mystery.

"I'm not sure what to do," I confess. I've danced my way through lessons and plenty of balls in Ryutoa, but always with a detached resistance. While I'm trying to resist my feelings right now, they're overwhelming me.

"Just follow my lead." The scruff of facial hair on Emeric's chin brushes my temple as he whispers to me. The cascade of tingles rushing through me crescendos with the tempo of the music, creating a symphony of incomparable proportions.

The intense feeling causes my body to shiver.

"Are you comfortable?" Emeric asks, sensing the tiny tremors of my body.

I tilt my chin to look at the man holding me in his arms. Emeric holds me tight enough it feels as if I'm floating. He has no idea if he keeps holding me like this, he could stop me from doing what I promised. As it is, it's going to be impossible to say goodbye, and I'm determined to leave without one.

"My leg is fine," I say. "It's the wedding. It's slightly uncomfortable and a little overwhelming."

It's the truth, even if part of it is concealed.

"Being confronted with true love is a little too much for you?" Emeric's lips tilt into a soft grin, as if he knows my secret.

But he can't.

How can he know he's my true love?

"True love doesn't exist," I say. "It's a legend. A myth."

I repeat the lie I once believed.

"You can't deny it when it's staring you right in the face." Emeric's dark eyes stare into mine, delving deeper than I've ever let anyone.

I normally resist eye contact, but I keep my eyes on Emeric, not breaking the bond with him.

"It's not-" I swallow hard and gulp for air. It's staring me in the face, and I need to deny it. I need to deny it with every being of my body, every sense, every cell, every feeling crying out. "True love is fiction."

"I've seen it." Emeric lifts his eyebrows in a way which says - try and deny me.

"Just because someone gets married doesn't mean it's true love."

"Jude and Amelie might not be the definition of true love, but you can't deny they're in love," Emeric says.

I can't deny it as I glance at the newlywed couple. Everyone can see they're in love as they gaze into each other's eyes during the dance. Amelie's face is lit brighter than a star in the night sky and Jude holds her as if she's the most treasured thing in all the kingdom.

Part of me aches because I want that, but at the same time I want to push it far, far away.

"They're in love," I agree, "but true love is different."

"True love is so powerful it can save a life." Emeric's eyes shift and I follow his gaze. It lands on his brother, Leo, dancing with Eira. "I was witness to it."

"What?" The word stutters out of me, part shock and part realization.

I need Emeric to deny true love. I need him to say he doesn't believe it. I need him to make this easier for me, but he's only making me feel.

And I don't want to feel.

"I saw true love." Emeric's voice is as soft as the breeze whispering over our skin with the night air. "Leo was hit with a witch's poisoned arrow. No one survives a poisoned arrow. He was bleeding and died, right there in Eira's arms."

Emeric must feel the hammering of my heart against his chest. Or maybe it's his heart beating wildly against mine. The vulnerability in Emeric's voice astonishes me. I know where this story is going, but I'm still anxious. What does it mean?

"She kissed him." Emeric presses his eyes shut. "I'll never forget the way Leo took a breath. The way he came back to life. It was true love's kiss."

"That is straight out of a fairytale." Leo and Eira have been busy with Jude and Amelie, and I haven't been able to talk to them.

"I'll never forget it." A deep sigh leaves Emeric, and I can't tell if it's one of pain or pleasure.

"Well, I've obviously forgotten everything," I say, trying to lighten the mood. "For all we know, I'm married."

I expect Emeric to chuckle, but tiny lines form between his eyes, as if it's a possibility he never thought of, and he doesn't like it.

"I doubt you are."

CHAPTER SIXTY

EMERIC

Fia can't be married.

She doesn't have a ring, and the only one who has come to claim her is a fake princess. The only husband worthy of Fia is one who would come to her rescue, and no one has.

"As much as I'd like for you to have your memory return…" I try to smirk at Fia to keep a joking attitude. "I don't think I want you remembering your wedding. There might be some jealousy."

"I remember weddings in general," Fia says. "Not mine. And I think you'd rather enjoy making someone jealous."

"I think you have it mixed up." My hands dip a little lower on Fia's waist as I readjust my hold on her. "I'd be jealous of your husband if you were married."

I don't miss how Fia's breath stills, and it gives me a soaring feeling of pleasure. She might only think I'm teasing her, and perhaps I am, but it's also something more. I like to take her breath away, even if she won't admit I'm doing it.

"I..." Fia sways a bit, as if something has tilted her off her axis. "Marriage would mean nothing for me. And you, as heir, you must be under pressure to marry and continue the line of Swen's."

The course of our conversation tonight, all during this one dance, has delved deeper than ever before. It's a beautiful night, and looking into Fia's eyes, I think my feelings about marriage are changing. If I confess my true feelings to Fia it'll scare her away.

My feelings scare me.

"I haven't planned on marrying," I say. "My family knows my wishes, even if they encourage me otherwise. But I don't have to marry."

"Interesting." Fia's fingers tickle the back of my neck, as if she's twirling my hair rather than her own. "I would think most royals are required or even forced to marry."

"I'm not most royals." I lift my eyebrows, trying to keep the mood light, but I feel Fia can see through my façade. "I want the right girl. The one who belongs in my arms."

"As heir, aren't you supposed to continue the line of Swen's?" Fia nervously clears her throat, and I find it an endearing measure. "Aren't you supposed to provide an heir with some eligible woman?"

I can't help but chuckle at Fia's cuteness.

"There are no rules which say I must marry and provide an heir."

"But you're royal," Fia insists. "Royals must continue the bloodline."

"This royal..." I tilt my chin down to Fia, "will never have children, which lessens the likelihood of certain women wanting to marry me."

There. I said it. To a woman. To the one whose opinion matters the most to me. To the one I could see myself marrying.

I told Fia I don't want children, but there's no reaction from her. At least not one I expected.

"I don't want children either," Fia says in a voice so quiet I almost miss it.

I can't believe she would utter a statement in agreement with me, especially one with underlying implications.

"I mean..." Fia's eyes widen as she suddenly realizes the implications of what she just said. "Just because I don't want children doesn't mean I want to marry someone who also doesn't want children. I don't want to get married. Ever."

"I know you're young," I say, not unsurprised at her quick turnaround. "We're both young. But it seems quite early for you to make such a decision. Why don't you want children?"

"Why don't you want children?" Fia throws the question back at me.

I wish I could tell her the truth. I wish I could say I don't want children because any male child of mine will be required to meet the decree. I won't have a child to put it through facing a dragon. I won't put a son through what I went through. I won't give him a death sentence. Nor will I have a girl who can be heir and pass on this decree.

And so, I tell a partial truth.

"I don't want children to have what's in my blood. I don't want them to be like me."

I expect Fia to ask what's in my blood, but she doesn't, she only replies to my initial question.

"That's why I don't want children," Fia says. "Because my family's blood is cursed."

It's as if time pauses for a second, letting the word "cursed" hang in the air and permeate me.

Is Fia's blood cursed?

While it's never been said my family's blood is cursed, it sure feels like it is.

"What kind of-"

"Emeric." A strong hand lands on my shoulder, and I twist my neck to find my father. "I need you. Right away."

Normally, I would make some excuse to finish a dance with a beautiful girl, but the look on Father's face tells me staying with Fia is not up for debate. Something has happened. Father's face is rigid and worry lines crease between his eyes.

"Excuse me," I tell a perplexed Fia, releasing her. I pivot quickly and fall in step next to Father. "What's wrong?"

"There's some pressing news," he replies. "I'll tell you back at the castle."

I look over my shoulder.

Fia remains where I left her, staring blankly after me. I twist my hand, which once was warm next to her body, but now cools quickly.

CHAPTER SIXTY-ONE

FIA

I watch Emeric and his father head off at a concerned pace. They're not rushing to alert anyone of danger, but they're also not walking away slowly as if nothing concerns them. There is unease behind their movements, and I can't help but worry.

From the opposite side of the dance area, I catch Queen Adelinde's eye. I dip my chin and slowly walk, trying not to limp, to a chair at a table. My quickened heartbeat slows, and my worry dissipates slightly.

Perhaps Prince Carmichael interrupted our dance to keep Emeric away from me. Perhaps there is nothing to be concerned about.

Queen Adelinde has warned me to keep my distance from Emeric, and tonight we were in full view of everyone. It's no wonder King Carmichael interrupted our dance. I'm only surprised he didn't interrupt sooner.

I never should have accepted the dance with Emeric. Yes, I owed him one, but not a dance where I nearly bared all my secrets and remarks which could identify me. It's becoming increasingly more difficult for me to not lay myself bare when I'm with Emeric, which is why I need to escape soon. I need to find Fynn. He's the only one who can help me now.

Sitting in the chair, I extend my left leg under the skirt of my dress. Liora has deemed I'm healing well and fast for a minor leg break. I should not have a problem leaving Swendale Castle, whether by foot or by horse. My only problem will be procuring the provisions I need for the long journey. This will entail obtaining some money or valuables I can sell along the way. I could part with my necklace if I need to, but I can't part with my royal ring I have hidden. It's the only thing linking me to my family and royal lineage.

"Where did Emeric go?" Adette ignores all rules of decorum and princess like behavior as she plops down with slumping posture into a chair next to me.

As it's a close friend's wedding and not a noble dignitary, I'm not going to suggest Adette act like a princess. I know how tiring it can get.

"I'm not sure," I reply. "Your father said he needed him right away."

"Curious." Adette looks in the direction her father and brother hurried off. "It makes me wonder."

"Wonder what?" Perhaps Adette can give me some clues to verify my hunch her father was only removing Emeric from my presence.

"I think something is happening at the castle," Adette says. "If Father and Emeric left in a hurry, it's not something little."

I glance in the direction of the castle. Spots of light shine through castle windows in the dark and lanterns light up the path to the entrance. The castle isn't far, but quite a distance for me to walk as my leg isn't back to full strength.

But...

But this might be the best time to leave with little notice. I need to return to the castle while everyone is occupied and find a way to set off on my journey.

"Perhaps-" Adette starts, but a handsome young man interrupts.

"Would you honor me with a dance, Princess Adette?" The young man looks so hopeful, as if it took him all night to work up the courage to ask her.

"But my lady-in-waiting-" Adette starts.

"Is headed back to the castle on her own because she's quite tired," I interrupt.

"It's too bad Emeric didn't take you with him." Adette gives me a sly look, as if she suspects I'm following her brother back to the castle.

"Go dance," I say. "I'll be quite fine on my own."

"Are you sure?" Adette widens her eyes, as if to say - you're not helping me here.

I'm not helping Adette. I'm helping the kind looking young man.

"It's one dance," I whisper to Adette. "You'll make his night. If he gets out of line, I know you have a dagger in your boot."

"Alright." Adette laughs and extends her hand out to the wide-eyed young man. Perhaps he heard the word dagger. "I'll dance with you."

"Have fun, Princess," I say.

Adette turns back to me. "You shouldn't walk far in the dark, especially with your leg. Can you ride a horse?"

"Yes." I nod.

Adette is always thoughtful. She'll be quite disappointed when she finds me missing later. It nearly breaks my heart to think how she's going to react.

"There are some horses tied up over there." Adette points to the opposite side of the field we're in. "Take one without packs, they're extras for those in the castle to ride back."

"Thank you." I push myself to stand as Adette heads to dance with her new partner. Luck is on my side.

The noise softens and the darkness envelopes me as I move further away from the party. Horses softly whinny and stomp on the ground as I approach where they're tied up. My mind is engrossed in detailing the plans of my escape. I could ride this saddled horse and leave the one I took from the bandits in the stables as a replacement. It shouldn't be hard to take a few food stores from the kitchen, and it wouldn't look unusual as Adette and I often get snacks from the kitchen. The only problem I might encounter is running into someone I know.

I reach out for the reins of a horse and my hand bumps into someone opposite me as they do the same.

"I'm taking this horse," the voice says.

My hand tingles, strongly, from where it touches the other person.

"Eike!" I stammer.

The woman next to me falters and steps back. She wears a cloak to conceal her figure and a hood to cover her face, but I know it's her.

"What are you doing back here?" I quickly gather my wits. Eike seems as surprised to see me as I am to see her. "You're not supposed to come back."

"I'm leaving," Eike says in a rush. "Give me the horse."

Before she realizes she can take another horse, I reach out and grab her wrist. It's covered with the cloak, and I'm protected from the tingling sensation by the cloth.

"Why did you come back?" I make my voice as threatening as I can. It would often scare Fynn's friends, but Eike already seems scared of something else.

"You don't know how long it's been. I couldn't refuse her deal. She said she would give me a potion to turn my brothers back if I helped her escape."

There are so many questions I could ask from that one sentence, but I narrow it to the most important one, even if I already suspect the answer.

"Who?"

"The witch, Morella." Eike's mesmerizing eyes peer out of the folds of her hood.

"She's out of her cell?" I look toward the castle. Is there more light coming from there than normal? "Does anyone know?"

"I'm sorry." Eike sounds repentant. "She wants you. You need to run."

"Me?" My hands drop from the reins and Eike now takes over being the clear headed one. She mounts the horse while I remain shocked.

"She knows who you are, Fia." Eike grips the reins. "You're in danger."

"Eike!" I yell after her, but she's already galloping away on the horse.

As fast as I can, I untie the next horse and manage to mount it with my good leg. Eike said to run, but I do the opposite. I head directly back to the castle.

The horse gallops over the bridge and I ride under the gate and through the entrance into the courtyard. This isn't good. If Emeric and his father knew Morella escaped, they would have shut the gate.

I pull the horse to a stop near an entrance into the castle when my name is called. It's either good fortune or rotten luck he found me right away.

"Fia!" Emeric clasps me around the waist and helps me to the ground. "Why are you back?"

"Morella!" I'm breathless. "Escape."

"It's a diversion! We've been tricked. It's not the garden." Emeric points at two guards standing behind him. "The dungeon! Now!"

Emeric starts to run after them.

"Emeric! No!" I shout. "She won't be there!"

He hears me and stops, his eyes confused when he turns back to me. "How do you know this?"

"I need to talk to you."

"I hate those words." Emeric runs his fingers through his hair in frustration. "Nothing good ever follows those words."

With furtive glances around, I tug Emeric into the castle.

"Someplace quiet," I say. "Where no one will hear us."

Emeric shoulder's drop and he sighs. This isn't an impossible task for him and I'm sure he knows every intimate corner in the castle. He leads me to one. It's a tiny room with linens and he pulls out a piece of wood to bar the door from being opened from the outside.

It's dark. Dark as a cave. Which might make it easier to tell Emeric everything and I won't have to see his expressions.

"Has Morella really escaped? Or was that a diversion to get me alone?" Emeric asks, but it's not his typical flirty voice. He sounds worn. And what I'm going to tell him will only amplify the feeling.

Or he might hate me.

Which isn't horrible, because it'll make it easier to leave after this.

"The girl who pretended to be Princess Fia from Ryutoa made a deal with the witch in the dungeon and came back to free her," I say.

"You said she wasn't going to return." Emeric sucks in a breath. "I need to tell my father."

"Just wait a minute, please. Let me explain."

"This can't wait." I hear Emeric move the board and I reach out to stop him.

"I'm the real Princess Fia from Ryutoa. I was kidnapped by the people who came here claiming to know me. I escaped during the storm, my horse fell and landed on me, and then you rescued me. I remember everything, everything except you rescuing me."

It's silent. If I didn't have a hand on Emeric, I would have thought he left.

"You're a princess?" Emeric's voice is faint. "A real princess? And your blood is cursed?"

"Yes," I admit. "My twin brother is heir to the throne, but he went missing, and I need to set out to find him. I need to leave to go look for him."

"Why didn't you tell me this sooner?"

"There's so much more, which is why I needed to keep this from you."

I hear Emeric slump against the door. "Tell me everything."

And I do.

Everything except for how he's my true love.

And how I've fallen for him.

I love him like I'm going to lose him.

Because I will lose him.

I need to lose him.

And he never needs to know what he lost.

"Wait." Emeric pauses my story when I get to the part about my deal with Eike. "We need to go to the dungeon. I need to see this for myself."

Emeric unbars the door and some light floods in.

"Morella found out who I was from Eike. After Eike left, I followed you down to the dungeon," I continue.

"You followed me?" Emeric runs a hand through his hair and walks out into the hall. He starts walking toward the dungeon and I once again follow, but he's faster than me.

"I'm sorry," I say loud. "I couldn't hear what you talked about, but I went to her cell after you left. She knew I was there. She wanted to make a deal with me. She would keep my secrets if I got her wand for her," I tell Emeric. "I swear I never gave it to her. I have no idea where it is."

"The wand!" Emeric slaps a palm against his forehead.

"Son, there's been an escape!" Prince Carmichael rushes toward us with guards flanking him.

"Let me explain to him," I say quickly.

"No." Emeric looks at me with sad eyes.

Then he reaches for me.

Chapter Sixty-Two

EMERIC

I wrap my hand around Fia's arm, not tight enough to alarm her, but secure enough I can grip her more if I need to.

"I really need to leave the castle. You're not safe with me around," Fia tells me. "Morella is after me."

"She'll kill you." It hits me like a ton of bricks. Morella will kill Fia to take her kingdom. Morella tried to kill Eira, and she'll do the same to Fia. "You're not safe."

"That's why I need to leave." A sheen of moisture covers Fia's eyes, and she blinks. "Will you help me?"

"Arrest her! Now!" A guard immediately obeys my instruction and grips Fia in a hold.

"Emeric!" Fia's voice cracks and her face drops.

"I'll explain later," I say with a hushed tone, but I'm not sure she hears me. I'm not sure she'll believe why I'm doing this.

"Emeric, what is the meaning of this?" Father steps forward.

"Morella escaped with Fia's help," I say. "She made a deal with Morella to get her wand."

"No." Fia adamantly shakes her head. The hurt across Fia's face guts me, but I need to do this.

"Check the vault," I say, knowing the wand is gone. "See if the wand is there."

"I didn't take the wand." Fia is outraged. "Why are you lying?"

The guard looks to Father for guidance.

"Do as Prince Emeric says." Father nods. "Take her to the dungeon until we sort this out."

"Emeric!" Fia yells. She thrashes and fights the guards, but they're well trained in dealing with unwilling prisoners. "You're not safe! You need to let me go."

But I can't let her go. I hate Fia has to go through this, but it's necessary. It's the only path I see for the moment.

"I'll check the vault," Father says with a withering glance at the furious Fia. "Do you want to join me?"

"I'll make sure Fia gets settled in a cell." I swallow a lump. "Bring me news of the wand when you have it."

"I was just in the dungeon. Morella had help getting out of her cell," Father says. "The guards were knocked out."

I clench my jaw and nod. "I'll question Fia."

"You need to let me out now!" Fia is blazing mad when I make it to her cell. She grips the bars and brandishes me with a stare I've never seen before. "Morella is after me. If she finds out I'm here, you'll all be in danger. Let me go and I'll run. She won't find me."

"She'll find you," I say, scared if I get close to the bars Fia will grab me through them. "She's a witch."

"Then let me go so I'm not near your family," Fia pleads. "I can be far away when she gets to me."

"I'm keeping you here to keep you safe," I tell her.

The enormity of how much I want to keep her safe is overwhelming. I'd rather die than see her taken by Morella, but I can't tell Fia that. She'd take offense.

"I need you to let me go to keep you safe," Fia counters. "Don't do this for some sort of ego boost. It's going to end badly."

"You're protected here. We took down Morella once, and we can do it again," I assure Fia, not entirely sure if we can, but I'll say anything to keep Fia here. "Why does she want you? She told me if she got free, I had better run as she would come after me."

"We're both in danger," Fia replies. "She thinks I'm the only Tanin alive who can produce an heir. If I'm gone and have no children, the throne is open."

A deep groan emerges from me. I wish I had known Fia earlier to protect her. "Your father was marrying you off to provide that heir, and if there's no one..." My chin drops. "Morella will seize it."

This is the opening Morella would need. She wouldn't even think twice about a kingdom she could easily take over. Just like Eira's family, Morella would kill Fia's mom and marry her dad, or do away with both of them and take over.

"That's why you need to let me go. She'll come for me."

"That's why I need to keep you here," I say again.

"Emeric!" Fia's knuckles turn white from gripping the bars. She doesn't have her gloves on. "Let me go."

"I can't," I say.

"I need to get out of here." Fia's hands slide down the bars as she slumps to the ground. She still wears the deep purple gown she wore to the wedding and reception. It bunches up around her. "I need to hide."

"Hide!" I exclaim. The word gives me an idea. "I know how to hide you from Morella. Jude has a magic cloak which hides the wearer from what hunts them. If Morella is hunting you, it'll hide you."

"How will it hide me if she knows I'm here?" Fia tilts her chin up, and her glassy eyes meet mine.

"I don't know." I shrug. "It's magic."

"I bet it doesn't work," Fia says. "There isn't much magic left in the Greater World."

"There's plenty," I say. "You're proof of it. You have a magic touch because you ate a magic pea."

Fia grunts and traces the outline of an embroidered sweet pea on the skirt of her dress. "Jude is at his wedding party. You shouldn't disturb him."

"Why are you resisting my help?" I wince. "Why are you always resisting everything I do?"

"Because you're not helping!" Fia's voice makes me step back from the bars. "I was never supposed to be here."

"But you are." I believe she's here for a reason, even if she doesn't believe it. There's a reason she was in the muddy field when I was passing by. "Maybe it's fate."

"Fate can be cruel." Fia's chin drops to her chest. "What kind of fate makes someone marry by eighteen or turn into a dragon?"

"That's not fate," I say. "That's a curse. And I'm sorry your family has a curse. Believe me when I say I understand."

If I had the choice between facing a dragon and dying at eighteen, or transforming into a dragon, I'd take the curse on Fia's family over the decree on mine.

"I need to find my brother." A tiny sob comes from the depths of Fia's chest. "Let me go."

She's breaking my heart, but I won't let her break.

"You're not safe yet," I remind her. "When it's safe, we'll let you out."

"You're not safe either." Fia quickly swipes at her cheek with the back of her hand to rid herself of a tear. "I need to go."

"You won't be going anywhere." My father's voice travels down the hall. His heavy footsteps approach. "The wand is gone."

He tells me what I already know. Fia didn't take the wand, but it's my only leverage to keep her locked up and safe.

"Looks like you'll be staying here," I say. "I'll see about getting you a cloak."

I turn and head off before Fia has a chance to say anything else, but I hear her yell my name.

"Emeric!"

It sounds like she hates me with everything in her.

But all I want is her love.

CHAPTER SIXTY-THREE

FIA

"Emeric." I say his name in the harshest voice I can muster. He's returned after leaving, and he does indeed carry a cloak in his arms.

"Fia." He clenches the cloak in his hands. It's as if he's waiting for a berating he knows will come. I'm nearly ready to give him one.

"You're lying to keep me locked in here," I hiss.

Emeric averts his gaze and doesn't look at me. "Here's the cloak I was telling you about. You should put it on."

"No." I defiantly stand in front of the bars between us and cross my arms over my chest. "If she's after you, you put it on."

Emeric's dark curls obscure his eyes, but he runs a hand through his curls and pushes them back off his forehead. His eyes are sunken in and dark circles ring them, more than usual. He's tired, worn.

"I once faced a dragon, the one from my nightmares, and I ran. I should have stayed and faced it for the ones I love, but I didn't. I won't make the same mistake again. I'll face whatever comes my way, even if it's a witch."

"Emeric." His name comes out in a sad breath.

I want to rage against him and hurl bitterness for what he's doing, but I can't ignore the fierce look in Emeric's eyes. Nor can I ignore the spark of compassion. I can tell Emeric hates having to lock me up.

"Please." Emeric holds the cloak out with a pleading look. "Take it."

"Fine." I grab at the cloak and yank it through the bars, and Emeric stumbles forward before he lets go of his end.

The cloak is wool, but the thick fibers are soft with age. I wrap the dark red dyed material around my body and it immediately warms me. I draw up the hood and it conceals my face.

"How do you know this will work?"

"It works," a female voice says. I look up to find Eira. "The cloak was once mine."

"What makes it magic?" I run my hand over a soft sleeve.

"What makes anything magic?" Eira places a hand on Emeric's forearm, as if she's trying to calm him. "The cloak hid me, and it will hide you."

"Who was it hiding you from?" I ask.

"From my stepmother. She threatened to kill me, and I ran away. I was gifted the cloak which I wore nonstop. I removed it four times, and each time she found me." Eira's brown eyes look golden as she looks at me. She's seen more in her life than most of the people in this castle.

"Your stepmother is-" I already know the answer.

"Morella."

I start to peel off the cloak. "Then you should be wearing it. She wants your kingdom too."

"No." Eira shakes her head. "You must wear it."

"The iron boots she was wearing are still here." Emeric's younger brother joins Eira and Emeric outside my cell. I haven't gotten to spend much time with Leo. "The fairy potion wore off. The good news is Morella shouldn't turn into a dragon."

"Wait." I grip the bars. "She was going to turn into a dragon."

"She drank a potion from a fairy," Eira starts, "and it would have turned her into a dragon except-"

"Dragons aren't allowed in Swendale," Leo finishes.

"You wouldn't like my family," I say, which causes Leo and Eira to look confused.

"Fia's family is cursed," Emeric fills in. "The males will turn into a dragon if they're not married by the time they turn eighteen."

"Fynn!" Leo and Eira exclaim at the same time.

My heart flutters inside my chest, like a hummingbird trying to get out of a basket.

"That's my brother!" I can't help smiling. "My twin brother. You know him?"

"We were with him before we came home," Leo replies. "In Somniara."

"He made it!" I don't even know where to start with asking questions, but I want their entire story.

"Tell me. Tell me everything!" I grip the bars and push my face through them. I need to know what happened to Fynn.

"I can't believe it," I say, after listening to Leo and Eira's tale. "He's alive."

"And no longer a dragon," Eira says.

"And he's on his way here," Leo says.

Then it dawns on all of us.

"You're not the only one in danger." Eira claps a hand to her mouth. "If Morella discovers Fynn is alive, she'll go after him."

"We need to draw her here," I say. "You need to use me as bait."

"No." Emeric shakes his head and presses his lips together.

"You're keeping me locked up here to keep me safe," I say. "You know she'll be back for me. You said you can handle her."

"I'll be the bait," Emeric says. "Morella said if she ever got free, I would need to run because she was going to finish what she started."

"Then we're all bait," Eira says. Her face shows determination more than fear.

"Emeric." Leo sets a hand on his brother's shoulder. "We need to talk with Mother and Father. We need to make some plans."

Before I know it, my visitors turn to leave.

"Wait!" I shout after them. "What about me?"

"You gave the witch her wand." Leo looks back. The light of a sconce on the wall makes his shadow dance as if he's an apparition. "You'll stay in the dungeon."

"But I didn't." I don't yell and I'm not sure Leo hears me.

It doesn't matter. Until Emeric tells the truth or I find a way to escape, I'm stuck here. The dungeon is always lit the same whether it's night or day, and I can't tell what time it is. But it must be late, because I'm weary and bone tired.

I wrap the cloak around me and lie on the cot. It can't hurt to close my eyes for a little bit.

Chapter Sixty-Four

EMERIC

My eyes fly open. I must have fallen asleep.

"Fia!"

"She's fine," Adette tells me. She stands in the door leading from her room to Fia's room smiling at me. "She's still locked up."

I'm in Fia's bed. I remember Mother saying we needed to adjourn for the night after a rushed family meeting. It reminded me of the night of my birthday and then Leo's when we met with my parents and they told us the truth of what it means to be a Swen male. We tried to make plans back then. Plans to make a date with death.

Last night we made plans to try to avoid death. Somehow, I made my way to Fia's bed, though I have no memory of it.

"I brought her breakfast in her cell and Eira's with her now. More guards than usual are assigned to her and we'll all take turns keeping her company, though she requested we don't send you. She's quite furious with you."

"Everyone can see that," I say.

"I told you she was a princess." Adette smirks. She secretly loves it when she can prove Leo and me wrong. I hate to admit it, but Adette is right a majority of the time.

"You did," I admit. "Do you believe she stole the wand and gave it to Morella?"

"Do know for sure Morella has the wand?" Adette asks and turns her head as a cat meows from somewhere in the room.

"Max!"

He's in the fireplace, which doesn't have a burning fire. I haven't seen a fire in it for quite some time. Max digs his front paws in a large pile of ash.

"What's he doing?" Adette leans over the cat to peer at the floor of the fireplace. "What do you have, boy?"

Adette reaches where Max paws and draws out an object. Her eyes widen as she grips it.

"Morella's wand!" Adette shakes her head in disbelief and keeps a death grip on the wand. "I can't believe she took it."

"Fia didn't take it." My shoulders sag. The wand was hidden in Fia's room the entire time. "Max took it, and he must have put it there."

"Emeric!" Adette shoves me hard enough I nearly fall over. "You lied."

"I had to." I try to take the wand from Adette, but she pulls her hand away. "Fia would be gone now if I didn't. She would have run away."

"Oh!" A knowing sound comes from Adette.

"You understand?" I stand back up. "That I had to lie to keep her safe?"

"I understand you love her." Adette points the wand at me.

"No." I hold my hands up, afraid Adette might be able to wield the wand. "You really shouldn't point that thing at me."

"You love her." Adette flicks the wand, as if she can use magic to get the truth out of me.

"Fia can't stand me," I say.

Adette waves the wand around like she's trying it out. "That's just a thing you two do. It's not real."

I always hoped so, but sometimes it sure feels real.

"Even if I love her," I start, but Adette's excitement doesn't let me finish.

"I knew it!" She grins widely and jumps up and down. "You love her!"

"But I don't deserve love," I finish. "And she deserves so much more."

"You're an idiot." Adette smacks me again. "A complete and stupid idiot."

"I'd like to keep that a secret," I say with a grimace.

"Love is not a secret, not something you should keep locked up in you," Adette says.

"You may be wise," I tell Adette, "but you've never been in love."

"I may have not experienced romantic love, but I know what love is," Adette says, taking a slight offense. "Our family is love. I've experienced and seen love. The way our parents try to protect us, the way Mother and Father love each other, even the way you and Leo set off to try and honor a decree which is impossible, all to save everyone else. I've seen true love's kiss, and I know if you don't tell someone you love them, you're letting them miss out on a great gift."

"Fia does not want to be loved. She doesn't want to marry or have kids," I tell my sister.

"That doesn't mean you can't tell her," Adette says. "Tell her you love her. She deserves to know."

"She deserves more," I say.

"That." Adette pokes me in the chest with a finger. "That is love. Tell her."

I bite back a grin. I do love Fia, a girl who probably won't love me back. A girl who deserves love and doesn't want it.

"First let's get a witch, and if I survive, I'll tell Fia I love her."

"You'll survive," Adette says. "I know how to throw a dagger."

Our blind optimism might kill us, but at least we'll be together.

"We have another wedding to attend," I say.

CHAPTER SIXTY-FIVE

FIA

There's a wedding while I sit helplessly in a dungeon cell. I have no part in the plan, other than to remain locked up while everyone draws Morella into their trap. Leo and Eira are having a fake wedding, knowing Morella won't be able to stay away.

I grip the iron bars, straining to listen for any noise. All I hear are the sounds of dripping water and the beating of my own torn heart. The stale air doesn't fill my lungs the way I need it to, but there's a fire raging inside of me. I can't sit here without action letting strangers protect me. Except they aren't strangers. They've become so much more to me, and I need to protect them.

I need to escape this cage and be free. Wander alone where no one can find me ever again. Perhaps my destiny is to move far away, forever having the image of Emeric behind my eyes. The image of him has faded as he fills my sights every day, but the image will return if I run.

If I run, I know he'll chase me. We're tethered, Emeric and me, even if he doesn't know it. I can keep pulling the string as tight as it goes, but he's always drawn back to me.

What will happen if I stop running and pulling the line? Is that why he's locked me in here?

"Hello?" I call out.

My only answer is a noise, a scuffling of feet on stone floors and a grunt.

"Meow."

Max saunters up and rubs his side against the iron bars. I reach my fingers through and rub his silky ears which starts a barrage of purring.

"What's going on, boy?" I ask the feline. "Are we going to get out of here?"

"Come, my lady." A female guard strides up, a key in her hand. "Prince Emeric has requested I escort you to safety before the prisoner is brought to the dungeon."

My chest seizes in tightness. "Did they catch her? Is everyone alright? Is Emeric okay?"

The guard lifts her eyes to me at Emeric's name and then resumes unlocking my cell. "There's no time for questions. You need to come with me quickly and he'll come for you."

I glance over my shoulder at the red cloak lying on the cot. It was removed to draw Morella in, but I no longer need it. The plan has worked as Emeric said it would. A fake wedding drew Morella in. She's been captured.

As quickly as my healing leg allows me, I follow after the silent guard.

"Where are we going?" I ask when she leads me to a horse waiting in a quiet part of the courtyard.

"Prince Emeric wants me to take you away from the castle." The guard helps lift me on a horse. She positions herself behind me and we ride out of the gate without hinderance.

The further we get from the castle, the more trepidation builds in me. Something doesn't feel right. I tug off a glove and place my fingertips on the bit of skin showing on the guard's wrist. I gasp.

She's royal.

"Don't do anything stupid, Princess." A dagger in the guard's left hand points at my throat while her right hand keeps guiding the horse.

I remain still as the point of the dagger points danger-ously close to the base of my neck. One wrong movement or jerk of the horse and I could impale myself on it. The blade catches the bit of sunshine streaming through the trees in the late afternoon. It seems my life is always at the end of a sharp object, and I won't let today be the one it ends on.

"What are you doing?" I demand. "Are you capturing me or rescuing me?"

"Haven't you figured out who I am?" An evil cackle sounds in my ear, chilling all the blood in me.

I may not know where I'm going, but I know who I'm with.

Morella.

I may never rule my kingdom, but I can save it. If a Tanin is to keep ruling Ryutoa and it takes a life, I'll be the silent hero. I do better in the background than I do in a crowd. And I'm not dead yet.

"You could have killed me in my cell," I say. "Why didn't you?"

"Oh, you foolish, foolish girl with simple thoughts." Morella adjusts the angle of the dagger and steers the horse toward a clump of trees. "Why take down one heir when I can take down the lot of you?"

"You won't succeed," I say.

She can't. Evil can't win, except the seer once told me everything must have a balance. If good has won before, is it time evil won?

"Love is a weapon. He'll come for you," Morella says.

"No." My breath stutters. "How do you know about my brother?"

"Oh." Morella chuckles in evil delight. "This is a delicious morsel. One more crumb I must take as I clear the buffet. But no, dearie, I wasn't talking about your brother, but the prince who loves you."

Emeric.

"No. He can't love me," I whisper hoarsely.

"Stubborn love." Morella sneers. "He'll come for you. I'm planning on it. One by one, everyone will come. And one by one I'll get rid of you all. I won't fail this time. The poison will find its mark."

My breath shudders at the sight of the dagger tip. It's covered in something thick with a dark green color, nearly black.

Witch's poison. The only thing which can counter witch's poison is – true love.

If the blade never touches me, true love doesn't need to be revealed. Morella hasn't made her mark on me yet, but with each passing second we move closer to her killing me. A second closer to her killing others, and I won't let that happen.

I escaped kidnapping once before and I can do it again. The horse slows as we enter the tightly bunched trees. The horse weaves through on a tight path, making it difficult for anyone to follow. And hard for anyone to give chase.

I need to distract Morella for a moment. Whether I appeal to her vanity or poke at her insecurities, I need only a few moments to grab onto a wild plan.

"There are more against you than with you." I keep my focus on a large branch ahead, hoping Morella keeps leading the horse in the direction of it.

"You can only count on yourself, dearie. It doesn't matter who is against you or for you, as long as they fall in line."

"If you haven't succeeded by now, you're going about this the wrong way," I say.

"Maybe I'm exactly where I want to be," Morella seethes into my ear.

I'm exactly where I need to be and with a quick motion, I push myself up and grab onto a low hanging branch. The horse keeps moving forward with Morella, but she's able to lash out with the dagger. The tip only manages to reach the tailing end of the long overcoat I wear. There's a tearing sound as the horse canters by and I cling to the branch. I drop to the ground with a grunt, careful to land only on my right leg. Then I dodge behind the tree.

I start to run with a limp, my leg crying out at the movements it hasn't done for some time. A glance over my shoulder shows Morella has dismounted the horse and follows me. She doesn't look like she's in a hurry and an evil smile clings to her face.

"You can run, dearie," she shouts after me. "But you'll always be chased."

That's what I'm counting on, except it seems Morella is too.

"Don't think for a moment I didn't plan this." Morella's eerie voice continues to follow me. "Why did the horse slow right before the low hanging branch? Why would I give you a means to escape? Why haven't I killed you yet?"

My breathing is heavy, and I push off the trunk of a tree to help me move forward. Am I taking the path Morella wants me to take? How do I change the course? She expects me to try and rescue myself while she also expects Emeric to come after me.

"Help!" This time I yell with abandon, not afraid to let someone rescue me.

My prince will come for me. My true love.

I only hope I'm not leading Emeric to the trap and death Morella has planned. But even if it plays out the way Morella wants it to, I can thwart her. Morella says love is a weapon, but she doesn't know the weapon I have.

True love.

CHAPTER SIXTY-SIX

EMERIC

"Fia!" I scream her name.

She's gone.

The iron bars of the cell door are open, and the only thing left is the red cloak. I pick it up and shake it as if I can make the woman I love materialize.

"It's not Morella we captured." Leo breathlessly runs up to me from further down the dungeon where the prisoner we thought Morella was placed. "She used a cloaking spell on someone to look like her."

"She has Fia." I toss the cloak at Leo. "I need to go after her."

I start to run before my brother can stop me. I ran from the dragon in the past, and this time I'm going to run towards it. I won't make the same mistake twice, even if it kills me this time.

"Emeric!" Leo's voice becomes an echo behind me. "Wait!"

I won't wait.

A lump in my throat builds as something in me pushes me beyond thought. Without knowing how it happens, I'm bent over a saddled horse sprinting out of the castle and over the bridge. My heart guides my hands, tugging the horse in a direction I'm sure Fia is. I don't know how I know where to go, I only know she left me an invisible trail, and I'll follow it.

"Fia." My breath is taken away as I focus on the woman I need to rescue. Rescuing her will rescue me. I need her next to me. She's the one who restores me, and even if it takes laying down my life to get her, I'll do it.

The horse gallops toward a stand of trees. Morella must have gone in, for I see no other path they could have taken.

"Fia!" I yell. I don't care who knows I'm chasing after her.

"Help!"

The cry is unmistakable. It's the same cry I heard in the muddy field, but this one is more piercing. More fearful. More heartfelt. It urges me forward.

I can't ride the horse fast through the thick trees and low hanging branches. I quickly dismount the horse and tie it to a tree.

"Fia!" I yell again as I break into a run.

"Emeric!"

The sound of Fia crying my name produces relief and worry at the same time. I push through some small locust trees, their sharp thorns reaching out and snagging on my waistcoat, leaving red scratches on my hands and wrists. Their sting is nothing compared to the sting of fear.

This fear propels me forward. It makes me chase rather than run away. I push out of the brambles into a narrow ravine. It's dry now, but water runs through it when it rains. One side of the ravine is hemmed in by craggy rocks, which reach a little beyond my height.

"Help!"

Fia's voice isn't far, and I run in the direction of it. I find her backed up against the rocks. She edges herself along it, trapped in place. Across the ravine from Fia is Morella.

Morella holds a dagger in her hand and hasn't yet spotted me. She stalks Fia like a predator stalks prey, slowly approaching a trapped and scared animal. I reach for my sword, but it's not there and I grit my teeth. It's back at the castle where I left it after I thought we had captured Morella. In my haste of discovering we were tricked, I left without it.

"Emeric!" Fia spots me and I clamp my jaw tight. There's no sneaking up on Morella now as the evil sorceress narrows her gaze on me.

Eira informed us she and her father believe Morella is a sorceress, rather than a witch, which makes sense with all the spells and evil she can unleash. Witches don't always aim to harm, and many attempt to perform magic to do good, though some turn bad. Sorceresses intentionally do magic to cause harm.

"Two birds with one dagger." Morella's lips twitch into an evil grin and she takes a sure step into the ravine and towards Fia.

I react with instinct and run.

I don't flee like I did with the water dragon. I rush toward Fia, my muscles burning and my lungs heaving.

"No!" I cry as Morella pulls back her hand with the dagger and Fia resolutely stares at her, not blinking or flinching as she awaits the thrust into her abdomen.

But the blade doesn't touch Fia.

Instead, a searing pain rips through my side and spreads out in a white hot blaze through my back, stomach, and chest.

"Emeric." Fia grips me as I slump forward, my chest to her chest. Her back slides against the rock wall as we lower to the ground. "Emeric."

I blink my eyes trying to focus. My cheek is pressed against Fia's chest, and she brushes hair out of my face with her hand. Something wet drops on my forehead.

"She wasn't supposed to stab you," Fia whispers. "It was supposed to be me. You were supposed to rescue me."

"I did." I can barely get the words out and I struggle for a breath. The pain is immense, more than I ever imagined possible. But the pain of leaving Fia is far greater than the pain of the wound, and I would choose to do it all over again. This pain is worth it. "I love you."

"Oh." I hear Morella's cackle as my eyes close. "This is a twist to our tale. Another Swen brother is taking the poison for the one he loves, but there won't be a happy ending this time. He was supposed to go second, but now you can."

"I'm in charge of my ending," Fia yells.

I feel someone grip the handle of the blade lodged in my side. It must be Fia. Then she pulls on it, and darkness overtakes me.

CHAPTER SIXTY-SEVEN

FIA

Blood seeps from the wound where I pull the dagger from Emeric. He wasn't supposed to take the blade. He stepped in between Morella and me as she was about to thrust the dagger into me. I was going to grab her second dagger as she was stabbing me.

Morella steps back to survey the scene, no longer within my reach. She isn't watching me as she reaches for the other dagger I saw sheathed at her side.

This is my only chance.

I sit on the ground with Emeric on top of me, and my position isn't the best with the rock behind me, but it's all I have.

"Please," I whisper as I contract my left arm and aim.

As if guided by magic or perhaps my hopes and wishes, the dagger slices a straight line through the air and digs into Morella's wrist right where her flesh shows. Whatever poison remains on the blade immediately sears into her and she cries out as the dagger falls to the ground. The dagger she holds in her hand drops and Morella cries out

397

again as the tip lodges in her boot. She rips the dagger out of her boot and throws it at me.

"You stupid girl! I don't have the antidote or my wand!"

The dagger bounces harmlessly near me, and I bend forward to retrieve it. Poison coats the blade, and I lift it as if to throw again. Morella ignores the blade I pulled from Emeric and threw at her. She starts to make a hasty retreat.

"Emeric." I grip his shoulders and use what strength I have to turn his upper body over. I run my hand across his forehead and the royal tingle runs through my hand and another energy surges through the rest of me. A tear drops from my eye to his cheek. "Why?"

"I took the blade for you," Emeric whispers, a faint smile on his face.

I want to cry and smile at the same time. "You really think you're the hero in this story?"

"Not a hero." Emeric's breathing is labored and it's hard to make out his words, but he keeps his eyes on me. "Only a man. In love with you."

A tear rolls down my cheek. He had to say it.

Love.

It's a weapon.

The poison makes its way through Emeric's body and his breathing slows to intermittent raspy breaths. He can't keep his eyes open and they flutter shut.

"Emeric." I sob, my chest heaving in bitter waves. It aches and I cry out; tears stream down my face like water rushing in a river. I clasp his face in the palms of my hands, and the tingling fades. "No!"

Love is a weapon, but true love is the strongest one. If Emeric has a chance of living, I need to wield it. I need to reveal my secret.

I bend over Emeric and press my lips to his. It's salty and sweet, and his lips stick to mine as I pull away from him.

"Emeric. Please," I whisper, and then I watch and wait.

I have no other weapons, no other magic, nothing else which can save this man. Only true love. I press my hand to Emeric's wound. True love can counteract the poison, but it can't counter the stab wound.

Suddenly, making my body shudder, Emeric inhales sharply and his eyes fly open.

"Emeric!" I keep a hand on his wound and press my other one to his cheek. The tingling sensation once again flows through my hand.

"Took you long enough to kiss me," Emeric says in a hoarse voice and coughs.

"Shh." I shush him. "Don't move."

Emeric's eyelids flutter and he relaxes into my hold. "You're my true love."

"Did you know?" I blink back at him. "Did you take the blade knowing my kiss could save you?"

"No." Emeric's head shakes against me. "I only had hope."

"That's a risky game to play." A strangled chuckle leaves my throat. "But just because you're my true love doesn't mean-"

"You love me," Emeric fills in. He takes a labored inhale, and I feel his pain in my bones. I tried to deny him, tried to deny what I feel, but it's impossible.

"I love you." It's only a whisper and I'm not sure if Emeric hears me. The words seem foreign to me, yet natural at the same time, but only with Emeric.

"I knew you wanted to kiss me." Emeric's lips flutter into a small smile and then he winces as he moves.

I keep my hand pressed to his wound. It looks as if the blade entered right near his hipbone. "You took a blade with witch's poison. I had to kiss you to save you."

"I could have gotten you to kiss me earlier, if I wanted you to." Emeric smirks, though it's not with his usual effort. He's weak.

"I recall you trying." I brush my thumb gently over his lips. "And I didn't kiss you."

"Will you kiss me again?" Emeric looks sleepy. "I wasn't fully aware for the first one."

"Emeric!" There's a shout not far away. "Fia!"

"Over here!" I shout, grateful for the distraction. "In the ravine."

"Are you going to kiss me?" Emeric asks again, the sweetest smile I've ever seen on his face.

I lift my eyes to see Leo pushing through the bramble, Eira right behind him.

"You're going to have to wait," I reply.

Emeric only continues to smile. "I'll wait forever for your kiss."

CHAPTER SIXTY-EIGHT

EMERIC

If she makes me wait for another kiss, I'll wait. I'll wait a lifetime for Fia.

"What happened?" Leo runs up.

"Morella stabbed him," Fia replies, her voice choked up.

"Where is she?" Leo plants his feet and reaches for the sword at his side. He looks around while I swell with pride at my brother. I trained him and he's using it. I wonder if the side effects of the poison are messing with my emotions.

"She's gone." I smack my lips. They feel dry.

"Emeric." Leo drops to his knees next to me.

"The blade was poisoned." Fia's voice still shakes. "Eira, careful! There's another blade on the incline of the ravine below us. There's witch's poison on it."

"Witch's poison!" Leo tears at the bottom of his shirt.

"Morella." I grunt in pain as Fia removes her hand from my wound and Leo presses the fabric to it. "Tried to kill."

"Shh." Fia shushes me and I clamp my lips together, but only because she's brushing her thumb over them and I

401

relish her touch. "Emeric pushed his way between Morella and me as she was about to stab me."

Eira holds the end of a dagger between her fingers, the blade pointing at the ground. "It's the same poison she used on you, Leo."

Leo's eyes widen as he looks at me and then draws his gaze up to Fia who holds me. "Witch's poison kills fast."

"This dagger has poison on it too." Fia holds out the other dagger and Eira takes it with a curious glance at both of us.

"How did Emeric survive?" Eira asks Fia.

"She saved me with-" I start and then cough.

"Be quiet," Fia scolds me. "Save your strength. We still need to get you back to Liora. You've been stabbed."

"Minor flesh wound." I close my eyes. I've never felt so weak, and yet, so strong.

"Did you kiss him?" Eira points a dagger at Fia. "Did you?"

"Um..." Fia looks at me and quirks her lips to the side. "I did."

"What are the chances?" Eira shakes her head in disbelief.

"You still can't let me have my moment." Leo shakes his head, but it's with a smile. "You have to go and take a dagger for your true love and then she saves you with a kiss."

"She's a dragon princess." I tilt my chin to get a better look at the woman who's my true love. Her eyes are swollen and red, she sniffs her runny nose, and dirt streaks her face. But she's the most beautiful woman I've ever seen.

"What did you call me?" Fia caresses my cheek with her hand.

"My dragon princess," I say. "You're as fierce as a dragon."

A small chuckle leaves Fia and my head bounces on her chest with the movement. "My brother is known as a dragon prince, but I've never been called a dragon princess."

"Your family is cursed." Leo keeps pressing the fabric of his shirt to my wound. The blood is starting to clot. "I know about your brother. Does the curse carry to you?"

"My male children will be cursed to turn into a dragon on their eighteenth birthday unless they marry," Fia replies.

"Wait!" Eira suddenly sounds excited. "If you and Emeric have children-"

"I don't want children," Fia and I say at the same time.

"Hear me out." Eira dangerously waves around the daggers in her hands. "Does Fia know your secret?"

"Ah, my love." Leo nods his chin at his bride-to-be. "Perhaps you should bury those poisoned daggers before you accidentally drop one on me and have to save me again."

"I won't drop them." Eira sets them on the ground. "Does she know?"

"Know what?" Fia asks and her eyes rove around the three of us.

"You can tell her. I trust her to keep it secret." I wince as I try to adjust my position. It's going to be painful getting back to the castle.

Leo quickly explains the decree to Fia and what eighteen-year-old Swen men are required to do.

"It can't be coincidence who our true loves are," Eira says, excitement in her voice. "I have dragon blood and Fia's blood carries a curse to turn into dragons, and our true loves must sacrifice to dragons. Leo and I may not have found a way to break the decree or change curses, but maybe it's right in front of us. Maybe we're the key to change."

"No." Fia shakes her head, and I understand. It's a little much to think of right now. "Our children...I mean...if Emeric and I..." Fia starts to blush like mad, and if it's possible, it makes me fall more madly in love with her.

"We'll talk about that later." I grunt.

"Right," Leo says. "We need to get you taken care of."

"True love." I sigh at Fia's touch. "Am I dreaming?"

"Emeric." Fia's tone is again scolding. "Can we keep that to ourselves for now?"

"If you don't want other girls chasing after me, you're going to have to let everyone know you hold my heart," I say.

Fia playfully swats at me as Leo laughs loudly.

"Pretty sure they'll still be chasing you even if you shout your love for Fia from the highest part of the castle," Leo says.

"Please don't do that," Fia says as her fingers tangle in my hair, twisting it around her finger.

"Fia knows how to use a dagger, she'll scare people away," I say. "She hit Morella with the poisoned tip."

"You did?" Eira looks down at the daggers on the ground and then at Fia. "What happened to Morella? Is she injured, dead, or coming back?"

"I don't know." Fia's finger twirls my hair. "She said she didn't have an antidote or wand and ran off."

"I feel a little lightheaded." I pinch my eyes tight. While I want to act strong and behave as if I haven't been stabbed, it hurts, and I don't feel good.

"We need to get Emeric back to the castle and send guards out," Eira says.

"So cold," I whisper. It's the cold of the breath of the water dragon. Like ice in my veins.

"You need to hang on," Leo says as I start to shiver. My brother puts his own waistcoat over me as Fia compresses my wound.

"Tired." My heart beats rapidly and my breathing becomes shallow.

"It might be quicker to bring Liora than move him," I hear Leo say.

"I'll get her," Eira says as my eyelids flutter.

"Need to save." There was a dragon attacking Fia. I didn't run away. I ran to her. "Dragon."

"He's sounding confused," Leo says, but I'm not confused. He is.

"It's you." I gaze at Fia, as if she's in a dream. There's a haze. "You're real. You're alive."

"He's lost too much blood," Leo says.

That's not true. Blood flows through me. My heart sings out. I have never felt more alive as my true love holds me.

"Emeric." Fia bends close and her hair drapes over my face, tickling the sensitive skin of my cheek. Her warm breath washes over me before her lips touch my clammy forehead. "Stay with me and I'll give you all the kisses you want when you're healed."

CHAPTER SIXTY-NINE

FIA

"You're still healing," I say.

"So are you."

Emeric and I stand together in the private royal garden for some fresh air and a break from the duties of being royal. A couple puppies scamper about at our feet.

"Am I holding you up or are you holding me up?" I clasp tightly to Emeric's back with my gloved hands. The magic of the pea still has a hold on me.

"We hold each other." Emeric's hands move from my waist to the small curve of my back.

It's been a week since Emeric was stabbed. We're healing together. From injuries, from self-doubt, from denial, from past mistakes, and so much more. While I still hold tight to stubbornness and my independence, it feels natural to let Emeric into my life. The less I deny he's my true love, the more he becomes engrained and a part of me. I can still be me with him, and I feel even more whole having his support.

"We're alone." Emeric's nose brushes against my temple and that simple touch alone sends a cascade of shivers down my backbone.

We don't often get a chance to be alone with Morella and kidnappers still on the loose, plans for Eira and Leo's wedding being made, and preparing for the arrival of my parents who were sent notice of my and Fynn's whereabouts. When Emeric and I are alone, we make every moment count.

"I'm guessing that means you want a kiss." I tilt my chin up to Emeric and bring a hand to his face.

I said I'd kiss him as much as he wants if he stayed with me, and he did. I won't deny him. I'd never thought I'd be a person to crave a kiss, but with Emeric it's like breathing air or eating food. A kiss with him sustains me and fills me. I used to think kisses were meaningless platitudes, but they aren't. They're an expression of love, and I will never fully be able to explain the love I feel for Emeric. It's beyond anything I can comprehend.

"It's like you can read my mind." Emeric lowers his lips to mine, and the shivers running down my back turn into a full body wave of pleasure. My fingers tangle in his hair as his lips dance with mine.

"Ahem." I hear Adette clear her throat.

Emeric only chuckles when I jump away from him like we've been caught stealing the royal jewels. Emeric might be used to having people see him kiss someone, but I'm a little more reserved. I suck in my slightly swollen lips and find Adette smirking at us.

"I hate to interrupt you two, but Fia has company," Adette says. "They're in the banquet hall."

"Is it my parents?" My stomach flutters. I'm nervous, but excited to see them. I'm not the same young woman who left Ryutoa.

"I'll take care of the puppies while you two head to the banquet hall." Adette bends over to pick up a puppy nibbling at her shoe.

"Are you ready for this?" Emeric asks when we stand outside the doors leading to the banquet room.

"No, and yes," I reply. "Will you stay with me?"

"You should know by now I'm never leaving your side." Emeric tilts his chin down and smiles while squeezing my hand. "If your father tries to make you marry the merchant ship owner, he's going to have to get rid of me first."

"He's going to think you're an upgrade," I say, "and that's what worries me. I don't want him using our relationship to his advantage."

"Is that what we're in?" Emeric smirks. "A relationship? My reputation is ruined if that gets out."

"I'm all about ruining your reputation." I nudge Emeric with my shoulder.

"Time to show them who you are." Emeric holds the door open for me.

It's not my parents I see standing near the table.

"Fynn!"

With a slight limp, I rush toward my twin brother.

"Fia!" Fynn runs at me, picks me up in his arms and spins me around. "This is a surprise! How are you here?"

"Leo and Eira didn't tell you I'm here?" I wrinkle my nose as Fynn sets me on the floor.

"How do you know Leo and Eira?" Fynn asks.

"I think we have some catching up to do," I say as Emeric waits quietly behind me.

Fynn sees me notice the young woman standing off to the side.

"This is my true love, Aeliana," Fynn says, and he beckons the young woman to join him. Fynn's true love is beautiful with blonde curly hair and big dark blue eyes. Her smile makes her glow.

"It's so nice to finally meet you," Aeliana says in a sweet voice. "Fynn has told me so much about you."

"You're the enchanted sleeping princess from Somniara?" I can't believe I'm looking at a fairytale.

"I was," Aeliana replies with a soft smile. "I understand I have you to thank for encouraging Fynn to come after me and wake me."

Emeric's hand lightly touches the small of my back.

"Oh." I grab Emeric's hand and pull him next to me. "This is Emeric. He's my..."

It's not that I'm hesitant to say what Emeric is to me, but I don't know how Fynn is going to react.

"I'm her true love." Emeric grins wide, pleased he gets to announce the title which he likes better than prince or heir. "And she's mine."

Fynn's eyes light up in brotherly amusement. "I knew you had one. Why didn't you tell me sooner?"

"I wish she would have told me sooner too." Emeric chuckles. "It took me nearly dying from a poisoned blade for her to admit it."

I jab Emeric in the arm with my elbow, but I can't help the smile coming to my face. "If you hadn't had to prove your princely braveness by taking the blade for me, I never would have been forced to give you true love's kiss."

"I wasn't about to let you die," Emeric says.

"Then you could have been the one to plant the kiss on me," I counter.

"I wouldn't have had to think twice about it, unlike you," Emeric banters back. "You waited until my heart stopped."

"It started back up."

"And that's why I will ever love you." Emeric leans over and plants a soft kiss on my temple.

Because my brother is here, I immediately turn pink, which makes Emeric grin with pleasure.

Fynn amusedly watches our back and forth. "It's obvious you two were made for each other."

"It sounds like you have a tale to tell," Aeliana says as Fynn takes her hand. "I'd love to hear it if you want to share."

"And we want to hear yours," I say, awed by the look of love in Fynn's face for his true love.

He found his true love.

And mine found me.

We may not have a happy ending yet, but this seems to be the happy beginning of something new.

THE NEXT EVERLOVE CHRONICLE

Oria is the daughter of a duke on the run and she's a lady without a land. Beckett is a prince with a kingdom and no direction. Best friends from childhood, they think they know each other well. When an enchantment takes hold of Beckett, their loyalties will be tested. Can Oria give up her dreams to help Beckett find his true love to break the enchantment or will Beckett remain a frog to let Oria live her dream? True love is put to the test in this Frog Prince retelling.

Golden and Green is the next standalone book in The Everlove Chronicles.

GRATITUDE

Thank you! I thank the same people over and over again. They are my lifelines, my support, my cheerleaders, and the ones I hold dear in my heart. My heart goes out to all of them again. I can be a quiet one, holding things deep inside. I like to think I always see the cup as more than half full, but when I think it's not full, it's these people who fill me up...my family and my dear friends.

And to you, my sweet reader...thank you from the depths of my heart. This is a heart calling, a joyful passion, a creative outlet, and it's the sweet comment, heartfelt review, a lovely rating, a social media share, and an encouraging word from you which keeps me working hard and hitting publish. Thank you.

Pleasant words are a honeycomb, sweet to the soul and healing to the bones. Proverbs 16:24

MORE SWEET ROMANCE

Find all Chrissy's books at her website
www.chrissyqmartin.com
And get the best deals on bundles at her direct author store
www.swimmergirlbooks.com

RUNNING ON LOVE AND DONUTS series
A romantic comedy series

DREAM PREP ACADEMY series
Standalone YA sweet romance books set at Dream Prep
Academy

LOVE IS A TRIATHLON series
A YA sports romance trilogy

FOR THE LOVE OF SPORTS series
Standalone YA sports romance books

About the Author

Chrissy Q Martin loves dreaming up stories with happy endings. She's a self-described awkward and shy girl with a love for chocolate, coffee, plants, and books. She loves to spend time with her family and friends, and also enjoys swimming, hiking and trail running. Adventures and budget travel get her excited, but she loves any moment she gets with her loved ones.

Check out Chrissy's website for fun stuff and find out where she pops in on social media. She loves to connect with readers!

www.chrissyqmartin.com

www.ingramcontent.com/pod-product-compliance
Lightning Source LLC
Chambersburg PA
CBHW031157310726
48969CB00001B/113